I0535749

Deadman's Trigger
The Raven & The Iris
Book 2

by Michael J & Alesia E. Matson

ISBN 978-0-9754107-9-0

Acknowledgments

This book took a very long time to get born. We'd like to acknowledge a few of the folks who midwived it.

Thanks to our sons Jon Eric, Zane, and Carl for taking care of things around the house for us when we couldn't.

Many thanks to our beta readers, Melissa Manes, Adam Smith, and Dr. Holly Wells for reading past typos, misspellings, and a herd of rogue commas to give us their honest feedback on the story to date, this manuscript in particular, and our writing style in general. Your words of encouragement were, at times, the only tie to sanity we had through the process. Thanks again to Melissa Manes, who was the copy editor for this book.

Alesia owes a real debt of thanks to all those who participate in the #ShakespeareSunday weekly hashtag party on Twitter. There were a few Sundays when those were the only words I could bear. And another round of gratitude to Suzanne Grainger, my stitchy sister and master ego-puncturer, for being everything a best friend is supposed to be.

iv

Preface

Welcome to the second book in *The Raven & the Iris* trilogy, a series that, in electronic format, re-imagines the way fantasy stories are told in the 21st century. As with most fantasy settings, there is so much more to Menelon than we could possibly have written into one romance trilogy. For all its size and wealth and glamor and grit, Fernwall is still only one city. The rest of the world is in there somewhere, and for ages its been every author's dream to have a way to share that information with readers.

Thanks to the internet, we're now able to use ebooks to do just that. This book is one way we can give you even more access to the world of Menelon. If you're reading the electronic version of this book, you'll find certain words are hyperlinked, like this one. Exactly what the links look like will depend on the device and software you're using to read the book, but regardless of appearance, the links will take you to web pages where we have provided further information via our wiki. There, you'll find a growing body of information about the culture, people, and history of Menelon. There's a map of Fernwall, updated with new locations with the release of each new book. You can read a brief history of The Great War, and follow links to other information on the religions, peoples, cultures, and sometimes cut scenes and background information on the characters.

To prevent clutter and distraction, we have attempted to refrain from highlighting the same entries when they are only a few paragraphs apart, but otherwise, links are redundant. If you miss an entry the first time, or if you want to double check something, follow a new thread of links through the wiki, or just want to check to see if we've updated the article, the next time the subject comes up, the word will be highlighted again.

While we have made every effort to ensure an enjoyable experience, the vast disparities in ebook formats (EPUB, MOBI, and Amazon's proprietary Kindle), reading devices, and e-reader apps, make it impossible for us to ensure that you will have the same experience on every device. We hope you enjoy the wiki links and will come back often to see new information about the world of Raven & Iris as it's created.

We hope you enjoy the story.

Michael & Alesia

For the dreamers, and the dream

Chapter 1

Blakesly House, Angels
11 Vilmath 580

Dawn was a far distant promise when the hot knives in Angel's head had withdrawn enough for her to risk opening her eyes. She removed the soft cotton cloth her maid had placed there, still damp and fragrant with the scent of herbs. Her vision swam. A fragrant beeswax candle burned upon a nightstand near her bed, and beyond it she could just make out the hearth screen, back lit by the glowing embers of the fire, and the familiar armchair just before it. Her eyes focused and refocused as they moved from item to item, at first unsure why they were there, then remembering why as swiftly as if it had been a reply to a question. She blinked again, and saw something strange among the watch-pin, water glass, handkerchief, night lamp, and other errata strewn atop the nightstand. The *kirpan*, the miniature sword pendant that was one-half of a Guardian Paladin's wedding token, had been stabbed into a wax candle that had been left to burn there.

That was odd. Why the candle? She had no memory of having asked for it, nor of having stabbed it with the *kirpan* when they'd returned her here from the Belton House some hours before, nor could she imagine young Clarice having done such a thing. The ornamental jewel and its companion sheath were honored by as symbols of a sacred mystery, not to be handled disrespectfully...

...though apparently an enraged betrothed who'd just learned that his "happily ever after" was a lie could treat a *kirpan* however he pleased. Angel's memories of that awful night were as keen as if they'd just happened, and those events had led to this latest one with a mournful inevitability that made her throat tighten.

There was simply no way to rest comfortably. Angel rolled upright, and instantly regretted it. Her head began to throb, as if her brain were oozing molten fire from a web of fracture lines that were also, somehow, all that held her skull together. She snatched up a pillow and screamed into it, rocking back and forth steadily until the onslaught under her scalp receded.

There had been lots of bad nights lately, but this one was already one of

1

the worst in recent memory. When she opened her eyes, she found that the room was somehow still intact, though everything had a strange, fluttering halo, or after-image, in her field of view. She drew a careful, unsteady breath, and blinked hard to clear her vision, once more spying the little *kirpan* in its candle-corpse. Leaning over, she braced the remains, then gingerly withdrew the little sword, wiping the ornamental blade clean with her little kerchief while she thought.

Distantly, she remembered when Louis had purchased it. They were still living in Püran-Khir then, and busily preparing for their return to Cascadia. She'd barely noted it at the time. It was merely another appropriate prop for the new role she'd just acquired. Like the gowns, the accent, and the religion, it had just been one more layer of gilt and paint for the facade that Lady Angelique Blakesly was to become.

And then Raven, angry, betrayed, had hurled it at her. She'd only just intercepted it with her hand, and it had pierced the flesh of her palm almost as deeply as it had been plunged it into the candle wax.

The memories no longer had the power to bring tears, though her heart still ached, and felt as if it always would. Angel clenched the ornamental jewel in her fist, eyes staring at the woman reflected in the vanity mirror across the room. Her long, pale hair was braided down her back, and her eyes were hard, like agates in the bottom of a well. They sat uneasily atop her cheekbones, angled and sharp-edged like the ornamental blade in her hand, like the knives it seemed she'd known how to use for as long as she could remember.

Her two very different lives had clashed before. Yet again, they'd done so disastrously. This time was no telling how far the damage would go.

Is he going to Hal Roland with what he knows? the dark-eyed woman in the mirror asked. In her mind, the voice was that of a Fernwall native, with the flat vowels and clipped consonants of someone born in the heart of Merchants' Quarter. The inner voice she thought she used had the familiar, rounded vowels and cadent phrases so characteristic of Cascadia's wine country, far to the south. The differences frightened her, as did the certain knowledge of whose voice it must be.

She shook her head. There were too many ramifications to this, and she hadn't had time to think them through. "Ah don't know. No, Ah don't think so," she corrected herself, shaking her head slightly. "If he could have arrested me, he likely would have by now."

But you don't know that for certain? her mirror image pressed.

"How can Ah know anythin' o' the sort?" Angel cried softly, "it's been weeks since he found out. Don't you think—?"

Guesses don't do us much good, Angel. The face in the mirror tilted slightly. *Roland's not the only possibility. He could just take it straight to Remington, you know.*

"Iris, he won't do that. He loves us. You have t' know that!"

I don't have to know anything of the sort. She slid out of bed and rather casually tossed the pendant toward the jewelry box. *You heard him, earlier.*

He wasn't as drunk as he pretended to be. If he can't arrest you because of "true love" or whatever, she went on, unable to resist making a silly gesture to mock the phrase, *he could still cut the barony out from under you. If you want to keep Carlisle, then we're going to have to take a few more precautions to safeguard it, and you—from him, and from Louis.*

Angel snatched at her own hands, clasping them tightly to keep them under control. There was some information that Iris needed to know that she did not know, but Iris was supposed to be her—she *was* Iris, wasn't she?—so how could she *not* know it? Angel herself had difficulty bringing them to mind. She could remember seeing the documents, the reports, the legal forms, but. . .

"Um, maybe we ought t' talk t' the baroness about that."

Aren't you and Angelique the same. . . ?

"Not anymore, it don't seem."

Since when?

Angel sighed and shrugged. "Since a few hours ago. Right before she hit Raven at the ball, Ah think."

Shit. Does she know? Iris's thoughts suddenly became quite loud in Angel's head. They were angry thoughts, sometimes violent, always disturbing, and now impossible to control.

"Ah don't think so. Not yet. Iris, stop it, Ah can't think over all that."

The face in the mirror taunted back with an edgy half-smile. *Make me.*

"Iris, that ain't helpin'! *Iris. . . !*"

Abruptly, the knives were back again, flashing and clashing inside her head and turning the space between her ears into a battle zone. She clenched her teeth to keep from screaming, and held the heels of both hands pressed against her temples to keep her skull intact. It went on and on, shredding her apart once more from the inside until at last blackness came down upon her like a mercy-stroke.

Dawn had become an immediate promise when consciousness at last returned. She lifted herself up from where she'd collapsed to the floor, but in cautious stages. First, to a careful kneeling position, while her fingers gingerly traced the features of a face and aching skull that, except for a bitten lip, seemed whole enough. Only then did she rise to her feet, slowly enough to keep her head from pounding in protest. The woman she saw reflected in the mirror had blood smears in her hair and on her face, and she knew, without knowing how she knew, that the hard eyes gazing at her there now were not entirely her own.

Angel tried to speak, but the words would not come out. Startled, she drew breath to try again.

Nothing.

And then, "Just let me do the talking for a while," Iris said, and Angel heard the flatly inflected words in her own ears, harsh and uncompromising. "We've got damage control to do." She found herself walking toward her bathing chamber, though it was not by her will.

3

Iris, stop it. Ah don't know how you're doin' this, but it ain't right!

"Hush. Nothing is any different. You just know about it now, that's all. Look, if you can tolerate it from Angelique, you can tolerate it from me," she said, muttering the words as she filled the basin. "Maybe it will make a few things easier. *That* would be novel."

Her heart was still racing, but her hands replaced the basin and took up a clean cloth without her volition. She felt almost as if she were in shock, and couldn't quite make herself understand that wetness of the water and its chill were sensations she could only experience distantly, and then only if Iris' attention drifted in the slightest. By the time those hands placed the cool, damp cloth over her face, they felt like the hands, and face, of a stranger.

"I'm no stranger, Angel," Iris said, barely muttering the words into the washcloth. "I've been here all along, trying to protect your neck for you while you seem determined to let anyone with half a brain to put a collar around it. It's just easier for me to do that, this way."

She lowered the cloth and gazed in the mirror once more. "You don't have to worry. I can do what needs to be done—and I hope the baroness has as much luck with her end."

Angel winced, or rather, felt as if she should. Her face still did not register the attempt. *Ah cain't imagine what she's goin' t' say about what happened at the ball last night,* she thought, and wondered, too, what the baroness was going to tell the servants.

"The less, the better," Iris said, with an impatient sigh. "You know Louis's got to have an informant below-stairs. You know he does."

It was comforting, in an odd sort of way, for Angel to hear her own voice speaking so confidently, as if she knew without equivocation precisely what had to be done. *But, what are we going t' do about Raven?* she wondered, finding it even more curious to think about herself in terms of "we" rather than "I". But then she remembered, with some chagrin, that there had always been more than one opinion within her on what the answer to that question should be.

"Nothing."

The word was tersely offered, and in a way that was meant to shut down discussion. It worked, for a moment, but her heart could not be so easily silenced. *We cain't just let him go like that.*

"Oh, yes we can," she muttered, rinsing the cloth to dab at the blood on her lip. "He's chosen a side. It wasn't us. Maybe he'll rat us out, maybe he won't. Either way, we can't trust him."

Her heart began to pound alarmingly, and the awful, clamoring noise within her grew so loud that Iris, in control up to that point, had to drop to her knees and clutch at her head as if to keep it from exploding. "We—have—to—let—him—go!" she said, snarling in order to silence the din. "Remember... the first thing we learned... in that hell-hole, the *Boeche-Briazel*," she hissed, regaining her feet with grim determination. "You don't

4

give anyone the chance to fuck you over—and you kill them before they get a chance to fuck you over twice. Remember?"

You are not going to kill him! Raven's just...!

"In a position to put your neck in a fucking collar for decades!" She glared grimly into the little looking glass above the wash basin as if the person she had to convince were reflected there. "Don't you get it yet? Pull your head out of that, that *bottomless* sentimental well and catch that clue cart rolling by, baby. Even *if* Raven doesn't have the hard evidence he needs to arrest you for the theft of the *Mâgun-Zak*, he still has found something in those documents Louis forged that exposes you for a fraud. He's been attempting to pickle himself instead, thankfully, and that's all that's saved you. If you can't imagine how infuriated all those self-righteous society hypocrites are going to be when they hear the news, then you haven't been paying attention.

"And hey, if that isn't enough? Louis and all his thuggy-boys are after you now, and you can't come clean with Remington either, not on this. You've told too many lies—to her face—and you've told them for too long. Paragon of honor that she is, she'll be among the first to want you eviscerated in The People's Square.

"No, Angel." Iris paused and drew a determined breath. Twice before in her life, she'd turned her wide-ranging anger in on herself and had succumbed to nearly anhedonic levels of despair, but not this time. "Raven's promises aren't worth any more than he is, and it's time you started acting like you knew it."

Iris, that's just not—

"If he'd had the stones to stick with you through this, he'd have found them well before that debacle last night."

No! He's hurt—we lied—!

"What? *Like he's never told a lie?*" Clenched jaws kept her from screaming it. She desperately wanted to hurl something in her rage, but there were sounds in the sitting room, likely the hall boy and scullery girl preparing it against the baroness' appearance. She drew a deep, steadying breath instead and considered the tasks ahead of her. Angel's inner voice rattled on while she thought.

Iris, you cain't just strike him off like that. You cain't. You've got t' get him back. We've got t' talk t' him! Now—this morning—before he has a chance t' do anythin' he'll regret!

She didn't roll her eyes, but it was an effort. "Maybe we should go to his office at police headquarters? Assuming he's not ass-end up in an ale barrel already, we can make it stupidly easy for him! Let's just get it over with *and* the farce of a trial that will follow. Louis can sweep up the price of your bond for your indenture to the city-state and *keep you like a bitch in his kennel!*"

There was no immediate reply to that. Iris nodded to the face reflected there the mirror, its mask-like expression as hard and cold as the words she'd just spoken. "That's right. Do you really want to go back to being

'Angela', again? By all means then, throw yourself on Raven's mercy—think he's learned *that* Paladin virtue any better than the others?"

Every question exploded vitriol in her heart. Angel could not stop weeping, but Iris drew strength from it. It schooled her into remembering why it was important to prevent anyone from hurting Angel like that, ever again. She dashed away the fresh tears that tumbled down her newly washed cheeks. "Right. Me neither. Your life here got infinitely more dangerous, so now we're playing this out my way."

She turned from the wet, sorrow-stricken face in the mirror and returned to the bedchamber. Categorizing and prioritizing the new threats to the life Angel had built here had made it easier to ignore how grief carved new runnels into what was left of her soul.

"Enough with the caterwauling. Better wake up the baroness, Angel. We've got work to do."

2313 Compton Place, Upper Merchants'
11 Vilmath, 580

Louis Arnot sat in the over upholstered chair in his opulently decorated drawing room in his expensively refurbished estate house, much as he had done every single morning for the last one hundred and twenty-five. His perfumed fingers toyed with an oblong object made of ivory or bone and about the size of a calling card. It clicked and clattered atop the polished bloodwood table as he tapped it and turned it and tapped it again. His unseeing eyes gazed out over grounds that were neither lush with summer's last heated breaths nor ripe with autumn's bawdy displays. For one hundred and twenty-five mornings he'd sat here, surrounded with the kind of wealth that would beggar the soul of any pirate, and yet for all its comforts he knew this had become little more than a well-padded holding pen.

He glanced at a truly beautiful, dark-haired girl who writhed upon a pile of soft furs before the hearth. She was completely naked, save for a diamond collar, and a waist chain that glinted against the creamy backdrop of her flawless skin. At first glance, she seemed to be lost in mindless, erotic ecstasy. A second glance at her puffy labia and glistening-wet thighs confirmed it. Even though his eyes lingered on her there—he'd forgotten her name—his mind ranged back to the girl who had captured his attention, and what was left of his heart, years before in a country far away from these cold Cascadian winters.

Oh, Angela... *No, I suppose I must call you "Iris" now, mustn't I. A pretty name to stand for some ugly deeds, Angela darling. Could you really pull the trigger on me, I wonder? After all we were to each other? After all I've given you?* There was a certain wistful melancholy in the thought, and he paused to savor it as he might the bouquet of a fine wine, or a new painting he intended to acquire. When it began to bore him, he dismissed it and returned to his contemplation of his former accomplice's flight and betrayal.

It had never occurred to him that she could have fallen in love with anyone, not really. She was no more capable of such weakness than he was, but in light of a certain item in the Standard's society pages, he did rather have a question or two about her sanity.

Evening Standard
11 Vilmath, 580
EARLY EDITION

Carlisle Feud! Wedding Off?

BELTON HOUSE—Late this past summer, readers will remember that this paper aired the rumors of the betrothal of Baroness Angelique Blakesly of Carlisle to Sir Vincent Sultaire, youngest son of the Baron of Valemont. Sir Vincent, our readers may further recall, is currently serving time as a chief inspecting detective (CID) for the Fernwall Police Department after several *youthful* peccadilloes left him on the wrong side of the railing in his first, ill-starred court appearance.

Hints of trouble brewing began to surface almost immediately thereafter. Lady Blakesly has been seen less and less among her peers in society, and was effectively absent from the Harvest-Fest celebrations. Reporters on the social circuit have noticed an increasing chill between the two at what few public appearances they have made together.

Last night's public row at the annual Belton House Winter Ball brought the months of speculation to a violent head. Though the exact grounds for the quarrel can only be speculated upon—Sir Vincent's recent behavior has been nothing short of notorious—it did seem to signal the imminent end of the relationship when Lady Blakesly *slapped* her betrothed so hard she drew blood!

In the aftermath, this reporter overheard Lady Blakesly heatedly declare that she has 'had all [she] can take' of Sir Vincent Sultaire.

A knock at the door interrupted his reading. and he looked up at his butler's entrance. "That... *man* is ready to see you now," he said stiffly.

Louis nodded once, then slowly folded up his paper and placed it on the side table. A short, stocky man strode past the disapproving butler with a rolling gait of a workman. Though he ducked and nodded respectfully to Louis, he rather quickly found himself having trouble keeping his eyes off the naked woman rolling languidly in the furs.

"Well?" Louis asked expectantly. "Look at me, man! Not at her."

"Yes, Goodman. Sorry, Goodman," the workman said quickly, forcing his attention back to his employer. "We been done, again. So sorry. I don't know what else to say. We got close this time, but... well... you'll see it on page twelve, goodman."

Louis scowled at the man and picked up the paper again. "I see noth—Ah, here's something. 'Chimney sweep slips on ice, falls to death'," he quoted the headline, lifting an inquiring eyebrow.

"That's it," he confirmed. "He's the one I hired. You said put the word out. I put the word out and this one comes in and says he's heard about a fresh quick-trigger, off-book client at that new law firm off the Wyechester Road there in Upper Gate. Badger & Carson, they is. And, the client is a *lady,* he says. So I offers him twenty-five pounds if he can get me the goods, see? He says he can prove it tonight if I gives him a fiver, so I does. And..."

"And he fell off of the roof of the Malmont Building," Louis finished.

"Yes, goodman."

The girl in the furs caught her breath in soft orgasm, causing the workman another bout of momentary distraction, but he recovered himself before Louis could say anything. "Them blue bottles from the local precinct call it an accident, but it weren't. They was two sets of boot prints in the snow, see? One a man's. Them would be his. The others was small, like a woman or a child. My money's on 'woman', though, and she knew what she was about, that one. Just like the others."

"She is an amazing woman," Louis sighed thoughtfully. His gaze drifted over to the girl, still in the grip of the drugs he'd given her. Her skin was damp from her latest string of orgasms, and it shimmered like fresh milk in the firelight, but the skin he saw didn't belong to the girl in the furs. "Perfect, in fact."

"Shall I kill her?"

It didn't even break Louis's reverie. "Kill such a fine jewel?" The girl's drugged gaze turned up to him longingly, wordlessly begging him for a release he couldn't give her. Even as his eyes caressed her familiarly, the fact of her presence barely registered with him. She was not the woman he wanted.

"No, my friend. She must not be killed. She must be... directed. Managed. Controlled." He gave the workman a hard look but spoke softly. "We must recapture Iris, dead man's trigger or no. I *must* possess her again. Everything depends on it."

He leaned over in his chair and cupped the vacant-eyed girl's chin. "I will make her more than she ever imagined she could be, as she will for me."

The Rose & Woodbine Tavern, Merchants
15 Vilmath, 580

It was never going to be a classy place. In fact, it was quite the opposite, and that was the point. It teemed with bad music, loaded dice, cheap beer, and even cheaper prostitutes. It didn't smell very good. It was not a place decent, upstanding citizens went to drink, eat, or fuck, but then, for the last month Vincent hadn't considered himself "decent", never mind "upstanding". So he'd eaten, drank, and examined every mole and pimple in every intimate place on every whore in the tavern, because...

That was the point. He couldn't find a point—to anything. As the youngest son of a baron, he had obligations, but no duties. He had a title (several, actually) but neither money nor station beyond what mere formality provided. He had education, but no cause in which it could be put to service. He was a cop sworn to uphold the law, but a slave because he'd broken the law. He was engaged, but estranged. He'd found a thief, but couldn't arrest her. She knew his past, but what he'd been told of hers was obviously a string of lies. It all ran around and around in his head until he could no longer tell the beginning from the end.

In the past few days, during the brief interludes when alcoholic numbness receded far enough, he found himself remembering the last time he'd seen Angelique, at the Belton House Ball. The annual winter festivity was attended by anyone and everyone who considered themselves to be part of "society", which, of course, meant that every society reporter in Cascadia was also going to be present.

He had not wanted to go. He had not wanted to see her. He had not wanted to be reminded of the one lie he couldn't make true. She had lied to him, she had played him just as she had played the Ladies' Auxiliary and everyone else in Fernwall, and what sickened him the worst was that in spite of it all, he still loved her. Deep down in his heart, he even admired her! He didn't want to admire her, he didn't want to love her, either. And, he told himself, he most *certainly* didn't want to attend the most talked about and written about public event of the autumn season with her! He wanted to hate her or, failing that, he'd settle for simply forgetting that he'd ever been in love with her.

On his way to the ball, he'd stopped for a celebratory ale with David Cooper's attorney, and another, a bit later, with Cooper himself. All the while, he told himself that he would go home, that he'd look up Barbara Cole instead, that there was paperwork to be done in his office, that he didn't have time to make the long trip up to the city of Angels' just to attend a ball. In the end, Vincent had gone after all, just as he knew he would, because he could not help himself.

He vividly recalled his first sight of her across the ballroom, looking like a wintry princess walking on clouds in a pale blue gown that sparkled and glinted like ice. Her face had lit up when she saw him, but before he'd taken two steps into the organized cacophony of the ballroom, he had been waylaid

9

by a gaggle of young noblewomen asking him questions about, of all things, the *Mâgun-Zak* case!

"Is there any news, Sir Vincent?" Lady Mariel of Waterstone had placed herself in his way to ask it. He had *not* wanted to be reminded about the case that night, of all nights, but before he could brush off the question, one of the decorative satin ribbons she wore around her wrists had tangled about one of his legs, causing her to shriek playfully and her friends to giggle.

"How goes the case, Sir Vincent? We're *so* looking forward to being able to put this horrible business behind us." Lady Magarit had asked then, flipping her fan open to get his attention. *He* too had been looking forward to putting this whole messy affair behind him as soon as he possibly could, but before he could say as much, a group of young knights joined them.

"Have you caught the thief, yet, Sir Vincent?" Sir Alain of Trobiere asked. Vincent's eyes had flicked to Angelique reflexively. He had, but there wasn't a damned thing he could do about it. It was as infuriating as the charade of their "betrothal" was intolerable. It occurred to him then to wonder if their betrothal hadn't been a part of her plan all along! *Oh, that's nicely played,* he fumed. *Hitch yourself to the cop, right in front of society, to make it impossible for him to arrest you without destroying his reputation, that of the commissioner, and the Law Enforcement Committee as well.*

It had worked like a charm, and he had been about to find her and tell her so when she had appeared there as if summoned.

"If you would excuse me, noble sirs." Angelique's voice had cut across the last question. He hadn't heard it, anyway. Dark circles under her eyes attested to the state of her health. She looked *tired,* and he could feel the tension in her fingers through the sleeves of his evening wear. "I believe Sir Vincent owes me a dance," she added, with an uncharacteristic note of steel under those polite sounding words that none of the young men who had gathered around him dared challenge.

"Do I indeed? Dance with my 'betrothed'? How positively unfashionable, Lady Blakesly," he'd quipped back, purposely slurring his words. It made him sound more inebriated than a couple of glasses of beer could have explained. For once, his reputation served his purposes. It had allowed him to show her just what he thought of being played, and if his behavior was seen as unseemly in the process, it would be written off as the bad behavior of a drunk at a party. He'd weathered much worse.

"These are the first words we've exchanged in weeks, Vincent," she had replied. Her phony Vin-Nôrëan accent was only slightly threaded through the softer, flat, vowels of what was apparently supposed to be Cascr. He wasn't sure which was more irritating, the phony accent or the phony accent papered over with what he knew to be her native voice. She was still trying to play him. "But, if we must discuss fashion to remain civil," she'd gone on, her eyes pleading with him, "then I am happy to do so."

For a brief instant, he couldn't maintain his drunken pose. She was so beautiful, and his heart ached for her. He wanted nothing more than to remain civil, to love her, to parade her around the room as his beloved, and the chosen partner of his life. Nor could he ignore just how much he loved her, enjoyed her wit, her vivacity, her lithe, trim... body.

A body well-maintained for a single purpose, and it *wasn't* their bedroom adventures. She had tried to play him again, and the thought of it infuriated him. He slipped back into his drunken pose.

"Oh, by all means, my lady. Will the season's trends in hemlines do, or would you prefer to discuss the proper bodice lace to cover a *set of concealed front-hooks?*" he said, every word dripping sarcasm.

"What would you know of either, Sir Vincent, other than what it took to get your hands on the body beneath?" There was little trace of a D'wanese accent in *that* riposte, and he felt the lissome figure in his arms stiffen and twitch under his hands.

"I haven't had any complaints," he shot back, "even from you."

"Except for a recent one, perhaps: neglect." Chameleon-like, she'd leaned toward him to breathe those words, her face tilted up to his, lips slightly parted. "Why not come back to Blakesly House with me tonight, *Mar-leven?* I've missed you dearly..." The words, aspirated with enough steam to make him want to drag her off the dance floor right then and there, and his eyes had said—his whole body had said—*I have missed you too*, and he knew it.

But she was *still* playing him, she had to be! Somehow, he had managed to dive back behind his drunken act in time to hide what he felt—from both of them.

"And will we tell truths, my love?" he asked instead, acid simmering under every word.

"I was not always—I could not... I have told you all the truths that were mine to tell, but—"

That tore it. *He* was supposed to be her betrothed, her soon-to-be husband. *He* was the one who was supposed to be privy to her secrets, to be privileged to help her in times of need! "Pardon me, my lady, but have you *any* idea what kind of havoc those... *limitations* of yours have wrought on others? Limitations that, had they not been in place, had you not exempted me from them—me! the man you are planning on marrying, remember? Had you told me the truth—I might have been able to use the information to *help* you and limit the collateral damage!" By the time he had finished he was shaking with suppressed rage and frustration. He hadn't felt so impotent, or so angry at his impotence since he'd stormed out of Valemont Manor.

They were still dancing, but their dance had almost turned into a mêlée. Angelique's body was as hard as stone again, and she knew how to use it like a weapon. She twisted slightly, then drove the heel of her shoe into the arch of his foot in calculated retaliation.

"Done is done!" she'd said, snapping off the words with calculated precision. "I cannot change the choices I made then. I was simply doing the best I could, in the circumstances. Can you not respect that, or at least attempt to understand it?"

In retrospect, he couldn't be proud of what he said next. It had ended the evening for them both. "Respect you," he'd shot back, rather louder than he had intended. It attracted attention neither of them needed at that moment, and it wasn't helpful. He lowered his voice, but what it lacked in volume was compensated for in sheer vitriol. "You want me to respect you for first lying to me, then *leaving me to deal with the consequences? Those are the actions of a selfish child!*"

She'd stiffened in his arms, reeling back and then forward again to hit him, hard! It showed him how the guards at Bishop-Florian must have felt that night. He'd been struck less forcefully by men!

The Paladins had closed ranks around Angelique after that, and a squad from their number had been dispatched to escort Sir Vincent Sultaire from the premises. After that, he had avoided their "society" and hers. He'd even stopped going to his flat. Thankfully, the Cooper trial was largely over, and after that, he'd completely dropped out of *everything*. Trish, a prostitute who'd known him since before he'd been collared, had taken pity on him and introduced him around The Rose & Woodbine. It was a safe place to lay low and think—or to drink and fuck. Same thing as far as he was concerned. The people there were simple and plainspoken. They were laborers: street sweeps, chimney sweeps, garbage collectors, cab drivers, dishwashers and launderers; the good, uncomplicated, illiterate folk that kept "society" running, and they were a blessed relief from the endless judgments and interrogations that characterized his most of his experience with his own class.

"*Who's the wicked, selfish, rotten crook who stole the* Mâgun-Zak *and why haven't you caught him yet?*"

"*Why are you and Lady Blakesly having so many problems now that you're engaged? You didn't really love her, did you?*"

"*Why was David Cooper acquitted? He stole it, didn't he? Why did you testify against the city-state and* for *him?*"

They all wanted answers to the burning questions that filled up the gossip columns of the major dailies, and he was the one who was supposed to have them. He *did* have them, and there was another point with no point: There were answers, but he couldn't reveal them. Not to anyone, not without betraying the one woman in the world that he still loved, in spite of himself—in spite of her! He hated himself for that. He loved a liar and was a liar. He hated the lies and the secrets because they were Angel's lies and Angel's secrets and his own honor demanded that he not betray her, even though she had betrayed him, again and again.

It was there that he always turned on himself, inner knives flashing. He was a con. He made money—a *lot* of money—playing both sides of the table. He hated that, too. He was a criminal mad at a criminal for acting like a criminal. It was all just another circle; another point with no point and no amount of cheap booze or cheaper sex could change the facts. Lacking any ideas better than those he'd found any other night, Vincent had once again filled himself with stale beer, grabbed the nearest willing whore, and dragged her off to his filthy room for a plunge into physical gratification and forgetfulness.

Docktown, Merchants
Early Morning

Iris lunged through shadows toward her nearest assailant, jerking him in front of her to intercept the knife his buddy had thrown. He grunted and sagged as the shock took him. The elbow she jammed into his ear assisted him to the ground. One of his partners closed the distance, another knife held low. She yanked the blade out of the dying man's chest and drove it into the belly of the living. His knees collapsed beneath him, and she knew she'd remember the astonished look on his face for the rest of her life.

It occurred to her then that she had lately been spending too much time having to fight for her life in dirty alleys.

It had been her own fault, of course. When she'd armed the "dead man's trigger" with the case file she'd stolen, she'd hoped it would keep Louis at bay for just long enough to hand the contents over to Raven, who by then should have been armed with the truth about her past and the choices she'd made. Instead, summer had ripened into autumn, then rotted toward winter without any change in the three-way standoff between Raven, Louis, and herself, and the dead man's trigger had become a millstone around her neck.

Louis, blast his black, oily guts, was now using it to play her just as ruthlessly as she was playing him. Publicly, it had done its job and held Louis at bay. Privately, he'd used up a half-dozen hirelings in his thus-far frustrated attempts to recover that dossier, or her, whichever his thugs could get their hands on, first.

The next candidate in line for that honor lunged toward her, wearing a thick, padded coat and swinging a heavy cudgel. The blow caught Iris on her right thigh and knocked her into a stack of crates—packed crates, as it turned out. She crumpled to the frozen ground, dazed and heaving for air. The third attacker, a heavily built woman in a thick, padded coat, moved in for the knock-out blow.

Iris braced herself, but a stuttering crash from further down the alley forestalled disaster. Her two attackers jumped and whirled, weapons held at the ready to face a new threat, but Iris didn't even pause to look. She leaped to her left, just barely scrambling past a patch of "black ice" before she slipped on it. Black ice was especially deadly for those who "worked the night shift" because it lie hidden in the dark places where the winter sun couldn't quite penetrate, and was almost impossible to spot until it was too late.

"Gardammit!" the woman shouted, wheeling in pursuit. "Getter, y' stupid pig!"

Stupid Pig growled something, but Iris was in the middle of heaving herself up to the first landing of a rusty, wrought-iron fire escape and had little time to spare for translation. The growl became a yelp of surprise, chopped short by a grunt of pain. Iris turned to see that the larger of the two figures (Stupid Pig, presumably) had measured his length out on the paving stones of the alleyway.

Cursing at him for his clumsiness, the woman lunged toward Iris. Her fate differed from her mate's only in that he was there to break her fall.

Neither had seen the black ice.

Breathing heavily, Iris leaped back down to the street, cushioning her own fall with two prostrate bodies that *whoosh*ed satisfyingly when she landed. She slammed their heads into the ice-slicked cobblestones once for good measure. Their abrupt loss of motor control gave her a moment to catch her breath, and another to look over her attackers. She couldn't see much detail of the face of the man she'd stabbed, and there was nothing in his pouch, or his dead mate's, to distinguish them from any of the others Louis had hired.

A low groan signaled the return to consciousness of at least one of the two survivors. She turned to kick a knife out of the man's meaty fist—some orcish ancestry there, from the look of him—and it clattered to a stop near a pile of broken pallets. That club also needed to go, and she lofted it further back into the alley, where it *thunked* hollowly a couple of times, then rolled to a stop.

"Hey. You two. Hold still," she panted, her words crystallized in clouds of frozen steam, "I need you to tell your boss something. Tell him I'm enjoying this current case-lot of dumbshit he's hired. You're all making this *so* much easier." From her sleeve she withdrew a small, thin plaque carved from whalebone, and tossed it toward them from between two gloved fingers. It sliced through the air to land corner down in a small, grimy pile of snow, and bore only the inked silhouette of an iris.

"You can give that to Louis," Iris instructed, turning to go. "He can add it to his collection."

She sidled out of the alley, and then half-sprinted, half-limped up one block to mount a drain spout on the side of the next building. Her leg had begun to throb, and the muscles across her shoulders ached, but there was no help for it. There were too many unanswered questions that kept her prowling the riverbanks at night.

Sure, she knew Louis was playing for time. The biggest question was, "time for what?"

The spreading bruise on her thigh reminded her of the most obvious answer: This armed truce simply could not last. As the late summer weeks lengthened into autumn, Iris felt as if she could almost sense Louis' brooding, scheming thoughts surrounding Blakesly House and its lady like a pall. She was having to spend more hours prying into his business dealings at night, and that meant fewer hours for Lady Blakesly to delve further into what was going on out at Carlisle during the days. She needed something else to play against him, but he was forcing her to burn her candle at both ends to get it. Eventually, her body would simply give out from the strain.

Iris sighed, then slid carefully across the ledge created by the building's cornice to reach her next objective. She liked simple solutions. If simply sticking a knife in his ribs would have done that, Louis Arnot would not have lived long enough to see the first snows fly.

No. Louis was a fat, steaming pile of complications, and murdering him would have done nothing but expose them, likely to Angel's detriment. Iris didn't care for the stilted formality of noble society in Fernwall, but even she had to admit that the food, the decor, and the smell were much better than she'd find anywhere else in this town.

She leaped back upon the iron fire escape ladder, clambering up it to the sharply peaked rooftops that characterized Fernwall's seaport, harbor district, and riverways, loosely known as Docktown. Ships of all types and sizes were berthed end to end and side by side as far up and down the river as she could see. Their irregular shapes stood out in the light of the lamp posts on the piers, and they lumbered restlessly against one another in the wind that had arisen as the larger of the two moons had set. Only the distant stars remained above, their light too small and feeble to dispel the long tendrils of darkness that rolled like fog among the masts, stacks, shacks, and warehouses that spread out before her.

It was an hour for fell deeds, when the honest and the innocent locked their doors and huddled in their beds for protection. Iris knew she was neither. Thanks to that fuck-around drunkard Vincent Sultaire, she was also quite alone. The only protections she had now were the dead man's trigger and her ability to out-think Louis.

Iris shook herself. The night was moving on, and recent events had added yet another reason to extend her nightly prowls: She needed to ascertain Raven's position and intentions, preferably without him finding out about it.

She didn't want to listen to the other voices inside her, clamoring in what was left of her heart. They cried out for her to find Raven, yes, but rather to throw herself on his mercy and beg for his help!

Why don't you, Iris? You've got t' try t' reason with him, or maybe scream at him, or fight with him if that's what you want—

Iris snarled as she jumped between rooftops, then yelped. Her injured leg collapsed beneath her and she tumbled down the far side of a peak, crumpling into an undignified pile along the raised frontage wall. It was all that had kept her from falling to her death on the street, three stories below.

"Fucking waste of skin," Iris said, muttering in disgust at the thoughts and feelings that she could no longer ignore or control. Not since that awful public row with Vincent—Raven—at that fancy party at the Belton House. "Get mad, get drunk, shout ugly names, storm out, whore around—he's a fucking spoiled, pampered child." She got back to her feet slowly, wincing briefly when she put her right foot down. "Forget him. We've got work to do."

Having put some needed distance between herself and the meat she'd left cooling in that alley, Iris took a much more decorous opportunity to drop down to street level, then changed direction, hiring an all night ferryman to take her across the river. Once safely onshore once more, she found another way up to the rooftops. The word on the street was that Fernwall's most notorious con-turned-cop had taken up temporary residence at one of the dive bars in Merchants'. She wanted to see if she could ascertain which it was, at least, before the lateness of the hour forced her to make the long trek back to Blakesly House.

As was her habit, Iris used a "switchback"—doubling back on her own trail, but at a higher or lower elevation—to throw off tails she might have accumulated. None of the night-shifters disposed to violence would dare follow her above the north bank of the Caspian and into Angels to do their dirty work. The noble classes tended to get muscular when nasty things happened in their clean streets and pretty neighborhoods, and none of them liked finding dead bodies littering up their fine streets when the sun arose in the mornings. It was the kind of thing that would have them frothing at the mouth to put more money into law enforcement in an attempt to sweep all of South End into the bay. It was also the kind of response that the syndicate bosses and crime lords feared, and so they tended to keep their activities north of the river well under wraps. Anywhere south of that, Iris knew she was fair game for any of the night's predators that might be foolish enough to make a try for her.

Once reasonably sure she'd not been followed, Iris made her way back toward the river near "The Poleman". It was a dive favored by the men and women who moved the barges up and down the Caspian River, and it perched on slanted timbers like a squat, fat vulture leering out over the river delta, waiting for the next tasty corpse to float by. The locals said, "Ye'll know The Poleman's open from two streets over," and so it held this night. Iris heard the drunken songs, the shouting, the fights, and rowdy games long before she laid eyes on the place, and dawn was only three hours away.

She paused briefly to orient herself, then clambered down a stack of pallets to the street. Her sharp ears quickly picked up the sickening, unmistakable sounds of fists pounding into flesh, of bones breaking, of a fragile, mortal body being smashed, over and over, into stone, and she stepped further back into the shadows.

Whoa. Not my cuppa, thanks anyway. Having no desire to crash anyone else's party at this late hour, Iris picked her way around where she thought the fight had to be, trying to stay out of sight until she was clear. As she watched, two large figures—they might have been Louis', for all she knew—emerged from a gap between a pair of ramshackle out-buildings, glancing and skulking so furtively it almost made her laugh out loud. The mirth died in her throat when she saw the blood trickling thickly onto the paving stones, glinting dully in a street lamp's distant glow.

She knew it was blood, though she couldn't have explained *how* she knew it, nor how she knew that the freezing air would have slowed the flow already, had the victim been dead. Curious now, Iris slipped across the alleyway and waited for her eyes to adjust, eventually locating the small, crumpled form partially covered with old tarps and the remnants of a broken barrel. Kneeling, she searched for a pulse, trying first a wrist—a woman's wrist—and then at her neck. The skull had been cracked behind the left ear, or so it seemed. Then the head shifted, rolling facial features into the light.

16

Iris's body went rigid with surprise and recognition.

Police Inspector Barbara Cole. What in Menelon brought you here at this time of night?

The Rose & Woodbine Tavern, Merchants
16 Vilmath, 580

Commissioner Hal Roland burst through the flimsy door of the hovel in which his most truant problem child was known to hide. It hadn't finished splintering before the he grabbed the edge of the mattress and heaved, up ending said problem child and onto the whore with whom he spent the night onto the floor in a mess of smelly blankets and tangled limbs.

"You're done here," he told the girl gruffly, jerking his head toward the now-permanent opening where the door had been. "If you didn't get your money up front, go back to hooker school. Go on, get out." He barely spared her a glance as she scrambled for her clothing and left. Hal Roland had a reputation among his cops as a man one never wanted to anger, or to be around when someone else had been foolish enough to do so. He wasn't particularly known for shortness of temper, nor was he extraordinarily tall or muscular. Though he'd never win a beauty contest he wasn't all that frightening of countenance, either. When he was moved to anger, however, he had a bearing that could melt stone walls. That morning, he was angry in that "simmering just under the boil" way that threatened to explode all over the first wise-assed word to come out of young Sultaire's mouth.

"Geez! You could have knocked!" Vincent obliged, from somewhere beneath the remains of his bed.

"I did," Roland said, snarling and brushing splinters of wood from his suit jacket. He waited with the coiled tension of a predator while the younger man clawed his way out of the wreckage, then slapped him in the head with a thick file folder for his pains.

"While you've been indulging yourself in your latest temper tantrum, the rest of us have been trying to cover your ass," he said, shouting down an irritated protest from his hungover charge. Weeks of repressed rage and frustration erupted right in the middle of Vincent's hangover and Roland let him have it without mercy. "Including Barbara Cole—remember her?—who was attacked and nearly *beaten to death* last night, all in the line of a *duty* she wasn't qualified to fulfill, and right now I'm about one breath away from snapping a real collar around your neck and hauling you back to the city auction block!" With a disgusted sneer, he slammed the folder down on the only other intact piece of furniture left in the room, an unfinished wooden stool.

"Wha...? Cole? Where? Why?" The younger man demanded, fumbling with blankets and sheets and bits of clothing all at once.

Roland watched him for two heartbeats. "The information's in there," he growled, gesturing with thick fingers at the bound stack of paperwork. "Preliminary report's on top. What ain't in there is that she'd been at The

Poleman to make contact with a bargeman who smuggled things up and down river he wasn't supposed to, or so he said. That was the last anyone at headquarters heard from her. Hours later—now, get this—a young woman with short, black hair and dressed in a dark blue bodysuit—desk sergeant thinks she's a mercenary—turns up at Docktown Precinct Three to tell them about the soon-to-be corpse. She gave the exact location—two blocks up from The Poleman—and a rough description of the two suspects and then disappeared. The blue jackets found Cole less than fifteen minutes later, in time to rush her over to the closest healer's hospice and save her life."

A young woman with short blue black hair and dressed in dark blue... Vincent stared at him for a heartbeat, then nearly twisted his ankle slipping on sheets and blankets to get to the folder. Word of a woman fitting that description had made the rounds lately: the dark blue suit, the short, irregularly cut hair...

"Name!" he blurted, ripping open the folder. "Do we have a name yet? The Poleman..." he mumbled, riffling through the file. "She saved a cop? Cole...?" This wasn't making any sense, but if Cole had risked her life tracking that lead down, it had to have been important.

"And you think this woman, whoever she is, knows more about who attacked Cole? Agreed. All right. I'm on it," he said, mumbling absently to Roland as he riffled through the papers for answers. "If she's involved in the things the rumor mill is wearing out its bearings over, then she's part of what's causing all the unrest locally, too."

The grizzled old cop managed to swallow about half the ire he hadn't yet expressed. "Unrest hell! We're headed for a trap war, which you'd know if you'd weren't so busy feeling sorry for yourself. You're the only cop I've got left who has the contacts to find that woman whoever she is, and figure out how to stop her. Be in my office in two hours to tell me how you're going to straighten this mess up," he ordered, adding, "clean and sober!" on his way out.

Police Headquarters, Merchants' Quarter

The office was musty and cold. The brazier had been neither lit nor cleaned, nor the floor swept in at least a month. His inbox was crammed to overflowing with reports, notes, calling cards (many from Angelique, that he tossed aside unopened), letters to "Chief Inspector Sultaire" and so on. He'd even managed to miss a few court dates, which he found laughable: a crook giving testimony, with a police officer's authority, on another crook? Perhaps the only saving grace to *that* particular point of idiocy was that Urilian judges were notoriously hard to convince of anything, whether it was guilt or innocence.

In any event, and to his surprise, despite his gruff exterior Roland had apparently covered for him. The official excuse was that he'd been ill, and everybody in this building knew that it had been just that: an excuse.

18

"Well!" an inspector named Braddock had snarked as they passed in the hall. "I see the last round of ale therapy agreed with you. Back to work, then?"

"I was actually looking for the tap," Vincent had tossed right back. "Regular administration, you know? Wouldn't want to relapse. You should try it some time."

Braddock's response stopped just short of insubordination, and he wasn't alone. Cold shoulders and backward glances followed him all the way to his office. Everyone knew about the attack on Barbara Cole, and there was no escaping the connection between that and his absence of late. In their minds, her blood was on his hands. He more or less agreed, so he didn't order a clerk to build his fire or fetch more badly needed coffee. He saw to it all himself, useful skills he'd once been taught as "punishment chores" by his incensed father. Now, they were just a bit of self-imposed penance, a pittance offered in contrition for his sins.

Once his office was put to rights, Vincent sat down at his desk to pour through the contents of the rather thick file Roland had left with him. It included not only the attack on Cole, but also information on all of the other cases he had been ignoring while living at the The Rose & Woodbine Tavern. Of particular interest was the packet that contained a copy of the official court record of the Cooper show trial. Skimming through it, Vincent found that he remembered it vividly.

"Sir Vincent, in your investigation of the defendant, did you find any evidence that the *Mâgun-Zak* was in, or ever had been in, Goodman Cooper's possession?" Cooper's attorney had asked. The prosecution had just put an "expert" on the stand, claiming that such rare artifacts as the *Zak* were always hot items, so it had probably been sold within an hour "of the defendant having stolen it." Since he was a cop, Vincent was supposed to have played along with the charade. That was how it was always done, but he'd had no intention of playing along.

"Since Goodman Cooper doesn't even have a bank account," Vincent had replied, using the opportunity to take a shot at the previous witness's biased testimony, "I would have thought the prosecution's expert witness might have explained just how a man who has never stolen anything worth more than a few hundred crowns or so suddenly learned how to hide 'close on a million' in hard currency, in his little flat—"

"Objection!" the City State's prosecutor had looked livid. This was *not* going according to the Law Enforcement Committee's script!

"Sir Vincent," the court's chief justice had said calmly, "this is not the place for sarcasm. Stick to the facts, please." She'd then cast Vincent a hard look, one that was mirrored by the two other judges at the bench. He'd scored.

"None," he'd replied flatly, turning back to the question. "Nor is there any evidence that he was at the scene that night. In fact, I can't even find a witness who will testify they've ever seen him enter the building—in his life!" The prosecutor had looked like he wanted to knife Vincent for that one.

"Oh come now, Sir Vincent!" Cooper's lawyer looked as if someone had handed him all his Winterfest gifts at once, wrapped in gold foil. "Everyone makes at least one trip to Bishop Florian Hall. It's a city landmark!"

That had provided an opportunity for Vincent to drive the knife into this travesty of justice and be done with it. "Obviously, you have as little idea about how the poor in this city live as the prosecutor over there. David Cooper lives in a small one-room flat. Not exactly the kind of digs one would expect for a thief able to afford the kind of magitech needed to defeat the security surrounding the *Zak*. Further, his legal history is long, making it possible to work out, at least loosely, what his average annual income has been for, oh, the last ten years or so. With a few exceptions, it's been less than five hundred pounds, yearly. Again, not exactly the kind of income necessary to buy or rent the magitech horsepower he needed to defeat the best security money can buy, or even to turn in the kinds of circles where such contacts can be found.

"The poor can't afford club memberships any more than they can afford sight seeing trips to Bishop Florian Hall. Nor can they afford the kinds of personal trainers who teach special forces grade, hand-to-hand combat—and Cooper was never in the military," Vincent had added, though of course these were things that everyone knew. It was part of the theater of justice—or perhaps "injustice"—that the courts had become in Fernwall. By stating the obvious, he got it written into the transcripts of the trial. That prevented the realities of poverty from being completely overlooked merely because they made the fat aristocrats that ran the legal system uncomfortable.

"And why would such highly specialized training be required?" Cooper's lawyer had asked, encouraging his new star witness to elaborate at will.

"Four armed guards were taken down in close quarters without a sound being made. They were not killed. As the prosecution's witnesses have already testified and the facts show, they were incapacitated, and incapacitating a victim is considerably more difficult than killing him," Vincent had explained, barely checking his own impatience. "Yet, the thief risked the increase in difficulty *rather* than killing, which means the thief not only had the requisite skills, but had them at a level that let him or her feel comfortable taking on the increased risks associated with at least three perfectly silent take-downs in quick succession. The prosecution is right to state that Goodman Cooper's record shows that he never kills, but to extrapolate from the lack of deaths involved in his thefts that he therefore possesses the training of a veteran special forces operative—or master assassin—is a leap too far."

It had been enough. Cooper had neither the skills nor the money to commit the crime of which he had been accused. The trial had ended pretty much as Vincent and Roland had known it would. The prosecution's flimsy circumstantial evidence wasn't enough. Cooper was found not guilty of the *Mâgun-Zak* theft.

That was the good news.

The bad news was that the hunt was still on for the ancient dwarven artifact and it seemed everybody had a way to make use of the popular crisis of the day. Officially, little to no progress had been made on finding either it or the *real* thief, and the political ramifications were building almost as fast as the trouble in the traps. The head of the Committee on Law Enforcement in the House of Commons was screaming her bloody head off, and so was old Henry Craigmont, Duke of Trobiere. Amusing though he found it, the political screeching wasn't the real problem.

People nobody cared about were being killed and wounded at an alarming rate, simply because they were in the way—*that* was the real problem.

He turned to Barbara Cole's notes. They were extensive but incomplete, and so practically useless. Cole had been snooping about in "River Trap", a part of town that extended about a kilometer around The Poleman. River Trap was where one went to move goods in and out of the city quietly. So far, so good, but traps were called "traps" for a reason: They kept insiders inside, but they also kept outsiders outside—once someone got inside they were "blood" and there was no going back. Betrayal of your trap was a death sentence. If someone wasn't "blood" they weren't getting access, end of discussion. Questions by strangers weren't appreciated. If someone got too nosy, they ended up like Cole.

On the surface it seemed simple, but it wasn't. While trap culture changed slowly, political structures in a trap could change overnight, especially at the street level. Every time the police made an arrest, shut down a smuggling operation, or closed off a supply line, the effects rippled out like a rock thrown into a pond. Very real and usually very poor people lost well-loved and much-needed family members, or a living, or their social status within the trap, and sometimes all three at once.

Bureaucrats and society busybodies called such operations things like "cleaning up the town", or "sending a message to the criminal elements that they can't operate with impunity", or "making our city safe for our children." Such heavy-handed law enforcement did none of those things, as anybody who had lived among the poor well knew. One thing it *did* do was make the traps very dangerous places for the uninitiated until a new equilibrium was established.

That's what troubled Vincent about Cole's attack. The killings and beatings were happening so fast that equilibrium couldn't be achieved. The normal political power structures in the traps were breaking down, leading to violence which led to greater destabilization and more violence in a vicious spiral of distrust that typically ended in a trap war.

The burning question was: Why? What set this off in the first place? Was it really the hunt for the *'Zak?* and if so, just *who* was doing the hunting, and the killing?

He tried cross-referencing Cole's notes with other police activity that could have set River Trap on edge and came up with... *nothing!* There were a couple of seemingly unrelated sightings of a woman matching the description of Cole's savior. One was from a beggar posing as a match seller, who claimed he saw her scale a warehouse wall. In another report he found a dock worker who thought he'd seen someone matching her description streak across Telladi-Pelletier Boulevard at the south end of Beacon Bridge. The only piece of information containing any possible relevance to the violence was a strange report about unknown sex workers frequenting the bars that the bargemen were known to patronize. The odd thing in that report was that the supposed prostitutes spent a lot of time cozying up to these equally unknown patrons, only to leave by the main door, rather than the bedroom door. In and of itself, it was a small thing, but small things had a way of setting off big things in a trap full of people who were already living on the edge. He filed that little tidbit of information away for future reference.

In a way, what he found and didn't find relieved him. Commissioner Roland knew first hand the result that law enforcement activity had on those who lived in the traps. Officially, his internal police policy had been *not* to interfere unless absolutely necessary, and then to use as light a hand as possible, but *something* had River Trap, in particular, teetering on a knife's edge. Just last night, one man had been killed outright and another died hours later from a knife wound in the belly. Why hadn't the deaths at *least* triggered retaliatory killings?

He turned back to the file on Cole's attack. A couple of uniformed officers had been working nearby and had filed reports. One was from a nearby shopkeeper, who told an officer one of the dead men had been around earlier that evening asking after a woman matching the same general description as Cole's savior. The deceased had told the shopkeeper he had "something to discuss" with her, and had even offered money in exchange for the information.

So, there's outside money being thrown around. That's guaranteed to set trap folks' teeth on edge. Nice, but not particularly useful.

In fact, there was very little useful in *any* of it. There was only one conclusion he could draw: The victims and the assailant—presumably the same dark-garbed woman as Cole's savior—were outsiders. That's why there had not been any retaliatory killings. It might also be the reason a trap war had looked imminent for weeks but had not yet started. There were "strange folk about" and more outsider deaths than insider deaths. The traps were confused, but also cautious. *Nobody* wanted a trap war. Nobody.

He sat back and stared into the fire thoughtfully. Had Cole been investigating River Trap because she had believed there was a correlation between the violence in River Trap and the *Mâgun-Zak?* Did she believe that it was there, or that someone in River Trap knew where it was, or where it had gone? If so, on that score Vincent was fairly certain she was wrong. An artifact as valuable as the *Mâgun-Zak* would not be found anywhere in the South End, never mind in River Trap. If there had been any serious negotiations going on about moving such a valuable item out of the city through the river trap underground, he'd have heard about it.

Upon further reflection, he had to admit that while he had his head stuck in an ale barrel, half the city could have disappeared and he might have missed it. In any event, it was safe to conclude that Cole had unknowingly stepped onto a battlefield where all sides had marked her as an enemy. The result was as inevitable as was the only possible conclusion: There were new players in town, players that either didn't know about the local rules or didn't care about them.

That description might have fit Angelique to a tee, but he'd made it his business to know that she had done little but attend to church and baronial matters since he'd caught her sneaking back into her own bedroom that night. So, who was this woman stalking through the traps, and who or what was after her?

Commissioner Roland's door was open when Vincent arrived. He was facing a wall in his office, fussing over a cabinet lock.

"Unless you have a thief in the house, a key usually works best, boss," he drawled, crossing over to Roland's liquor cabinet.

"Maybe a *locksmith*. You might remember that we try to keep thieves in pens downstairs," Roland said, giving him a *very* unhappy look. "This damn thing's rusty, that's all. And you keep your nose out of that, you're not even dried out yet, dammit." He turned to pluck the glass from Vincent's hand, then slammed it upside down on the tray. "You got a lot of credibility to earn back around here. From now on, that only happens when you're sober."

Vincent paused in the act of unstoppering a bottle, then thought better of it and reached for the coffee pot, instead. None of this was going to be easy, but he'd asked for—no, he'd *demanded*—the freedom to do as he wished with his life when he'd stormed out of his father's house. Now came the part he'd never wanted to face: the responsibility.

What was that about being pulled into the vortex, ol' boy?

"I know I have a lot of apologies to make, and I know I'm indebted to you." Vincent turned to face the older man and tried to smile. "You could have sold me out and nobody would have blamed you. Even me."

Roland allowed himself to be mollified, if only a little. The younger man had charm enough, but not even his uncustomary candor could dispel the weight of the burdens on the older man's broad shoulders. He shrugged that off and gestured Vincent toward a chair. "Had no one to blame but myself, son. I took you on as a personal responsibility, and that effectively tied my career to your sentence. I haven't done such a great job of it. I'm just sorry Cole's the one who had to pay the price."

Vincent stared at the steam rising from his coffee for a long minute before answering. "You... can put that one on my shoulders too, Chief. If I had..."

He stopped and suddenly stood back up. *If you'd what? If you'd not been duped by Angelique? If you'd sold her out?* He walked over to the windows, and stared down at the streets. They had been his home for seven, going on eight years. He knew things about this city that no cop, nobleman, or politician would ever know, and what had he done with that knowledge? Damned little! Sure, he had conned some crooked business owners out of the money they were bilking out of the locals—and had turned a nice profit in the process—but so what? He hadn't changed anything. The poor were still poor, and truth to tell, most of them were proud to be what they were. They didn't want money, his or anybody else's. They wanted work and the dignity that came with honest work. They wanted fair pay to provide for their families. It was the kind of thing the Raven couldn't provide, and no amount of sympathizing on his part was going to help. If he was ever going to make a difference, to *find a point* to all this, he had to do something differently, and that had to begin now.

"If I had done the job you asked me to do, it probably wouldn't have happened, and you probably wouldn't be looking at a trap war for your troubles," he finally managed to say, glancing over at his warden once before turning back to the street. "If you have any other officers in the traps, I'd suggest you get them out before it happens to them, because it will."

"Give me an alternative." Roland's voice slashed through his half-voiced reverie. "You're supposed to be the Raven. *Give me a choice!*"

Vincent walked slowly back to his chair, sat down, and met Roland's gaze. "The MARCUS Agency," he said. "Maybe Rubiyet's. They've got the manpower, and inside access to the kind of information needed to do what needs to be done without triggering trap-wide violence."

Roland's jaw clenched, and he got up to close his office door, effectively rendering whatever was said next "off the record". He and his department had tangled with MARCUS agents from time to time over the years, and there were bruises on both sides to show for it.

"MARCUS is a private agency. They're not servants to anyone or anything but Goodman Marcus' bottom line. If his people wanted to be involved, they'd be all over it already. Thing is, they know what shit smells like and they've got the gods-given good sense to stay out of it. Gaust is too stupid to risk anywhere near that part of town, and Cole's damned near dead. Unless I want to use the assignment as an indirect way to kill off useless time-servers like Braddock and his cronies, I got no one else.

"That just leaves you and me," he said, concluding the refutation by collapsing into his loudly-protesting chair. "You read the file. Lady Emilia isn't going to stand between us and that fat-mouthed Trobiere forever. I'm frankly surprised she hasn't summoned us both up to Angel Heights to rake us over the coals. She can't wait all that much longer for you to extract your head from your ass, Vince, and neither can I. So, if you're going, we're going together—and we're rolling for the whole house."

In plain language, Roland was telling him that he was prepared to ignore the legal limits, to accept the risks involved, to do what needed to be done to take down as much of Fernwall's criminal underworld as necessary to set this right.

Vincent gave him a long, hard look. Being the son of a baron, even the youngest son, he knew just how ugly power games could get, especially when they were played for territory. That's *exactly* what Fernwall's Police Chief was saying he was willing to risk: not just a trap war, but a city wide turf war!

24

In his rush to leave his father, Vincent was also leaving power and wealth as he understood them. He'd since learned the hard way that he'd just run from one form to another. In the end, power was power, markets were markets, and capital was capital. All the rest, the fancy titles and tall buildings and the expensive suits, those were just the window dressing that made the nobility and aristocracy feel better about themselves.

On the other side of it, the generosity to the poor in the traps made the crime lords and gang leaders feel better about themselves. It was all a game that was played with human lives even if it didn't kill, and sometimes it did. In a turf war, there would most certainly be killing. With the traps already on edge, it would only take one mistake to set off a conflagration that could cover the city from Three Quarters to South End.

"This could get away from everyone in a hurry, boss. You're sure you want to do this?" he asked, his voice still quiet.

The weight of his years seemed to settle on him abruptly, and Roland suddenly looked old. "What a question," he rasped. "I came into this job with the personal mission to make law enforcement less burdensome for the vast majority of working day folk in this city. Used to be, the old-time crime bosses felt the same way—they did their crimes, but everyone knew the rules, and they never made it harder on the locals. The end of the war changed all that. The war profiteers have found a way to exploit everything they can get their hands on, and most of it his happening in parts of the city-state that I can't see. Things have gotten so much worse for everyone that at least one of them can arrange for the theft of the *Zak*, and make an attempt to frame Cooper for it. Not content with that, they've moved on to beatings and murders in River Trap and are managing to keep South End on edge.

"Now, a few months ago," Roland went on, leaning back in his chair tiredly, "I sent a cop out to investigate the theft of the *Mâgun-Zak*. It was all going along more or less according to schedule when that cop—you—dropped his line of investigation like a hot poker. You held yourself together long enough, just barely, to keep Cooper out of a collar, and then you disappeared. When you resurfaced, it was just long enough to have a huge public fight with the only noblewoman in this city besotted enough with you to agree to marry you. Then you ditched again."

The silence around them built for several moments while Vincent braced himself for the inevitable conclusion. "I'm an old cop, Vince," Roland finally said. "I know a causality chain when I see one. You dropped the investigation because you discovered who did it and you could not make the arrest. You couldn't even let Cole or Gaust do it. Why? Because you felt compelled to protect the real thief's identity. That's easy.

"The list of persons for whom you would be willing to compromise yourself and your sentence? Extremely short, I'd say, and there would have to be some pretty hefty *extenuating circumstances*."

Roland paused in his recounting, underscoring those last words and their significance with silence before he continued. "And, that's about as far as

I've been willing to think it over. I've got a lot of important people screaming at me to find the *'Zak*, or failing that, they'd like me to collar the one who stole it. Thing is? They're just as gods-be-damned indiscriminate about ruined lives as that crime boss is, and I've had all I can stomach of the pack of 'em. All they really want is a scapegoat, another fancy show trial to make things right all around. I swore an oath to protect and serve the parliament and the people of this city-state. The best way to do that as I see it is to stop this trap war before it starts.

"You asked me if I was sure I wanted to do this?" Roland stood up from his chair, knuckles planted as he leaned over the top of his desk. "Yeah. I'm sure. You're my last trump, Vince. Make it *right*."

The younger man swallowed hard, wondering at how wildly Roland differed from his father. Both men were angry, but unlike his father's rages, Roland's ire was pointed at things that mattered, at injustice and cruelty, at corrupted power, and at the notion of disposable people. He was angry at the same things that made Vincent angry. He just came at it from a different angle.

When he had left his office, Vincent had known this case was big. Now he had a better idea of how just how big it was, and how far into that old vortex he'd been drawn, but he saw no way out. If there was a way out it had to be down, right down into it. Down was the only way left he could go.

"Then get your people out," he said standing up, "and I'll need my tools back." He offered Roland his hand, meeting the older man's gaze and holding it, his own steady. There was no arrogance in his eyes, but no fear either. He was in a place he'd never been before: over the edge with a perfectly clear mind.

Roland clasped his hand, looked into Raven's eyes, then nodded once. "I'll send a couple of 'cruits down to the vault for the trunk. Anything else?"

"Get a few body bags ready," Vincent said. "It's time a few of the *right* people started dying."

Chapter 2

Blakesly House, Angels
17 Vilmath, 580

Once again, morning had found Iris once again sprinting across the lawns of Blakesly House in a hazy, predawn hour, heading for the trellis that led to the second story bedroom window of the Baroness of Carlisle. The trellis was a barren, thorn-ridden thing in winter, bearing little resemblance to the riot of color and bloom it became in fairer seasons. She'd had it reinforced several months ago when the increased tempo of her secret comings and goings had taken an almost fatal toll on the woodwork. It didn't so much as creak as she covered the vertical distance to the unlocked window, shimmying through it, and then into the relative safety of the bedchamber of the baroness.

A heavily shaded crystal lamp stood upon the nightstand near the bed— the lady suffered terrible nightmares, as most of her staff well knew—but Iris spared little attention for the elegance of the surroundings. Some of the servants were already awake and preparing for the appearance of Lady Blakesly, and that meant she had little time for smirking over the decor. Iris sat at the vanity, peeling her long, deep blue winter gloves from her arms and then the short-haired black wig from her scalp with precise, efficient movements. Items were folded and placed in a box as she removed them, including the rest of the close-fitting blue suit she'd worn, all fatally edged implements, and even the boots—*Thank you Raven, you son of a bitch, for pointing* that *mistake out to me!*—which she wrapped in canvas for protection.

With that thought, she placed the locked storage chest into its hidden recess under the bed, then replaced the floor boards. One last glance about told her that all was in order. She donned the lady's silken-soft nightgown, mussed her hair thoroughly, laid down in the bed with the covers pulled over and promptly fell fast asleep.

Less than two hours later, a very distressed Clarice desperately attempted to awaken her mistress, who could not seem to keep her eyes open long enough to complete a sentence. "My lady, please... you must try to stay awake."

Angelique roused herself out of a doze once again, shaking her head ruefully. "I am trying, my dear," she said, the end of it getting swallowed by an indelicate yawn. "Are you quite sure of . . . the time. . . ?"

"Of course I am, my dear lady. What a thing to—oh dear, she's fallen off again. My lady," the girl said, as loudly as she dared. Two of the new housemaids were in the sitting room just without, preparing a morning tray for the baroness. She really did not want to attract their attention or give them, and especially that nosy girl Patsy any reason—any *more* reasons—to gossip.

"You really must awaken. The countess of Remington has sent you word, she wishes to see you *today,* I'm afraid you cannot sleep!"

Word of dear Lady Emilia forced Angelique to breathe deeply and swing her legs over the edge of her bed, pulling herself upright by sheer will. She muttered something in D'waanese that Clarice couldn't quite make out, but then cleared her throat and spoke a bit more loudly.

"Lady Emilia? Very well, dear girl, no need to summon the *galdünë,* ah, the 'cavalry' I think we say here. I shall be seeing her at the Auxiliary meeting this afternoon, shall I not?" She yawned again, covering it with the back of her hand this time. Her maid's hesitation cut it short, and she glanced at her in hazy confusion.

"Clarice?"

"The Ladies' Auxiliary meeting was yesterday, my lady," the girl said, eyes downcast.

The news, as well as the shame and dread that washed over her on hearing it, had become all too familiar in the past weeks. "I see," Angelique said, though of course she didn't. She had no memories of any of it, but the mere fact of it was so odd—how did one say such a thing?

"Do you think you can stay awake now, my lady? Shall I bring you some tea from your tray? It's just without," her young maid asked anxiously.

"Please, my dear," she replied, swallowing her growing dismay with the tail end of a yawn she couldn't stifle. It looked to be another long day of trying to remain alert enough to manage her struggling barony, and to meet the demands of a social position that had become as hollow as she looked and felt. She glanced toward the drawer of her nightstand. In it was an alchemical tincture which her physician had prescribed against fatigue. Derived from a potion created during the war to help soldiers offset the effects of prolonged combat operations, a milder version of it was prescribed in the post-war decades by healers as a way to manage any temporary period of insomnia. If it didn't quite have the same potency of the "mule's kick" a veteran knew, in Angelique's experience, a few drops in a cup of tea would clear most of the fog from her head. It would allow her to get through her meeting with her friend and mentor, who also happened to be one of the most powerful women in the city-state *and* one of the co-chairs of the Ladies' Auxiliary of the Guardian Paladin Church.

Of course, there were unpleasant side effects if the drug were used to replace sleep entirely: tremors, headaches, dizziness, nausea, hallucinations, psychotic episodes, even heart failure in extreme cases. These hardly concerned her, for she felt she could be in no danger of abusing it, even though she could not recall how she had obtained more when she had run out, the week before.

Clarice returned with her morning tray. Smiling her thanks, Angelique waited until the girl had turned to the wardrobe before dosing her cup, managing to replace the tiny flask in its drawer before the girl could see. It was impossible, however, to hide the livid bruise on her thigh and the long scrapes and scratches on her arms. Clarice's innocent eyes pleaded with her for the explanations, but there had already been so many cuts and bruises that she had not been able to explain. In the end, it was just easier to add these to the list.

The rest of the routine went more smoothly once the drug took effect. After she was dressed, Angelique read passages from *The Lady's Book of Hours,* the folio of religious poetry and short prose works that had given her comfort and guidance during the last few difficult months. Too weary to cultivate new acquaintances or even maintain the ones she had, she found herself returning to the collected works of her adopted church in the long, dark hours when loneliness and grief threatened to overwhelm her.

Once at her vanity, she read through her correspondence, only looking up as her maid finished tucking the last few blond locks into the demure coil she typically wore at the back of her neck. The pink and dove-gray gown she'd chosen had brightened her complexion decently, but nothing short of a miracle would hide the dark circles under her eyes. If she looked hag-ridden of late, it hadn't slowed down the flood of introductory cards and invitations that had begun to arrive shortly after the spectacle she had made of herself at the Belton House Winter Ball. Most of them were from other young noblemen, each of whom hoped to turn a rich and titled widow's affections in his direction. She pushed away the cynical thoughts about auction blocks and high bidders, having accustomed herself to ignoring such idle mental exercises on topics she did not wish to dignify by paying them attention. They soon subsided, allowing her to catch her maid's questioning gaze, reflected in the mirror.

"Well done, as always, Clarice," she assured the girl, arising with fatigue she couldn't quite disguise.The medicinal draft had cleared her head, but her body still felt as if overnight, it had become lead. "Be so good as to ask Verlinden to have the carriage brought around. No, I do not wish to break my fast," she added, seeing how the girl turned toward where a light repast had been set for her in her sitting room. "I am not hungry, dear. Now go and speak to our new butler as I bade you. I shall be down directly."

Only when she was alone did she pick up the card which bore the embossed family crest of Lady Emilia Fauré-Nielsen. Angelique knew that Emilia's mother had once been a high-ranking priestess in Vin-Nôrë. It had been the Vin-Nôrean tie between them that had given Lady Blakesly a widow's honorable introduction to position and society in Fernwall, the city-state that remained after the kingdom of Cascadia fractured into its constituent duchies and earldoms. That this tie had been based upon a lie was something that pained Angelique terribly.

From the desk of Lady Emilia Nielsen

16 Vilmath, 580

To Lady Angelique Blakesly
Blakesly House

I look forward to seeing you in my private sitting room at Fourteen-Hundred Hours this very day, my dear, for afternoon tea and some conversation. Your repeated absences from the meetings of the Women's Auxiliary have been much remarked upon, and I am afraid some of your conduct of late has called into question certain matters that I thought you might wish to discuss. I have ever been your friend here in Fernwall, Angelique. I hope you will always regard me as such, and find it in your heart to trust me with whatever has been weighing so heavily upon you.

Faithfully Yours,

A personal seal was affixed just below the ornate signature letter: Emilia's monogram backed by the Lady's Rose, in blood-red wax.

"Well, perhaps it might do me good to speak about my decisions regarding Vincent," Angelique mused, placing the letter upon her writing desk before gathering what she needed on her way out. "If I have transgressed against the Lady's commandments and committed blasphemies in the heat of unlawful lust, then I do need her counsel. My conflicted soul can find no peace, not even in slumber. If anyone will know how I am to win free of this, it will be Lady Emilia."

Nodding to herself, Lady Blakesly picked up her hand purse and swept down the stairs, as prepared as she could be for the meeting to come.

"My lady." It was Clarice's voice, once again bringing Angelique to wakefulness. "We're here."

Lady Emilia's home in Fernwall was one of the grandest estates that graced the city of "Angels", originally named so for the dozens of sculptures of the same name that decorated the edifice of the Grand Cathedral of the Guardian Paladin. The church had been one of the first structures built in the hills north of Fernwall proper and remained an iconic sight even in the modern world.

Remington Hall was perhaps a league's distance from the cathedral, nestled in a trio of hills and up a long drive through copses of oak and alder. The gray and green marble edifice gleamed through hazy morning sun, almost a shadow under the weak, late-autumn sunshine that momentarily burned through the high clouds. The hall was a showpiece for the old Llamázi style. Rows of arches guarded the ground floor while rectangular, mullioned windows marched across the upper floors like reflective soldiers. The towers were round with only a few, small windows. It was all topped with ornate, room-like chimney structures. Later additions showed the less colorful, but more functional Llamázi revival style, while the newest addition, constructed late in the Nadrean era, was a fine example of garish excesses in glass and ornate detail typical of the period.

"Thank you, my dear," Angelique murmured, straightening in her seat. She hadn't truly been sleeping. The draft she'd taken earlier prevented that, but it seemed as if she had fallen into something of a doze as they traveled, for she dreamed she'd been listening in on an argument between several women over topics she could not now quite recall.

The horses clattered to a stop beneath the portico. A liveried footman approached to open the door, assisting the baroness and then her lady's maid safely to the ground.

"Welcome, Lady Blakesly," Armand smiled as he came forward to greet her. The gentle old duffer was Remington's butler and was unreasonably fond of her, ostensibly for their shared Vin-Nôrean heritage. "We haven't seen much of you here at Remington Hall of late. I trust you've been well?"

"As well as may be expected, dear Armand," Angelique replied, grateful for his concern. "And you?"

"As well as may be expected," he agreed, handing her cloak off to a footman. "Ah, and here is Lady Rebecca to accompany us," he said then, gesturing to where the middle-aged woman who served Lady Emilia as ladies' maid, scribe, and long-time companion descended the grand staircase. Rebecca had been the one who had trained Clarice in service, and the two had remained close in the months since. Their chatter covered Angelique's silence as they traversed the beautifully appointed halls toward the countess's personal sitting room. Though she'd spent many an hour within its confines since coming to Fernwall, Angelique had never actually been "summoned" there until that moment. She was not entirely sure that her mentor was not terribly displeased with her for more than her frequent absences of late.

Armand stepped smartly ahead of them and opened one of the great double doors. "Lady Angelique Blakesly," he announced.

The three women glided past him into the richly appointed room. For all its beauty, Lady Emilia's private sitting room was a study of simplicity and comfort. The tables and cupboards were finely crafted and hand-rubbed to a soft glow. The chairs around the great hearth were comfortable, not pretentious. The tables were utilitarian, rather than ostentatious. Everything was ordered, had its place, and was kept *in* its place. This was only partly due to Lady Emilia's blindness, but also because she believed that a disciplined and ordered home led to a disciplined and ordered life, a righteous life free from the temptations of impulse and excess. She was a Guardian Paladin who lived her religion every day, and she had been an inspiration to Angelique Blakesly, who was on the short list of the nobly born who rated access to this most intimate sanctum.

Blind or not, Lady Emilia was making herself a cup of tea when they arrived. Rebecca immediately moved to take over the task, *tsking* at her in the old, familiar way they'd shared ever since Angelique had known them. Emilia smiled fondly as she returned to the hearth.

"Do sit down, Angelique." The elderly matron settled back into her seat. She had spoken softly, but there was a note of steel in her voice that Angelique was not accustomed to hearing. Heart sinking, she smoothed the front of her gown and sat as she'd been bade.

"My dear lady Emilia," she began, casting about for the words to frame an apology. The older woman merely picked up her prayer beads and waited patiently for her protégé to continue. There was little left for Angelique to do but straighten her spine and forge ahead.

"Allow me to apologize for missing the last Auxiliary meeting," she finally said, not knowing where else to begin. The worst part about all this was that she had no idea where she'd actually *been* during that time.

Lady Emilia's beads continued to click as they passed through her fingers, but she remained silent, expectant. The soft ticking of the mantel clock expanded into the tomb-like quiet of the room, filling it with an insistent prompting to speak. Speak. Speak. Speak. Angelique clamped her lips together to keep a stream of incoherent babble from spewing forth, for it came from several different points of view, and all of them were located behind her own eyes.

She shook her head in an attempt to clear it. "My lady, I have no reasons that do not sound like excuses. I don't wish to offend either of us by offering them. I did wish to speak with you today about a rather painful decision I've reached," she added, fighting down the stubborn lump that had formed in her throat. "After much thought and prayer, I find I must put an official end to the betrothal with Vincent. He has all but ended it, unofficially."

"Then why, my dear child, have you not been taking advantage of the many invitations you have since received?"

Stung, Angelique glanced swiftly at Emilia. "I will not be forsworn, my lady," she murmured, grateful for the cup of tea Clarice offered. "I have made promises. Somewhat rashly perhaps, in hindsight, but they were made in good faith on my part. I must end it with him before I may look elsewhere for... male companionship." She sipped her tea to avoid adding that such companionship was at the uttermost bottom of her list of things to acquire then, or in the near future.

Lady Emilia set her prayer beads aside momentarily to sample from her own cup. "And yet..." she murmured over the steaming rim, "you have not done *that* either."

The snort that followed was unladylike and though it came from Angelique, it startled her more than it did her mentor. "Your pardon, my dear lady. I meant only to say that I have been attempting to arrange a meeting with Sir Vincent. He cannot be found. The desk officer at Police Headquarters says only that Chief Inspector Sultaire is not there. My inquiries to his office have received no response. Messengers sent to his home are never answered."

A voice from deep within her wailed in grief. Angelique did her best to ignore it. "Short of hiring a private investigator to track him down," she said, throat clenching tightly around the words, "I am left with little choice but to wait for him to be dragged out of whatever gutter or brothel he has fallen into this time."

The beads clicked, the clock ticked. The older woman seemed to be thinking. Angelique knew that Emilia's duties on the upper house's Law Enforcement Committee had given her access to reports on the progress of Vincent's indenture, but what wound her nerves almost to the breaking point was the impression that Lady Emilia was "looking into" the matter, and the reminder that she didn't need eyes to see what she most needed to see.

"The determined, clear-minded woman I knew a year ago would have camped out at Vincent's doorstep until he relented," Emilia said at last, "or stood in front of Commissioner Roland's desk until he'd sent a squad out to fetch her betrothed back. I cannot 'see' the reasons why you have not, my dear, but I *can* 'see' with perfect clarity that there are things about this matter that you have not told me. I would like to invite you to do so, now."

"My dear Lady Emilia, I cannot think—"

"I agree. You're exhausted, and you have been so for weeks. You are normally known to be resourceful and energetic, but those resources are clearly being spent elsewhere, and rather prodigiously, it seems."

Emilia didn't need eyes to notice the blank look on the younger woman's face, either.

"I beg your pardon, my lady?" Angelique asked, a bit bewildered.

"Why else would you be so exhausted all the time that Clarice can't even keep you awake?"

The girl at least had the good grace to blush at the exposure, though she did not betray in any other way that she'd heard. Clarice and Rebecca were both bound to their mistresses by vows both holy and secular, as the Guardian Paladins had always done. Under normal circumstances, their loyalty to their mistress was unquestioning and unquestionable. Apparently these were not normal circumstances for either of them.

She reached for the obvious excuse. "It is only that I have not been sleeping well, my lady."

It was Emilia's turn to snort. With one hand, she gestured somewhat impatiently for Angelique to continue. Swallowing heavily, she did.

"I simply... cannot seem to rest, when I sleep. I awaken feeling even more fatigued than I was the night before. I have nightmares, and there have been... interludes, recently, when I cannot for the sake of my soul remember where I have been, or what I have done.

"I fear Our Lady punishes me now for acts of... blasphemy, I believe I must call them, though it burns me with shame now to have to say it." Angelique let those last words out in a rush, placing her teacup back upon the low table before she could spill it.

Lady Emilia frowned. "Blasphemy? That seems unlike you, Angelique."

Close to tears now, the younger woman allowed her face to drop into her hands. "In a moment of heated passion," she began miserably, "I called upon the Lord and Lady of Paladins. While coupled unlawfully, I swore an oath, before our God, to Vincent. There was a passage from *Cantons of Ecstasy...*"

"The bit about any two or more joining in communion in the Paladin's name?"

Emilia's casually-guessed reply startled Angelique. "That's the one," she admitted miserably. "We were not betrothed, at the time. He offered no oath in return..."

Angelique abruptly went still. It seemed that there had been some *other* event attached to that night. Something monumental had happened—no, not *happened... The* Mâgun-Zak *had been stolen... That I stole it? Why should I feel as if I had anything to do with that? I would not even know how!* She sat in the ticking silence as something akin to horror and shame spread through her, but it was not at the confession she'd just made to her friend and mentor.

The countess sipped her tea calmly as she waited for the tension in the air to dissipate. "Before our Lady could possibly punish you for your sins, She would have to accept the Judge's punishment for Her own transgressions," she finally pointed out.

"She is punished," Angelique said, hardly daring to whisper it. "Every day She must bear witness to the evil Her acts released into this world." It was derived from Paladin scripture, however loosely. As the Lady, the Paladin had joined with Eldar to bring forth Valïa, a holy child of purest goodness to advocate compassion for the poor, sick, and needy. It was a noble intention, but it was an act committed against the universal laws of creation laid down for the Gods by *their* Father. He, it was told, had hurled himself into the fabric of creation to stop the unending waves of insect-like demon-hordes which poured into the world in response to the wildly unbalancing effect of the divine child's birth.

"And though I am but a mortal woman," Angelique went on miserably, "I bear witness to the evil my own acts have wrought. Had I been of stronger character, had I taken the Lady's lessons about honor and restraint to heart... but I did not. Our relationship was not strong enough to withstand it... and now he is lost to me."

Lady Emilia remained silent and thought about that while each tick of the clock seemed to truncate time rather than simply mark its passing. Though it was true that the Lady exhorted young people to channel their sexual power into lawful and ordained marriage—for the good of society—

nowhere in the Paladin religion was it *forbidden* to have sexual relations before marriage. Rather, the concept of wrong-doing was focused on bringing an unsupported child into the world, a child devoid of the family, fortune, and connections that the social institution of "marriage" provided. This was why Lady Emilia had ruthlessly quashed the rumors swimming around her protégé. It had less to do with Angelique's private life than it did with keeping Church dogma grounded in scripture. Sex outside of marriage *of itself* was not a sin, something the conservatives within the Paladin Church frequently liked to forget. These were *basic* teachings, and Angelique knew them well—so well that she had, at one time, considered her relationship with Vincent to be blessed. Now she was calling it sin. The question was, why?

"Angelique, I'm going to have to insist that you be entirely forthcoming with me," Lady Emilia said, suddenly changing tacks and startling Angelique with her brusqueness. "My dear, no son of the Baron of Valemont is going to fall apart simply because he asked a pretty girl to marry him. There is more here. *Much* more, and if you want my help, you must tell me *everything.*"

"I...my lady Emilia, I have confessed—"

"Angelique!" Emilia turned sightless eyes unerringly to where her lady's maid stood. "Rebecca my dear, I think Baroness Blakesly and I need to talk privately for a bit." Clarice was as startled as her mistress at this, but Rebecca gathered the girl with one arm and escorted her into the hallway, then closed the door, leaving the two noblewomen in the room. Their servants would stand guard against any interruption until they were summoned from within. Angelique couldn't wait that long.

"My dear Lady Emilia, I swear I have told you all I know!"

Again, Lady Emilia held her peace. Seconds turned into minutes while in her way she examined not the words, but rather the soul of the woman who spoke them. When they had been introduced, Angelique had been possessed of a cast-iron will and more life experience than many people twice her age. Now she used what little will she had left to fend off inquiry like a native Cascadian aristocrat, but it was an insufficient cover for a soul so tormented it no longer even knew itself. *Something* was eating away at her internal resources like a cancer, but the older woman could not quite discern what it was.

However, she thought there might be a way to force it to reveal itself. "I believe you are telling me the truth, or most of it," Lady Emilia finally said, setting her prayer beads aside. She levered herself out of her chair, then stepped hesitantly toward the chair where Angelique sat. "But a thing can be true, and still not be true. There is something hiding inside you, Angelique. Will you let me help you bring it into the open?"

She could sense the firestorm of conflict that the offer had raised within the younger woman. She clearly wished for Emilia's help, but it was not with a whole heart. Hearing neither objection nor consent, the lady lifted one hand and gently placed it on Angelique's head and began to pray. With the fingers of the other, she traced the sign of the benedictory of the Lady.

35

Something passed between them at the touch. Whether it was some spark of divine power as a priest of any religion might have invoked, or simply that Angelique's newfound piety would not allow her to maintain any manner of deception before such a blessing, Angel never knew. She had been paying close attention to the conversation, but it had been easier to let Angelique speak and act since she understood the ins and outs of Paladin society so well. Angel had only just realized that she could not call the intimate knowledge that the baroness possessed to the fore of her mind, nor the delicate Vin-Nôrean accent with which she had only just been speaking. She looked up at the formidable old lady's face in sudden horror, not really knowing what to say, or how to explain any of it. When she did speak, the voice in her ears was full of the soft consonants and gently rounded vowels of the south country.

South *Cascadia*.

"I—Ah... Ah b-beg your pardon. Milady. Milady *Countess*," she stammered. Lady Emilia staggered back. "Ah m-most humbly beg it, but Ah don't know what t' say."

Eyebrow arched, Emilia groped for her chair, then collapsed into it when she found it. No one else had entered this room, but someone else was *definitely* seated in it now. The shifts she sensed were much, much more subtle than the change in accent. Though she had no eyes by which to see the physical changes before her, she could *hear* them and *feel* them with perfect clarity. If it had not come about from a holy benediction, she might have suspected necromantic possession, but no spirit could have withstood the Benedictory of the Lady.

"For the love of the Lord," she breathed. "The duchy of Asbury, yes?"

Angel covered her mouth, hand trembling badly. "Yes, milady," she said, hardly daring to speak. "The Siddoway family seat, at Carolin' Dell." The ducal family held some of the best of the wine country directly, including the network of valleys known and named for the way the vine-tenders called to one another from the slope of one hill to another.

"I visited that country many years ago as a young woman," Emilia replied quietly, clearly taken aback by what the Lady had revealed in this interview. "I still had my sight then, and I remember the extraordinary green of the vineyards in summer. Row after row of vines rolling across the gentle hills. And the smells in the fall..." She smiled at the memory. Those had been hard times. The Asbury wine country had been a refuge for her during the latter years of the war. Its stately manor houses and manicured gardens provided a welcome rest to her, and to other souls tired of the struggle of holding together a world that seemed to prefer tp tear itself apart.

Angel did not know what to say. Lady Emilia drew a breath and continued. "You know I am a countess, but do you know who?"

"The Countess of Remington," Angel said, nodding promptly to the question. She'd sidled over to the lovely worked-marble mantel and stood before it, her hands clenching its smoothly wrought grooves with all her might.

"Lady Emilia, Ah know you mean well, you've helped us—me—so much. . . ." Her words tumbled to a stop, sensing the danger in that topic if she followed it too far.

"Go on, child," Lady Emilia said, coaxing her as gently as she could to continue. "I want only to help you. I promise that is true."

"Ah cain't," Angel gasped, fear naked in her voice. "Oh Lady Emilia, it's all just awful now, Ah cain't even keep it all straight anymore, and there are. . . things, *times,* Ah just don't remember, no matter how hard Ah try." The r-sounds were as soft as baby's breath, rolling atop the words like a shape more than a sound. "You've been so kind, but that—that would change, if you knew. . . ."

Once again the elderly woman struggled out of her chair. She stepped across the fine carpet to engulf a frightened young girl in her arms, soothing her with a profound sense of calm and serenity. "Gently, Angelique," she said softly, caressing her hair. "It's all right."

"No, it isn't," Angel said, voice muffled, trembling violently in the older woman's embrace. "It hasn't been right in a long time. The baroness isn't here right now. Ah'm Angel. Just. . . Angel."

Again, Emilia's eyebrow arched. "You are from Caroling Dell, but Angelique is from Vin-Nôrë, is that correct?"

A long silence followed that question. Angel's body stilled. "She says she is," she finally whispered. "Oh, milady p-please, Ah beg your mercy. She'll come back t' run things, she c-cain't help it. And Ah'll find a way t' keep her from missin' any more meetin's, but Ah'm s-so afraid—Ah'm afraid she means it about Raven, and Ah don't want t' lose him."

"Then. . . you are *not* Angelique Blakesly? Where has she gone?"

Angel tensed, nodded, then shook her head and shrugged. "Ah'm sorry. Ah don't know how t' answer."

"I see." Emilia worked hard to make sense of what she was hearing. In this instance, peculiarly, her blindness was more a help than a hindrance. The girl in her arms sounded and *felt* like an entirely different person, and that made it easier to accept her as such, strange though it was. "Let me see if I have this sorted properly. You're afraid Angelique will end the engagement with Vincent—Raven—and you don't want her to do that, but you can't stop her?"

Angel nodded, pushing away from the larger woman's embrace as carefully as she could. It felt warm, safe, and protected, but the younger woman knew that she did not have the luxury to be any of those things now. In fact, she was becoming more and more exposed with every word they exchanged. Tears streamed from her eyes, and though it took her a moment, she at last remembered the handkerchief that Angelique always tucked into the wrist of her long sleeves. There was a very real conflict going on within her, as someone that felt like Angelique tried to reassert control over the words being spoken. Though she desperately *wanted* the lady to come back to talk them all out of this situation, some other part of her seemed to be holding the baroness part back—by force. Angel still didn't understand any of it, but

Lady Emilia was clearly awaiting an answer.

"She the one who runs things," she managed to explain at last. "It's just easiest t' let her, because she knows how. But, she has collected some fearsome grudges against Raven—Vincent, Ah mean—and won't admit—" Angel audibly bit off the end of that sentence before it could emerge, then followed it up hard with the next thing she could think up to escape the dangers in what the baroness couldn't face. "Well, he won't talk t' her now anyway, so it don't make any difference."

Emilia made her way back to her seat. "Come and sit back down, dear. Please. You are in no danger from me. I swear it by our Lady's love, my sole wish is to help in any way I can. Please tell me what it is that Angelique won't admit that has made Sir Vincent not want to talk to her anymore."

Casting about for an escape and not finding one—other than to run for the doors, guarded on the other side by the two ladies in waiting—Angel sighed and did her best to reclaim her chair in the lovely pink and gray linen day dress that was so fashionable that season. There was a trick to sitting down without crushing the fabric unduly, but Angel wasn't really sure she knew what it was. In her mind, not mussing a such a fancy dress was only a little less important than guarding the secrets into which Emilia was probing.

"Ah'm not sure how Ah can answer you," she finally confessed, twisting the delicate lawn handkerchief in tense, unhappy hands. "Ah don't know how t' trust you. Ah don't know what promises could bind you t' keep those secrets. All Ah do know. . ."

The clock chimed the half hour delicately as Angel struggled to finish her sentence. "Ah know this can't go on," she finally concluded, nodding firmly. "Ah'm the one who knows that."

The prayer beads found their way back into Emilia's weathered old hands and her fingers began to work the beads in a practiced rhythm as she searched for a way to calm the scared, fidgeting sparrow across from her. "Perhaps it would help you to trust me if I told you something I already know," she suggested. "If I tell you what secrets I keep for Angelique, will it help you tell me the secrets *you* keep for her?"

Angel nodded. "Ah didn't even know you were keepin' secrets for the lady," she admitted. "Ah just know she hasn't trusted you with *this* one."

"Obviously not," Emilia said, and couldn't help smiling. Angel's forthrightness was like a breath of fresh air. "Very well. My dear, I suppose you might say I *overheard* some of the quarrel between you and Vinc—between *Angelique* and Vincent—at the Belton House Ball. Vincent said some things that made me curious, so I had my herald investigate some things, very discreetly, you understand. She performed some tests on the age of the documents filed with the Heraldric Registry. She tells me that from the results she saw, it is nearly certain that Angelique is not a true heiress of the Blakesly family."

A vast silence bloomed inside Angel at this. She thought Angelique might have fainted outright, for her presence had disappeared. Angel herself felt as if she might be sick, but Lady Emilia's next words spared her the search for a bowl.

"The documents were good enough to make it into the Registry, but not good enough to pass a detailed investigation. Herald has since corrected those oversights at my directive. No one now could ever use those documents to disprove Angelique's claim to Carlisle."

The blond head tilted slightly, but Angel was breathing more easily already. "So you have known she, um, isn't really a baroness. That *Ah* am not a baroness, Ah suppose Ah ought t' say. And you kept that secret, my lady, when you knew it was a lie? Why?"

"Why should I not?" the countess tossed back. "Carlisle isn't the only demesne that lost its entire family to one hundred years of war, hunger, and disease. If Angelique Blakesly can pull Carlisle back together and assume her duties as its ruler, then that is much better for everyone than for there to be no baron at all."

Angel blinked, going through that sentence slowly to make sure she understood it. "So it's a matter of practicality, then?" she suggested, looking relieved when Lady Emilia nodded. "All right. As a practical matter, you're certainly not goin' t' want Lady Blakesly's name dragged through the mud and across the front pages of the major dailies, Ah should think?"

At Emilia's next and slower nod, Angel's eyebrows twitched. "All right," she repeated, taking a last, deep breath before saying a thing that could never be unsaid.

"Angelique knows who really stole the *Mâgun-Zak*," she said in a very quiet voice, "though she likes to act like she doesn't. And now, Sir Vincent thinks he knows, too. That's why he can't be around her—me—anymore."

Lady Emilia stared at her—or would have if she could have. "She knows who. . . ?" A painful twisting sensation in her gut made her stop speaking abruptly. A great many facts to the mystery swirling around the *Mâgun-Zak* had just clicked into place, and all of them implicated the woman seated in the room with her. In spite of, or perhaps because of the many enigmas that had always surrounded Angelique Blakesly, Emilia had grown extraordinarily fond of her. In a sudden flash she knew what had to be said, and repeating what Angel had said wasn't it.

"Angel. You must listen to me very, *very* carefully. You must do all that you can to get you and Angelique on-side, and you must—attend me carefully, Angel—you *must* get Sir Vincent back on-side, too. You need him. That is no longer open for debate. If you don't, we lose Angelique, Carlisle, and probably a good deal more. Do you understand?"

It was the last response any of them expected. In the back of her mind, a stream of invective erupted in flat vowels and clipped consonants. Angel foundered for a moment, trying to silence the shouting in her head, now more frightened than she'd been before, just in a different way. "Ah think Ah understand you, and Ah'm still not sure what you mean by it," she admitted at last.

"You and Vincent got into this situation together," the old woman said, striving for calm even as vague, distorted inner visions danced just out of easy comprehension. "Your choices and his have created it together. You *and* Vincent must set it right, and it *will* take Sir Vincent Sultaire to help. His cleverness, his quick mind, and most of all, his shall we say 'extralegal' knowledge and connections. You can't do this alone."

As Angel nodded, Emilia got the clearest sense of a young girl seated there, one who had been playing dress-up in her mother's fine clothes. They were still lovely, but they didn't quite fit. And that voice, when she spoke—as familiar as Angelique's, but utterly strange, too. She continued to absorb the subtly nuanced differences in the woman before her while Angel wrestled with the advice she'd just been given.

"Yes," she said at last, and very quietly. "Ah've said so all along. Ah love him, milady. It's just... there are some... parts of me, Ah guess... who want t' kill him, instead."

There was a pause in the clicking of the prayer beads. For the briefest moment, Emilia thought the woman in the room with her had once again transformed into someone else, a looming thunderhead whose knives flashed like lightning, but in utter silence. Just behind and beyond her were other, less distinct presences, some feral, some grieving, each with its own set of memories, fears, and personal agendas. The impression lasted only a moment, but it left Emilia privately aghast. When the older woman spoke at last her voice shook slightly, and she knew it was not merely from wonder.

"I am not sure how such a thing can have happened, but your soul is in pieces, my dear, shattered, like a mirror. I can sense many reflections inside you now, many voices. As you said, they do not all agree with one another. What you did not say is that some of them are dangerous."

Uncertain how to answer that, but sensing that it required one, Angel fingered her handkerchief. "Ah would never allow anyone t' hurt you, milady," she managed at last.

"You told me that you were not the one who decides."

"Well, Ah can at least decide that much," Angel said, a slight smile flickering over her lips.

"You're going to have to accustom yourself to deciding more than that, I'm afraid, Angel my dear." Emilia retrieved her prayer beads and her fingers resumed the comforting rhythm they'd first learned over half a century before. "You're going to have to gather together the parts of yourself who know how you got into this situation, and require them to help you get out of it. For your sake, and for Vincent's."

Angel nodded right away, every centimeter the "biddable young girl" that Paladins prized so highly in their serving class. "All right," she murmured, and then she did smile though Lady Emilia only heard it in the words she spoke. "Ah think maybe there is someone who might help. She doesn't have much use for Angelique, but Ah think she trusts me. She might be willin'."

Emilia nodded. "Very good dear. And if you ever need me, come and see me. I will explain to Rebecca. Now, are you able to speak for Angelique?"

After a moment, Angel shrugged. "Ah could, but it would probably just

40

be easier t'... t' let her do her own talkin'," she said, knowing it sounded absurd. "Ah do want t' thank you, Lady Emilia. Ah know it sounds strange, but... it truly has been a pleasure t' speak with you."

The older woman sensed the change in the body across from her, as distinct as a cool breeze after a warm one. It was Lady Angelique Blakesly who straightened in her seat then, frowning at the twisted, tattered state of the fine handkerchief in her grip. She loosened it right away and cast about for something to say.

"B-b-by the Lord," she finally stammered, not knowing how else to begin. Her heart was pounding, and her hands were shaking as she fought to control her fear at what had just transpired. "P-please, my lady, allow me to apologize, to *beg* your forgiveness for what I've done."

The older woman dismissed that with a wave of her hand. "Enough, Angelique. Please try to calm yourself. We are past such things now. Do you remember any of what just transpired?"

"All of it, I am afraid." Angelique arose and walked unsteadily to one of the large bay windows. It overlooked Lady Emilia's garden, now wintered over, much like her own. "I wish I had found a way to tell you, myself. I am so sorry. It was a poor way to repay your friendship."

"I'll accept that apology," Emilia said, "it *was* a poor way to treat a friend, but until I know the details, Angelique, I will not take it personally." A smile flickered over her lips and was quickly gone. "I meant what I said about Vincent, my dear. You're going to need him, and the man he is becoming, to help you. Sorting out the troubles that have separated you must be your first priority. I would also advise you to put aside your needless guilt over that oath. You're hardly the first woman who's sworn extravagantly over a man, and you're unlikely to be the last."

The younger woman did a double-take. "That is a strange attitude, my lady. My illicit behavior with Vincent can hardly be righteous in the Paladin's sight. In the last issue of *Isen's Banner, Sijainen* Moro was careful to say—"

"Those ultra-orthodox teachings have been rejected by the mainstream church for centuries, and that publication you mention has been censured by the Justiciar's Office. I would urge you not to take them too seriously until you've had a chance to compare them to more recent thinking on moral matters. Besides that—do you think I took you under my wing solely because of your religious piety?"

It was a moment before Angelique could bring herself to answer. "I confess I had hoped our mutual devotion to the Lady played some part in your favor towards me. If you tell me it did not, I will believe you, of course."

Again, that eyebrow arched. Angelique Blakesly seemed to have just transformed from a vibrant young woman into a weary, older woman whose entire life had vaporized right in front of her.

"Your devotion to the Lady was a large part of it, yes," Emilia agreed, choosing a gentler tone, "but by that I mean your *true* devotion to the living heart and soul of our Lady, not these pious mouthings of doctrine that's questionable, at best. If blind fealty to doctrine could save the world, then

41

Menelon would be a paradise. You'll note it is not."

"And yet, there must be law," Angelique retorted, spine as achingly straight as if she were being rebuked. "Without law, without restraint, we are little better than despots. If we as society's guardians lay waste to law and tradition in our private lives, then how can we deserve to function as leaders in public? My own hypocrisy poisons me," she concluded, twisting up that poor piece of linen once again, "and it should."

"It poisons you because *you do nothing to set it right!*" Lady Emilia snapped emphatically. "Casting aside the truth of your birth for the moment, you are now a *noble* woman, Angelique. The burden of your sins rests doubly on you precisely because you are a baroness now. You are the adjudicator of the laws of your lands and you are bound by those laws, whether they are written down or not. *Act,* Angelique. Let Angel help you where you cannot help yourself."

Angelique nodded, then murmured her assent when she remembered the lady did not see with fleshly eyes. She turned away from the window, retracing with measured steps her path to the chair she'd formerly occupied. "I do not doubt you are correct, but... Lady's tears... If you say Angel can set this right, again I shall accept it, my lady, but she seems little more than a child. I must ask: Are you certain she can do this?"

"She can do what she needs to do," Emilia assured her, "until those other parts of your soul are collected together and put to good work. The Lady never tasks us beyond our strength, but the Lord may task us to the utter limits of our being. There, my dear, is where you and Vincent must go if you wish to become the people, the *leaders* I know you can be."

There was a long moment of silence after that as Angelique attempted to resist or refuse what her mentor advised, but she had become too much a Guardian Paladin to reject it outright. In the end, she bowed before authority, as she always had done. "Strength was never my burden to carry," she said at last, "but it is not out of reach entirely. I shall obey you, my lady, to whatever end."

Chapter 3

Blakesly House, later that day

Like nearly every other home in the hills of southern Angels, just north of Three Quarters, Blakesly House had been constructed at the very height of the Nadrean Era and was, like most other homes nestled in those hills a picture perfect study of the flowing, ornate style of the period. Glass was everywhere, including in some of the brick work. Taking advantage of what had then been new advances in magitech, some of glass brickwork was even lit. Corners were rounded, or became towers with soaring peaks, and no self-respecting Nadrean building was complete if it didn't have a full skirt of decks, guarded by pillars.

Blakesly House hummed with quiet activity when the lady's carriage returned. Verlinden, the new butler Angelique had hired, and Mrs. Reynolds, the old housekeeper, had wrangled fiercely over duties, personnel, and responsibilities in the past few months, but between them they'd managed to transform Carlisle's summer home in Fernwall into a showcase of Nadrean elegance, influenced heavily by her western, Vin-Nôrëan origins. It had become a fully functional baronial residence at last, and as Angelique crossed the threshold she realized, for the first time, that she felt grateful to be *home*. It was a new sensation, yet another oddity to add to the growing stack of them that her life had somehow become.

Before she could retreat to the safety and privacy of her rooms, however, there were duties to manage. She rattled off a list of instructions to Verlinden and Clarice as she crossed to the grand staircase without paying either of them much mind. Her engagements for the afternoon and evening were to be canceled regretfully due to illness. No visitors were to be admitted to the house. She would take dinner in her rooms. All trays were to be left on the table in the hall. No one but Clarice was to enter, and that only if she was summoned.

The door closed behind her at last, and her knees nearly buckled beneath her before she could make it to a chair. She collapsed into the upholstered wingback chair near the window, unseeing eyes gazing far beyond to the warships anchored in the secured Merchant Marine harbor, hazy and indistinct

43

in the distance.

"It would seem I am not alone in here," she finally murmured, saying the words aloud if only to prove that she could.

That's true. The thought emerged delicately, wreathed once again in the gentle consonants and soft vowels of southern Cascadia. It pebbled the skin on her arms and legs like a dash of icy cold air.

"This is not normal," she hissed, clutching the delicate silver shield amulet that hung on a silver chain at her neck. "What a stupid thing to say. Of course it is not 'normal.' By the Lord, have I gone mad?"

Ah don't know. How can you know what 'mad' feels like? Nothin' about your—our—life ever was ever sane, or normal, milady. The mental voice was unequivocal, but not unkind. *You've just been ignorin' the parts of it you don't want t' remember.*

"What parts?"

Angel sighed, though it was strictly internal. *Like the fact that we're really from Carolin' Dell and not Püran-Khir? That we lived for a good long time there with Louis? And that we're responsible for stealin' the Mâgun-Zak and lyin' to Raven and—*

"Enough." Slender hands covered a face gone pale. "I can't remember any of that."

Ah know. You used t' know, but Ah guess you don't have t' remember it t' be a baroness. It's just that a baroness isn't all that you—we—are. There's a big mess that's swirlin' around just outside of what you want t' remember, and you don't really know how t' deal with any of it.

She folded her trembling hands into her lap and studied them for several moments. Though they had been carefully filed and buffed at some point, the nails were terribly short and one had been broken right down to the quick. She remembered the ugly, fresh bruise on her thigh—it was a serious one. The bump or fall that had caused it must have been extremely painful, and yet she could not recall it. As she'd told Lady Emilia, this kind of thing had been going on for weeks, but without any kind of glimmer of an idea about their origins, she'd done her best to ignore them, too.

"And you do?" she asked. The question hung there for almost a quarter of an hour without an answer, and Angelique's unease increased with every tick of her mantelpiece clock. Troubled, unsure if an answer was forthcoming despite Emilia's earlier assurances about Angel's reliability, she arose from her chair and passed into her private sitting room, pouring a cup of tea from the pot that had been left there. *Something* was going on just beneath the surface of her awareness that brought her to a state of anxiety bordering on panic. She had just turned to ring the bell to summon Clarice when Angel's mental voice resurfaced to stop her.

Beg pardon, this isn't easy, milady. Let's just say Ah know who does know, which has to be as good as the same thing, just now. There was another long-ish pause that left Angelique in an anxious state, as if she were quarreling with someone instead of merely waiting for a response. *Lady Emilia is right, Ah'm afraid. You're not going t' want t' hear this, but we truly do need Raven*

44

back on our side, t' help us out-think Louis. He's not the only one we need, there are at least two others, but the only thing all three have in common right now is that they detest you.

"Me?"

'Fraid so, milady.

Startled, Angelique took another sip of tea to calm herself. "This is all really rather extraordinary. I know I offended Vincent, of course, but how can I possibly have offended *myself* and not been aware of it?"

There was an internal shrug at that. *It ain't just you in here anymore, Baroness. And, well, most of that isn't personal, not really. The issues with Raven, though? Those are personal, but it's because he only has part of the truth. He's obviously sufferin' somethin' terrible. Ah swear to you, once he knows all the truth, he'll understand. He might even want t' love us again. Cain't you find a way t' talk t' him?*

Angelique snorted, and anger flared as she remembered, with painful clarity, the last encounter she'd had with Sir Vincent Sultaire at the Belton House Winter Ball. It was the seasonal event that began the official round of Winterfest celebrations. This year's theme had been "Fire and Ice," and she'd felt so beautiful in the ice-blue satin dress she'd worn that it had been easy to dismiss the weariness she'd been dealing with for weeks. Vincent, of course, was scandalously late. Though he'd managed to dress correctly for the occasion, he had also consumed a vast quantity of ale at some point, if his loud voice and clumsiness were any indications.

His eyes found hers from across the grand foyer almost immediately, and for one fragile moment Angelique swore she had seen some thaw in Vincent's manner. Hope kindled brilliantly within her. It seemed there might be a way forward for them after all, leaving the theft of the *Mâgun-Zak* in the past. That hope was immediately extinguished, however, when the young knight's expression slammed closed as tight as a vault door. He turned instead to flirt his way around the edges of the room, away from where she had been left standing near a knot of her peers in the Ladies' Auxiliary with only their silly simpering for comfort.

Still desperate for his forgiveness, Lady Blakesly had at last excused herself from her "friends" and made her way at a deliberate pace toward Vincent. His hunting expedition had been firmly thwarted by a rank of noblemen who wanted, with the worst possible timing, to ask him about the progress of the *Mâgun-Zak* case. It was on everyone's lips, mostly because the trial transcripts were being released to the newspapers almost on a daily basis. The nobility hadn't been the only ones following it avidly, but they were perhaps the most well-read.

"If you would excuse me, noble sirs," Angelique said, offering the polite intrusion with a carefully crafted smile. Her gloved hands had come to rest on Vincent's arm, and she was neatly cutting him out of the group even as she spoke. "I believe Sir Vincent owes me a dance."

"Do I indeed?" Vincent arched an eyebrow. "Dance with my 'betrothed'? How positively unfashionable, Lady Blakesly." The assembled nobles around them chuckled uneasily, but Angelique saw his eyes as he led her onto the floor. They flashed with the pain of a most intimate betrayal, followed immediately by anger and flippant irony, two weapons he wielded to devastating effect.

At that moment, however, Angelique wanted peace with him more than she wanted the Lady's grace. "These are the first words we've exchanged in weeks, Vincent," she'd said instead, attempting to dampen the Vin-Nôrean accent that had seemed to infuriate him in several previous attempts. Now that she had his attention, she found herself trembling, and not entirely due to nerves. Drunk or sober, the baron of Valemont's youngest son remained almost irresistibly attractive to her. His merest touch made her ache with hunger for him. "But, if we must discuss fashion in order to remain civil, then I am happy to do so."

The fire in his eyes flared again, passion and anger burning away some of the drunken fog. For that single moment, Angelique was able to see that he still loved her, somehow, some way, but it was all tangled up in things neither of them seemed able to change. "Oh, by all means, my lady," he'd replied, scathing sarcasm running like a current just below the surface. "Will the season's trends in hemlines do, or would you prefer to discuss the proper bodice lace to cover a *set of concealed front-hooks*?"

It stung her, and the retort was across her lips before she could censor it. "And what would you know of either, Sir Vincent, other than what it took to get your hands on the body beneath?"

"I haven't had any complaints," he shot back, "even from you."

What was most bitter to remember was how her body had leaned into his at those words, for it did remember what his hands were like, and wanted to experience them again, very much, and in the near future, please. Chin lifted slightly, Angelique summoned what wit she could to answer that.

"Except for a recent one, perhaps: neglect," she'd breathed, willing him to relent and agree with her. "Why not come back to Blakesly House with me tonight, *Mar-leven*? I've missed you dearly, and we need to talk. . . "

His eyes said *I have missed you too*, and in that moment, Angelique felt she might have wept in relief. The next, well-aimed thrust brought quick tears to her eyes, but they were not tears of joy.

"And will we tell truths, my love?" he'd asked, hand caressing her cheek.

"I was not always. . . " She'd had to breathe the words past a dangerously thick lump in her throat. She needed and wanted to tell him, things, and they were so important, but they were all trying to come out of her at once. "I could not—I have told you all the truths that were mine to tell, but—"

Vincent's snort brought her up short. When their eyes met it was all she could do to keep from cringing.

"Pardon me, my lady," he hissed. The veneer was gone. Only a lifetime of training in genteel manners kept his voice in check, and that training was obviously wearing thin. "But have you *any* idea what kind of havoc those. . . *limitations* of yours have wrought on others?"

46

He spun her out into a pirouette with so much force that, had he let go of her hand, he would have hurled her into the guests standing nearby. Instead, he'd pulled her back into his embrace just as forcefully, drawing shocked glares and concerned murmurs from those who had seen it.

"Limitations that, had they not been in place," he went on, fuming, "had you not exempted me from them—me! The man you are planning on marrying, remember? Had you told me the truth—I might have been able to use the information to *help* you and limit the collateral damage!"

Vincent shook with rage and frustration, and the muscles in his jaw worked fitfully as he held her gaze. Somehow, he was still dancing. *They* were still dancing. Expression flickering edgily, temper snapping, Angelique had taken the opportunity to drive one of her heels into his instep, injury repaying insult with a bit of interest. She remembered smiling in satisfaction at his grunt of pain even as her heart had howled in utter horror at what was happening.

"Done is done!" she'd hissed, chin lifting even higher to face down what she saw then as her own cowardice. "I cannot change the choices I made then. I was simply doing the best I could, in the *circumstances*." Angelique lowered her voice in sudden compunction, for they were once again dancing uncomfortably close to other couples. "Can you not respect that, or at least attempt to understand it?"

"Respect you," he'd snarled back, his voice rather louder than either of them would have liked. "You want me to respect you for first lying to me, then *leaving me to deal with the consequences?* Those are the actions of a selfish child!"

Angelique had never been quite sure of the events that followed that moment and had been forced to rely on the ghastly recounting in the society pages afterward. She remembered that her ears began to ring loudly, and her entire body had stiffened so suddenly that her steps faltered. Someone was shouting. It might have been her. After that, she only clearly remembered Vincent staggering back, bleeding from three scratches across his freshly slapped cheek. Everyone agreed that she'd certainly struck him hard, even unflinchingly. The papers reported that she'd hissed a furious *"How do you dare?"* and this had been corroborated by the ladies Anne and Mercía, afterward—mostly because they were trying to discover the extent of the insult he'd offered her, there in the middle of the Belton House's grand ballroom.

Before you get twisted up too badly by alla' that, Angel's soft voice said, interrupting the memory of Lady Emilia's blind eyes staring at her in the tumult afterward. *You might ought t' want t' notice that before that argument with Raven? You* remembered *committin' the theft. You had been thinkin' about how t' explain it all t' him. Remember?*

Angelique's eyes closed at this, conceding the point. "I suppose I did. But, I cannot remember it now, Angel. Can you?"

Her body drew a deep breath. *No. Ah remember that we did it, but I couldn't do it again, now.*

Something in that made Angelique sit up straight. "But you know who knows, isn't that right? There is someone... else... in here?"

Angel sighed out the breath. *Ah... It's more than one. At least two. One of 'em is the reason you're not gettin' any sleep at night. She's been prowling around South End, tryin' t' figure out what Louis has got goin' on down there.*

She dropped her face into her hands. "By the Lord's justice... the killings in Docktown." She'd been reading about them in the papers, just like everyone else had. "How many...?"

Ah wouldn't worry—

That's because you don't need to. The thought was clear and concise, and it cut across the other as cleanly as any blade. *You and the baroness there just need to go on minding your own business-es.* The addendum referenced an uncomfortable truth and caused a moment of equally uncomfortable silence. It lasted less than a heartbeat. *Neither of you are capable of managing anything more dangerous than a tea party. Just stay out of my way. Leave the rest of this to me.*

Angelique stiffened. She'd always been her own worst critic, but this voice was more than critical. It was angry, hateful, and so foreign to her that she felt the first stirrings of fear. "What *are* you?"

Same thing you are, Baroness - someone who's here to keep Angel's neck out of a collar.

Iris... Angel seemed to sigh quietly, her irritation clearly at war with her circumspection. *That ain't helpin'. The last thing any of us wants is for the lady t' run t' the priesthood for an exorcism.*

Angelique groped for the Lady's shield pendant she'd taken to wearing in place of the detested *kirpan*. It was one of the most sacred symbols of her religion, but it gave her little comfort in spite of its meaning. After her interview with Emilia and the blessing she'd received—after Emilia's tacit acceptance of her plight and its ramifications—it had never occurred to her that necromancy or some other fell magic might have caused her current predicament.

No, milady, of course it's not, Angel was quick to say. *Ah don't know what this is, or how it happened, but—*

"Then how can you certain of that?" Angelique Blakesly lifted her head and looked into her mirror, registering profound relief when she recognized the face there as her own. "Can you account for every moment of every day of your life? I cannot even recall what happened last night!" She paused then, circumspection causing her to lower her voice back to the murmur she'd been using for convenience. Before she could resume, Iris' flatly inflected tones interrupted.

You don't need to know. You just don't. Look, I don't like it anymore than you do, Baroness, but I like that crowd you run with—

"The crowd *I* run with??"

—even less. That's why I want you to stay focused on the Paladin side of things. Angel says she doesn't know how any more, but it's what she wants. If

48

you can manage that much—including taking care of the informant Louis's got belowstairs—I'll take care of everything else.

"Just who do you think you—"

Iris, that's not goin' t' work, not anymore. Angel's inner voice soothed after Iris' caustic diatribe, and Angelique bit back the rest of what she had been about to say. *We've got t' work together now, and we cain't do it alone. Lady Emilia is right—we need you t' help us with Raven.*

Snide, bitter laughter stuck in her throat.

We've already had this discussion, Angel. It's adorable how the nobles stick up for one another, but honestly, Remington's got no idea what she's talking about.

Angelique swallowed heavily, then arose to stand at her bedroom window, gazing out as the western sky darkened over the waters of the Great Northern Sea. "Lady Emilia has lived through more than you give her credit for, and she sees more than you can possibly understand," she said, her breath fogging the pane as she spoke. A pair of smudged fingerprint lines emerged on the glass, and she frowned to see them there, but went on, murmuring in low tones. "She says we must have Vincent's help. I don't have to like it any more than you do, Iris," she went on, deliberately mimicking the implicit threat in the words as she repeated them aloud, "but it means we must find a way to mend the rift with him."

Her breath had revealed two more lines. The third seemed to slant into the second, and the fourth looked as if it had the hint of a cross-bar at the bottom. Wondering if they weren't somehow deliberately placed there, she exhaled again.

Ah agree, Angel had added, chiming in quickly on the tail-end of the spoken words. *Somehow, we have t' get him t' listen t' the truth—all of it, this time. Ah just don't know how. He cain't even be in the same room with us, anymore.*

The truth doesn't exactly exonerate us anyway, you know. Wait, what is that? Iris had noticed what the lettering that was emerging with each exhaled breath, thereby making it the focus of all three awarenesses.

The letters read:

BURN THE CANDLE
BY YOUR BED
TIL THE MAKSAAR COMES
TO CHOP OFF YOUR HEAD

"*Maksaar?*" Barely aware she'd whispered the word, Angelique took a step back from the window, then took up a lit candle to examine the window more closely. After an uncomfortable moment, it was Angel who replied, albeit reluctantly.

Maksaar is a street slang word. A... D'waanese slang word.

"And it means?"

The pressure in her chest seemed to expand by the heartbeat, blossoming into anxiety within moments. It was Iris who answered.

It means that Cricket's back.

The words that had been smeared into the glass of her bedchamber window evaporated with the steam that had revealed them.

"Who is Cricket?" The only reply she received to that was wreathed in silence and visible letters that disappeared with her breath, just as the spoken ones did. The return of inner quiet at this moment did nothing but unsettle her further. Just beyond the glass, she saw that an early winter evening had fallen, cloaked in a similar silence. She stood at her bedroom window until even the lights in the bay were snuffed by the night and the mist. The only light visible came from Blakesly House itself; beyond that, only darkness and danger.

Upon a moment's further consideration, Angelique thought that facing unknown dangers in that *outer* darkness might make an entertaining change from the horrifying reality of what was happening within her. A walk in the safety of her garden, in the cool, fresh night air, would be a sweet remedy to clear a mind that had become uncomfortably cluttered, of late. Even Angel's gentle voice seemed to have deserted her. Bemused, unsure whether she ought to be frightened or grateful, she gathered up a shawl and made her way through the darkened house, inhaling the faint scent of new paint and fresh rugs that lingered in the air, even though the renovations to the house were complete. She paused only to speak to one of the new undermaids about her dinner, then let herself out of the framed glass doors, and into her rose gardens.

She had not bothered to ask for the exterior lights to be lit. There was enough ambient light from the house itself for her to see well enough. All was wintered-over at that time of year, of course, and covered in straw. Old mounds of snow were left piled in the sheltered places here and there, bone-white and mostly undisturbed. Even the stumps of her rose bushes looked like misshapen lumps against the white-dusted hedge. Just beyond, fog was creeping back into town along the river and its channels, consuming its bridges, swallowing its sounds, shrouding everything in its cold, dank embrace.

She pulled her shawl tightly about her shoulders and stepped slowly along the stone path. It all felt as dead as she did inside, as if spring would never return, as if had there had never been such things as daylight, or sunshine. Even bringing to mind the Paladin's promises about the surety of the coming dawn could not comfort her. The words had to compete with too many other thoughts and feelings. None of them were under her control.

Do you know how it happened?

It was Iris again, of course. Angel's thoughts were usually more diffident. "I do not. Do you?"

NnOo. The inner response was oddly doubled, and loud, as both "voices" echoed it, but it Angel who continued. *It wasn't always this way.*

The agreement to that was unanimous. "I should much like to know how it happened," Angelique said, watching her words escape in wisps of steam. "I remember being myself as early as Püran-Khir. Just before we boarded the ship, but I don't remember either of you."

That's all right, Baroness. I remember you. I remember when Louis created you.

Iris! Angel's burst of anger was as brief as it was uncharacteristic. *That's just not fair, and it's not even right,* she went on, and in much gentler tones. *We were all the same then, Ah know we were.*

Then you know more than I do, Angel. So tell me this, since you know so much: What are your earliest memories of Louis? You too, Baroness. How far back can you recall?

The cold seemed to creep in through Angelique's pores as she began to ponder that, and she could sense that the same could be said for the other two consciousness involved. "Just flickers," she admitted at last. "I remember him reminding me of where he found me, how he'd saved me and protected me..."

Iris snorted. *That's one version of it.*

But not the only one, Angel agreed grimly. *Why do you want t' know?*

Because I'm losing the battle against time, to put it plainly. I need something else on Louis to get him off our backs about that dead man's trigger. Look, Louis had to have had a life before he arrived in Püran-Khir. He was no more a native of that place than you were, and I'm betting that whatever drove him to venture overseas to Vin-Nôrë must have been as dirty as what he did while he was there. If I can find out who he was, at least, that'll give me a place to start.

But, I don't have all our memories anymore, Iris went on, clearly frustrated by the same lapses that irritated Angelique. *So if either of you can think of anything that might help, don't keep it to yourself. Time's running out.*

They'd moved beyond the reach of the illumination offered by the windows in the house. Angelique's steps slowed, eyes drifting sightlessly over the dead ground at her feet while her mind recalled three differing sets of memories. A headache took root just between her brows.

Ah remember livin' in one o' the shantytowns in what we called "low port," Angel told them, her voice sober and quiet. *An' Ah remember he used to make us... well—*

Though she had only an inkling of what that inner voice didn't want to reveal, hot shame flooded through her and Angelique caught her breath. "He what, Angel? What?"

You don't remember actually doing *those things any more than I do,* Iris interrupted, ignoring the spoken words to address Angel, instead. *At least, I hope you don't. So who does?*

Iris, Ah don't think we need to go borrowin' more trouble at this point, Angel said, her thoughts both pleading and placating. *If Cricket really is back, maybe she knows.*

Exasperated, Angelique cut in. "Would you one of you like to tell me who this 'Cricket' is?"

They were near the bottom of the gently sloping lawns that terminated in a hedge behind Blakesly House. It had been left to grow without much supervision by her gardeners. It had been a tradition among all Guardian Paladin landholders to leave at least one wild place on their lands, a token of respect for nature, and the land, and the things in this world that were beyond their control. *Duke or dairyman, nature always laughs last,* the saying went. Angelique's steps had carried her in that direction, though the hedge—berry briers, for the most part—was barren at this time of year.

She hadn't gotten to the end of the path before she felt she was being watched.

Angelique halted, and the hairs on the back of her neck stood up straight. *Something* had moved deep in the hedge, she'd have taken an oath on it— and that 'something' was bigger than the rabbits and raccoons and foxes that sometimes made this hedge their home. For just a moment, there was a smell in the back of her nose, the scent of something dreadful, like rotting meat mixed with offal, and old, wet fur. She took a hesitant step back.

It's all right, Baroness. You're not in any danger.

"How can you possibly know that?" she said, gasping over her body's natural threat response.

Because I know what this is. Iris suddenly sounded quite smug. It was almost as if she smiled a little, though Angelique could not see any reason for it. *You wanted to know who Cricket is? Well, why don't you call out to her and see if you can get her to answer?*

"Do you mean to say there is someone in my hedge?" Shadows shifted within it, and Angelique was sure she'd caught two yellow eyes gazing at her slyly.

Oh, for the love of the Lord, would you get a grip on yourself, Angelique! I mean to say what I said. If anyone's got a lock on who Louis was before Püran-Khir, it'll be Cricket, but she doesn't trust 'stones'— that's what the street orphans call folks like you and Lady Emilia. You're going to have to convince her to help.

"The child doesn't trust me, but she's in my hedge?" Angelique whispered, kneeling down to get a better look.

It was Angel's sigh that got breathed, at that. *She's in a bit more than that. Just... speak t' her, milady. Call her name, and ask her for her help.*

Angelique cleared her throat. This night had been chock-full of astonishing things, but this might well be the most unbelievable.

"Hello? Cricket? Are you there?" The mists muffled her voice, and it somehow sounded distant and hollow in her own ears. There wasn't an answer immediately, though surely those were more than branches and twigs shifting there within the darkness.

"Cricket? Is that you? Won't you come speak with me?"

I'm here. The voice was lilting when it finally emerged, if a little broken and uneven. *What do you want, stone lady?*

It took Angelique aback. Had she heard that voice with her ears? The uncertainty was followed by a flush of horror, and she stood slowly, clutching her shawl about her.

Go on, Angel's voice urged. *It may not be easy, milady. but we need her help. We do.*

Angelique bit her lower lip, worrying it between sharp, white teeth while she debated with herself—a concept that had lost all proper context of late, she had to admit. On one side, she wasn't sure that it was good to encourage whatever was going on, here. On the other, she realized that she had little choice.

"I... Angel says I need your help," she finally said. It sounded silly. "But I'm not sure who you are. I'm not sure about any of this."

There was no reply. A damp, chill breeze riffled the mists and made them swirl.

Try again. Cricket's a little... fragile. Angel's interior voice was whisper-soft in her mind, barely there against the background drone of uncertainty and sorrow.

"Cricket? Are you there? If you are, will you show yourself?"

Yes, I won't
No, I will
Bones are grist for every mill.

Angelique recognized the tune. It was a children's rhyming game, though the words of this one had a grisly twist.

"You are so clever, Cricket, that I cannot understand your answer," she said, peering into the thorn-brake. She thought for a moment that she'd seen a small, dirty hand withdraw from a bare branch, and was frustrated that she could not be certain.

Oh, that was good, Angel murmured, bringing her attention back to the conversation, if it was one. *Be nice to her, just don't try anythin' too grand or she'll disappear.*

Not as clever as you, stone lady. Angelique swore she caught a glimpse of those yellow eyes again, shifty, fey, assessing her anew with every word. *I just pretend to be who I am. That's easy. You're not pretending. You are always someone else, and everyone believes none of it. Even you.*

It was nonsense, madness—wasn't it? In light of recent events, Angelique hardly felt qualified to own an opinion. "That's a pretty fair summation, I suppose, but if you would tell me, do you know a man named Louis Arnot?"

All rustling stilled, then Cricket's sing-song voice began to recite. *A dragon found a dolly, and made it come to life—*

She's got a thing for nonsense rhymes, doesn't she.

"Iris, do be still! Cricket," Angelique said, bending over slightly, and feeling more than a little silly about it, "do go on. Do you know Louis? Do you remember him?"

A dragon found a dolly and made it come to life.
If he could but love her, he'd make her be his wife.

But dragons have no heart, you see, and this became his woe.
He tore her heart from 'neath her breast...

... and fed it to the crows.

The chant drifted off, the last words hazing frostily into the air around her. It was Iris who shook off the spell.
Look, you can stand out here in the cold and listen to this drivel if you—
"How do you know Louis, Cricket?" Angelique tried to speak over the argument within, but it just made it more difficult to hear the fey one when she answered.

I met him 'neath a ruined gate
he'd said I'd made him very late,
but late, he said, was just on time
and that concludes this stupid rhyme.

Oh, for the love of the—!
Angelique, however, was chuckling. Whoever or whatever this was, she was either terribly mad or terribly clever. "You said that just to infuriate Iris, didn't you."
The night breeze drifted through the thorn-brake, rustling the dead leaves. *I know she hates Louis, and I know you do, too.*
After a moment's hesitation, Angelique crouched down, pulling the fabric of her skirt around her knees and hugging them to herself tightly. She watched the hedge closely, though she still wasn't convinced she should be looking *out*side herself for the source of this strange voice.
"I don't hate Louis, Cricket," she said then, whispering it like a confession. "I'm afraid of him."
You should be. He is not a nice man.
"Why aren't you afraid of him, then?"
There was no answer to that, not for many long minutes. Anxiety built within her once more, but before she could give up and seek the warmth and safety of the house, Cricket's voice returned.
Because I'm not nice, either.
Maybe we'd be better off t' let me try, milady. Cricket... your loyalty t' Louis cain't protect you, now. He's goin' t' hurt us all if we cain't figure out how t' stop him.
Fog swirled around her body for several minutes, and she'd stood up at last to give her knees some relief when she heard Cricket's lilting cadences once more.
Don't you want to be his dolly, anymore?
Tears stung Angelique's eyes at that, but it was Angel's retort that rose first. *He hurt me when Ah was his dolly, too. So no, Ah don't want him to hurt me anymore, Cricket. Ah want a life without havin' t' hurt all the time, where the person Ah love just loves me for who Ah am. Ah want t' make peace with Raven, try t' make things right with him. Won't you help us?*

54

Ravens?

Well, just the one, Cricket. Raven's a man, not a bird.

One for sorrow.
Two for joy.
Three for a girl.
Four for a boy.
Five for silver.
Six for gold.
Seven for a secret, never to be told.

That was an old, old rhyme. Angelique recognized it as a counting game for magpies—but she knew that an entire generation of children in Vin-Nôrë had learned it by counting ravens in city streets full of the dead.

"*Me and ravens share a secret. Never, never to be told—the others don't like it. I'm* sure *you won't like it. Shall I tell you anyway?*"

The menace in the child—she assumed it was a child, if it was anything at all—caused Angelique to take another inadvertent step back.

"I think I would rather hear you tell me you'll help us," Angelique said. A picture was forming in her imagination as they spoke, just the barest sketch of a slight child with extremely pale skin, tangled, colorless hair, gaunt face, gangly body, and large yellow eyes that reflected twisted dreams, broken memories, and secrets that no child should ever have had to keep.

Why should I?

Angelique struggled with her answer, or rather, with an answer she thought such a child might accept. In the end, she chose the simplest. "Because Angel tells me that you can. Because we don't want Louis to hurt us, anymore."

Silence descended after this, broken only by rustling brush and tree branches creaking as they settled for the night. When Cricket's answer came, it was as quiet and cold as the mist itself.

That doesn't mean I have to, stone lady. It doesn't mean I should. But I will help, because Angel asked me so nicely. I will ask you a riddle: What does a dragon do when it doesn't like its name?

She had the strangest sense that all of them were holding the same breath. *Oh come on, Cricket,* Angel said, wheedling much like a child, herself. *you don't need t' tease. What's the answer?*

Something rasped and skittered in the hedge like laughter. *He gives himself a new one.*

Now we're getting somewhere, Iris' thoughts whispered. *Cricket, did Louis have another name, when you knew him?*

You don't remember? It was asked slyly, as if Cricket were certain Iris should have remembered. "*Angela does. He used to love that name best when Angela screamed it.*"

This is fucking ridic—

"Silence, Iris." Angelique barely realized she'd said it. She remembered that Angela had been her birth name, but no one other than Louis ever called her that. "Cricket—if you mean me, I truly do not remember. What was that name?"

Fey, lilting laughter whispered in the air around her.

"Of course I don't mean you. What does a stone lady know about running and fighting, or hiding in the dark, or killing for the right to eat? Nothing, that's what! Angela knows! The name he loved best, the name that Angela just loved to scream was... RALPHY!"

Chapter 4

A beat-up old army trunk was waiting for Vincent in his office the next morning. It was made of slats of hard oak and bound in brass. The oval name plate on the front said simply KT.COL. H.B-SULTAIRE. It had once belonged to Sir Colonel Harrison Blackmore-Sultaire, Vincent's paternal grandfather. The trunk, along with the rest of his wartime belongings, had been stored in an attic after he resigned his commission in '51.

Young Vincent had found the trunk one day while prowling through little-used parts of the attics in Valemont Manor. Inside it, he'd found a great black cloak made of a strange material. It was heavy and had a low luster, like it had been polished and waxed, but felt soft as down and flowed through his fingers like satin. When squeezed or compressed, however, it became strangely hard and resilient. The label was equally enigmatic. It merely said "RAVEN WING M14A3 SN0103 IMMC".

He was fifteen years old when he made the discovery. A voracious reader, he'd been reading everything he could get his hands on about mageborn flyers since he was ten, but he'd never seen a mention of a device that allowed a non-mage to fly!

A highly intelligent child, Vincent was impossibly curious and very quick-witted, traits that had regularly driven his oldest brother and his father into rages. Even his last tutor, the lovable but crotchety Master Slagter, often had trouble keeping him motivated—and challenged—until the Raven Wing came along. Vincent had been excited and intrigued, and the clever old school master knew a figurative gold mine when he saw one. He turned his pupil's research into the cloak into an adventure that sent him on a journey into the past that few of his generation would ever have the opportunity to take.

Valemont's crusty old excuse for a library quickly proved to be useless, so Master Slagter had arranged to accompany him to the libraries at City College, the Royal Academy, and the fine public archives at Bellington University, all to no avail. The Bardic College Archival Library would likely have had the material, but was closed to the general public. No exception would be made for a minor baron's adolescent son.

Finally, in a fit of pique, Vincent wrote to the public affairs officer at the Headquarters of the International Merchant Marine Corps—the IMMC itself. The global headquarters of the IMMC was right there, in the city of Angels. After a few weeks of earnest correspondence, he was granted access to the recently declassified records of "The Raven Wing Project," but only under Master Slagter's close supervision.

If the tutor had been pleased with the results of his pupil's irrepressible tenacity, young Vincent was elated! The Raven Wing Project had been one of many highly classified research projects into human flight funded by the allies during the opening decades of the sixth century. Officially, the project was canceled after ten years. By that time, it had been discovered that it was both faster and cheaper to locate young humans with a little magical talent and teach them how to use it to grow wings for flight.

The Raven Wing was only an alchemically enhanced glide wing. It was expensive to make, and required an equally expensive, ground-based launch system. It's only advantage had been that a Raven Wing could function like armor, where feathers could not. That was the *official* story.

The real story had remained classified until recently: The Raven Wing project had never truly been canceled. Rather, like many dead end projects during the war, it became a secret pet project for a close-knit group of officers, all of whom had financial interests in it. But, even under their care, supply records showed that only two thousand Raven Wings were ever requisitioned. His grandfather's was the one hundred and third, manufactured in Fernwall, in 521.

That meant his grandfather couldn't have been the original owner of Raven Wing 103, but he *had* owned it, and used it, and that made his Raven Wing special to Vincent. Raven Wings were also by that time quite rare. So rare, in fact, that five years earlier the Bardic College of Fernwall declared them a "wartime artifact." That, too, made his Raven Wing special.

After the excitement had passed, however, young Vincent decided his grandfather's approach to acknowledging the existence of the Raven Wing was best: He kept his mouth shut about it. It had been his and Master Slagter's secret, but once he'd mastered the cloak, he was no longer the captive his father thought he was.

That spring and summer, under Master Slagter's watchful eye, he learned how to soar by studying the military manuals, and by climbing trees and rock formations to watch the great raptors hunt and the ravens soar. The old man dug up stacks of books on meteorology and aeronautics and assigned Vincent long lists of assignments on each. As a youth, he learned the value of large chimney stacks, and of the enormous power of the mighty Caspian to create waves of rising air that could take him so high into the sky he found it hard to breathe. He learned how to read the air currents in the clouds, and how rivers of air moved up and down mountainsides, sometimes creating deadly down drafts! He learned the mechanics of birds' wings and studied how they used their feathers to increase lift, turn, stop, swoop, and land, and then used nearly every hour of available daylight to practice. In the evenings, he studied every journal and pamphlet he could locate on topics the names of which most nobles couldn't pronounce, let alone discuss.

At the time, Master Slagter couldn't have been more smug. Vincent Sultaire was no longer a bored, reluctant, recalcitrant student. He had begun to soak up information like a parched sponge picked up water. His obsession with the Raven Wing had become the tool Slagter used to direct the parts of Vincent's personality that irritated his father the most into activities that taught him what he needed to learn. Once he had Vincent engaged, there seemed to be no stopping him.

Less than a year after finding his grandfather's trunk, it wasn't un- usual to find Vincent well over a hundred kilometers from Valemont Manor, exploring a forest, lying on a log at the beach, or rolling in the hay with some farmer's daughter on the far side of the valley. In exchange for Master Slagter's cover, each trip also came with a lesson attached. Trips to the beach included exercises in measuring tidal surges or marine biology. His secret rendezvous with Salia became a ground survey problem that required him to use his trigonometry and an old war-surplus theodolite he borrowed from the steward. An afternoon spent in an old forest became a lesson in forestry, or in studying ecosystems. The result was a more rounded education than any he could have gotten in a preparatory school or prestigious college.

Back in his office in Fernwall, Vincent shook himself out of his reverie and turned to the remaining gear in the trunk. Wrinkling his nose against the smell of camphor, placed there as mothballs to ward off pests, he rummaged past the pair of standard IMMC issue "owl sight" flight goggles, still in their leather flight-case, and the folded woolen scarf. The pot of grease that would have protected his skin against cold air had gone rancid, but the sight of a familiar-looking handle in the bottom of the trunk gave him pause.

The final nail in the coffin of the Raven Wing project had been the challenge of getting a squadron of gliders off the ground. The IMMC had commissioned research, but then killed the Raven Wing Project when it discovered what constructing and maintaining the launch systems would cost. During a unit on mechanical engineering, Master Slagter had helped Vincent refine those early military concepts down into something easily portable. He called it a "line plier". Then the older man contacted a friend of his who ran a small shop for manufacturing magitech items there in town. The engineer assured them that it was not only possible to make much lighter "lifting lines" with fine gear-works able to move him up and down vertical surfaces, but also much heavier lines capable of projecting a hook or grapple over a distance, then in retraction, of towing him far enough and fast enough to launch the Raven Wing.

Roland had let him keep his lifting line pliers, but had taken the heavier set, the Raven Wing and all the other flying gear, and locked it all safely out of his reach for what was supposed to have been the duration of his sentence. No doubt, the old cop had thought that with his Raven Wing and tow line pliers, his troublesome charge would have simply flown away. In retrospect, Vincent had to admit that, at the time, he might actually have.

Setting the big towline plier aside, he stood and swung the great cloak around his shoulders. It was something he used to do nearly every morning, but on this morning he was startled by the surge of raw emotion that accompanied the old, familiar gesture. His body remembered its weight, the silky flow of the fabric, the weighted feel of it as it fell from his shoulders, and its peculiar smell: mothballs, old oak planks, human sweat, and traces of some other odor that Vincent had never been able to place. A torrent of memories and emotions that he had fought to ignore since the day of his arrest poured through him, and for a long, long moment he simply stood there, lost in what he could no longer push away. There it was again, the feeling that had always tightened his chest and choked off his voice: the desperate need to fly away to safety, to leave the strife and heartache his life had become, to find some place peaceful and calm. That feeling was always accompanied by the equally keen yearning to do *something* he knew he was good at, to *have* something his father couldn't cut away from him with his razor sharp tongue. With what acerbic commentary would his father regale him now, he wondered, if he knew to what purpose his youngest son was about to put grandfather's old cloak?

After collecting the rest of his gear, Vincent left police headquarters via the landing pad on the roof, rather than the front door. Landing pads for air couriers were becoming more common throughout the city because, after the war, air couriers were more commonly used to carry information from place to place. The increased use of air mail was causing problems at the street level in the busy city center. Twenty-meter wing spans took up a lot of space, and interfered dangerously with pretty much everything, especially when they dropped unexpectedly out of the sky. Therefore, increasingly, roof top landing pads were becoming the required take-off and landing area for buildings from Merchants' all the way north to Angels.

When he'd arrived, early that morning, the city had been blanketed in a frozen haze. It was now dissipating fast before the rising winter sun, though the air remained crisp and cold. He took out one of his tow line pliers and shot a line over to one of the chimneys on the building opposite, grabbed the cloak, and squeezed the trigger. The Raven Wing unfurled and transformed into wings, and he swooped over the street below like a great black bird. Pulled along by the powerful tow line, he rose higher and higher until, just as he approached the chimney, he released the catch, stowed the line plier in a pocket, and took control of the wing. It always "locked" itself in a neutral glide position, but there were hand controls on both wings.

When open, the Raven Wing looked pretty much like every other flyer's wings. Though the main part of the wing was solid, the ends and trailing edge softened out into bird-like feathers that gave the operator as much control over the glide wing as flyers had over their feathered wings. A tail piece also ended in feather-like control surfaces and served the same purpose as any bird's tail feathers. Garbed in a dark overcoat, in flight, Vincent did

60

indeed look like a giant raven in flight. The only difference was, his wings didn't flap.

Catching the hot air coming up the chimney flues, he circled around them to gain altitude, then swooped away, barely stifling an urge to sing out in pure triumph as he roared off to the southeast. The wind sang in his face again. The city spread out below him like an obstacle course, then an ever-shrinking maze. He could see at least a dozen air couriers in the distance, wings beating as they hurried this way and that across the north end of the city. The bay was to his right, shrinking by the minute, and ahead and to his left, the great Caspian Valley opened up, the wide ribbon of the river cutting its way nearly due east across the valley floor. Below him, the lines of the streets wound and crisscrossed confusingly. Chimneys, water towers, and lightning rods all jutted up at him from the rooftops, the sentinels of the city skyscape and, in the case of the chimneys at least, a highway of hot convection currents that would take him anywhere he needed to go.

He wanted to shout with joy and punch the air. He wanted to do aerial acrobatics, just for the thrill of it. He wanted to roar across the surface of the river, then veer off toward the river bank just as the down draft threatened to splash him into the water, soaring high out over the valley in the good, free air. He'd reach the convergence zone, where the cool river air met the warm air of the valley. From there, he knew he could soar so high that the entire Caspian Valley would resemble a great round bowl adorned with a sky-blue sash. The skills he'd first mastered as a teen were still there, if he didn't over-think them, and now that his body was stronger and more like that of the adults for whom the Raven Wing had been designed, the entire device seemed to respond more readily to his commands.

As desperate as Raven was to spend the rest of the daylight hours in flight, his body was simply no longer accustomed to the exercise. By the end of the first hour, he could feel the familiar aches across his shoulders and in the muscles of his abdomen. It would take time to recondition them back to peak functioning. It was all right, though. As that was happening, he'd begin the work he'd set out to do, critically important work, work that had a point, and a purpose.

He needed to find Trish, and at this time of the day, Trish was usually to be found in the Foc'sle, in Docktown. The file Roland had dropped in his lap contained precious few leads about the new talent in the traps. It seemed that neither was conversant with local trap culture. One was a mysterious woman in the interesting clothes. The other player was, as yet, a variable identifiable only by the death of their operatives. He had only one tangible though tangential lead: the unknown prostitutes working over local clients for information, but for neither money nor sex. The easiest way to find a prostitute who didn't belong was to talk to one who *did* belong.

In what would have been an hour's drive by trap, Vincent was walking through the front door in ten minutes after making his decision.

The Foc'sle was a huge place with an eatery, tavern, and gambling hall that catered to sailors, carpenters, sailmakers, mapmakers, longshoremen, teamsters, and every other kind of profession required to keep the Port of Fernwall, still the largest and busiest port in the world, humming along. Like the port itself, the Foc'sle never really closed. There were just times when the place was insanely busy, like afternoons and early evenings, and times when the place was cavernously empty. As Raven strode in from the entry hall, he could clearly see the bar, opposite him across a sea of empty tables. Most were card tables or "Bullet and Anchor" tables, a dice game popular with seamen. Most were there for eating, drinking, and socializing. A foursome of tired-looking workmen were playing cards at one, and a few other regulars sprawled in various stages of alcoholic stupor at others. A knot of prostitutes sat talking quietly around one of the dining tables. Vincent recognized a couple of them and headed in their direction.

"Morning," he said, realizing only afterward that the greeting was likely a little too loud. Almost everyone at the table was slumping, bleary-eyed, over their steaming cups. The two he knew, however—Sal and Stella—looked up and beamed.

"Raven!" Sal gushed, getting up to give Vincent a hug. Blond and muscular, he was more handsome than any young man had a right to be, and had a winning personality to match. Trish had once quipped she wished she made the coin Sal made every day. He was probably the highest paid prostitute in the place, and so was a favorite of the owners as well.

"Morning, Sal," Raven replied, once the room re-settled. Whatever he'd been about to add got cut off by a drunken shout from the corner.

"RAVEN!" Sal's greeting had roused Pashel, who'd been getting drunk in that corner for as long as Vincent had been coming to the Foc'sle. The old woman—he'd assumed she was a woman, though no one had ever said—heaved herself upright in her chair to shout out a slurred, half-growled version of his street name, then slumped back in her chair once more, head lolling back.

The night shifters glanced at one another, some shrugging, a few chuckling wryly. Raven grinned along with them.

"Morning Raven," Shela greeted him from her chair. She had mousy hair, just enough freckles on her cheeks to make her look girlishly cute, and the lean, elegant build of a dancer. She was also tiredly nursing a steaming mug of coffee.

"Late night?" he asked.

"No night," Shela chortled. "Just got here. Money was good though. Fiver for an all-night stand."

"And you're still alive," Raven replied, chuckling. He greeted the others, then looked at them as a group. "Is Trish in her room?" Sal, who still had an arm around him, deflated. Vincent grinned at him. "Sorry, Sal. It's work." He patted the younger man's ass playfully.

"What are you payin'?" the oldest of the women asked in a husky voice. Vincent had seen her once or twice, but didn't know her name. She had tawny hair and fine features that were softening as she matured.

"Trish didn't come in til after midnight," Sal put in, cutting off any answer to the older woman's question, to her irritation. "What was it Ellé, about two bells?"

Ellé, a dark-haired beauty about Sal's age, shrugged. "She's still here, far as I know, but we were all busy," she added, picking up where Sal left off. Even her voice was gorgeous, Raven thought. "She might have left before we came down."

"I been up awhile," the older woman repeated. "What are you payin'?"

"Depends on what you know," Vincent countered pointedly, "and what it's worth to me."

"He pays well enough," Sal purred, running a long finger suggestively along Raven's cheek. "Plays well too."

Again, the older woman's look turned sour, and she crossed her arms over her chest in disgust.

Vincent winked at him. "Know who the mystery competition is?"

"Who...?"

"The new talent, Sal," Ellé said, offering an answer after Sal shrugged. "I don't know who the prostitutes are, but we've had those armed enforcers in here in twos and threes almost every night for a month. They're hunting for someone called Inis." She pronounced it like "eye-niss", and the others nodded agreement.

"*Inis?* You're sure?"

"I don't think those prostitutes are real sex workers," came Trish's voice from the stairwell. Her hair was still mussed from bed, and she was groggy with sleep, or rather, the lack of it. "Or at least, they're not local talent."

"TRISHhhhaaarrraauuuggh...!" Once again, Pashel jerked herself awake to shout something, finishing the spray of spittle off with an incoherent growl of approbation.

Even the card players laughed, though the one closest to the drunken old reprobate jumped up and started cursing. A suspicious-looking puddle was growing beneath Pashel, whose bladder had apparently lapsed with her alertness.

"It's all right, Trish. I'll see to her," Shela said, nose wrinkling as she arose to tend to Pashel, who was clearly no longer able to tend to herself. The people here tended to look after their own, as they could. *Blood was blood, after all,* Raven mused to himself, watching the young woman escort Pashel into the back with the help of one of the scullery boys.

Then Trish was talking, and he was remembering just how good it was to spend time, *any* time, in her company.

"Thanks, honey. Give me a hug, Raven," she said, smiling tiredly. "I haven't seen you since the Rose & Woodbine." Groggy from sleep or not, Trish could strut her luscious curves with the best of them. She pushed Sal out of the way and burrowed into Raven's cloak.

"You're warm," she murmured from somewhere beneath the great cloak, "and you smell like mothballs. That's just sad. You've been away for far too long!"

"Truly," Sal huffed. He had retaken his seat. Highest paid whore in the place or not, it was Trish who wielded the real power in the Foc'sle, and several other establishments as well. Once a poor street-walker, she was now about as close to a madam as one could get without owning a place of her own, which meant that, like all madams, she was now *very* well-informed.

Vincent pried Trish out from under his Raven Wing and handed her into an empty chair, then grabbed another for himself. "Sorry," he sighed. "I'd rather not talk about that..."

The barmaid planted cups of coffee in front of them both before he settled in his seat, leaving an awkward silence behind.

"Well, you got your cloak back!" It was Trish who said it, unable to allow anyone to feel uncomfortable around her for long. "You out of your collar then, too?"

"'Fraid not," he drawled, putting his other troubles from his mind for the moment. "I'm on a fact-finding mission this morning. What can you tell me about these enforcers? Ever seen them before? What do they say they're doing?"

All four shook their heads in negation. "Well, that's not entirely true, I suppose," Trish frowned. "I've seen some of them before, but only when they're not working."

"Bad for business," the older woman said. She wasn't happy the others had volunteered information she was hoping would earn her some coin, and wasn't bothering to hide her annoyance.

"So are trap wars," Trish said flatly. "Raven, meet Vera and Ellé." Raven raised his coffee mug in greeting. Ellé, at least, smiled and did the same.

"Vera needs a job," Trish was saying, casting Vera a pointed look. "A *different* job. She's about done with this one."

"About too old, you mean," Vera corrected.

"It's only your attitude that's old," Trish sniffed, "and tired. I've told you—"

"Let's not get into that again, please?" Ellé stepped in to cut off what had apparently become a regular row between them. "Raven, I don't know who those so-called 'whores' were," she said, turning the conversation back to the subject at hand. "I've seen three different girls. One is a redhead almost as curvy as Trish, another is a brunette like me, but with short-cropped hair and a very athletic build, like Shela. The third one is a skinny, mousy-haired girl with eyes way too experienced for her age."

"I saw them too," Shela nodded. "About the only thing the three have in common is that they tied up potential customers, but didn't take any of them up stairs."

"What were they looking for?" Vincent asked.

"Information," Sal replied. "I only saw one of them. It was the brunette, I think. Dressed in something vaguely 'Llamazi. I overheard her grilling Sailor Sam pretty hard about someone called 'Ralphy'." Sailor Sam was a colorful local; a retired sailor who now spent his days in the Foc'sle nursing a mug of grog at the Bullet and Anchor table. Whoever the brunette was, she knew how to pick a mark!

Unfortunately, none of them knew anything more about "Ralphy", the new batch of enforcers, or Inis. Raven stayed long enough to buy them all breakfast and gave them each a gold crown for their information. He also left Vera directions to Emma's. If anyone could help Vera find her next life after sex work, it would be Emma. She was the next person on his list to see, anyway.

Back in the air, now headed east, he thought over what he had learned. He now had a name for the mysterious woman: Inis. He knew that the enforcers were looking for Inis, and since the women posing as prostitutes were digging for information about the enforcers, he had to wonder if they weren't on Inis' payroll. It made sense. It was a good start to the day.

After leaving the Foc'sle, Raven couldn't resist taking to the air again, but he had barely made it airborne before he spotted a fight on the streets below, just a few blocks away from Spice Market Square. A pimp, it appeared, was having to protect one of his prostitutes from a thug. He circled around a nearby six flue chimney to watch. Vincent didn't like pimps. They always bought slaves, and they always treated them poorly, despite the protections the courts tried to enforce. The fight didn't last very long. Like them or not, by necessity, pimps were good at hand-to-hand fighting. The aggressor, it appeared, was just a thug.

Or was he? After the thug took off, trailing blood from his broken nose, Vincent swooped off toward the square itself and spiraled down to land on a back street near the rear door of Mae's Emporium. Mae Leeford, the founder, was long dead. Her grandson Wade now ran the old store and kept it well stocked with goods that weren't easily found in the stalls that clogged the streets every fair-weather day of the year. Wade had known Vincent since he first came to town, and so wasn't at all surprised to see the younger man enter his cozy common room from the back of the building, and help himself to the steaming coffee pot, warming at the back of the stove.

"Early start, then?" Wade asked, wiping his hands on the bottom of his shop keeper's apron. "Go on," he waved as Vincent held up the coffee pot. "It's fresh. You might pour me one while you're at it. Shalah!" he yelled toward the front of the store. "Take over, will you? She's a good girl, but she ain't all there in the head," he told Vincent, taking the cup Vincent had just filled. "She'd be about right for a scullery or housemaid, and her folks need the money, but can't afford cab fare for her to look up a job up in Angels every day, so. . . " he shrugged.

"So you took her on," Vincent said, smiling knowingly. That was how the traps worked. They looked after their own. "I just saw a pimp break some idiot's nose for messing with one of his girls. They were both pretty heavily armed for this part of town." He let the unsaid question hang in the air.

"Happening more often," Wade said quietly, sitting down at his table. He motioned Vincent to sit as well. "Lots of strange folk about, lately. Lots of deaths, beatings. . . Word from River Trap is, they are missing a couple.

Don't know who though. Just had a customer come in yesterday to tell me that."

"So now everyone's armed to the teeth," Vincent murmured into his coffee cup. Wade just nodded. "Ever heard of a woman called Inis?" Wade shook his head. "How about a woman with short black hair, slender but not skinny, maybe dressed as a hooker? No idea what her name is."

"Her I seen," Wade shook a finger at Vincent. "Finnegan's, across the street, a few nights ago. 'Llamazi girl, looked to be. Saw her come out with a couple of guys. She was dressed like a local girl, but I never seen her before, and they went off in different directions."

"So got any ideas who's causing the local trouble?" Vincent asked. Wade shrugged again.

"They ain't local, as I've heard it. I get customers in here from all over. Ain't none of them knows any of them. It's probably the only reason there ain't blood in the streets yet, but I did hear," Wade leaned over like he was about to tell Vincent a state secret, "that they all work for a mercenary outfit. I also heard they're looking for some woman." There was *that* tidbit again. This was the third time. He arched an eyebrow to let Wade think he'd scored.

"But you don't know who the enforcers work for, and you've never seen this woman?"

"Not that I know of. But I think them enforcers is from Harborside."

"How do you know that?" Vincent asked wonderingly.

"Cuz I had one come in here to buy a Sudaani teapot, big gal, she was, and wore a heavy, padded coat, and she smelled like the bay," Wade said proudly.

"Go on, you!" Vincent beamed at him, though privately he thought that a rather thin line of reasoning. There were other, equally plausible reasons for her to smell like the bay. She might have just come from the port, for instance, and had bay mud, or bilge water, on her shoes or clothes. Still, he filed that little fact for future reference, and pushed his half empty coffee cup away as well.

"I've got to go," he told Wade. "Send word to Emma's if you hear or see anything else, would you? And, thank you for the coffee."

"Welcome any time, Raven. Don't be such a stranger."

Two minutes later, the Raven was back in the air.

The rest of Raven's day had gone much the same. In between exhilarating episodes of soaring above the streets that were much too short, he learned over and over again what he'd already heard. The strange enforcers were on the hunt for a woman. Who they worked for, who the woman worked for, why they were fighting it out in Docktown–and mostly in River Trap—was a complete mystery to everybody, but it *was* the reason a war hadn't started yet. Everyone had questions, nobody had answers, and so everybody was armed to the teeth with hands ready to reach for weapons. It was only a matter of time before someone who was a bit too twitchy killed the wrong person, and a free-fall spiral into anarchy followed.

By evening, he needed food and drink and a place out of the cold to sit down and think for a bit. In the shadowy world of South End, Emma's place was better than most. She lived in a small, run-down tenement flat near the river that she rented from the Bargemen's Guild. Her husband had been a carpenter until the army came to collect him. That had been ten or eleven years ago, just at the end of the war. Wally had died building a bridge in southern Vin-Llamáz, they'd said. Since then, Emma had lived by her wits, at first supporting herself and the twins Wally had never met, and later two more children from men who had paid well for her services, but whom she didn't really know. Sex work had never been her calling; her biggest talent had turned out to be making herself indispensable to the good folk of River Trap, and that is what had saved her.

That evening, her warm kitchen and calm demeanor were invaluable to Raven, who flopped into one of her heavy wooden chairs unceremoniously, and smiled at her tiredly. "Is there *anybody* in this town who knows why Docktown is suddenly a kill zone for strangers?" he asked the room at large. At one point, the wall that had separated the dining area from the kitchen had been knocked down, leaving one spacious common room from which Emma held court. There were usually at least three or four locals around to pass on, or pick up, information about the comings and goings in River Trap, but this hour, the only other person awake in the room sagged on a bench near the fire, nursing a mug of ale.

"I've got paid knives on one side," Raven went on quietly, "and a mystery woman who seems to be good enough to keep the whole lot of them at bay on the other." He paused, and snorted disgustedly. "Maybe I'll send 'em a note: 'Please take your private little war somewhere else. Thank you. Raven.'"

He chuckled ruefully at his little joke, but it fell somewhat flat. No one else was laughing. "Guess I'd need some o' that high-brow humor t' get the joke," the man on the bench said. "Don't seem so funny when ye can't jus' run off, an ye got t' live in it every day."

"Hey, Raven. Don't mind Arn," Emma said then, placing a warm, savory roll and a hot cup of coffee in front of her new arrival. "He had to talk to a blue jacket after the last killings and hasn't gotten over it yet." A bowl of stew followed the roll and the coffee, then Emma kissed his cheek and settled into the empty chair next to him. "Is that why you've come back? It's good to see you again."

Raven gave Emma a grateful smile and tore a chunk off of the roll to use it to stir his stew. "This has to stop," he said quietly. "I've been drunk long enough. Too long, from the look of things." His smile contained no mirth. He was under no illusion that he held the world together, or even just this little patch of Docktown, but guilt gnawed at him. Had he been sober, he had every reason to suspect that he could have stopped things before they'd gotten this far.

"So, where you been all this time?" she asked, handing off her youngest to one of the twins. "I wondered if you finally slipped your collar and ran off for good, it's been so long."

"I wish," Raven drawled sardonically. "Things aren't going well with. . ."
He paused to take another look around the room, then continued in a lower voice. "Angelique—and I don't know what to do about it. I've been trying to drown myself at The Rose & Woodbine for a while, to help me ignore it. Then, a detective I've worked with up at the cop shop was nearly killed trying to trace the *Mâgun-Zak* through the traps. Roland came to pull my head out of. . ."

His smile turned as sardonic as his voice. He didn't need to finish that thought aloud. He wasn't proud of his behavior, but it was factual, it was truth, and he'd run from it long enough. *Too* long. "Emma, he doesn't want a trap war anymore than *you* do. What's going on down here, really? Why are these outsiders fighting it out *here?* There has to be a reason."

She shook her head soberly. When she spoke, she matched her tone to his, leaning in close in order to be heard. "I don't know, Raven. There are new enforcers everywhere now. They all run around armed. *Some* of them are people we know, but *they're* working for people we know. The others. . . "

She twisted her mug in her hands, clearly thinking about how to explain what she knew. "Some of them have been hired to escort barges up and down the river. That's all they do. They call themselves 'independents' because they're not wearing their unit badges, and they won't talk about who's hiring them. That's one group.

"A second group is searching for something, or maybe someone, or maybe both. They're willing enough to throw coin around, but you know how it is here, Raven. No one's going to talk to outsiders."

Three groups—or sides. This was getting complicated. He dunked another piece of roll in his stew and chewed thoughtfully for a moment.

"Okay, let me see if I've got all this straight: One group of enforcers is looking for this woman, and they're dumb enough to try to throw money around in the traps, which isn't working out well for them. Then there's another tight-lipped group that keeps pretty much to themselves and escorts who knows what up and down the river; and then there's this unknown woman running around killing people. Is that about it?"

"More or less. There may be more cross-over between the groups than I think, but I haven't had anyone I can trust be able to back that. Do you know anything about the woman?"

"Only her name," Raven sighed. "Inis, I guess. I can infer a bit more, but that's about it."

Emma frowned. "*Inis?* You sure about that?" She got up and crossed to her hearth. Patting a sullen Arn on the shoulder comfortingly, she reached down the box and carried it back to the table.

"I heard 'Iris'," she said quietly, withdrawing a small, oblong object from her little box, which she then placed on the table between them.

It clattered like ivory, or bone, and was the size of a calling card. Upon it was the inked silhouette of the eponymous flower. "My boy Del found that and brought it to me. He'd been snooping around the places where the

68

bodies have been found, when he thinks I can't catch him at it. He found that about two days ago, over near Catscratch Alley, I think he said."

Raven picked it up and turned it over in his hands. The cool, smooth surface immediately reminded him of the many ivory pots on Angelique's vanity. He pushed that thought away and ran his fingers over the indigo engraving. "Inis, Iris," he murmured, tapping the engraving with a fingernail. "Makes perfect sense. So, I'm looking for information about a woman named Iris with formidable combat skills. Mind if I keep this?" At Emma's shrug, he pocketed the expensive calling card. "And she's obviously got money. *Lots* of money, if she can afford polished bone calling cards.

"Next question: Why in the seven hells is she in River Trap? If those enforcers are hunting her, it's not likely she's hunting them back."

"I suppose that depends on why they want her, or why she's fighting them," Emma said musingly.

Raven swirled that bread crust around in his stew morosely as he thought. "Of course!" he blurted suddenly. "She's hunting for something, maybe something in those heavily guarded barges—I'll wager it isn't 'Llamázi coffee!—and those enforcers are trying to stop her."

Emma wasn't convinced. "If that were true, they could stay close to those barges and set traps for her. They wouldn't have to hunt her down through all of River Trap and beyond."

He seemed to deflate instantly. "True," he replied glumly, but then rallied facts to support this theory. "On the other hand, it would probably take better kit than they've got to trap her, from what I've learned. If she's looking for something specific, she seems smart enough to know its easier to get to before it's packed up for shipment and buried in a pile of tuns on a barge."

Emma's food was always good. Too good, really. After a bowl of stew and a hot roll, he was ready for a nap, or a good night's sleep, neither of which he was likely to get. "These are murky waters, Emma," he sighed tiredly.

From near the fire, a snore punctuated Raven's complaint. Arn's head lolled upon his chest, mug still clutched between his hands. Emma glanced over at him and snorted softly.

"Is it the waters that are murky, or your heart?" she asked. Her twins were bedding down their younger siblings for the night. This was about as "private" as Emma's kitchen ever got. "We've known each other for a long time now, Raven. I've never seen you like this. Your arrest and conviction didn't knock you on your ass so badly. You think you can't see clearly? Well, I believe it. I'm just asking you to make sure you know the real reason why that is."

Raven huffed a mirthless chuckle. "I know the reason. I just don't know what to do about it."

She nodded once and reached up to smooth his hair as if he were one of her own children in need of comfort. "Damn, man," she finally said, drawing the obvious conclusion. "What did she *do*?"

What did she do? It was a straightforward question that had a straightforward answer. Emma was one of the first people he'd taken into his confidence when he'd moved into town. He had been young, then, and had never been entirely on his own before. She had seen something in the teenager and had taken him under her wing, another chick for River Trap's mother hen. She had given him some of his first contacts in the shadowy world of the big city's underground and had taught him the customs and courtesies of trap culture. He had always trusted her, but never divulged information she didn't need to know. That was no more than expected. It was a survival trait in the traps. He had first learned it at home, out of necessity, for many of the same reasons. She didn't *need* to know this. Not really. It was of such importance that it was a matter of state, of *international* politics, but this was Emma, and he needed someone in whom he could confide.

Raven cast his eyes around the room one more time. The only one left by that point was Arn, and he was nodding off by the fire. Satisfied, Raven leaned over and whispered his answer into Emma's ear.

"She's the one who stole the *Mâgun-Zak*. And don't you *dare* breathe a word of that to anyone!"

Emma sat motionless for several minutes after this. She stared thoughtfully into her almost-empty cup, putting what she already knew together with what she'd just learned. "I suppose she must have led you on quite the chase," she said at last, ignoring for the moment the larger consequences that the event had had on all of them. "Did you have any idea she didn't trust you? She agreed to marry you, didn't she?"

"That sort of gets right to the point, yes," he agreed glumly. "Roland's a clever old cop. He figured it out, too. Told me privately and intends to do nothing. He's put it on me to make this right all around and pretty much given me free reign to do so, but I don't know how, Emma," he finished in a hoarse whisper. He hadn't realized how frustrated he was, how close to tears. "I just... don't know how."

She put her cup down and leaned over to gather him up in her arms, holding him gently until he felt the tears begin to flow, and the lump in his throat loosen. "Raven, you're so strung out I'm surprised you're still upright. This is all going to look much clearer in the morning. Want to stay over? There's a storm coming in, all the old folk are saying so. The first bad one of the winter. There are worse places to hole up for it." As he straightened and pulled himself upright, he found a rueful grin on her soft, round face. "And my bed doesn't come with... complications."

Her offer made him feel worse—or better, it was difficult to say. He didn't feel particularly lovable just then, but once again this generous woman had offered him aid. She'd fed him, she'd listened to his tale of woe, and now she offered him a place to sleep, even though her bed was the only the bed available; a tiny refuge from the storm swirling around him, and from the winter gale bearing down on the city. "Thank you," he finally sniffed. "Again."

She huffed at him fondly, then leaned over to kiss his temple. "Thank me by finding us a kitten," she said then, arising to gather the dirty dishes. "The weather is driving the rats up from wharves. We could use some help keeping them out of the storage bins."

That got him to chuckling and broke the mood. As she cleared the table, he got up and assisted old Arn into the tiny cot along the far wall. He'd probably still be there in the morning. Then he helped her clean up the kitchen and get the rest of the children put down, so they could go to bed themselves. It was a routine he knew well, from years of being in and out of Emma's life. On this darkest of nights, he found the routine chores, the simple acceptance, the warmth of her soft body laying next to him in her small bed, a rare, healing gift, but sleep did not come with it.

She must have led you on quite the chase. But she hadn't. Fresh in the flush of new love, he and Angelique had spent considerable time together. She had her duties to her church and Lady Emilia, which took up a considerable amount of her time, and she had her house. That was about it. When he wasn't working and she wasn't busy with church duties, they were usually together. Rarely did a week go by that they hadn't spent at least *some* time together. He'd have sworn her life was as transparent to criticism as his own was ripe for it.

But then, her claim to Carlisle had been forged and her Vin-Nôrëan accent, though perfect, had been as phony as her claim to the baronial estate had been.

Why? Why the act? In retrospect, he supposed he should have suspected it was an act when he discovered her personal morals to be so wildly out of line with the public persona the entire Paladin Church thought was the "real" Angelique Blakesly. He'd been too infatuated with her, and too pleased with himself at having "corrupted" a conservative Paladin woman of high station to notice.

So again he had to ask, why? Obviously she was no more a starched-up conservative Paladin than she was a baroness, but she *was* a master thief! A master thief with sufficient knowledge of magitech security, enough money, and enough access to the underground magitech world, to defeat a state of the art security system.

Had she really duped him that badly? Had she so thoroughly blinded him with her beauty and sensuality he had seen nothing else? Everything inside him was screaming *no!* After the last couple of months, however, he wondered if he could dare trust his instincts and judgment. If she had duped him so absolutely, then the answer was self-evident: No! If he hadn't seen through a woman with whom he'd spent hours and hours, how could he be sure he was seeing anything else correctly?

Doubt paralyzed him momentarily, and he forced himself to relax, to breathe through it so as not to wake the woman slumbering in the crook of his arm. The other possibility, he slowly realized, was that she hadn't been acting from her own free will, that her actions had been constrained by some other agency who had power over her. It was a tantalizing possibility, but he'd seen no evidence of *that* either. Just clouds, vapor-like hints that, at the time, seemed unimportant, trivial reactions of the moment, rather than symptoms of something deeper, but were they?

71

It was an interesting line of reasoning and one that came with a blessed perk. It allowed him, without guilt or recrimination, to turn every memory of their time together over and over in his mind, looking for tells of something hidden, of anything that would have revealed her silent captivity to an agency so far beyond her she dared not betray its existence by even so much as a glance.

It made him feel better to believe that. Eventually, he drifted off to sleep while his mind traced its way through their days together, the most beloved face in his life held there fixed in perpetuity: Her bright smile... the color shifts in her hazel eyes... her quick wit... her pale, ash-blond hair...

Chapter 5

2313 Compton Place, Upper Merchants'
19 Vilmath 580

Nobody was ever going to accuse Patsy of being pretty. She was a plump little thing with a round, pock-marked face and chubby hands. She wasn't particularly bright, though as an undermaid to Blakesly House, the house-keeper Mrs. Reynolds had no complaints with her work. She was dutiful, diligent, and had enough wit to solve the sorts of problems that cropped up in a maid's life on a daily basis. Single and only in her early twenties, by personal preference Patsy lived at Blakesly House. If one had to be poor, she had told Mrs. Reynolds in her hiring interview, at least she could live in a nice house. Besides, she'd said, her family lived clear in South End, and a maid's wages made paying such long cab fairs on a daily basis at least as impractical as the hours-long drives each way. It was just easier, and it made requests for a half a day off to visit her family seem reasonable.

But in truth, Patsy had no family. The same pox that had so cruelly marked her face had killed her mother and the war had claimed the lives of her father and both of her older brothers. No, Patsy hadn't wanted the half day to travel to South End—though she could easily have done so, and in style too. No, she had other reasons, reasons that made her somewhat nervous as she knocked on the door of Louis Arnot's Compton Place townhouse.

"Mistress Patsy," the butler intoned, stepping aside to let her enter. He turned on his heel, then led her to the parlor. "If you will wait here, I will let Goodman Arnot know you're here."

Patsy looked around, not sure whether she should sit down or not. The place was every bit as fine as Blakesly House, though considerably more ostentatious. The parquet floor had been polished to mirror perfection, as had the wood paneling on the walls. The rugs were expensive, and all looked like imports from Vin-Llamáz and Sudaan. The paintings were huge and their frames ornate, and she had cause to know that the fine velvet upholstery on the over-stuffed chairs was hard to clean, and that the pile wore down so quickly it had to be replaced every few years.

"Ah, Mistress Patsy," Louis said airily as he glided into the room. "Sit, sit, my dear. Enjoy the comforts you spend your days keeping in perfect order for the rest of us. Brandy? Thesker? Wine?" He snapped his fingers and a young woman dressed in nothing more than heels and expensive lingerie quickly came through the door, her heels clicking loudly on the parquet floor. She went to the sideboard to pour drinks.

"Uh, just wine, if you please," Patsy said, taking a seat in one of the crushed velvet chairs.

Louis took a seat across from her. "So, what do you have for me?" he asked, taking a snifter of brandy from the woman in lingerie.

Patsy tried not to look as she took her glass of wine. Not because she was embarrassed, but because she considered it rude to stare.

"Lady Blakesly has an event upcoming." She said it as calmly as she could, then sipped carefully from her glass.

"Indeed!" Louis said, pleased. "I saw as much in the papers. Is that all you have for me?"

"No, it's something else. How much?" she asked, not dropping Louis' gaze.

"A pound for now," Louis sniffed. "More if your information is accurate."

Patsy calmly set her wine glass on the side table and stood up. "Good day, Goodman Arnot," she said formally. "I think that concludes our business dealings."

Louis snapped his fingers but once, and the door out into the hall snapped shut. "That would not be wise," he said calmly. "I did say, 'more if your information is accurate'," he reminded her.

Patsy smoothed the front of her dress while considering her answer. "How much does this cost?" she finally asked, running her hands over the velvet she had just been sitting on. "And you have three such chairs in this room alone," she went on, not waiting for him to answer. "You're rich, you're powerful, you're a lawyer with a reputation for getting even the most incorrigible criminals off. You could probably have me killed this instant." She sat back down into the chair. "But it wouldn't get you what you want, now, would it? And all I want is the price of one of these chairs. Just one. How is that unfair? How does that wrong you?"

Louis sat back and considered. The girl had a spine, there was that, and nerve too, to have been working for months right under Angelique's nose without the baroness even suspecting her. That made her too valuable a resource to kill in a moment of pique. Too, she was the only spy he had in Blakesly House. Just after Patsy was hired the baroness had quit hiring altogether. Even workmen were no longer allowed in the house, and he thought he knew why. So, Patsy was the only resource he had, or ever *would* have, in Blakesly House, for some time. "You drive a hard bargain, Mistress Patsy," he finally allowed. "But I think you may be more in the right on this point than I. Very well, twenty pounds then. Would you like a check, or shall I just hand you coin?"

74

"Coin if you please, goodman," Patsy replied politely. "Not surprisingly, I don't trust you. But, business is business and fair is fair."

"It is, indeed."

Patsy dipped a chubby hand into her coat pocket and pulled out a small, blue bottle with an eyedropper lid. "It seems Lady Blakesly is using this, whatever it is, very regularly," she said, handing Louis the bottle. "I find those in the glass bin every three to four weeks, and they all smell the same."

Louis unscrewed the cap and sniffed. It was "Mule's Kick", as the soldiers called it. Even used infrequently, Mule's Kick—or MOED, its official military acronym—had side effects. Emotional instability was chief on that list, but it was only the first. Prince Athos had so disliked the drug that, soon after regaining control over their country, he banned it from use in the Vin-Nôrëan military.

This, he concluded, must be how Angelique was managing to work both ends of the clock, playing her role of baroness during the day, while working the streets as Iris at night, and if it had been going on since she and Sir Vincent's estrangement... Well! There was scope in that. *Lots* of scope. "Well done, Patsy," he told the girl. "You've earned your twenty pounds."

Blakesly House
22 Vilmath 580

The first bitter winter storm arrived the next day with gale force winds and sub-freezing temperatures, icing down everything in the city and coating it with a dusting of fresh snow. Too much was happening out there that was out of her direct control, and the enforced rest made Iris edgy and irritable. In the nights before the weather had turned foul, the folk in the traps along the river had begun to talk animatedly about seeing "raven in the skies again," which hadn't seemed remarkable at all until she'd seen it for herself. The sight had simultaneously thrilled her and made her want to throw up - Raven was indeed in the skies again, soaring up and above the channels of the Caspian, and she'd have given half Angelique's fortune to get a good look at how he'd done it.

One of her consolations was that the foul weather had certainly grounded Raven and had likely kept the activity of Louis' thugs to an unwilling minimum. The other was that it had given Angel time to tease more details of her early life in Püran-Khir out of Cricket. Not the days before Louis, of course. What she knew about that time was that it was little more than an extended nightmare, now locked securely away if not forgotten, and that for the best. These were instead the first days she *could* remember, back when Louis used to have his little Angela call him "Ralphy" sometimes, usually in bed.

As she'd told the others, Louis had had a life before Püran-Khir. He was almost certainly from Cascadia, and probably from Fernwall. He had to have had a history here, in addition to a criminal record, and it just might have been under the name of "Ralphy." That, combined with what she knew of his life in Püran-Khir—forgery, smuggling, illegal drugs—had given her enough of a description to begin asking around Docktown and Near Thieves', in a variety of guises, for anyone matching that description from before the war's end.

Until nature had dumped centimeters of ice on the entire city, that is. Iris fretted restlessly, but for the baroness, the timing of the storm couldn't have been better. Unable to take part in the hunt for Raven or the search for incriminating evidence on Louis, and unwilling to risk facing Vincent in public again, Angelique instead concentrated on domestic matters. She was long overdue for a return to Carlisle and had begun preparations for that weeks-long, eastward journey in the spring when the passes cleared.

Vincent's estrangement had not halted the plans the two of them had put into motion before it. Air couriers had been arriving about once every week or ten days from Sir Dale Merkline's estate agents, and from the platoon of B'nachian mercenaries she'd sent to assess the state of the defenses along the frontier. Her troops, such as they were, had been in such disarray that Commander Rolfang had dismissed the entire officer corps, on her authority, and were rebuilding them for a push-back against the orcs, goblins, and trolls that were running amok on her borders. Her manor house, the historic seat of the Barony of Carlisle, was in such disrepair that it was a question as to whether demolition was a better option than restoration. The farmers had been treated little better than serfs by most of the knights and gentry, and the fields were producing little more than subsistence nutrition (and taxes, of course) for those who lived upon them. Malnutrition and disease were the biggest killers, even accounting for the losses to demihuman predation, and the mines, the ancestral source of wealth of Carlisle, were so overrun by them that all but a very few had been closed. In short, bereft of its ruling family, Carlisle had been exploited and abandoned, and both land and people were suffering mightily from the neglect.

And it was all on her shoulders, now. All of it.

There had been a time when such news would have caused Angelique to panic. She'd known nothing of running a barony when Louis had thrown this one at her to keep her quiet and preoccupied while he finished setting up his law practice there in Fernwall. He had failed to understand, however, how taking on those responsibilities would shape the malleable, amoral girl she'd been. As Lady Emilia had repeatedly pointed out, these burdens had become hers when they'd handed her the title. She was now all that stood between the thousands of souls who inhabited Carlisle and the continued exploitation by those who should have known better. What was happening there infuriated her in ways she couldn't easily explain. Angelique had conceded to herself the probability that she had never had an independent existence apart from Angel, but with each report she read, document she wrote, and solution she implemented, she strengthened her newfound resolve to bring justice and prosperity back to the people of Carlisle, regardless of personal cost.

She was *learning* how to be a "noble woman" at last, a *real* Guardian Paladin, the same way most cats learned how to swim. Thanks in large part to help and advice from Lady Emilia—-and from Vincent, just a few short months ago—she thought perhaps she might not drown before she got the hang of it.

With one other notable exception, her remaining hours had been spent repairing the recent damage done to her reputation—to Carlisle's reputation—there in the city-state. Her recent interactions with Vincent had tarnished much of the good will she'd garnered from her peers in her charitable work, nor had she remained untouched from the scandal that still lingered on the Ladies' Auxiliary in the wake of the theft of the *Mâgun-Zak*. Fortunately, Guardian Paladins loved nothing so much as to gather together to enjoy art and beauty. Her first art show as "patron of name" had been on the late-autumn schedule at Morahan's for months, and if that didn't draw the Paladins out of their opulent winter caves, nothing would.

The last remaining matter that was hers to tend had been that of discovering the identity of Louis' informant belowstairs. To that end, she'd sent Clarice to bid their new butler join her after breakfast that morning. Verlinden was nearly a stereotypical Vin-Norëan: tall, dark-haired, bronze-skinned, with an imposing, hatchet-like nose that looked all the longer when he was staring down at her over it. An older man, his dark hair was liberally streaked with gray, and his manner, on the few occasions she'd gotten behind his stern reserve, was rather gentle and deferent. His recommendations from Armand had been impeccable, but it was his military service that, in Angelique's mind, had been the deciding factor: His time spent on campaign with Prince Athos far to the north had effectively isolated him from any possible influence by Louis Arnot.

Angelique had accepted Verlinden's oath of service to Carlisle at the end of Ilian, and she watched him that morning as he directed her small staff in clearing away her breakfast. Though they'd interacted regularly over household matters in the weeks since, "trust" was still not a word she could toss around easily. Verlinden and Clarice, at least, had the distinction of being the only two in her immediate employ who were also oath-bound to her. If it wasn't "trust", it was at least a way to control the damage if the worst happened.

"Do please sit, if you wish," Angelique said, stalling for time until Clarice had returned from clearing her chambers of all other staff. "I have heard that your hip still troubles you when the weather turns foul. I have not grown so grand that I insist others suffer to flatter my vanity." She smiled and gestured to a chair, but Verlinden merely shook his head slightly, bowing his thanks rather than speak them.

"That is very kind of you, but it would simply be more difficult to arise again later, my lady," he said, pouring her another cup of tea while they waited. His D'wanese accent twanged of his roots in the great stronghold of Núrinen, Vin-Nôrë's northernmost province, and ancestral home to its king.

"Then you must join me here at tea," she protested, but her smile eroded any exasperation in her tone. "And pour for Clarice, too, if you would. I drink enough tea alone, and am rather tired of it."

"Very well, my lady." Angelique thought she detected a slight thaw in that reserve of his, the barest twitch in the corner of his mouth that might have been just the tiniest seed of a smile, and it made her smile, too.

He went to the sideboard and did as she'd bade him. Clarice returned a few moments later and sat near her mistress on a nearby chair. Verlinden served her a cup too, then moved to stand by the picture window framing the view of the bay, and waited for the lady to speak. Angelique began by relating what anyone in Fernwall might have known about her previous relationship with Louis Arnot. He'd been "her family's solicitor" and had indeed been the one who'd handled (forged documents had to be "handled") all the legal paperwork regarding her claim to Carlisle.

"All of that is a matter of public record," she said, concluding her preamble by reaching for her teacup. "What is less well known is that I dismissed him as my solicitor, this past Amerian."

She paused to sip her tea, blowing across the steaming surface to give herself time to think. *No more lies* had become her motto, but the unadulterated truth was still dangerous to them all, in differing ways. "There is no need to air the tedious details with you at this time. Suffice it to say that I became aware of some less-than-savory aspects of his professional career here in Fernwall that are most distressing. In combination with his continued, and unwanted, attentions to my person, I have to conclude that Goodman Arnot's intentions toward me and in Carlisle did not end with his dismissal."

Her little fire popped and shifted, sending a shower of sparks up the chimney. "In short, I believe he may still have an informant belowstairs. I am tasking the two of you to discover who it is."

Verlinden's face was mostly backlit, but she could sense how his protective Paladin instincts bristled in response. With the instincts of a battlefield survivor, however, he waited until his first reaction had passed, then thought for another moment before he spoke. "Vin-Nôrë was often a difficult and complicated place to be, in those years," he said, keeping his countenance neutral, "and as you said, Baroness, there is much you have not told us. Before I act on your orders, I should only like to ask you, as a matter of honor: Did you ever promise yourself to this man in any way that would encourage his attentions?"

She drew a swift breath to refute that but immediately thought the better of it. Even with her partial memories of that time, she knew that the relationship between herself and Louis was much more complicated than an unthinking response could have honestly covered. Clarice gazed at her with her sweet, trusting brown eyes, and for a moment, Angelique found herself paralyzed with indecision.

"Have I offended you, my lady?" Verlinden's soft baritone soothed rather than irritated, even in question. Angelique offered him a rueful smile for it. In Vin-Nôrë, she knew, these kinds of exchanges occurred much more often between a noblewoman and her servants. This was the first time they'd put it to the test in Fernwall, where it was somewhat frowned upon as a regular practice.

"Of course not. You have not been in my service long enough to know me. It is a just question, and as such, one not lightly answered." She sipped her tea again and watched as Clarice rose to check that the exterior hall remained empty. "Goodman Arnot never asked to marry me, nor ever made a marriage any kind of condition for his assistance," she said, as her maid returned to her chair. "Nor did I ever promise him any sort of domestic arrangement, no, nor a romantic one. He charged for his services, and believe me, I have paid. In full."

The words left a bitter taste in her mouth, and in the ears of her servants too, if their uncertain, questioning expressions were an indication. Angelique offered a smile, humorless though it was, to break the mood. "I am not certain what encourages Goodman Arnot's attentions and what does not, but I am certain that I have been unequivocal in my insistence that he leave me—personally, and as Carlisle—alone. Will that serve for an honorable answer, Verlinden? Until time and circumstance allow for a fuller one?"

He nodded slowly, thinking it through before he spoke. "You, too, came highly recommended from Armand, you know," he reminded her, then did smile, just a little. "With that in mind, I may begin the search for your informant with a will, my lady. How would you like us to begin?"

Clarice nodded happily, for Angelique well knew the girl's devotion to her, little though she felt she deserved it. "Very well. In addition to taking risks to get their information, whoever it is will have to venture to Goodman Arnot's residence in Merchants' to deliver it. That is several hours ride by taxi into the city, then back. That kind of extra time away from duties is recorded by Reynolds, even if it is not gossiped about by the other servants. That's where you should start."

They glanced at each other, then Clarice nodded. "We'll find this person, my lady, but what would you like us to do, once we have?"

"Nothing," Angelique said, firmly. "Your task is to identify them, then to inform me. I'll take care of the rest."

Verlinden nodded and put his teacup down with an unmistakable air of finality. "Then it shall be done."

*   *   *

Morahan's, a Fine Art Gallery, Three-Quarters

Morahan's was not a museum. As galleries went, it was a relatively small shop in the ever-popular "Three Quarters" section of town, where Three Lions Bridge crossed the northernmost branch of the Caspian nearest the bay. Docktown, Angels, and Merchants' converged there, lending the shops and neighborhoods an eclectic, sophisticated air that appealed to nearly everyone in the city who had meetings to make and money to spend. Its parks were well-kept in all seasons, and its winding, irregular side streets teemed with tiny shops and restaurants that had good patronage all year around. However, the location of Morahan's had been only one of the keys to its success. The other was Ramora Morahan's uncanny ability to connect promising young artists to wealthy, hopeful patrons, then exhibiting the results of these fruitful endeavors in her gallery in a list of top-line shows that ran through the entire social season.

Baroness Angelique Blakesly of Carlisle was just the latest in a succession of nobility and moneyed aristocracy who had sponsored artists and shows at Morahan's. Her chosen artist, Madilayn Sover-Behrens, primarily painted boldly-colored landscapes in oil-based pigments, but had ventured into watercolors for her portrait of her patron, which featured centrally in the exhibit. She'd draped Angelique's body in sea-green silks, then placed her in her garden, in three-quarter profile, overlooking the distant bay. Angelique could barely remember sitting for it. Though the woman portrayed there maintained a placid expression as she gazed out at the harbor in the distance, an aura of such profound sorrow pervaded the portrait that the artist had subtitled it simply, "Danaït Waits," after the reckless and impatient heroine of one of the Guardian Paladin myth cycles who was tasked by the Paladin to "learn to wait, and ever to wait, beyond patience, beyond sorrow, beyond redemption, and beyond hope… "

"It is a lovely work, Lady Angelique." Lady Thérèse Landers-Teasdale was the countess of Wilburn, and she was accompanied by her sister, Lady Valére Landers-Islington, the duchess of Perrault. They'd already exchanged greetings in the way that women of their station did, then had turned to the painting as one.

"Is it your first portrait?" Thérèse asked.

"It is, my lady," Angelique said.

"I cannot think why it should seem such a melancholy scene," Perrault said musingly. She had lately returned to her duties after a troublesome childbirth and was accounted by all who knew her as a pleasant, gregarious woman in society, as well as a keen-tongued debater in the House of Lords.

"Perhaps it is only that those are the last roses of autumn, and they remind us how transitory everything in this life is, Your Grace," Angelique replied. In point of fact, it seemed every Guardian Paladin in Fernwall must have known why she'd been grieving, but it wasn't a subject she was prepared to discuss in public.

Lady Valére nodded right away, as happy to avoid an unpleasant topic as Angelique was. "You likely have the right of it, Carlisle. The artist has a gift for suggestion, I must say. I see that this piece is not on offer," she added then, with a knowing smile. "Does that mean we will see this fine work featured in the drawing room at Blakesly House this season? We heard that the renovations to that fine old house have been completed at last?"

When Angelique hesitated, Thérése spoke up. "Oh, you must, Angelique. It's quite done, you know. It will be expected."

"Of course, Lady Therése. It is only that I am uncertain how much entertaining I will do, this year." Something, or rather, several somethings stirred uneasily inside Angelique at this. She offered a swift smile to cover her seemingly-distracted air, then added, "I'm afraid I still have not acclimated to this weather, Your Grace. I've been unwell of late."

"Yes, so my sister has told me. Oh, look, here is dear Lady Beatrice," Valére said then, smiling encouragingly to the Countess of Liberaune, who was just stepping toward them. Of greater station than Angelique, the three spent several moments greeting one another, giving her a moment or two to stifle the pangs of guilt she felt at Beatrice Wilkinson-Foster's presence. The entire family had suffered a terrible blow to their reputation and to social standing after the theft of the *Mâgun-Zak* the previous summer. Though she still could not quite remember how she'd done it, Angelique could no longer avoid acknowledging it, or the consequences of having done it. Lady Beatrice looked as if she had aged a decade in just the past few months, and very much as if she needed a friend.

"Lady Beatrice, thank you for coming," Angelique managed to say at last, once Valére and Therése had turned to include her in their conversation. "It was good of you to make the trip."

Her welcoming smile nearly froze on her lips, however, when the tall, fair-haired form of Eric Wilkinson-Foster stepped from behind his mother to bow politely to their host for the event. Eric, she now recalled, had sent a card inquiring after her health some weeks before, but otherwise had not attempted to speak with her since the night of his mother's last party.

"It was kind of you to invite me specifically, Lady Angelique, especially after some of the harsh things I said to you, this summer past." Beatrice's manner was as direct as ever, but much of the caustic self-righteousness that had characterized her manner the summer past had evaporated. "I hope you do not mind that my son Eric accompanies me this evening," she added, turning to create space for him to join them.

"Of course not, I'm delighted to see you, Sir Eric. I hope the earl is not unwell?"

"Not at all," Sir Eric replied. "He has been, uh, keeping more to himself lately," he went on, poorly papering over what all of society knew. Since the theft, the man could not appear in public without being questioned repeatedly about his responsibility to the city-state and to the powerful Santí family of Vin-Nôrë if the *Mâgun-Zak* was never recovered. "And, I suspect he finds this wintry air disagreeable at the best of times."

The ladies around them chuckled at this, and Angelique reminded herself to smile, too. "Please convey my regards to him," she said, squeezing Eric's fingers lightly before releasing them. "We are the poorer for his absence."

Lady Beatrice looked relieved. "And we have been the poorer for yours of late, you know," she told Angelique sincerely. "Your presence has been missed among us, and not only at the Auxiliary meetings. I had not realized your steadying effect on the younger women until you were no longer about to provide it."

"Lady Angelique was just mentioning that her health has not been the best," Therése said, sidling over to stand with the young baroness, who was not only outnumbered by the renewed interest in her health but outranked as well. She took Angelique's hand in both of hers with a swift smile, and held it companionably, offering physical touch in support. It was a simple gesture, but it meant something to Angelique, who squeezed the other woman's fingers gently, surprised at the rush of affection she felt.

Eric, too amiable to loom protectively, did rather lean over both women in concern as he spoke. "Lady Georgiana spoke of it to us at dinner recently," he said, too kind-souled himself to credit Georgiana's gossip as anything other than friendly interest. "I hope you will take better care, Lady Blakesly. All of Carlisle relies upon you, after all."

There was a silent beat before Angelique realized they were all looking at her, expecting her to answer. "I shall endeavor to remember it, Sir Eric," she said at last, offering it as a platitude because she wasn't certain what else there was to say. It seemed a witty reply to the others, who chuckled knowingly, and even Eric grinned at her as if she'd said something terribly clever.

This was followed by a beat of silence, as they registered the moment between the two and mistook it for something it wasn't, at least, not on Angelique's part. Before anyone could remark on it, Lady Valére smirked. "Oh, Liberaune, look. I see Demorest over there. I had not thought Lady Eva would risk the trip down from Angel Heights. Would you excuse us, Sir Eric, Lady Angelique?" she said then, gathering her sister and their friend by the arms. "Come along, Therése. Lady Bea? I'd like to greet her properly." Therése seemed reluctant to leave, but Beatrice nodded right away, directing a glance at her son that Angelique was certain she had not been meant to see.

"I hope we'll speak again soon, Lady Angelique," Therése said in parting. "My sister and I have been discussing some charitable events, the arts, and access for poor children. May we contact you? You'd be the perfect fit, I should think."

The Landers family was one of the most powerful in the country. Angelique tried not to stammer as Valére led her sister away. "I'd be most delighted, my lady. Thank you."

"We'll send 'round a note in the morning!" Valére smiled over her shoulder knowingly as they left. The mass departure left her temporarily alone in Eric's company, still searching for something to say. Eric, ever the gentleman, saved her the trouble.

"Lady Blakesly, I—"

"My dear friend," Angelique said, cutting across his thought before he could complete it. "There was a time when you would append my first name to that honorific, not my last. May I not convince you to resume it? Surely we are better friends than such formality would warrant."

To his credit, Eric's smile evinced neither self-pity nor acrimony at her manner of address. He simply reached for her hand and held it gently in both of his as he spoke. "I have heard the rumors, but I do not know your heart, my lady. I did not wish you to think I would presume. . ."

The room around them was filling slowly as more and more guests braved the weather to join in a bit of pre-holiday festivity. Angelique looked back up into Eric's earnest face, nodded a little, and managed a smile of her own. "I have never thought you capable of presumption, Sir Eric. That is the truth. From all I know of you, you have ever been my friend, and I'm grateful for it."

"Very well, then," he said, offering a tentative smile. "I was merely going to say, *Lady Angelique,* how good it is to see you among us again, and as 'patron of name' for your first show. It suits you, if I may be so bold. You're looking extraordinarily well, this evening."

She chuckled at that, unable to be anything but pleased. the gown was new, in sea-green silks almost the same shade as those in the portrait, but cut and tailored much more simply than most of those on display that evening—a newer, modern kind of elegance, for new, and very modern decade. It had been one of her favorites for that season, and she'd chosen it for this event for that reason.

"I think perhaps you are being kind again," Angelique said, "but let's allow it to stand. I do feel so much better and I am enjoying being in society again," she told him, withdrawing her hand from his to place it companionably upon his forearm. "Is there another work of Mistress Sover-Behrens which you'd like to see? There's a magnificent landscape of Angels' Bridge you would perhaps enjoy just over here."

"Indeed, my lady, thank you. If you would indulge me, though," he said, barely glancing at the painting as they approached. "You are from Vin-Nôrë, may I ask you something?"

"What an intriguing preamble, Sir Eric," she replied, stilling the uneasy murmuring that arose within her at those words. "I'll answer what I can, of course."

He offered her his arm again and walked them instead toward a wall in a quieter part of the room. "It's something my father, the earl, has been asking since the theft," he said quietly, gazing at the still life hanging there, but not truly seeing it. "He wonders, why would anyone steal the *Mâgun-Zak?* It's a relic, yes, but the metallurgy is unknown to us, and it's construction is so unique that it can't be forged. It can't be sold, or so we're told. Too notorious. So, what *was* the purpose?"

She was startled by the question, and knew it showed. "I have no idea, Sir Eric. I am not sure why you thought I would know."

His look turned apologetic immediately. "I'm sorry. I thought I remembered that you lived in Püran-Khir, where the *Mâgun-Zak* was on display for all those years."

The quiet murmuring in the back of her mind suddenly silenced itself. No rude commentary, no ironic suggestions, nothing. Angelique's mouth twitched wryly, an expression directed more at her inner audience than outer, and answered him.

"And so I did," she told Eric easily, parrying the query with a measured dose of truth, "but I know no more about it than you do—indeed, much less, if I may judge from the questions you ask."

"Forgive me," he quickly apologized again, "I assumed the presentation of the gift to King Cashëmin would have been even more widely published in Püran-Khir than it was here in Fernwall."

She patted his arm reassuringly. "It may have been, Sir Eric," she said, feeling the eyes of the ladies Beatrice and Eva upon them along with those of several others. She gestured then toward another painting, a still life of tulips in a chipped porcelain vase, to give them cover for their talk. "I have never had a head for such technical details. I am sorry to prove so inadequate a friend. I have no answer to your father's questions."

"If you have no answers, dear lady, then you have no answers," Sir Eric replied, casting her an understanding smile.

Smoothly done, Baroness. The words were clear and distinct in Angelique's mind as Iris weighed in with her grudging approval. The hair on the back of her neck, however, lifted straight up at her next observation. *Don't drop your guard just yet, though. That was the warm-up round. The main event just got here.*

"I hope you won't think it too forward of me to ask for the honor of calling on you at Blakesly House sometime soon," Eric was saying, his eyes on the painting before them. He therefore missed the searching glance she directed about the room as she attempted to locate the reason for the warning.

"I've..." Her prepared answer to this question died in her throat, for her gaze had just fallen upon the tall, lightly built, pale-haired man who'd featured prominently in her nightmares of late.

Louis. He had barely entered the gallery before being spotted by a long-legged woman dressed in a vanishingly short skirt and impeccably tailored business jacket that marked her as a Urilian. She moved to intercept Louis immediately, dripping saucy sensuality as she went. Louis smiled his professional smile, the smile Angel had come to know meant he'd identified a 'mark' and met the woman half-way. He wore his perfectly tailored gray suit, mirror-polished shoes, and immaculately coiffed hair with an air that was just a touch too self-conscious, or perhaps self-aggrandizing for the Paladins present. His mark, however, lit up at whatever Louis had said as he bent over her hand.

"Milady?" Eric said. Having seen her face, he followed her gaze to Louis, who placed that woman—definitely a Urilian, from the vulgar way she was behaving—on his arm. "Do you know this man? Is there a problem?"

That's putting it kindly, don't you think?

"I—Yes. I know him," Angelique finally said, having to concentrate to hear her own voice in her ears over the stream of caustic remarks in her head since Louis' arrival. "I simply did not expect to see him here this evening."

Nor did Ah, Angel's voice said uneasily. *What nerve. Whatever he wants here, it cain't be good.*

"I was about to make my excuses—I know you have many duties this evening as patron of name—but if you'd rather I stay and escort you, Lady Angelique...?"

It was in her to agree to it. Eric Wilkinson-Foster was a knight of the Guardian Paladin from fingertips to toenails, and those protective instincts, as Verlinden had earlier demonstrated, ran deep.

An escort might *make him behave,* Angel's voice said, somewhat dubiously, but the next thoughts—from Iris—put an end to the speculation.

If he brings the trick over with him, keep your rescuer at your side, Iris advised coolly. *Don't let Louis have the advantage of numbers.*

Though it pained her somewhat, Angelique found that she agreed. "Stay for but a moment if you would, Sir Eric. I've no idea what Goodman Arnot wants here, nor who that... woman might be," she added, flashing him a look that was half-plea and half-caution.

"Who is he?" Eric asked. Louis shared but a few words with the woman, both gesturing at the painting they were examining and exchanging business cards before he bowed and left her to it. He paused to look about the room again, then was spotted by a portly aristocrat with a grizzled beard who waved him down, using his program as a flag. Again Louis put on his professional smile and greeted the man with infectious enthusiasm.

"He is my former solicitor," Angelique said evenly, only just then realizing that he had not yet spotted her in the room, or perhaps, that he did not wish her to know he had. She drew a determined breath, and her chin came up slightly. "His name is Louis Arnot."

And every bit of that, Iris hissed quietly in the back of her mind, *is all for show. Every bit of it.*

"I know," Angelique said, momentarily unaware that she'd murmured it aloud.

"Your pardon, my lady?" Eric turned his gaze back to Angelique. Across the room, the rotund man had already moved on. Louis' searching gaze had just begun to sweep the room again when a nobleman Angelique didn't know greeted him much as had the other two.

Angelique glanced at him distractedly. "Ar-not," she said, covering her slip with a quick tutorial on D'waanese pronunciation. "It rhymes with 'mar-low'. Tell me, can you see what the flower is on his lapel? I can't quite make it out from here."

"What? Oh. Yes, it's an... iris, a dark blue iris," her companion supplied. "Is that significant somehow?"

Pale eyebrows flickered slightly at this. *Dismiss him,* Iris instructed curtly. *You won't need him. That's a flag of truce.*

Or stalemate, more likely, Angel added. *But Ah agree. He ain't gonna cause trouble, not here. Ah think he wants t' talk.*

"I've no idea," Angelique said in answer to Eric, dissembling so skillfully that she half-believed it, herself. "It's just odd to see one this time of year. Forgive my earlier anxiety, Sir Eric. Goodman Arnot's appearance seems to be harmless. He is a... collector. Of sorts. Oh, isn't your mother looking for you?" she added then, nodding over toward where Lady Beatrice stood in conversation with the countess of Demorest and a young, attractively dressed woman who bore more than a slight resemblance to Lady Eva Marelle. "It will be all right, my dear friend. Truly. Thank you for your concern."

Sir Eric didn't look entirely convinced, but he clearly did not wish to be rude, either. "As you wish then, Lady Angelique." He bowed over her hand, then excused himself. His departure caught Louis's eye, which then landed on Angelique with an unwholesome kind of satisfaction. He quickly deflected another client—or mark, more likely—on his way over to reach her.

Eric had left her in their quiet little spot, and it was a better place for this confrontation than most. Angelique stood her ground and let him cross the distance to her, her face an expressionless mask.

"Very nice, Lady Blakesly," he murmured, taking her hand to bow over it much more floridly than Sir Eric had. "A lovely show, so far. I must confess, I was surprised to receive an invitation."

"You needn't have gone to the trouble to... obtain one," she retorted, jerking her hand free of his as discreetly as she could manage. "Morahan's is open to the public for this event. Invitations were sent as a courtesy, and I owe you none. What do you want, Louis?"

"Oh, I took no trouble," he assured her, pausing to sniff lightly at the flower on his lapel, "Not all invitations come by post, after all. The question isn't what I want, Lady Blakesly. The question is, what do *you* want?"

Unable to help herself, Angelique lifted an eyebrow. "Oh, please. If you were at all interested in what I wanted, you wouldn't have come within a league of me," she told him flatly. "Don't make me repeat myself, Louis. You don't have the hand you're trying to play."

Neither do you, Baroness, Iris reminded her. *Be careful. There's a lot here you don't know, and I don't have time to tell you. Stall him.*

"Don't I?" Louis purred, apparently far more amused than perturbed by her intimation. "I would have thought you knew me better than that, after all these years. Just a hint, then. One card, and only one card: Sir Vincent Sultaire is innocent of the crimes for which he's wearing a collar. He's due a retrial, and I daresay an acquittal. Does that interest you?"

She shot him a glance and resisted the urge to sidle away from him precisely because she did know him. That statement was little more than bait.

But it cain't hurt t' hear what he has t' say, can it? Angel hedged.

Damned effective bait, I'd say, Iris's inner voice drawled. *I don't give a damn. That makes you the tie-breaker, Baroness. You called for the card. Now you have to decide what it is that he's really showing you.*

"Had it come from anyone but you, perhaps," Angelique retorted, deliberately looking away from him to take in the room. A knot of younger persons had gathered in front of *Danaït Waits,* among them Lady Georgiana Dawes. "You're attempting to manipulate me. Again. I'm surprised you'd pick so trite and obvious a tactic."

Nice counter, Iris conceded. *Let's see if he takes it.*

His answering smile was surprisingly, hauntingly, gentle. "So much anger," he murmured. "To my great regret, your choices, since we parted, have placed you under great stress. Perhaps that is why you don't see the obvious contradiction. I can't be both obvious *and* manipulative, but if you must choose, then choose 'manipulative.' It will better serve your future baron—at least I assume you still want Sir Vincent to be your baron?" he asked, casting her a questioning look.

It earned him an odd-feeling, off-balance double-take, as Angel's surge of hope collided with Iris' more vulgar repudiation. Angelique blinked, studying Louis' countenance closely, looking for any sign of the barbed hook she knew had to be buried somewhere in the offer.

"Sir Vincent no longer wishes to be Carlisle's baron, which you most certainly know," Angelique said at last, tearing her eyes from his to cast her gaze about the room once more. "I can only think the card a particularly cruel one to show me, under the circumstances, for all your pretense of caring."

"Perhaps," Louis smiled serenely. "Or perhaps I have come to believe that, if you continue on the course you're pursuing, it will ruin your health and probably your life. I would rather have you whole and well—even if at a distance—than incapacitated by drug use."

Lord protect us, he's playin' this hard, an' Ah cain't see his game.

Wait. How does he know about the drug?

Angelique had caught that too, but the debate had stirred a third voice from a place of inner stillness that she only noticed when it seemed to crack.

Louis is my favorite playmate.

The words hissed and crackled, like the skittering of dead leaves on cobblestones, like the voice she'd have sworn was in the hedge at the back of her estate and not right there in her own mind, taunting her with glimpses of things better left in the dark.

He always plays hard, and the harder you play him back, the harder he loves you for it until everyone is dead, dead, dead.

Momentarily overwhelmed, Angelique bowed her head and placed the tips of her fingers against her brow, willing the endless internal splintering to *stop.* "If you want me whole and well, then let me go. The information I'm holding isn't going anywhere as long as I'm well enough to maintain its container," she managed to say at last, recovering her composure before any sign of distress attracted unwanted attention from the other Paladins nearby. "Please, Louis. Leave me to the cold consequences of my choices—all of them—so I *can* rest, and recover. If you really mean what you're saying, you can at least grant me that much grace."

Iris began to crow happily about how adeptly Angelique had turned the tables, but it collapsed into an inner groan almost as soon as Louis opened his mouth.

"Then do I have your permission to pursue his case?" he asked, leaning over her solicitously. "It might help. It's certainly better than trying to work both the day and the 'night shift,' as they say."

"*No!*" She said it louder than she'd intended, and Eva Marelle and Eric Foster weren't the only nobles who turned instinctively at the sound. Louis had not missed the naked fear in her negation, either. She drew herself upright, lifted her chin, and continued in the baroness' most cultured Vin-Nôrëan tones. "Stay away from him, Louis. Stay out of his case, out of his way, out his life—and out of mine." She swept him once with a disdainful gaze. "You are excused. Leave the premises before I have you thrown out into the street."

The dismissal was the best in her arsenal, and she deployed it to sweep past the man before Iris found a way to punctuate the command by sliding a knife between his ribs. Without a backward glance, Angelique strode toward the refreshment table at the rear of the room to claim a tall, fluted glass of sparkling wine. The first half of it disappeared in a single swallow, and the resultant flush of inebriation was more effective at silencing the persistent, double-sided headache she'd developed than anything else she'd tried.

Neither Iris nor Angel had ever been particularly interested in the reports coming back from Carlisle. The problems were worse than she'd feared, and she had no idea how much of it was Louis' doing. Now, he was offering to serve in Vincent's defense to get his sentence overturned so that the two of them might wed? What could he possibly hope to gain by a baron with easy access to law enforcement and a point to prove about proper baronial management?

Ah know why. The words of the thought surfaced one by one, as if encased in the bubbles in the wine. Angel's voice was as implacable as either of the other two awarenesses had ever heard it. *And both of you do too, though you're tryin' hard t' pretend you don't. Once Louis' got his slimy, blood-suckin' tentacles dug into Raven, he can make him dance however he pleases. Ah'd do anythin' to keep that from happenin'.* There was a moment of silence as the last word bubbles sizzled to the surface almost at the same time, then stopped momentarily. *An' so will you.*

* * *

Mercy Hospital, Merchants' Quarter
23 Vilmath 580

Mercy Hospital was an epic display of post-war modernity, as was the medicine practiced within its walls. Unlike the excess of the pre-war Nadrean style, the building was orderly, plain, and functional, from the top of its simple brick chimney stacks to the plain, marble columns that supported the portico. The drive was made of close-laid, brown brick. Hedges provided enclosed, semi-private spaces, and in summer, the many flower gardens would add touches of color and life to what was otherwise a very sterile setting. It was both research center and patient hospital, and all who were fortunate enough to find themselves admitted were guaranteed the best treatment the medical arts could provide, irrespective of the ability to pay. In the sea of gloom that was the typical Valïan "healers hospice", Mercy was a rare beacon of hope.

A note from Roland had brought Vincent there. Typically pithy, all it had said was, "Cole's awake. She has information you need." He seriously hoped Roland was right. At the moment, all he had was a collection of questions. Was Iris also one of the nosy prostitutes? Was she an independent, or was she working with the independents who were guarding the barges? Was there any connection between the different armed groups milling around that part of town? And, what was in those barges, anyway?

Questions. That's all he had, and he couldn't make any of them fit together in a coherent fashion. He knew there had to be a plan. There was *always* a plan. That's how humans did things. They planned, then they executed the plan, usually making as few changes as possible. Changes cost time and money, both of which were typically in short supply.

He was still pondering the data, and the questions the data posed as he bounded up the stairs into the hospital. Cole was on the third floor, and the Valïan lay-worker in charge of the ward directed him to the convalescent's hall at the end of the corridor. It was an open, airy room with comfortably-upholstered chairs for visitors and low tables full of books and newspapers, blessed with windows that filled it from wall to wall with bright late-autumn sunshine.

Barbara was seated near one of the big picture windows in the far corner. There were braces supporting her arms and her left leg from the knee down, but the most ominous sign of her recent troubles was the large wad of bandaging that was wrapped about her head, heavily padded in the back where her skull was still in the process of knitting itself back together. There were others also convalescing in the room, but they'd congregated at a distant table to talk and play cards with their visitors, leaving the young police inspector to gaze out the window at the busy city street, three stories below.

She looked up when he came in, though, and was alert enough to ask the question no one else had dared. "Sultaire," she nodded. "Is it still 'Chief Inpector' Sultaire? Or did Roland bust you down after all?"

"It's gotten more complicated than that," he replied evasively. He grabbed another chair and sat down. "I'm so sorry, Barbara," he sighed. "You shouldn't be here. You shouldn't have been *there*. That was my job, and I—" He stopped himself, then sighed explosively. "I didn't do it."

Barbara snorted at him. "Not even you can be arrogant enough to think you can take my beatings for me. I was warned not to go in alone." She looked away from him then, her dark eyes returning to the view of the street. "But I was arrogant, too. I didn't listen."

"To whom?"

"To Roland, mostly. Gaust too." She drew a slow, careful breath, exhaling it nasally, then continuing. "I stopped asking for opinions, after that. So, you've got no cause to apologize to me, but I won't deny that I wished you at my back down there more than once."

That made him feel a tiny bit better, though he was sure he shouldn't be feeling better at all. "Was it worth it?"

"You're going to have to tell me," she replied, smiling a little. "I went on the theory that whoever was in possession of the *Mâgun-Zak* had to move it some how, and that I might learn more about that if I went down to some of the smugglers' dens to see what I could pick up from the local chatter. My uncle draws up contracts for the local longshoremen sometimes, he was the one who told me about the tensions in the traps, the new talent on the river with all the armament that doesn't like talking about who they work for, or even who hired them. So, I bought some second-hand clothes from a local pawnbroker, then went into The Poleman dressed as one of the bargers. Kept my head down, stayed inconspicuous—like you said to do—and listened.

"I won't bore you with what happened for most of that night," she said, her soft voice taking on a wry note. "Your stories failed to mention how boring most of these undercover ops can be. Anyway, the excitement happened after two bells into the night watch. I was in position to overhear a group of these armed strangers grousing about some of their sergeant's recent behavior. I won't go into it, you don't need any fresh ideas, but from what they said, I figured out where they'd left their latest assignment, and snuck down there to have a look around.

"I got lucky. The longshoremen were offloading the barge onto wagons. The lid was off one of the crates when I arrived, and they had wandered off to deal with a drunken brawl further up the dock. So I looked up the piece number for that box in the manifest book. It didn't match what was in the box. Then I noticed that there were two different numbering sequences. Some were just a number, you know, like 123456? but the open box with the mismatched contents had a prefix letter in front of the number. I just took a quick look, but a lot of the boxes had piece numbers with an 'A' prefix."

"So you're thinking the other boxes with the 'A' prefix also contain something other than what the manifests declare. Reasonable."

Barbara nodded. "I didn't get any further than that. The crew came back and spotted me leaving the barge. I ran for it, but they caught up with me before I could make it to safety. I woke up yesterday in the deep care ward and had no idea how I'd gotten there."

"You were found by someone who goes by the name Iris, who's also been snooping around that part of town," he told her. "Don't suppose you've heard the name?"

Her brow furrowed, and she shifted in her seat, or tried to, as she struggled to recall more of what she'd heard that night. "It may be nothing. I mean, I know it's past the season and all, but 'fifty gold for a live iris' strikes me as pretty steep, when you could probably get one at any greenhouse for a fraction of that. I heard a trio of women laughing about it. They made it sound kind of vulgar, actually. It just didn't make any sense at the time, but do you think it might have had something to do with my rescuer?"

"Probably," he admitted. "Word on the street is, at least one set of goons is hunting her, and this," he fished the bone calling card out of his jacket, "was found near a couple of dead mercs. Whoever she is, she has money."

"And whoever put the bounty out wants her alive, not dead. That's why the women were laughing. One of them said something about 'a warm body makes you rich, a dead one makes you dead.' The bounty's transferable."

He arched an eyebrow. Transferable bounties guaranteed only a certain class of bounty hunter would take the job: The kind nobody wanted to meet in a dark alley. Because, if the bounty hunter killed the target, the offered bounty automatically transferred to *them*. They became the target, who would then be wanted dead, not alive.

"Did you hear anything about a prostitute whose more interested in information about some dude called 'Ralphy' than selling her services?" he asked, moving on. "Slender build, short, dark hair..." he gave her a questioning look, but she shook her head.

"You're still in the market?" she asked, her usual poker-face enhanced greatly by the giant white bandage around her head.

"Always. You available later?" he deadpanned, arching an eyebrow. He held the pose for a dramatic heartbeat while she snorted at him disgustedly— their usual exchange, when the subject came up—then moved on. "Seriously, she's not *on* the market. That's the problem. She's also interested in the barges. Anyway," he stood up and made to put his chair back where he'd gotten it. "Get well soon. I need you, and so does Roland. Even if you can't do field work, you can organize and analyze, and we need another brain."

"Sultaire, you're not really going to walk out of here without telling me what you're working on, are you?" If the bandage enhanced her poker-face, it did nothing to hide the frank, pleading note in her voice. "I can't hold a book *or* a newspaper, and they won't let me off the floor. I'm bored out of my mind, here. What's happening?"

He sympathized with her predicament and thought about how he could help. Finally, deciding he had to tell her *something*, he looked around the room, grabbed his chair again and sat down. There were no sound barriers, but the room was sparsely populated, and it was fairly large. "All right," he said quietly. "The, uh, public consumption version then..."

Chapter 6

Louis Arnot sat at his overly ornate desk, staring at a dark-haired beauty who was, at that moment, lying upon a divan near the fire, her back curved in a lovely arc as the last throes of ecstasy faded. She eased back down to the cushions, smiling at him dreamily, her eyes as glassy as crystal.

"Beautiful, darling," he said, but in truth, he'd paid very little attention. While his eyes had been on her, his mind had been elsewhere, pondering a couple of persistent problems. One was summarized in a letter that was in front of him. Non-delivery of goods had always been an issue for many of his less-savory clients. Law enforcement was always finding new ways to disrupt, however temporarily, the flow of real commerce in the city's underworld. For some, the situation had reached critical proportions, but nobody knew why it had happened. Some thought competitors were stealing from them, others had no idea at all how their smuggled goods, paid for in advance, of course—no smuggler was about to work on credit—could be vanishing in such quantities.

Except, things didn't just *vanish*. Though none of his idiot clients seemed to have figured it out, *that* was a violation of the basic laws of physics. So if they couldn't vanish, then they had to have been diverted; and in those quantities, diversion meant that a needle somewhere else in Cascadia had to have moved. A price point had to have noticeably changed. Louis intended to find it.

His other problem was dearer to his heart: Angelique! Or, when on "the night shift", the Iris. The intent of his meeting with her at Morahan's had not been met. He had hoped that, in her drug-induced emotional state, she would be ecstatic that he had found a way to free her idiot boyfriend from his collar so they could marry. That, he reasoned, should have calmed her down and kept her happily preoccupied long enough for him to complete his plan. Instead, she had foolishly spurned both him and his offer. Meanwhile, said idiot boyfriend had sobered up and was attending to his police duties with a vengeance. Louis would have loved to know how old Roland had managed *that*.

In any event, between Sultaire's interminable nosing around and Angelique's growing instability, the project was in danger of falling behind schedule. Clearly, this would not do. Fortunately, he expected the arrival of his answer at any moment. He had met Archibald "Lucky Chance" Thackery a couple of years before he'd left Püran-Khir. Captain Thackery, as he was then known, had been mustered out of the IMMC's Elite Forces Corps, the arcane arm of the Alliance's military forces. He had spent his war commanding Special Air Services, or SAS teams in southern SAS units were small, special forces teams sent behind enemy lines to disrupt enemy operations. In addition to a commanding officer like Thackery, every team also had a flyer, a medic, and three special forces soldiers capable of infiltration. Every member of the team knew signal code, allowing them not only to call in their flyer for a strike but to communicate with other team members at great distances. In these post-war times, Thackery's old SAS team had grown into a mercenary company composed of many former SAS troops and their support units and made his living hiring them out for jobs large and small.

He was also late. Louis' wall clock said it was 0900, or as the locals preferred, two bells a'fore noon. As if to punctuate the point, he heard the Clocktower ring out twice. A few moments later, there was a firm knock. The door to his study opened, and his butler appeared.

"Goodman Archibald Thackery," he said formally, stepping aside to allow Thackery to enter.

The mage was a tall, bald man with a wiry build and dark, deep set eyes set over a broad, square jawline. His gaze touched briefly upon the naked woman who purred with arousal on the divan, then flicked back to Louis. "Nice," he murmured without any real show of interest. "I don't appreciate being summoned, Arnot. You, of all people, should know better. What do you want?"

"I 'want' your services," Louis said, his bright smile insincere enough to put even saintly Valïa's teeth on edge. He jabbed his chin at his butler, then pointed at the sideboard. "Drink?"

"I'd prefer an answer to my question," the mage said, forestalling the butler with a wave of his hand. "What do you want?"

"I 'want' to hire you, obviously." He leaned back in his desk chair and began twiddling with his pen. "And your Lucky Lads, for a rather—how shall I put it—a 'delicate' job. Interested?"

"Cash up front. Your reputation hasn't improved one jot since you left that rotting corpse they jokingly call Püran-Khir."

"Then we're even," Louis shrugged. "Mercenary life has modernized your morals considerably, from what I hear," he went on, pointing his pen at Thackery. "Murders, assassinations, kidnappings, arson," he ticked the list off on his fingers with his pen, "tell me, Archie, is there *anything* you wouldn't do for the right amount of coin?"

He reached into his desk drawer and pulled out a heavy money pouch, then dropped it on his desk. It made a satisfying "thunk" when it landed, jingling merrily in the key of gold. "Five hundred pounds if you succeed," he went on. "This is just a down payment. Say..." He picked up the sack and jiggled it. "Fifty crowns? the rest on delivery of goods?" he gave Thackery a questioning look.

The mage eyed the gold for a heartbeat, then his eyes drifted back up to Louis. "To do what?"

"To capture the woman known as 'the Iris'," Louis said. He was *almost* apologetic. "*Alive.* That's all."

"Five hundred pounds to kidnap *one* woman?" Thackery blurted incredulously. "Is she a war veteran? A mage? What?"

"No. She's a highly trained combatant, thief, and assassin, however."

"Have you gone daft?"

"Too hard for you?"

"Too hard?" Thackery snorted. "I'll tell you what," he drawled sarcastically, "I'll put a few of my lads on it."

"She's already killed quite a few 'lads'."

"That's why you don't hire amateurs, dumbass."

"Tell you what then, Archie," Louis purred, scooping his sack of gold back into his desk drawer. "Double or nothing. If your lads get her, I'll pay you a thousand pounds. If they fail, you finish the job for nothing."

Thackery chuckled and shook his head. "It's just taking your money, Arnot, but if that's the way you want it, deal."

Louis smirked again, and carefully placed his pen in its holder. "Oh and, as a personal favor," he said casually, getting up from his desk to walk over to stand in front of Thackery, "if her boyfriend, the collared cop—I'm sure you've heard of him—happens to get in your way and gets hurt? So much the better."

Thackery arched an eyebrow questioningly. "What are you playing at, Arnot?"

"Just testing a theory," Louis waved. He headed over to his pet sex toy and began caressing her hair, ignoring her responsive, aroused sighs. "But just 'hurt,' mind you. Incapacitated for a while, nothing more. Do we have an understanding?"

Thackery's eyes drifted from Louis down to the girl and back up again. "You're a fucking slime ball, Louis."

"Then, I guess we have an understanding."

Chapter 7

Hey. Cricket.

Cricket? Come on, don't go all shy on me. You saw him, at the show. You know his game. Better than anyone, you know how he plays. I need your help.

> Where is Angel?

Sleeping. So's the baroness. We're alone, for now.

> And Angela?

Fuck Angela.

> She likes that. She learned to like it.

Stop it. No, all right, fine. You want to talk about Angela? Let's talk about what the two of you know about Ralphy.

> A dragon found a dolly, then—

No, Cricket. Before all that. This is from back in the before-time, the things you won't let me or Angel remember.

> Those are dragon secrets. He made me promise not to tell.

I know. Look, I know, all right? He made you believe he loved you, too.

> Louis always loved me. He said so. He said he'd never give me away to anyone. And he always lit the candles to keep the maksaar away.

... Cricket, Louis is really good at pretending—

> Not as good as you are.

—and who do you think taught me how? Who do you think taught Angela to like the disgusting things she likes? Things have changed since the Boeche-Briazel, honey. Angel is afraid of Louis, now. Yeah, sure, he's "a dragon" if you want to call him that, but if I can't find a way to stop him soon, he's going to hurt Angel—and she does not like it when he hurts her. We've got to protect her.

97

. . . are you going to hurt Louis again?

As all the Gods witness, Cricket—I really just want to be free of him. And Angel wants a life with Raven, now.

One for sorrow. . .

I'd say that about sums it up.

. . . and the stone lady?

The baroness will want whatever Angel wants. She'll always protect Angel too, in her own, vapidly insipid way. She's going to take care of things so Angel doesn't have to worry about men like Louis, ever again.

Cricket? Come on. Please? Just a name, a phrase, a direction. . . ? I can't turn to anyone else for this.

Well. . . Ralphy used to tell stories, with names like 'Oakwell Lane' and 'Double Knuckle Corner,' and 'Kinstroke Alley.' Do you remember what he likes best, on the nights when the rain moves in and makes a ruin of the tar-paper roof on our little twisty shack and he wraps us up in an old cloak and on the old torn mattress he gets between our legs and says—

Cricket!

What? No, don't be stupid. It was Marley.

He started saying 'Marley?'

Uh-huh. Do you want to know what happened after that?

. . . I'm not—

'Fraidy britches.

If I need to know, then tell me.

Heehee! Ralphy banged us so hard he almost broke us! He almost broke us so hard that Lame Lennie couldn't put us back together again!

He what?

We woke up with Lame Lennie's fingers up our—

Lame Lennie had no business putting his filthy hands—

That wasn't all he liked to put—

Cricket, does this have a point, other than trying to make me throw up?

...I don't know.

Right. That's it. I've had all I can take of this. Good night, Cricket.

Don't forget to light the candle.

Chapter 8

It had taken until the next day for Iris to figure out what Cricket was trying to tell her. That was because it had taken her almost that long to consult with the other streams of thought that still co-existed in her own head—despite her regular attempts to ignore them out of existence. That morning, the baroness was on her way to Pearl Haven, the beautiful estate home of the duke and duchess of Perrault.

There had been a card waiting for her when she awakened the next morning, urging her to come by at her earliest convenience so they could begin discussing a collaborative artistic endeavor for poor youth in the city-state. Pleased and excited by the prospect, Angelique bundled herself and Clarice into the carriage that morning and set off for Angel Heights. Her maid pretended to read from a romance novel but was in truth watching her mistress rather closely. Angelique ignored her, for the most part, and bent her head over a looped strand of prayer beads that she'd taken to carrying, much as Lady Emilia did. In these latter, troubled days, they served to disguise her part in these often contentious internal debates, and were oddly comforting, besides. Clarice likely credited it to piety, and as an emulation of Lady Emilia; either was an explanation that would serve.

"They're place names," Angelique said, whispering the words over her hands as Iris' thoughts had finished relating the tale of what had happened with Cricket the night before. "Real place names. If they are here in Fernwall somewhere, we could find them on the map at City Hall."

We're going in the wrong direction for that, Iris' thoughts drawled, rubbing Angelique the wrong way instantly. *But that's all right, thank you, Baroness. Maybe Cricket was trying to tell me where Ralphy lived, or where he worked when he lived here. And since she's mad as a bag full of bats...*

"And because she truly does not like you," Angelique added, unable to stop herself from whispering it with a certain amount of relish.

She doesn't like either of you, Angel reminded them. *Ah don't think Cricket really likes anyone.*

Except Louis. Is that going to be a problem?

101

They all held silence for several moments while they contemplated that question.

"How could it be? She doesn't. . . leave the house. Does she?"

There wasn't an answer to that. *Well, I'll begin looking into them this evening,* Iris decided. *Do we have a name for that informant, yet? Louis knows we're taking the stimulant, so whoever it is has access to your chambers, Baroness.*

Angelique nodded to herself, then looked up from her beads and cleared her throat. The carriage had just begun the climb up to Angel Heights, the part of the city-state where the most powerful lived, in their rolling, expansive parks. "Excuse me, Clarice, but I wished to know whether you and Verlinden have discovered aught about our informant?"

Offering a swift smile, her maid closed her book and nodded once. "I believe so, my lady. Reynolds has said that one of the undermaids, Patsy, recently asked for a half-day to visit her sick sister, but I know for a fact that she has no family here at all. So I, well, I had *occasion* to look for her in her room the other day," Clarice added, blushing a bit at her own boldness, "and she has a pair of very costly pearl earrings, and some silk underclothes that, um, well, I know I couldn't afford them, my lady, and you are generous with your coin."

"Perhaps she has a rich lover, and they were gifts?" Angelique suggested, raising her eyebrows as a way of inviting the younger woman to support her point.

Clarice shook her head. "No, my lady. She doesn't. She has no one, she's said it more than once—she claims she's happiest, that way."

Give that girl a prize. She's done well.

"Hm." A smile began to flicker in the corners of Angelique's mouth, one that not even Iris' autocratic orders could diminish. It softened Clarice's determined expression, and the girl began to smile, too, as her lady nodded in approval.

"Well, then. I think you may have done it, my girl. Share your findings with Verlinden, if you have not, but neither of you are to say or do anything to indicate what you think you know. I prefer to deal with Mistress Patsy, personally. Is that clear?"

"*Crystal* clear, my lady." It occurred to Angelique, as she watched Clarice nod and smile in satisfaction, then that her maid was at least partially descended of the ancient Medini people, and a Guardian Paladin, too. As if she'd heard those thoughts, Clarice added, "And I hope you will allow me to witness it when you do."

"Oh, I daresay it shall be you, Verlinden, and all the household who can be mustered," Angelique said, chuckling when even Iris grudgingly conceded a job well done. "'There is only one way to shame a traitor,' after all."

It was an ancient maxim. She knew it as well as Angelique did. "As publicly as possible," Clarice said, happily returning to her book.

The only remarkable thing about the rest of the day was the detour to City Hall, where the baroness of Carlisle was shown the impressively large map of the combined municipalities that made up the city-state of Fernwall. It took a few enthusiastic young clerks a half-hour of searching on her behalf, but when she finally left the building, even Iris was gratified. The unplanned detour had saved her several hours of beating around South End in the cold.

Those streets were in what the locals had begun to call "Near-Thieves'," and not-so-coincidentally, near River Trap, too.

Don't make any plans tonight, Baroness. We've got to get to Raven.

Later that night, legs and arms and lungs pumping in time like a furnace bellows, Iris cut across the darkened stable-yards at the end of Little Farthing Lane and jumped for the lowest branch of the sturdy old oak that anchored the far end of the yard. Devoid of all its leaves, it made for an admirable emergency escape; she hoisted herself up, then lay prone on the branch, out of the light. Her three pursuers pelted heedlessly into the yard and slipped on semi-frozen piles of shit for their trouble. Two of them lost their footing completely and ended up rolling around in it a bit before they managed to lurch back up to their feet.

Iris suppressed a grin as they cursed and shouted at one another, then agreed to search the stables. Or rather, they agreed that they *should.* The stable boy, who'd been sleeping on his shift rather than shoveling piles of horse dung from the yard, awoke to the racket and piped up with a squeaky, tremulous challenge. The leader pushed the lad back into the shelter of the overhanging awning while the other two knocked semi-frozen horse turds from their clothing. Stammering in his fear, the lad could barely spit out any kind of answer. The two rejoined their leader then, brushing the filth from their jackets and trousers and forming a menacing semi-circle around the lad, whom they'd trapped.

Iris sighed in frustration. *Why are they always bullies?* Seeing an opportunity in that unemployed shovel, she let herself down to the ground, then hefted it a few times to get the feel of it. The boy had just started to sob when, with a certain satisfaction, Iris swung that shovel like a club and smacked a few more smelly turds into their backs.

They were semi-solid and *splatted* gratifyingly when they hit.

"Gardammit!" a familiar woman's voice shouted. She wheeled to catch sight of Iris standing there at the edge of the lamplight, shovel-handle resting on her shoulder.

"Oh, it's you again," Iris said, recognizing the large woman and her padded coat from their previous encounter. "Look, it's not the boy's fault you're all stupid—"

There was no time to finish baiting them. The three rushed her, and Iris had to drop the shovel and bolt toward Three Lions Bridge, hoping for a head start on those thugs for the run toward Halmore's Mercantile. The three plunged after her, but Iris easily outpaced them, striding toward the south end of the bridge and the city beyond, where the buildings were taller and closer together, shifting the odds of the chase in her favor. She darted into one of the numerous unlit side streets, hurdling over a trash midden and only just managing to dodge a couple making "the two-backed beast."

Badly off-balance, Iris shouted a jaunty, "So sorry, there!" and twisted herself for a leap up to the bottom rung of an iron fire escape. Without warning, her boot slipped out from under her.

Black ice! Her knee twisted beneath her as she fell, and she cracked her head against bricks and paving stones in quick succession. Ears ringing, blinking her eyes to get them to refocus, she scrambled for footing nonetheless when her three pursuers entered the alley at a dead run and caromed into the coupling pair. Amid the renewed cursing and shrieks, two of them fell into the trash heap while the third was trying to divest himself of an armful of a half-naked woman, and an all-angry man.

"So much for Louis' 'concern' about Angelique's health. Or mine." Iris clung to the rough surface of the wall and got to her feet, staggering into the courtyard just beyond the alley. She found a sheltered archway to use for cover while she assessed her injuries. Her knee ached, but her head was clearing, which meant it was time to put these clods behind her. She heard the big woman shouting orders at her companions and decided that her situation required a change in elevation.

Another nearby tree provided a route to the rooftops, and a handy escape from her trio of pursuers, and she dismissed them from her mind. She had weightier things to concern her. Louis' plans, whatever they were, had obviously progressed to the point where he felt safe confronting Angelique in public while her own efforts were having to be split between finding a way to Raven that wouldn't cause him to distrust her on sight, and finding the dirt she needed on Louis. Even with Angelique's help with pattern analysis and Angel's extensive knowledge of Louis, this city was simply too big to tackle alone. Raven might have decided that he hated Carlisle's guts, but Iris had to admit that she was going to need his help to have any hope of finding what she sought.

She limbered her shoulders and hips briefly, then began to run, attempting to quiet her mind so her body could find the rhythm of it. Each run was unique, and she'd discovered that the secret to covering long distances with relative ease was in discovering what that rhythm was and losing herself in it.

Her injuries were troubling her, and she had to work harder at it than she should. She therefore missed the repetitive flashes of light that were signaling just behind her. Circling overhead, hidden by the inky black sky,

Raven had seen most of the encounter. He followed as the object of pursuit made her way deeper into Docktown via the main branch of the Caspian River, and took pains to stay well out of sight, above the glow of the street lamps and not coincidentally, any chimney stacks that might impede his flight. The weather wasn't great for this kind of work. A freezing haze had hung over the city most of the day and had coated everything in ice before sundown. The haze made it difficult to see for any distance unaided, and the Owlsight goggles weren't helping much.

However, if it made things difficult for him, it was making conditions on the ground downright treacherous. The icy streets, roofs, and hand-holds had slowed his target down, too. She— from that distance he was reasonably certain it was female—darted in and out of sight, vaulting alleys and narrow streets in display after display of strength and grace, power and control, scampering up and down drainpipes with the casual flair of a street rat. Every move brought her closer to Fairmile Road, the Morrissant Bridge crossing, and so to River Trap.

She was really quite good, he decided, as he watched from the hot air plume of a chimney stack he was circling. The warm air was managing to thaw his frozen cheeks, and he had just resolved to spend as much time as possible watching her from its relative comfort when he saw a series of flashes from near the courtyard Iris had just left. He twitched the "feathers" on the ends of his wings to steepen his roll just in time to see an answering flash from ahead her.

Signal flashes? Maybe. Fliers and ground control teams used small hand-held flashes equipped with spring-loaded shutters to communicate during the war, as had special forces units. If he was right, Iris was running right into a trap, a trap set by someone with enough brains to have thought things through at least a little.

It was time to move. If it was a trap, they'd cut her off and he needed to be closer, though he had no idea what he should do. Should he help Iris? Should he just watch and let her take her lumps—or not—as skill and chance would determine? Was she important enough for him to risk getting involved? If the people signaling did, indeed, attack, was disabling them the right thing to do? From the air, he knew, his weapons were just as likely to kill as stun. Roland had given him an unwritten license to kill, and had even smiled knowingly at his quip about preparing a few body bags, but unwritten permission was dangerous. If he killed the wrong people, even for the right reasons, he knew how quickly that permission would be disavowed, and how certainly he'd end up being a convict cop for life, afterward.

Iris drew up as she reached the roof of Halmore's Mercantile, a single, four-story building that comprised an entire city block there on the island. It had become a nexus point among the routes she'd painstakingly constructed since she'd begun living and working in Fernwall. Her head was aching, and the frigid night air made her knee ache regardless of how hard she worked to stay warm, but the many chimneys, peaks, water tanks, and entrance sheds made easy concealment for aggressors. It was just too cluttered for her to feel comfortable staying long. It was a place to rest, regroup, and reroute, but not a place to linger.

"'ello, ducks."

The arrogant drawl gave her just that precious moment of warning. Iris dove toward one of the water storage tanks just as a two-meter rope net hissed through the air to cover the surface where she'd been.

"You stupid prick! Now look what you've done!"

"Stow it! Ess-Pee-See, now!"

Iris winced. If the "SP" part of that stood for "search pattern", her troubles had just multiplied exponentially. These weren't stupid amateurs! She heard two sets of heavy boots land on the roof nearby, then all three of her pursuers went quiet. She took a quick glance around to orient herself. There was only the weak, partially occluded light of the moons for illumination, but she knew this particular stretch of the thieves' highway as well as anyone. She sprawled flat and rolled beneath the vast expanse of the tank. The roof level dropped a meter on the other side, and she prepared to let herself down quietly, focusing on a dash to the iron railing on the far side of the roof. If she could make it cleanly, she could vault from the top of it to reach the sharply sloped roof of three-story Monmouth Hotel next door.

From the black sky above the Monmouth Hotel, Raven watched three armed soldiers—from the look of them—close on the water tank under which Iris had just dove. The one with the net was gathering it back up for another throw while the other two tried to cut off her escape. One lifted an arm and held up something he angled toward a lamp, and Raven saw it flash. Again he banked hard, just in time to catch a quick reply from further east. *Whoever they are, these people are damned serious!*

Suddenly the man with the net went down and was immediately tangled in his own net. Another flew back from what looked like a water-tank as if he'd been struck by a ballista bolt. Raven heard the cursing then, as Iris shot from her hiding place and ran for the edge of the building, diving off the edge with what seemed like reckless abandon to sail across the span of empty air between the buildings, then tumbling onto the flat porch at the edge of the Monmouth's roof. She was right below him then, rolling with her momentum and using it to spring up the side of one of the brick chimneys, and from there to the long ridge atop the peak. She landed on her booted feet, then erupted once more into a dead run.

He was close enough that he could see her clearly now. The Owlsight goggles let him see through the night as though it were day, and with more detail than he ever expected, but the price was loss of color. She seemed to be about average height, and extraordinarily fit. Her hair was rendered black through the lenses, which only told him it had to be dark. But, if it was black, and if that strange, mottling effect in the fabric she wore were any indication of a pattern, then, he thought, this might indeed be the Iris, at last.

She was as lithe as any cat, he thought, as she jumped between peaks in her route across the Monmouth roof. From behind, he could hear her pursuers. The weren't cursing, as thugs might have, but rather organizing. The orders were curt and sharp, and they weren't argued. Once again, he saw flashes from one that were answered by another, now only a few buildings away from where Iris was heading.

This time, Iris saw the flashes. Her heart would have sunk, had it not been pushed to bursting by her recent sprint across a steep slope, crusty-frozen rather than slippery, but still treacherous. She took quick stock, then half-shrugged and plunged over the side of the Monmouth. It was a three-meter free-fall to catch the sail-cloth banner advertising something called the "Riverwell Court", and she winced to hear the iron supports creaking in protest as it broke her fall, but it was enough to get her to the covered second-story balcony that surrounded the Monmouth on three sides. She dashed toward the colonnaded courtyard she knew was just beyond, with vaulting, ivy-covered archways of the River Walk, hoping the dodge would confuse her pursuers.

The River Walk was a beautiful place in the summer sunshine. Angelique's wistful memories of her time there with Vincent Sultaire had begun to interfere with Iris' tactical analysis, and the hammering thunder between her ears made everything more difficult. She pushed sentiment aside and leaped from the balcony railing to the top of the nearest arch, using the tenacious, woody ivy vines to haul herself up to the wide, timbered trellises that stretched between each archway. Under other circumstances, running them lengthwise wouldn't have been any more of a challenge than running down a hallway. This night, however, she knew it was going to require all the concentration she could muster.

Iris took a deep breath, and began her run, forcing herself to focus on the surface just under and in front of her boots. By the time she was up to full speed, it seemed she could just make out the entrance to the park at the foot of the massive Morrisant Bridge. With a last surge of energy, she pushed herself into an arching leap, and with a stretching *reach* caught one of the iron poles that supported floral displays in season, but before her grip could close something stuck her in the back of the shoulder with such force it sent her sailing through the air to crash into an empty vendor's cart, left just beyond the park's entrance.

Dammit! The situation was making his choices for him.

One of the men pelting after Iris had stopped just long enough to throw something, and it had hit her. It was four against one, and she was obviously injured, and that was all Raven needed to make his choice. Whatever it was that Iris knew that was so damned important to these people, he was fairly sure it was going be important to him, too. He dove after them, swooped overhead, then banked hard to circle back around from a better angle—and flinched in time to feel the long, curved throwing stick crack off the armored surface of his Raven Wing. It rebounded, striking him a glancing blow to the thigh before falling to the ground. He hadn't managed to level out before he saw another streaking up at him.

Shit! Raven rolled and collapsed the wing just as the stick streaked by, then threw his arms out with all his strength to deploy it again. It worked! The stick had missed, but the dodge had cost him precious altitude. He was now no higher above the river than the bridge, still several hundred meters upriver.

The immense Morrisant bridge was a study in stone arches. There were three of them, each one three-quarters of a kilometer long as it spanned the wide southern fork of the river. The central arch was highest and rose an amazing twenty meters above the river at high tide. Above the three main arches were smaller arches that reached up to support the road deck as it soared up and over the river. Guard rails, also ornately carved in stone, guarded each side of the bridge.

"Two can play that game, gentlemen!" He pointed a tow plier at the man plunging toward where Iris had fallen and fired. The lead weight caught the man in the chest and hurled him into a nearby wall. Before the other men could react, Raven had retrieved his line and shot it at the bridge, letting it pull him skyward once more.

The blackness was clearing from the edges of Iris' vision just as the man approaching her—armored and armed—disappeared off to the side with a loud *crack!* She shook her head, catching only a glimpse of an enormous black shape as it banked hard overhead and vanished into the night skies.

Lady's garters, they've got a flyer, too? That's just cheatin'!

That flyer was not allied with them, Angel! Is someone else after us?

Heart hammering once more, Iris ignored the commentary and tried to lever herself out of the wreckage of the wooden cart, but her left arm had gone numb and would not obey her. She shifted to one side and rolled to her feet, then cradled her left arm in her right and ran to put some distance between herself and the attackers on the ground. She emerged onto the surface of the bridge, mostly devoid of traffic at this late hour, and her pursuers were right behind her. It was only one direction left to her. Without the use of both arms to change elevation, and knowing the chances of surviving a jump into the river were too slim to reckon, Iris ducked her head and lengthened her stride into an all-out, best-speed sprint for the other side.

Wounded as she was, she wasn't going to make it. From his vantage point, Raven could see that the three remaining soldiers would catch her before she reached the middle of the bridge. Worse, as he dove for the river once again he saw four *more* emerging at the southern end, waiting for her.

Hounds to hunters. It was one of the oldest tactics in anyone's book because it worked. Another club whizzed by Raven's head, and he banked hard and roared northward across the river again, line plier in hand. As he approached the north end, he aimed and fired. The lead weight sailed between two stone stanchions in the railing right in front of the three soldiers. He opened the grapnel, locked the line, tucked the Raven Wing, and hung on as the line came tight and sang, vaulting him up, over the railing, and onto the bridge. He flared the Raven Wing at the last moment to stall momentum, landing right between Iris and her three pursuers, who tripped on his line to land almost at Iris' feet.

"I've heard of falling for a woman," Raven drawled, his line hissing back into the line plier's housing, "but boys, boys! That's just bad form!"

The lead weight snicked back into the plier, and he stowed it. "Evening, Iris! I had no idea you were so popular."

She staggered back, still holding her injured arm to her body, instinctively not trusting help she hadn't requested. "Yeah? Who the fuck are you?" she gasped, even as Angel's thoughts in her mind sang out *By th' Lady's love—it's Raven!*

The three fallen soldiers were struggling to regain their feet. "Introductions can come later. You have more friends arriving from the sound end of the bridge. Your expertise must be 'trouble' because it looks like everybody's trying to bring you some." He drew his sword and readied himself for the first attack.

It took a single look to tell her what he said about the new trouble was just fact. They were trapped, or she was, at least—if that strange-looking cloak he wore explained his ability to fly—and he was drawing a sword?

"I hate to break it to you," she said, adding Angel's teary-eyed excitement to the list of detriments she had to manage, "but we're pretty badly outnumbered here, considering. Are you good enough with that thing to kill seven?"

"If you'd rather have dinner, I could arrange that," he replied, backing away from the three who had fallen. They were spreading out, apparently more intent on capturing them—or her—than fighting. "We can talk about where, later," he added hastily. "Right now, I'd say anywhere will soon be better than here."

"Oy! Iris! Enough, I'm out of breath. Give us a truce, love. Let's talk this out like adults, eh?"

It was one of the four approaching from the south, and he didn't look as if he'd been overly exercised any time recently. The bridge was fairly well lit—city ordinance—and she could see that he too wore leather armor, and that he bore a weapons belt with quite a few dangerous-looking pieces of armament. There were three others behind him, all garbed similarly, though their kits looked different. They walked a few paces behind the speaker, fanning out as they drew near.

"And just who the fuck are you?" she demanded, trying not to wince openly as she let her left arm hang free.

"Name's Willis. me girl. Squad leader for Lucky's Lads. Maybe you've heard." It was a suggestion, not a question, and he was prudently holding his hands away from his weapons as he approached.

Raven had heard of them, not that he put much stock in *what* he'd heard. The rumor mill said Lucky's Lads were former SAS troopers turned mercenaries, after the war, but from the look of Willis, they weren't exactly wearing out the parade grounds keeping in shape.

"I wouldn't trust this any further than we could pitch fat boy, there," he whispered to Iris.

"No shit," she muttered, growing angrier by the moment. "Stall them."

"And what the fuck do you want with this woman, Willis?" Raven demanded, maneuvering, as Iris was, in an attempt to keep all seven soldiers in view.

"Oh, you *must* be the Raven." Willis' tone was one of ease. He clearly was certain he had the upper hand in this engagement. "A con that got collared and sentenced to be a cop. I can appreciate the irony, by the way—but I've got business with the lady. It doesn't involve cops."

"It doesn't involve me, either," Iris said, spitting the words like bolts. "I don't care who you are. I'll jump the rail over there before I'll let you take me anywhere."

Willis laughed. "Ah, so y'do know who sent us, then?"

She spat at him. "I know he's a fool for hiring you."

The mercenary laughed again. "He didn't tell us you were such a delightful conversationalist! Look now, you don't need to make this any harder on yourself. Just ditch your pretend-cop there, luvvie, so's we can go cuddle someplace warmer, shall we? Be nice to me, and I won't even have to tie you up for the trip."

"Unless you've got a warrant and a badge, if you attack this woman again, you just might have an unscheduled appointment with the inside of Commissioner Roland's jail," Raven said, hoping it might at least give the idiot pause. "The one on the right has another of those damned nets," he went on, pitching his voice for Iris' ears. "If we're lucky, maybe he'll throw it at us."

She did a double-take, sure she'd misheard him. "What?"

"Oh, do be reasonable, Chief Inspector," Willis was saying, sidling to his left as he spoke. "I've got orders, you know, and there's just the one of you. You can walk away from this alive and whole, Raven. Just say the word. The lads'll let you pass. There's an ale barrel just down river there, with your name on it, ain't there?"

Iris snorted, but regardless of Raven's words and no matter how often she looked around, she couldn't see a way out that didn't involve the aforementioned plunge over the side of the bridge, into the icy waters of the Caspian, far below.

"Go on," she told Raven, as calmly as she could manage in the circumstances. "Get clear. You're no good to Roland or anyone else if they take you too. I'm too banged up to be sure I could rescue us both."

Angel's thoughts raced over the end of the spoken words like pebbles cast across glass. *He won't leave us, he cain't, not Raven—*

"There. See? The Iris is capable of reason after all. Of a sort." Willis laughed. So did his men.

Capable of love, too. Iris hadn't the time to decipher what Angelique meant before Raven's rejoinder made Angel begin to weep tears of joy.

"But we haven't even *kissed* yet," Raven protested outrageously. The tears were in Iris' eyes too, of a sudden, but only she knew that they weren't entirely from the throbbing pain behind her eyes.

"See?" he said, turning back to Willis, in mockingly tragic tones. "I can't leave yet, and you're sort of interfering with our evening. So, if you'd be so kind as to either leave or attack, I'd be much indebted to you," he went on, pressing his mocking display. "We've got a lot of other things to do, tonight."

Willis sighed in open disappointment, and shrugged. At that signal, one of his men hurled that net. It was what Raven had been awaiting. He grabbed Iris and threw his cloak over them both. They ducked the net, which then neatly landed on top of them.

"Shit!" Iris squealed, working hard to stay conscious. He'd grabbed her by the left arm, and there weren't words for what was going on in her shoulder.

"Finally!" Raven whispered. "Thought he was going to yammer all night. Put your good arm around me, here," he said, ignoring the names she was calling him. "Grab my waist with your legs, and hang on tight!"

"Why does this sound like a *really bad* idea?" she asked—rhetorically, for she was snaking her right arm around him, using her body to trap her injured arm between them. As dangerous and stupid as it sounded, it was going to be a lot better than leaving with Willis and company. Assuming they survived it, of course.

They both heard the boot steps approaching. Raven drew both line pliers. "Because it is," he said, half-apologetically, "but it's the best I could come up with on short notice. I usually plan much more thoroughly for a first date, I promise."

He stood up then, pushing up the cloak with one powerful thrust of his shoulders. Light and cold air rushed around Iris and she saw the cloak spread out and harden, then slam into three of the men with the force of a hammer, sending them flying. The net had sailed clear with the momentum and came back down to land on top of Willis and two of his three companions.

"Ha! Gotcha!" Raven grinned fiercely, then whirled to assess their foes. Out of the corner of his eye, he saw one of the three to the north rear back one arm, a curved throwing club in his hand.

Raven pulled a trigger. The lead weight from the end of the line plier caught the man in the chest and hurled him back. In the next heartbeat he'd shot the other line to the south end of the river. He had time to shout "Hang on!" to his passenger before they were both jerked up from the surface of the bridge, leaving Lucky's Lads in strife and confusion far below. The tow line screamed like an angry wildcat under the strain, but it worked!

Another of the silly throwing sticks ricocheted off the Raven Wing, but they had rolled so that his back was toward the ground, and it rebounded away harmlessly.

"They're a little slow at times, aren't they?" he quipped to Iris as he rolled them over.

She'd begun to laugh. It wasn't particularly loud or vigorous, but laughter it was, and it was her way of coping when life tumbled her over like this and spat her out to ride the rapids with nothing but her wits to protect her. "Maybe," she gasped, gripping him tightly, "But they'll be after us soon enough."

"Yeah, but this time they'll be on my turf, not theirs." Now able to look at the ground rather than the clouds above, he began to scan for a place to land. It wasn't the best choice he could think of, but still, they would be in River Trap. Here, he knew he could get help keeping Willis and his men busy while he and Iris escaped.

There it was, the stable yard just off the east end of the Fairmile Road. He headed that way and began to flare the wing to land.

Iris kept her mouth shut, reasoning correctly that it added to her chances of living through the landing if she let him concentrate on it. The possibility was good that, if he knew who he was really rescuing, he'd probably drop her and be done with it.

Iris, that's just not true. This could be our one chance. Please...

Hush, Angel. Not now. Angelique's voice was so subdued she could barely detect it. *We are not out of peril yet.*

Raven flared the glide wing, stalling them just above the fence line of the stable yard, then let it settle them to the ground. He hadn't carried anybody with him since Saliah, ten years ago. He was rather proud that he had pulled it off so smoothly but kept that to himself.

"There. Now we've got to get out of here, and find someplace to get that arm looked at." He helped her to her feet, then pulled off the goggles and jammed them into a pocket and took a quick look around. The side gate let back out onto Fairmile Road, but Willis and company would no doubt be headed that way a matter of minutes, so he opted instead to head for the stables. Hopefully, one of the stable boys would be on duty.

The stable yard was better lit. Iris kept her face averted as he led them both in but stepped back when he paused so she could lean against a door post. She knew she was vulnerable here. Raven claimed this as "his turf", and that implied access to allies and resources. It was an advantage, a serious one, as the setting for an encounter that could well turn ugly, despite Angel's sentimental protestations.

"Thank you," she said, fishing in her pouch for the vial of alchemically-enhanced analgesic she kept there against need. "You've done enough, though. Maybe too much, but I suspect Willis' boss is smart enough to keep him out of your way, in future. What I don't understand is *why*."

"Hulloo!" Raven called into the stable. "Why what, exactly?" he asked. A moment later, there was a rumbling and thumping from somewhere in the stable loft. Vial in hand, Iris uncapped it and tipped the contents into her mouth. They were bland enough, but tingled as they went down.

"Why you intervened," she said then, wiping her mouth with the back of her glove. "You could have just let them take me, you know."

"Yeah," he agreed, leading her into the stables. Several horses nickered grumpily at being awakened at such an obnoxious hour, and from the thumping on the stairs, an equally groggy stable boy was coming down the stairs from the loft. "Except you were wounded and outnumbered, which is hardly fair, and I've got questions of my own."

His answer unsettled her further. A tall, muscular teenage lad entered from across the stable and looked at them.

"Raven? What are y—"

"Jasper, there are seven stones coming across the bridge after my ass," he said quickly, cutting across the young man's words in his haste. "Well, her ass, but I've stuck my nose in. Keep 'em busy for me? Put the word out, and let Emma know, will ya? We'll get clear of the trap." He flicked the kid a coin that flashed gold.

Jasper caught it, yawned, nodded sleepily, then yelled something unintelligible back up to the loft. Raven chuckled, then turned to find Iris slumping against the door frame. He took her gently by her good arm, and led her out the side door, but she prudently disengaged from his grip there and tried walking on her own. The pain in her knee was quickly dulling to a grinding ache, and the ongoing riot in her head had subsided to sharp, jabbing flashes that kept time with her heartbeat. The bones in her shoulder, however, seemed to be broken, for she couldn't move it at all, and every attempt caused pain to spike through the relief the pain-killer had provided.

"Who is Emma?" she asked, shaking her head as if to clear it. "Your mistress?"

Likely one of them, at least, Angelique's thoughts savored of her wounded pride, but Iris couldn't have spared any energy for consolation, even had she wished it.

Raven chuckled, but reached for her again and pulled her in closer. His body helped support her weight on her right side, but she didn't want to be that close to him. Her reaction to his nearness was scrambling what few wits she had left with which to reason. She'd never cared much for the suave urbanity of Sir Vincent Sultaire, scion of Valemont, but the Raven in his element was every bit as attractive to her as he was dangerous. He was also warm, and helping, and Angel's inclination to throw herself at him was getting more and more difficult to resist with every step they took.

Fortunately for her struggles, they were still in danger, and Raven hadn't seemed to notice her distraction. He looked around once more, then got them across the street and into a small alley that led west. "Emma rules this part of town," he said, offering the explanation in subdued tones as they walked. "She's a trap lord, *the* trap lord here in River Trap, and the one that got me on the inside here. She's a very old friend."

"It seems you've picked your friends reasonably well, then," Iris said, forcing herself to concentrate on what to say, and on where she was putting her feet. "And your gear. Where'd you get that cloak and those clever line-shooting things you use?"

Raven paused as they reached an intersection. They could hear shouts echoing back at the south end of the bridge. Apparently Willis was still healthy enough to order his men around.

"It's a Mark 14a3 Raven Wing," he said, then ducked his head out to look up and down the street. It seemed clear, so he headed them across. "It was my grandfather's, from the war. I designed the tow lines from drawings I saw of the big bulky contraptions that the military was thinking of using to get whole squadrons of the wings up into the air. I've got smaller ones too. Good for lifting and lowering. They're not nearly powerful enough to launch the wing, but handy for scaling walls or getting back down to the street."

They'd reached the other side of the street, and Raven turned them both down a delivery alleyway, hoping to find signs of some street kids about, but so far, he'd seen and heard nothing.

"Now it's your turn," he told her. They were barely creeping ahead, and Raven seemed to be feeling his way along the wall with one hand as they went. "Who hired Willis and his boys?"

The question came too soon, and set off a tumult inside Iris' head that was louder than the headache and made her wince, and stumble.

Do you dare answer that? With the truth?

Yes! Please, both of you! Angel's thoughts were soaked with tears of desperation. *Ah mean it. Tell him.* Trust *him. He'll do the right thing, he cain't help it. We need him—AH need him, an' Ah don't want t' go on without him any more!*

Iris took a deep, shuddering breath, feeling fear for the first time that night. "Louis Arnot," she told him, praying to gods she couldn't name that Angel was right. "His name is Louis Arnot."

It caused Raven to miss a step, and he hissed under his breath. Louis Arnot had ruined detective Vincent Sultaire's first high-profile case. He'd had Baron Van Trapp of Glouden dead to rights, caught red-handed with his hands elbow deep, figuratively speaking, in the illegal and addictive substance known as "slave milk".

"*The* Louis Arnot?" he asked. "Wealthy, well-connected in the rich crime circles of the north? Gets rich, titled slave traffickers off? *That* Louis Arnot?"

Face averted, Iris nodded. "Sounds like the same one. Add forgery, smuggling, and drug-dealing to that list, while you're at it. He's as slimy as they come."

"I've been wanting a rematch with that man for over a year," he muttered. What he didn't say, of course, was that if he was honest, he had cause to be grateful for the pasting Arnot had given him in court. The lawyer probably didn't know it, but in getting Van Trapp off, he'd given Vincent an intensive education as to how the rich and powerful crime bosses in the north end worked their deals, and traded information, money, and property, not to mention how they manipulated the courts and the cops. He'd used that information for his own purposes—and profit—ever since.

"I hope you mean that," Iris told him, stumbling to a stop suddenly. Her eyesight had narrowed to a tunnel, a sure warning that she'd concussed herself in that fall, earlier. It wasn't making walking in the dark any easier. "Because he is stone-cold crazy, Raven, and someone needs to help me put him down."

Raven stiffened, then flattened them both against a the wall. They heard the slow, uneven boot steps. Whoever owned those boots was searching.

"I know someone else who will want a piece of that action too," he said, breathing the words into Iris's ear. She clung to his jacket, dizziness and desire playing tricks on all her senses. The vertigo, at least, made it easier for her to wait until the footsteps passed them by before attempting to speak.

"I don't know how much longer I'm going to stay awake," she said, requiring herself to breathe deeply, to remain conscious, at least semi-alert, and hopefully somewhat in control of Raven's access to her person. "If you know someplace safe... I'm not going after anyone... until my head clears..."

A man appeared in the intersection. It was one of Lucky's Lads, peering down the dark alley where they were hidden and silhouetted against the light from the burning brazier just behind him. He scowled in their direction several times, then moved on down the street.

"Dammit!" Raven's frustration was palpable. They weren't clear of River Trap, and Willis' boys were closing on them. "We need help—or a cab. Where are the street rats when you need one?"

...down the ladder, up the wall... around the corner, behind the stall...

Cricket's rhyme screamed like fury in her mind, and she cringed, comprehension dawning. "Hiding," she gasped, dropping her injured arm to press the heel of her palm against her forehead. The cold leather crushed like jagged ice, and the harder she pressed, the better it hurt. "Strangers... armed, searching... they won't come out..."

Raven stared at her for a heartbeat, then nodded. "Good point. Where's a drain pipe?" He looked around. "Over there. Other side of the street." He half supported her, half carried her to the storm drain, then took out his parrying sword and started tapping a rhythm of two tones with the blade and pommel. Iris couldn't chuckle, her head hurt too badly, but she heard Cricket's response to it in her mind.

Raven waited a few seconds, then repeated the rhythm, and waited again. He was just about to repeat it a third time when they heard an answering rhythm on another drain pipe, somewhere else nearby. Raven tapped out a different rhythm, then put his blade away.

He'd just told them to lead the strangers on a chase, and someone had agreed. Cricket's glee was manic; Iris would have preferred the bliss of ignorance if it had meant less noise between her ears.

"Now," Raven said, "let's get a cab, shall we?" Putting her on his arm again, he led her back to South Bank Road, where the cabs ran. If they could hop a cab before being spotted by Lucky's Lads, they could clear the area while the kids kept the soldiers busy. He was pushing, he knew, but Iris wasn't going to last much longer.

She didn't protest. They crossed the street, then had to duck into the cover of a shadowed alcove once to avoid detection—Willis and another of his squad, moving stealthily up both sides of the street, weapons drawn—but a shriek, followed by a clatter of wooden sticks and breaking glass drew them both off at a trot.

"Nice to have friends about, eh?" he quipped. A hansom appeared, and he flagged it and gave instructions for the driver to drop them at a cross street just over a kilometer ahead. Then they were inside the dim interior, and the horse's hooves were clopping steadily away from Willis and his bully boys.

Iris sagged into the cold leather, clutching her left arm, grimly willing herself to stay alert. Her body wanted to relax, but she couldn't allow it.

They were still outnumbered. "And that the other Lads don't think to stop cabs with fares at this hour. Is it much farther?"

"The closest discreet doctor I know is about an hour away," he replied, settling in across from her. "And we're headed in that direction. Now, tell me: Why are you after Arnot?"

Chapter 9

Iris shot him a glance, but whatever she meant to convey was largely lost in the darkness. "That's going to take more than an hour to answer," she told him, turning her gaze away from him, and toward the street just beyond the window. "I'm going to want a clear head for it. Can it wait?"

"Just trying to give you something to focus on," he said, settling in across from her in an attempt to get a better look at the dark-haired, dangerous woman he'd been tracking down for the better part of ten days. "Then how about a précis?"

Iris huffed softly. It was a fancy word to use. She wondered if he realized how incongruous it seemed from the raw-edged, dangerous man occupying the cab with her. The trouble was that there wasn't a short or easy answer to his question. There never was, where Louis was concerned.

"Because he and I have differing ideas about my future," she told him at last, pressing her forehead against the chilled, polished wood of the door frame. "He wants me at his disposal. I'd prefer a life where I can look at myself in the mirror every morning and respect the woman I see there."

"You *worked* for him?" Raven blurted it in his surprise, and she flinched slightly in response, but his mind was already racing.

Louis Arnot had emerged in Fernwall's Urilian-run legal arena two years previous, then had quickly made a name for himself as one of the best criminal defense lawyers in the city. He was wealthy—though nobody seemed to know how he came by that wealth—well-coiffed and smooth-spoken, and though shunned by the nobility was generally considered good company by the primarily Urilian aristocracy. Raven had deduced by the end of the Van Trapp trial that, despite the pains he took to appear otherwise, Arnot had to have been a Cascadian native. He knew the laws and culture too intimately, and his rise to power in the legal world had come too quickly after his arrival for him not to be well-connected, particularly to organized crime. It had meant that, like every other rich crime boss in the city, Louis Arnot was a master at never letting the slime from his underground dealings tarnish his shining public character. It also meant there was rarely ever enough dirt to trace back to him, let alone to accumulate so that the cops could obtain warrants to search his offices.

According to the story, Arnot had left Püran-Khir four years ago after helping the city rebuild its legal system. That was the story he fed to the press, anyway. That same year, the *Mâgun-Zak* had also left Püran-Khir for Glorédil on the first leg of a ten-year journey through "the lands of the Medini people". Its highly publicized departure had been accompanied by the publication of its world-crossing schedule. Therefore, its arrival in Fernwall this year had, of course, been planned long before the artifact ever left King Cashëmin's palace.

That rather put a different light on Arnot's activities, and if Iris had worked for him, it shed a new light on her, as well. He looked at her anew, pulling his flash from his belt and filtering the light through gloved fingers so he could actually get a good, long look at her. For the first time, he was close enough, and had time enough to devote his full attention to what his eyes were trying to tell him. She kept her face pressed against the window frame, and her short, irregularly cut hair rather inconveniently masked the lines of her face from his view. He could see that she was lithe, though, like a cat, quick and deadly. She had demonstrated a quick mind in high pressure situations, and had the physique of dancer, or a soldier...

The truth hit him like an avalanche. Angelique had that kind of physique. Like Iris, Angel's body was lean and compact. She had never just "moved", she'd *floated* from place to place, and flowed over him when they'd made love. Watching Angelique's face during orgasm had very nearly been an act of worship for him, and he had adored how intensity rendered her lovely face into something rather sublime. And, Iris... scenes of her from earlier that night clicked into place with his memories of Angelique, how she had tilted her head a certain way when she was listening intently, or the particular pose she would strike when challenging him—provocatively or defiantly— Iris had struck that pose on Morrisant Bridge! Marred by her injury, but still... Could it be?

His own words from Cooper's trial came back to him.

> *"Three guards were taken down... They were not killed... incapacitating a victim is considerably more difficult than killing him... comfortable taking on the increased risks associated with at least three perfectly silent take-downs... a veteran special forces operative... or master assassin..."*

Iris had expertly demonstrated that kind of training tonight, too—and her free running skill made the rooftop escape from Bishop-Florian Hall, after the theft of the *Mâgun Zak,* perfectly explicable. The logic trail was inescapable, and it solidified there at the end in a lump at the back of his throat.

She was here, right in front of him. The costume was new, as were the wig, the cosmetics, and the name, but the underlying lie hadn't changed.

"I'd ask you to take off the wig," he began pointedly, recapping his flash and replacing it on his belt in crisp, business-like movements, "but right now Iris and Angelique Blakesly are universally considered two different people, and Carlisle's name has already been dragged through the muck quite enough. Beyond that, I think its time to dispense with the pretense, don't you?"

Shit. It's now.

Iris froze. She'd been running hard toward this moment for weeks, but found herself completely flat-footed when it caught up with her. Dreading what was to come even more for the complete and utter lack of advice from the gallery in her head, she straightened on the seat slowly, and took a deep breath.

"I suppose that depends," she said, trying to gauge his expression in the cab's dim interior, but without much success. "Am I under arrest?"

"Are you the one who needs arresting?" After months of trying to forget her, to carve her out of his heart, she was here, in the same cab with him. She was injured and vulnerable, and he could feel the fear she kept at bay with every word she spoke. Even so, she was also more deadly than a viper, something he found intoxicating, and more than a little unnerving.

It took a long moment to figure out how to answer that. Her throat was too tight, every jolt of the carriage rained hellfire in her shoulder, and all Angel wanted to do was crawl into his lap and sob. The rest of her watched him intently, and tried to deny it was because she'd been nearly starved for the sight of him.

"I've needed arresting for months, Raven," she offered at last, not knowing what else to say. "You've known that."

"I know Roland thinks that," he said, flinging the words over the end of hers. "He'd *happily* clap you in irons. Personally, I've never found it all that efficacious to prosecute the weapon for the wielder's actions. Those I can easily lay at Louis' feet. But *you*," he went on, his look darkening, "You lied to me, and you lied to Lady Emilia—*repeatedly!* the man you are supposed to marry and the matron who trusted you the most; and then, just to add to the fun, you start tromping around down here in the traps, killing people in a bloody trail from the Fairmile Road to the foot of the Great Western Bridge! You've come closer than anyone in over a hundred years to setting this whole stinking city ablaze, did you realize that?"

"I've never killed anyone 'just for fun.' Killing is serious business," Iris retorted, pushing down Angel's shrieking wail of protest. "I tried to explain everything to you last summer, if you'll remember. In fact, I'd only just returned from *running to your damned flat* in Merchants' to throw myself at your feet and explain *everything*—"

"Right! Brilliant! *After* you've stolen the *Zak, after* you've deliberately hung Spider out to dry, *after* you've ruined the reputation of the Ladies' Auxiliary! Lady Emilia remains untouched only because she's been the one holding this country together for the last forty years. Everyone else, including me, is what? An afterthought?"

"*How was I supposed to trust you?*" Iris shrieked, then regretted it instantly. The other two voices in her mind began to shriek, and then

Cricket's joined them, words and phrases of the three disparate personalities circling around one another like a demented, three-cornered jig, and she pressed the heel of her hand into her temple in hopes it would keep them from bursting through it. "Did you think you were the only one who can read tells? Can you imagine even Angelique couldn't figure out you were lying *in your throat* about almost everything you told her? I was *going* to find a way to trust you, but you'd better believe I was going to cover my ass, first!"

"Oh I see. I was lying when I told you I loved you, *lying* when I told you I wanted to marry you," Raven said, bringing bitter sarcasm to bear, "and I was *certainly* only looking after my own interests when I helped you start actually ruling a barony you had no idea what to do with. Tell me, sunshine: since you were able to 'tell' so much, did it ever occur to you that, if you wanted out so damned bad, that the guy to talk to might just be the criminal you'd been fucking for months? You know, the con who just happens to have some of the biggest criminals in this city by the short hairs?"

"Yeah," she said, trying not to snarl, but mostly failing. "You, and Louis Arnot. Two of a kind. Trusting him implicitly didn't work out so well for me."

"*Did you have a choice?*" He nearly shouted it, but checked himself at the last minute, and snarled it, instead. These taxi cabs weren't sound-proofed. "I've made my share of stupid mistakes, *Iris,*" he went on, his voice low and thick with barely checked emotion, "and I've hurt a lot of the wrong people. I *earned* my collar, all right, but not for the so-called 'crimes' for which I was convicted. For those, I'll answer to the Judge Herself, but I don't have to answer to *you.*"

In the absence of traffic, the cab rolled along quickly. They'd entered the edges of the part of town were where the money lived, and so the street lamps were placed more closely together. They slashed light through the dark air between them, now heavy with grief and regret. The angry words she and Raven were hurling at each other were like knives driven into her heart—no, no, into *Angel's* heart—and for all her bitterness, Iris simply couldn't sustain her rage in the face of Angel's despair.

"I'm sorry. I shouldn't have said those things," Iris said, whispering the words as the returning darkness erupted into light once more. "I'm supposed to be begging your forgiveness, and I know I need to, but I don't know how."

"As you've so aptly pointed out, we've both made mistakes. *Bad* mistakes." The cab lurched and rolled as it negotiated a parked delivery wagon. He reached out to brace himself against the motion, damping down the sympathetic response as Iris groaned aloud as her injured shoulder smashed into the side wall, then grimly shifted herself on the cushion so she could remain facing him.

"A criminal judging someone else for being a criminal requires a special kind of arrogance," he said at last, "and a con judging someone else for playing fast and loose with the truth is completely ludicrous, if you think about it." He snorted in self-disgust. "If I really loved you as much as I said I did, then why didn't I try to help, rather than diving into an ale barrel?"

"That's been asked. Repeatedly," Iris admitted, unable to spare the concentration needed to convince Angel to still her weepy protests. Angelique showed no signs of intervening. In fact, the thief got the distinct impression that she was tapping her foot, rather impatiently awaiting the answer. "So, is it because you didn't know any more about love than I did, or because you really didn't give a shit?"

"Oh I gave a shit," Raven retorted forcefully. "That was the problem, *has been* the problem! I really, really *do* give a shit, so much so that I convinced myself I needed to forget you. Trust me, Angelique, I dove into that ale barrel in an attempt *not* to give a shit, and to this day there are times when I really wish it had worked. But it didn't."

He huffed short, humorless laughter and tore his gaze away from her to stare out into the night. "I have no idea what love is," he snorted. "Not really. Maybe that's what it is: Not being able to *not* care. Having to know, to understand. I don't know. All I know is that I can't make you go away. You're here," he tapped his chest, then looked directly at her, "inside me, and I can't get you out."

The instinctive protest about who she was—and wasn't—died in her throat long before he'd finished speaking. Iris searched his eyes and face for a long moment after that, defenses crumbling, hurting inside in all the wrong ways, and uncertain what she expected to find. "Well. If that's not what love is," she finally said, swallowing hard against the storm of tears that threatened to break, "at least it's something I can understand. I know what it's like to have things inside you that you can't escape, but you're the very first I've ever had that I've wanted to keep."

The horses' hooves, suddenly loud on the cobblestone road, were all the broke up the sudden silence as their carriage rolled on toward South Merchants'. It wasn't the answer he had expected, but then, if he was honest, he wasn't sure what he thought he was going to hear. A part of him still wanted to be hurt and angry over the lies, some of which were right in front of him. That short, black-haired wig was quickly becoming a festering sore in his sight, a perpetual reminder that on one level, none of this was real.

Or, maybe it was all *too* real. Maybe this *was* the truth of her, and he found himself asking it again: *Who was she, really?*

"I don't know whether I'm in love with you," he said, as if the words had to be excavated one by one, "or in love with your lies."

Something in her deflated at that, something that felt like the baroness' resolve in the face of what he'd just said. It didn't take a logician to realize that "Angelique Blakesly" constituted the bulk of the lies he referenced. But then, she looked at him again, this very armed and dangerous "Raven" who claimed a stinking stretch of River Town as "his turf," and suddenly knew she wasn't the only one who had a secret life which really ought to be explained.

"I don't know either, Raven, but you're nothing like the too-charming and over-groomed young knight that romanced Baroness Blakesly of Carlisle for over a year. Is this who *you* really are?"

The flip response popped into his head immediately, but he swallowed it. This wasn't the time to dodge or turn away. If he couldn't get this woman out of his soul, then he had to learn how to be honest, and hope for honesty in return. It was no small task for a young man who, as a child, had the true cost of honesty beaten into him at a very early age. Truth was dangerous. It left one vulnerable, open to attack, with no available defense. Truth hurt—the truth-teller most of all.

"I don't know how to answer you," he finally admitted. "Yes—and no, I suppose. This is probably closer to the truth, but it's not all of it."

"Then that's two ways we are similar. I like this side of you, for what it's worth." Incoming light lingered on her eyes as they once again took in the bulky cloak, gloves, the weapons-belt, and the well-used sheath that held the blade he'd drawn to defend her, just that hour past. The merest ghost of a smile flickered in one shadowed corner of her mouth. "Well, frankly, it's more than 'like.' A lot more than that."

He stared at her blankly for a few seconds, then chuckled knowingly. It broke the dark mood and dispelled the gloom that was beginning to hang in the air of the carriage like a cloud. "Well then, I guess we're even," he murmured, stripping off his gloves, then sliding over next to her. He put a hand on her cheek and ran a single finger down her jaw. It was hard-set now, and made her face look like it was carved out of alabaster. Her eyes burned with all the intensity of someone who'd lived on the edge, who in fact sought out that edge and danced upon it, every chance she got. He'd never seen it from her before, likely because she could never risk letting him see it before, but he recognized it at once.

"The 'Iris' adds to your other charms, as the overused saying goes," he said, brushing his lips against hers. "Just think of the trouble we can get into, together..."

"Gods' breath, I was hoping you'd say that." She kissed him then, leaning into him with her uninjured side, ignoring the prickling stabs that made it past the pain-killer's buffer. Perhaps he *would* throw over the noble facade— and Angelique Blakesly—in order to help her find enough trouble to keep them both amused, and that prospect made her happier than she'd been in a very long time.

Iris couldn't recall having kissed anyone purely of her own volition before, but kissing Raven turned out to be one of the most intoxicating things she'd ever done, and as thrilling in its own way as a full-bore run across the top of Three Lions Bridge. It caused her to wonder just what it might be like to do other pleasurable things with Raven, things that involved a more comfortable place to roll around, and a lot fewer clothes.

It used t' be our favorite way t' lose sleep. Angel's voice was wistful, but mostly smothered under the desire that fought a strong rearguard action against the grinding bones in her shoulder. It reminded her of the lies that had been told, and of the consequences of her choices.

Iris, we promised Lady Emilia. You cannot turn away from his caste. You must not allow him turn away from it. He might enjoy it for a time, but inevitably, he would come to resent you—and I doubt he would never forgive you for it.

Iris groaned a little, protesting at Angelique's reminder of what awaited them both just on the other side of the carriage walls, and pulled her mouth away from his most reluctantly. Right or wrong, they'd made promises to Remington, and Louis' appearance at Morahan's had changed everything.

"I'm sorry. I'd love to run away with you, Raven, but I know I can't outrun Louis forever." Her eyes searched his again, half-hooded in such intimate proximity. "Mostly because this time, he's coming after you."

Raven stared at her for several long heartbeats. He had no direct connection to Louis Arnot, but he was very involved in the business of some of his richest criminal clients, including Baron Van Trapp. Louis may have gotten Van Trapp off, but Raven had made sure the crooked nobleman was paying a price, none-the-less. A very *high* price. Like any good con, he was always scrupulous about making sure one end of his connections never knew about the other, but there was always a chance someone had talked. "What does he say about me?" he asked warily, leaning back just far enough to watch her face as they spoke.

Her mouth twisted once, briefly. Louis' latest move still made Iris' blood boil. "He's going to pry into your legal case, that's what. He claims you're 'innocent of the charges' and he's hinting that he can get you out of that collar—all if it will make the baroness happy, ostensibly, and clear the way for the marriage. Of course, it's utter orc shit. He knows it, I know it. But, once he's got his hooks into you, he won't willingly let you go. He knows..."

Of course Louis knows, but do you?

And have you got th' guts t' say it?

Iris swallowed. She'd never lacked for courage, and neither of them had time for any more lies. "He knows that I will do anything he says in order to protect you."

Raven's mind was racing before she'd finished. His eyes scanned her face again, drinking in every subtle shift in her expression, registering the fear there without really marking it. "Now why would Louis want me out of a collar?" he murmured, mostly to himself.

His gaze drifted to the window, but he wasn't really seeing what passed by without. Instead, he was going through the cons he had running, twisting them around, trying to work out some advantage to Louis or a client. Only one came to mind: If he married, then he and Angelique would be busy building their barony. He would, in theory, have no time to keep his cons running. "In theory," sure, but theory didn't win cases any more than positive thinking did. It took facts, and the hard work of building evidence, step by step.

"It makes no sense," he finally muttered. "Or maybe, better stated, the sense it makes is so theoretical it borders on faith."

Iris shook her head. "No, listen. I fired Louis last summer, but Louis never lets anyone go, not willingly. So, to make it stick, I broke into his storage room to steal the Van Trapp case files, then placed them with an anonymous attorney on what Louis always called a 'dead man's trigger', though I've heard them named other things, like 'the final word' or a 'last will and testament'. You know what I mean?"

He nodded. "Is that what you were doing the night I caught you?"

"More or less." She searched his face, letting him read what he would in hers. Any secrets she had left were his for the plundering. "That particular night, I'd just come back from letting him know what I'd done, by way of your flat." It echoed what she'd flung at him in acrimony, earlier. She turned what bitterness remained on herself, and it savored of regret.

Raven's smile echoed that. Master Slagter had tried to teach him that there was no such thing as a single side to a truth. His new understanding of what had really happened that night had added an exclamation point to his old tutor's truism.

"Done is done," he said firmly, unconsciously echoing her very words at the Belton House Ball. "But I still don't get this," he turned back to their conundrum. "Okay, you stole documents to make him behave. So what? What's the connection between your dead man's trigger and me?"

"I—" The question froze her, or perhaps it was the answer to it. *Love* wasn't a word that fit easily in her mouth, so she dodged around it, instead. "Me," she said, huffing it softly into the heat between them. "He wants me back, willingly if it works out that way, but 'unwillingly' is always an option that's on the table where Louis is concerned. Hence Lucky's Lads, tonight, and the thugs he's had on my tail whenever I cross one of the bridges into Merchants'. He wants me back—and if he can use you to get what he wants, then he will. You're just collateral to him—and if what you were saying earlier is true, you're probably an easier target *out* of a collar than you are in one."

"Because my collar has FPD stamped on it," he mused. "Yeah, I can see that, but darling, this still isn't logical. To turn this a different way, you're basically saying Louis thinks you'll cooperate if he plays the hero and gets my conviction overturned. Even assuming he still knows nothing about what I'm doing, he knows damned good and well what I've done in public, and he knows what you've done. Is he really so naive as to think we wouldn't join forces to make sure he could never hurt either of us again?"

Her gaze never wavered. "It's the slimy, disgusting things he'll do to get you exonerated, Raven, things he'll find a way to pin back on you, just to be sure you're good and caught. That way, he owns your soul, or at least has a good chance to purchase the lease on it. I think once you go through the Van Trapp dossier, you'll see what I mean. He'll have you, just like he has Van Trapp, and I'll come back willingly because it will all have been my fault.

"You're something I value, and I failed to protect you," she concluded, hating the next truth she had to admit. "This is all a game to Louis, and he just let me know that I've been out-played. He is very good at exploiting an opponent's 'undefended fortresses'. He turned up at Morahan's last night to let me know he had one of mine surrounded."

Raven's eyes went wide. "So *that's* it!" He banged himself on the forehead.

"How stupid of me. It makes perfect sense!" He was so excited he could barely sit still, in spite of the fatigue. "Let's assume Louis knows that he really *doesn't* own Van Trapp. Not anymore. I do—more or less. If he starts working on my case, then he'll get a chance to dig into things he suspects I'm doing, but can't prove. Boom! I have to cooperate, or he'll take me down, *hard.* So he wins, twice: He gets you, which is what he really wants, and he gets me out of the way, so he looks like a bloody genius to all the rich crime bosses in Fernwall."

"Wow." Iris' eyebrows had gotten terribly cozy with her hairline as he'd shared his revelation, and the smile that curled the corners of that expressive mouth was positively steeped in the kind of cynicism she could never have gotten from living an honest life. "Sure could have used *that* information before I tried nailing Louis' foot to the floor. Figuratively speaking, of course." She leaned into him then, pressing into the space he'd gained in their little revelatory interlude, and would have been purring if she hadn't also had to cradle her arm to keep it stable in the taxi's swaying interior. "Exactly *what* are you doing to the elusive and much out-of-favor baron Van Trapp of Glouden? You do realize he shares a liege lord with Carlisle in the earl of Camrose, do you not?"

"I do," Raven nodded, "and Camrose has his fingers in this too, though I have yet to figure out how. He's not into slave milk or slaves, like Van Trapp. Anyway, for the last year or so, the price of opium-based pharmecuticals from Valïan alchemists has been dropping, for some strange reason. Slave milk is built off of an opium base, and it takes a lot of it to make very little of the drug. Somehow, a significant portion of Van Trapp's deliveries—paid in cash in advance, of course—have been disappearing!" He looked positively puzzled for a few heartbeats, then grinned at her.

She shook her head ruefully for just a moment, then laughed softly. Their cab lurched to a stop, and they could clearly hear the sounds of cross-traffic ahead. "How much did you make off that extraordinary transaction?" she asked, abruptly curious. It wasn't often a question one got the opportunity to ask.

"Oh, it's an ongoing thing," he chortled. "There are only so many people, even in this town, who are willing to divert shiploads of opium into the black market, and Van Trapp has customers to satisfy— customers who don't like being told 'no'. So, I get his money, he gets a pittance of what he paid for, but has no where else to turn, and I sell the rest to the Valïans at a small discount so it doesn't screw up the market. Everybody wins but Van Trapp," he shrugged and looked out the window. They were well and truly in South Merchants' by then. "I've got to stop by the office for a few minutes. Willis recognized me. I can't believe Louis won't know what to do with that information, so we need to give him something else to occupy his time."

She nodded. "He's going to think I've been lying to him, or that we were playing him all along. But hey, listen." Pausing to fumble at her pouch with her good hand, she withdrew a few coins. "A vendor in Morrisant Park lost their income tonight when their cart broke my fall. Could you ask someone to see that these," she went on, handing them to him, "get to where they can make that right?"

"Must have been some cart," he drawled as the carriage eased off of South Bank Road and turned south. "But very thoughtful of you," he added, deliberately making it sound as pretentious as possible. She wrinkled her nose at him for it, sure they both got more than enough of that kind of thing up in Angel Heights. He stuffed the coins into his waistcoat pocket, just as the carriage rolled to a stop in front of the august police building. "I'll be having the desk sergeant send a runner up to my flat in the morning. Give me five minutes."

It took longer than five minutes, but not by much. Two police fliers emerged from the main doors, sprouted wings, and flew off in different directions while Iris watched, and waited, and did her best not to give in to the waves of paranoia that made her twitch each time a blue jacket strode her way. At last, Raven bounded back down the steps, and Iris let herself relax. She'd been certain enough of him, but there was still too much she didn't understand about how he was bound to Commissioner Roland. His prompt return—without reinforcements—had helped her learn how to trust him, and how to believe in what her heart, most often speaking in Angel's voice, was telling her.

"Four ninety-two Queens Street," he told the driver, before easing back into the seat next to her. "There!" he exclaimed, then pecked her on the lips for emphasis. "That's done. Now, what say we get rid of that wig? Since you banged your head, old Flint's going to look it over. Assuming he's sober enough to even notice, explaining why you're wearing it might be rather awkward."

Iris cast him a swift, speculative look, and considered it. It was difficult to surrender something that had become so intimately entwined with her independent identity, but what if his healer friend needed access to her scalp? In the end, her health had to be more important than vanity, didn't it?

Reluctantly, she reached for her belt pouch again, but then winced and stopped. "Takes two hands," she said, feeling awkward and foolish. It wasn't the real reason she was hesitating, but it was the easier with which to grapple. "I've only got just the one. Do I have to?"

"Yes," he insisted, perhaps a bit too quickly. "But, if you'll let me, I'll do it."

"Raven. . ." She'd begun to stall him, knowing the reasons for her reluctance would sound irrational. She probably *was* crazy, after all. Not too many people had voices in their heads that talked back.

He's not askin' you to give it up forever, Iris, Angel whispered softly. *It's a good thing the baroness isn't around t' be asked, Ah guess.* Before Iris could ask the question, Angel answered it. *Ah don't know. She might be sleepin'. She stopped talkin' awhile back and Ah cain't find her anywhere.*

"Shit." Profanity served to cover her concern at what Angel said, but it was mostly reluctant capitulation and they all knew it. Her fingers fumbled at the pouch's leather tie for a moment, then she held out a glass vial wrapped in several layers of cotton cloth.

"That's the solvent," she told him softly. "Apply it to the skin just before the hairline, then it should just peel back, using your fingers."

Raven quickly doused the cloth with the sweet-smelling solvent, worked the it around the edge of Iris' hair piece, then carefully peeled it back. Below it was an odd-looking, neutral-colored skullcap that covered Angelique's long, ash blond hair. With her good hand, she reached over the top of her head from behind, peeling gently at where her hairline ought to be. In a few moments, it pulled loose; with the abrupt introduction of air, the hair expanded and the cap curled back all at once, releasing it in long, flat locks that lay like rumpled ribbons upon her shoulders.

Raven smiled in spite of himself, set the wig aside, then slid his fingers into her fine, soft hair. He'd always loved how it looked, and how it felt in his hands, shining pale like silver and gold, flowing over his naked body like liquid silk in moonlight. "There," he murmured, entranced by the feel of it. "That's better."

"Is it?" Iris tried to read his expression, but couldn't hold his gaze for long. She felt exposed, vulnerable, and recognized that how much of her wanted to melt into him, how much she wanted to let go of the burdens of the responsibilities she'd assumed, how deeply she wanted him to be there to help her with them—and how ill-equipped she was to know what to do with any of it.

"Yes," he asserted. "I love your hair," he added, letting it fall from his hands so he could resettle himself next to her.

"Oh, good," she said, taking up the wig skullcap and handing them to him with an unrepentant flick of an eyebrow. "because you'll need to hold it for me until we're safely in your flat."

He gave the thing a disgusted look, then shoved it into a pocket. A part of him knew that his dislike of the wig was irrational. The lies were theirs. The wig was just a symbol. On the other hand, it served to protect the truth, and for those reasons alone, it was a necessary part of her disguise. "I understand the reason for it," he said as the carriage slowed and rolled through the turn down Queens Street, "but that doesn't mean I have to like it."

"Well, I do," she said, regretting the need to disagree with him before they'd even gotten out of the taxi, but unwilling to lie to him, even by omission. "Try not to let it rumple too much. It's worth more than a year's lease on your flat."

Chapter 10

In Flint's experience, awakening to the sound of pounding on his door in the middle of the night almost never meant good news. It was usually someone wanting money, or a quick, no-questions-asked healing, with never a thought to his convenience or how much a man needed proper sleep. He rolled over and tried to ignore it, but when it returned it was louder, and threatened to set off the morning-after headache that he wasn't yet ready to face. Shouting something bleary and unintelligible to silence the noise, he pulled on his robe against the chill and staggered toward the front door of his flat.

The pounding resumed before he got there. Momentarily enraged, he pounded back on his side of the door, shouting "Who are you and what the *fuck* do you want?"

"Well it isn't a fuck, Flint," Raven shot back, loud enough to be heard through the door. "So unless you've got money for next month's rent and booze, how about opening the damned door! Fucking alcoholic." He whispered the last two words to Iris, who was leaning against him while they waited. "If he'd stay sober, he could make good money."

This wasn't to be her first off-book treatment, not by several dozen, but the door opened before she could do more than nod. The man standing there was dressed in warm nightclothes. The front of his robe hung open, and he was fumbling for a pair of spectacles in one of his pockets. He was a stocky man, and balding into late middle-age. What was left of his dark hair was thoroughly shot through with silver, and it looked as if he hadn't groomed his beard in days. He clearly wasn't happy at the intrusion, and had drawn breath to tell him so—loudly—but then caught sight of what was tucked under Raven's arm, and blinked owlishly.

"Sultaire, you bug-fucker," he said, smashing his glasses onto his face, then peering at them both accusingly. "Oh, this can't be good. If it involves a woman and *any* kind of injury, it's *never* good."

"Thanks," Iris said, her acerbic drawl not nearly as deadly as usual, "that happens to mirror my experiences with off-book healers."

"Come on, Flint," Raven said, pushing past into his flat, dragging Iris along with him. "Let's get this over with before she bleeds to death, shall we?" He turned for the examining table at the other end of the common room.

"Oh, so you're going to drag her, bleeding, across my rugs. Nice," Flint said, tying up his robe as he followed them. "What the hell are you doing with bleeding women at this time of night? I thought you swore off?"

Iris' head came up at this, and she tried to glare at Flint, then Raven, but couldn't bring either into focus. "You had to swear off bloody women?" she said, handing Raven her pouch and gloves. "What the fuck have you been doing with yourself, anyway?"

"Long story," he told her, then helped her onto the table and turned back to Flint. "Look, can we worry about your damned rug later? It would be really nice if you managed to accomplish something *before* she dies."

There was something in his tone. Iris heard it, and tried to catch his eye. The effect was marred due to both hers being crossed. Flint, however, had growled something unimaginably foul involving Raven's ancestry, but had settled a high-backed chair in front of his latest patient and turned his attention to her.

"Right. What you got?"

She grimaced. He clearly didn't intend to waste his power on anything as professional as a diagnosis. Off-book healers fixed what their patients requested, asked no questions, and got hard coin in exchange for it.

"Right knee," Iris said, running through the list of aches and pains she'd accumulated that night. She tried to watch him, but the dizziness was getting worse by the second. "Left arm and shoulder. Dizziness and headache—banged my head in a bad fall."

"Hmph." Flint was clearly dubious, but also just as clearly didn't care enough to pursue it. He took a deep breath, held his hand over her knee, and frowned.

She felt the familiar sensation, almost a heat-like wave as it flowed into her knee. It pooled for a long moment, then began to radiate to the injuries above and below it. After a few seconds, the joint *popped,* but the ache began to recede almost before she could react.

As if bored, Flint moved his attention to her shoulder, repeating the procedure twice. The first one caused another, more painful popping sensation deep in the joint, and she grunted in protest. On Flint's second breath, the heat wave penetrated her shoulder blade and made it feel as if he were ringing it like a bell, and she gritted her teeth to keep from snarling at him for it. By the time he'd moved his hand away, that pain too had nearly vanished.

Iris sagged against Raven in relief, but Flint reached over to place two fingers beneath her chin, turning it up to face the light so he could look into her eyes. "Look at her pupils," he muttered, tilting them toward Raven so he could see for himself. The were markedly differing sizes, and slightly off-focus.

Raven arched an eyebrow. "You sure you're not still drunk?" he asked dubiously. "That's not normal."

"I'm not done yet," Flint said disgustedly. "Try to pay attention, Sultaire. If you ever want to know if someone's concussed, get a look into their eyes. The pupils look like that. Now... let's see what got rattled around in there."

He peered into her eyes again, but then closed his so he could see with his gift. He wasn't a brain specialist, but serving ten years aboard warships had taught him how to recognize and treat a concussion when he saw one. It was more challenging than either a sprained knee or broken shoulder, one requiring a more delicate and precise use of his faculties. Given that he'd been soaking them in *thesker* for most of the night, it took a bit more concentration than he might have liked.

Flint put his hand on her head and closed his eyes. Healing energy poured into her scalp, then penetrated past her skull in one very odd-feeling *push*. Iris grunted once, more in startlement than in pain, but the sensation had begun to recede again almost before she could register it.

He looked into her eyes again—Raven saw that the pupils were evenly dilated again—then nodded and asked, "How do you feel?"

Iris shifted her shoulder around and took a quick internal inventory. *I don't suppose he got rid of the lot of you with that?*

Nice, but you're not gettin' off so lucky.

She grimaced. There still had been no sign of the baroness, however, and that was something. Flint drew breath to question her further, but she was able to speak up in time to forestall him.

"Better," Iris told him truthfully. "The pain and dizziness are gone. Everything feels as if it works, again."

"You hesitated," he said, but it was a mocking, sing-song sort of accusation that told her he didn't really care. His thumb brushed her left cheekbone once, dissipating the bruise that had begun to surface in an almost idle way. "But, no matter. There," he said, and turned her face up by the chin once more for Raven's perusal. "She could be a poster model for the women of the wine district, don't you think?"

Raven arched an eyebrow. So did Iris. The predilection among the ruling families of south Cascadia for requiring sexual service from their servants was perhaps the worst kept secret of Cascadian history; and because the Cascadian nobility historically held on to power through family connections, certain features were now more common than they should have been amongst those from that region.

"So she could," he replied, looking at Iris anew. "I'd never noticed it before."

She couldn't conceal the slow flush that covered her cheeks as both men gazed openly at the secret she'd kept the longest. She brushed aside Flint's fingers, then rotated her newly-healed shoulder once more."Yes, well, it's a common enough face. Unless you want to start discussions about my pedigree right here," she said, looking directly at Raven, "we'd probably better be going."

Flint shrugged and turned toward his sideboard once again, having used up whatever interest he had in her, or in anything that wasn't inside one of the bottles waiting there. "Drink before you go?"

The keys rattled and the door opened, and then they were in the unlit parlor of Raven's cold flat. He shrugged off the Raven Wing and his overcoat, and tossed them at the coat rack in the corner. "So, how does a girl from the wine district end up in Püran-Khir?" he asked, unbuckling his weapons belt.

Without thinking about it, she dropped her gloves in a chair, followed by her belt, noting only after the fact that it was the same chair Angelique had used for her things during her visits there. Her own memories of this place were vague and somewhat disjointed, for they had, in a real way, come from another life and time. The same could be said of what she needed to recall in order to answer his question. She hadn't needed those memories in order function here, and so she'd left them behind, in Angel's keeping, and in Angelique's.

"This isn't going to be easy to talk about, or to hear," Iris said, uncovering the crystal in the lamp he kept near the chair. The shadows still concealed more of the room around them than the light revealed, but she could at least watch him as he crouched in front of the furnace to coax it back to life.

He tossed a match onto the coal and paper and watched it grow into a flame. "That sounds ominous. If you'd like something better than Flint's paint thinner, there ought to be some Cairnbrooks on the side board." In truth, he hadn't been here in a couple of months, and he wasn't really sure what was left where.

"Only if there's anything worth eating here that the mice haven't gotten." The shot she'd taken at Flint's had neatly silenced Angel for the moment, and there was still no sign of the baroness. Liquor wasn't going to help that, but food might. In his pantry she found a tin of flat-breads that hadn't gone too stale and a sealed jar of apple preserves, bringing them back to the parlor on a tray.

"I hope you weren't saving this for sentimental reasons, because I'm about to make at least half of it disappear," she advised him, placing it on the low table near the sofa. "You might as well just bring the bottle over. Neither of us is going anywhere for a while."

"Oh this is *really* beginning to sound bad," he drawled, closing the door to the stove. He stood up, brushed off his hands, and went over to open the sole bottle of liquor that remained on the sideboard. "You're not going to tell me you want a divorce, are you? Because we haven't even gotten married, yet."

"I'm not even holding you to the betrothal," she promised him, working the latches of her boots so she could slide out of them. "I don't mean to sound melodramatic, but I let you propose marriage last summer to a lie. I want to make that right, if I can. While I can. And if you still want me after that, I'll know that it's for real. That *we're* for real."

Raven pulled the stopper from the Cairnbrooks and poured two snifters. "Angelique Blakesly, you mean." He pushed a glass over to her. "She's a persona, created by Louis to facilitate the theft of the *Zak,* isn't she?"

She drew breath to agree to that, but was quickly forestalled.

Iris, don't you dare. She's as real as you are, and we don't get out of this without her, too!

Ballocks. She's a dialog sheet for a role, and always was.

Can you *run Carlisle? Talk to the other Paladins, or make sense o' what they're sayin'? Ah sure cain't, an' Ah don't want to give that up!*

Iris exhaled nasally, curling her legs beneath herself to settle in one corner of the sofa. She picked up the glass he'd offered, and silently conceded defeat. If Angel wanted the barony, then it meant that she and Angelique were going to have to find a way to work together, assuming she hadn't disappeared for good.

"She was, yes. Originally." She glanced up at him apologetically. "It's not that simple, anymore."

"Because that persona is now a member of the Cascadian nobility, with lands and titles?" he suggested. He dipped a piece of flat bread in the jam, and offered to feed it to her. She flickered an appreciative grin, but opened her mouth to accept the bite, truly hungrier than their meager little feast could hope to requite.

"And, unfortunately, with her own will and ideas about how things should be done, which usually differ pretty fundamentally from mine," Iris said, after clearing most of the food from her mouth. He shot her an inquiring look, and she nodded back at him. "You heard that right. I wish I could explain it, but I can't."

That earned her an arched eyebrow, as Raven began to realize that it wasn't the first time tonight that she'd referred to Angelique as a separate "she" rather than simply "I". "You did it again," he pointed out, pointing at her with his own bit of jam-laden flat bread. "Referred to Angelique as if she were someone else, with ideas separate from yourself."

She nodded, and then shrugged. "She is. Look, I know how it sounds, believe me. From the outside, it's got to look like it's all just one woman, but we're not. I accept responsibility for the choices and decisions I was part of making, though—and that includes accepting your proposal of marriage last summer. In fact," she added, reaching for more food, "I'll own my part in everything up to the morning after our fight in Angelique's bedroom at Blakesly House. Anything after that isn't as straight-forward."

"I don't understand."

"No one does." It was difficult to make herself eat with any semblance of civility, and she forced herself to slow down, mostly so she could concentrate on what she was saying. "I just know it's true. I don't recall any details of the life we had before Püran-Khir. I know it happened, but it's as if it happened to someone else."

Raven stared at her for a heartbeat, then picked up his glass. Mental illness had become wide-spread in all the allied countries, and had been for generations, since the walking wounded began returning from multiple fronts. "Battle fatigue" was by far the most commonly referenced problem, but there were others with names he couldn't even pronounce, let alone describe, or begin to understand.

He took a slow sip of the honey-sweet liquor, and rolled it across his tongue as he thought. Angel was too young to have fought the battles to free Vin-Nôrë, but it appeared that she'd been caught up in the aftermath of a war, nonetheless.

"All right," he said quietly. Like their other problems, the only way he could see to get through this was to dive in to the heart of it. "I gather from the way you put that, that this 'other person,' the one before Püran-Khir, isn't Angelique?"

That earned him a rueful tip of her glass in tribute. "Just so. We call her 'Angel'." It was odd to feel the smile flickering on her mouth and then to realize, instinctively, that it wasn't her own. Angel's presence hovered in an almost palpable way just behind her own thoughts, swirling amid riptides of affection, passion, and regret, yearning for him in a way that Iris found almost painfully embarrassing. She tore her eyes away from Raven's, and swallowed a mouthful of the sweet liquor, playing for time while she got her own emotions sorted.

"We?"

It earned him a strangely sympathetic glance. "Yeah. It's pretty crowded in here, sometimes. As far as I know, the baroness and I are the ones running things, if not always harmoniously." She pulled her fingers through her hair as she thought it over, frowning once at the color of it before flipping it back over her shoulder. "There are others, but they don't seem to have much interest in doing anything. Angel's the one who keeps the peace, and never for an instant lets any of the rest of us forget how much she lo—"

The word itself stopped her mouth, but the truth behind it would not be denied. As much as she might have wanted to, as much as it scared her, Iris could not look away from him. For once, Angel would not allow it.

"How much she loves you."

He smiled affectionately, but again, that dark eyebrow arched as his mind turned over what he'd just heard, and tried to make sense of it. As she had suggested, he'd never heard of such a thing, yet the off-handed way in which she spoke made it seem little more than an eccentricity. She didn't seem to be emotionally distressed about her situation—well, beyond reasons that were easily called to mind—and it hadn't seemed to hinder her, so far as he'd seen. In fact, her performance earlier that night had been spectacular.

None of which made what he was hearing from her sound anything close to "normal."

"So... Let me see if I'm getting this. You're Iris, and you speak metropolitan Cascr like a native—"

"And much prefer black hair to this colorless mop."

"—but since you and Angelique aren't the same," he pressed on, ignoring the temptation to argue it with her, "should I assume Angelique still speaks with a D'wanese accent?"

"She does. She's the only one who does. Angel speaks like a native Asburine."

"And she's the one who remembers your childhood?"

Iris nodded. The old furnace had at last managed to raise the tempera-ture in the room as they'd spoken, and she stood up to begin unhooking the fastenings on the front of her jacket. "Most of it. There are parts of it that we don't want to remember. They're locked away pretty tightly, and that's for the best."

"Those would be from what?" he mused, "your time in Püran-Khir?"

"From the holding facility on one of the islands in the bay, actually. They tell me it used to be a royal palace, with singing fountains and gardens for every flower under the sun, a theater, and a chapel to the Lady of Paladins in rose-pink marble." The last of the hooks on the front placket came free, and she started on the ones at her wrists, looking at them intently so she wouldn't have to look at him. "There wasn't much left of any of that, by the time we arrived."

"From what I've read, there wasn't much of any part of Püran-Khir when the IMMC left. I've never been there, so..." he shrugged. "That was in the 'Boeche-Briazel', then?"

It surprised her, that he'd heard of it. She glanced at him, then nodded again. "That's the place. All new arrivals were quarantined there until we could be cleared for entry. The Püranki didn't want plague entering the kingdom through the city, and I understand now that they were screening for Confederation deserters, too. I was just a child then. Maybe eight, maybe ten years old."

He did the quick math in his head. That had been some fifteen years ago. By that time, Vin-Nôrë's Champion, Prince Athos, had crushed everything military and Confederation in the northern half of the country. However, Confederation-driven corruption was still rampant, feeding largely off of the massive amounts of money King Cashëmin was throwing around to rebuild his capital. "I've only read about it, of course, but I understand things were relatively unpleasant in Püran-Khir then—unless you had money, of course."

"That's a nice way to put it." The last of the hooks at her wrists came free, and she slithered out of the jacket, then placed it in the chair with her other things.

Be nice, Iris. It ain't his fault. How could he know?

"Louis had picked Angela up in the Boeche, at some point," she said, damping down the sarcasm for Angel's sake. "He always did like playthings young, and apparently he found something in her appealing enough to 'adopt' her, spuriously, at least to get us into the harbor district—we called it 'Low Town'. I don't know what the Norëans in the city proper called it. By the time I got to live up there, I knew better than to ask."

She turned away him then, loosening the buttons on her waistband, then slithering out of the tightly-tailored trousers. It left her in her under-leggings, pale-colored, quilted, and shimmering like silk in the low light. "Those are some of the earliest, discrete memories I have. I lost some of my attraction for Louis when I got my hips and breasts, but he could always find a way to put an asset to another use. There were lots of lonely, frightened, hurting men—and women—in Low Town in those years. Lots of them liked

135

having access to a girl who cried prettily and begged them to stop."

Anger shot through Raven, a bolt that seared like molten metal at the thought of her being so abused, and so trapped. He carefully took another sip from his glass, and realized that he was holding it so tightly his knuckles were white. "And then?" was all he could manage to say without the words coming out as a snarl. If he really needed another reason to kill Arnot, he now had it, though he didn't doubt Iris would make him pay far more dearly.

She rejoined him on the sofa, opting for more food rather than drink. Though she could relate the events of that time with some detachment, in those intervening years a little girl's pain and despair and had deepened and darkened, into something much more potent, a kind of rage that sometimes slumbered, but never completely left her. Iris had fed on it, *thrived* on it for so long that she had become inured to it. It allowed her to face his anger with the kind of equanimity and respect that none of the other awarenesses in her could have managed.

"We did the best we could to survive there," she told him, and shrugged. "When he wasn't renting me out, he and I would go hunting—for anything to steal, or sell. I was so much better at it than he was that he turned it over to me, while he began pulling together what he needed for more complicated, and lucrative, jobs. When I'd get caught, I'd turn on the little girl-charm, and as a consequence I usually got a chance to escape. The only time I didn't, I got beaten to within a whisker of my life and left for dead on Louis' doorstep.

"After that," she said, sighing as she reached for her glass, "he got a bit more serious about getting me exposure to some better trade-craft. About that time, a local man named Kor Delvin owed Louis for a hot 'quick-ship' out of Low Town. Part of the payback was teaching me more about the art of disguise. It included some acting. Mimicry. They said I had a gift for it, and that's what eventually gave Louis the idea for Angelique Blakesly."

Raven dipped another piece of bread in the jam and fed it to her, then dipped another for himself. He found it highly ironic that he an Angelique had been together for a year, and he had known none of this. Their romance had been too hot, their infatuation too complete to admit such mundane matters as personal biography. "This must have been after the big ceremony, after the *Zak's* travel plans had been made public," he surmised.

Iris shrugged. "I suppose. I don't really know. Something came over me in those months, I don't know what it was." She paused to think about it, chasing a sticky crumb at the corner of her mouth with the pad of her third finger as daintily as the baroness might have. When her voice resumed, it was quiet, and thoughtful. Of all the things she did and did not remember, these were the memories that worried her the most.

"I saw Angelique go through something like it again, last summer. I just remember not being able to make myself care about anything. The entire world seemed ugly and dirty and defiled, just like me. There was no point to going on, no point to living, not to anything. I just... I think if I could have cared just a little more, I'd have wanted to die, but I just... couldn't... make myself care. About anything."

He supposed it was only natural, given how she'd been used, abused, sold, traded, and who knew what else, but he didn't have to like it. In fact, her revelations put some of his behavior last summer in a whole new light, and it wasn't a good one. "But, in spite of all that, you did manage to learn enough to pull off infiltrating the Cascadian nobility."

The sound she made at that was indelicate. "Child's play, really. Once I had access to better clothing, clean water, good food, and safe housing? I could take in anything Louis could put in front of me, and I did. We discovered that, in Cashëmin's Phoenix Court, the Cascadian nobility were widely regarded as notoriously corrupt, but they all spoke well of Remington. She was the arbiter of what was socially acceptable to Paladins here, so they all said. As such, it looked as if the biggest challenge after arriving would be in convincing Lady Emilia of the authenticity of Angelique Blakesly—and Raven, it was hardly even an effort. I have to give credit to the baroness—the best way to deceive is to believe, and by the time we got here, she believed it so well she had almost convinced herself."

"Well," he huffed. "That explains the lack of concern over all those neat and tidy Paladin morals, *and* your ability to cover it up completely. I'm impressed," he smiled. "I'd say thank you, but I doubt you did it for me."

"I didn't do it at all," she reminded him, taking up the bottle to refill both their glasses. "Not in the sense that I'd know anything about it, now. Morals are the baroness' business." Her nose wrinkled briefly. "And, she's become very good at them, of late."

It was very strange. A few minutes ago, when she was talking about Louis renting her out, she was speaking of herself in the first person, and many of her gestures were as naturally graceful as he remembered them to be. Now, the edge was back, the same edge to her countenance that he had felt on the bridge, and in the carriage. She said, "Angelique did it," not her—Iris—even though they were the same person.

He wondered if perhaps Iris was the part of her that dealt with matters not easily squared with church dogma. "Iris" was the thief, the killer, the amoral pragmatist, while "Angelique" was the law giver, the rationalist, the moral center. It was total speculation by a complete layman, but it was certainly worth pondering. "Of late," he repeated aloud. "So you—uh, she—wasn't before?"

Iris snickered over that for a long moment. "You were such a corrupting influence, you know," she said, eyes gleaming. "Honestly, she never stood a chance."

He blinked. "Me?" he pointed at his chest. "What about *you?*" he chortled. "You're not exactly a paragon of virtue, you know. She could have dumped me. She's sort of stuck with you."

"Not from lack of trying, on both our sides," she drawled, toasting him with her glass again before she put it back on the table. "I haven't sensed her presence since sometime during that carriage ride, but I can't hope that she's gone for good. I couldn't get that lucky twice in one night."

"Why would you want to?" he asked, his heart sinking a bit. "She's as

137

important to who you are as you are—if that made any sense." It was still difficult to talk about Angelique as a separate person when she sat right in front of him—or a part of her was. Right now it was all Iris, but as the edge softened, more of Angelique would again emerge. "I've heard you call her 'the baroness' in a disparaging way, but how do you plan on ruling a barony without her?"

"I don't," she shrugged, smiling easily. It was mostly an act, however, and she dropped that part of her response almost at once. "I don't have to, let's just put it that way. I have to rest, sometimes. That gives her time to do whatever the fuck she wants about Carlisle and the other Paladins. She and Angel must both be resting now, come to think of it. I haven't sensed anything from either in some time."

No, Ah'm here. That more tender inner presence, Iris realized, had been entirely enrapt with Raven's presence, and content just with the sight of him, and the sound of his voice not turned bitter in anger.

"Iris," Raven said, his drawl pulling her out of her reverie, "that makes no sense. If you're not resting, *she's* not resting. You're, uh, living in the same body, you know?" It was a strange thing to hear himself saying. "If you get the crap beat out of you, she has to wear it—out in society, probably."

She shrugged again, and turned her palms up to signal surrender. "I don't understand it, I don't know how else to say it, so I can't argue it. All I do know is that a lot of what the baroness—Angelique, if you like—does on her time, I don't understand and I don't really care to understand. I'd sooner knife most of those gossipy bitches and supercilious bastards than have them using up my air, but *she. . .* I don't know. She understands them, and she seems to enjoy being around them as much as Angel does. So, that's usually when I check out—I'm a liability in those situations, and I know it."

"Wow!" It was out of his mouth before he could check himself. "How did this happen? I mean, I know I miss things, but I never even suspected there was this side to—you, I guess. I'm not sure how else to put it. I'm beginning to feel like I missed out on about half the fun."

She laughed at him, then tossed off the last of the sweet brown liquor in her glass. "You didn't seem to think it was so much fun," she reminded him then, mirth fading, "when you were standing in the middle of a crime scene at Bishop-Florian."

"That's different," he said, sobering slightly. "You used your skill to harm, not to help. Anyway, reading between the lines a bit, it took both of you to get the job done, didn't it? Angelique sat on every committee. She made sure she knew the right things, and got the right things to happen at the right time. It was her diplomatic and organizational skill that set things up for you."

Her nose wrinkled again. "Her, and Louis, yes. He had—has—the connections and access to the right resources. The floor plans, the extra keys, the detailed knowledge of magitech? All from his sources. He put it down in front of her—us, I guess, back then—but now, I don't know how she smashes all that information together and gets anything coherent out of it."

She paused then, head cocked as if listening for something, but after a moment, grinned conspiratorially at him. "She really must be out of it. Not a peep about using brains instead of muscles or anything like that."

"How does this work?" he asked, a note of exasperation threading through his tone. "I mean, you almost talk about all these other—what are they, personalities?"

"Identities?" she suggested.

"Right. Anyway, as though you all are in different rooms of a house and sort of pop into the drawing room to chat with each other, or hurl insults, apparently, from time to time."

Her eyebrows rippled. "How charmingly you put it."

"Well, am I right?"

"I doubt it's that organized," she said, chuckling, "but that's as good an analogy for it as any. I work the night shift. The baroness runs around in her pretty dresses and does baronial things during the days. Angel pops in and out as she pleases, and runs interference with a few more troubling aspects of this psychotic 'break-up melodrama' so Angelique and I can do what needs to be done."

An eyebrow arched again, but he was chuckling. "Psychotic break-up melodrama?"

"The other choices were less flattering." Her smile lingered, though once again much of the humor drained out of it. "I'm pretty sure I'm crazy, Raven. Now do you see why I wouldn't hold you to that betrothal? If there's anything I haven't told you, any secret I've got left that you don't know, at least in part, it's only because we haven't gotten to it yet. Now, I think, you have what you need to know to make a smarter decision about hitching yourself to me—and to Carlisle—than the one you made, last time."

He poured himself another shot of Cairnbrooks while he thought about that. There had only ever been one real regret to his engagement with Angelique, and that was the prospect of giving up—or scaling back, at least—on his thrill-seeking. He was attracted to danger, and he knew it. He'd known it since the first time he'd jumped off the eastern tower of Valemont Manor, strapped into the Raven Wing. His con games had always appealed to him in much the same way, as dangerous and exciting ways to pit his wits against others, rather than against the elements. So, while he found Angelique's situation to be strange, in it he'd found a jewel, right inside the woman he'd promised to marry. He'd found it, free running across the rooftops of Merchants', and on the Morrisant Bridge, shouting defiance at her would-be captors. Maybe he was losing something, with this psychological problem of hers. There was much he didn't know about this new "she" that was many "shes", but so far, if there was a downside, he couldn't be sure what it might be.

"I know I have a lot yet to learn about all of this, but so far I'm not seeing the problem," he confessed, giving voice to his thought.

That brought her smile back. "Don't let it get too far ahead of you," Iris said, risking a little more irreverence with him. "You haven't made it up with the baroness, yet."

"I'm sure I shall be properly contrite." Almost idly, he watched her lean over to reach for her empty glass. Rather than refill it, her long fingers turned it over on the tray. It was the kind of small, yet common gesture he could never have imagined from his dainty baroness, but the woman wearing her face at the moment evidently had gained some familiarity with the customs of the lower classes, and the dive bars they frequented.

"Good luck with that," Iris said, twisting her pale hair into a loose knot at the back of her neck. "I'm sure you'll get a chance to try it out on her, first thing in the morning."

"Having fun, are you?" He picked up their glasses, and the bottle of Cairnbrooks, and took them back on the sideboard. "So, are you not going to remember any of this in the morning then? As Angelique, I mean."

She shrugged, but unfolded herself from the sofa to peel off the long-sleeved undershirt she wore. It left her standing in her undertrousers and some kind of short, tightly laced vest that covered her torso from the tops of her shoulders to the bottom of her ribcage. "I don't know how much she'll remember," she told him, applying her fingers to the knots that held the lacing secure. "She was thrilled and appalled by turns at what was going on, earlier. I don't remember her saying anything once you and I started enjoying some trade-talk."

He had headed over to the stove to adjust it, now that it was heating properly. Neither of them had said anything, but it was obvious they were heading to bed. "I assume that means you having a committee meeting in your head is off the table," he observed dryly.

She shot him an arch look. "You want *me* to intervene in your relationship issues with the baroness? *Me?* This is the first discussion I've had with any man that didn't involve a knife in I can't remember how long. You're the one who thinks he's in love with her. *You* talk to her."

"I had no idea you were into that kind of thing," he grinned as he shrugged out of his jacket. "I'm learning all kinds of things about you tonight," he went on outrageously.

"Your hearing may be suffering for it." The knots were tight, and most of her attention was on teasing the ribbons apart without shredding them. It muffled the words somewhat, but even so it was evident that she wasn't sharing the humor he found in the subject. "I said 'discussion,' though given the history here, I suppose I can see why you would just assume that she'd be fucking around on you. I, on the other hand, don't fuck around, especially not when it involves knives. It's too damned dangerous."

"Relax." He tossed his waist coat on top of his jacket and came over to help her. "I was teasing." He began helping her loosen the lacing, and Iris kept her eyes on their fingers so that she didn't have to risk looking up into his face. The garment was designed to hold her breasts securely against her chest during her physical exertions, and her relief as they were released from it was profound.

"Well, that helps," she admitted, more than a little unnerved at her

140

yearning to press into his hands, to lean into him as if she had the least idea what it had been like to make love to him, or to anyone. He pulled the ribbon free, and such was her distraction that he pulled her right along with it, the exposed flesh of her belly and tender, erect nipples pressing into him just enough to want more.

"Um. I don't actually know if I'm going to be very good at this," she said then, not afraid of him just then, not *precisely*, but not knowing how to proceed, either.

Raven caught her by the waist, then ran his hands up the soft skin of her back. She shuddered hard, gripping the front of his shirt with both fists and sighed into his chest. He tangled his fingers in her hair, then he turned her face up, and brushed her lips with his.

"You spend a lot of time second-guessing yourself, you know that?" he said, breathing the question into her mouth, then closed her lips with his again, and any hope she had of answering him in words evaporated.

In her experience, sexual intercourse hadn't had much to do with love, or joy, or sharing, or tenderness. Sex had always been about control, and whoever controlled the encounter was usually the one who got the better of it. So she'd learned how to keep enough of herself removed from the engagement to get control, even if it was only a little, and at a very young age. And yet, Raven's hands were twisted up in her hair and his tongue twined intimately with hers. He had seized control as easily as he breathed, and rather than fight him, Iris suddenly found she couldn't help him hard enough. Her fists released the fabric of his shirt, and she wrapped her arms around his neck and pulled his head down to hers, kissing him crazily, desperately, a woman in love for the very first time with a man she'd only just met, and had almost lost.

Raven clasped her tightly, drowning in the memories this woman when she'd been the one he'd desperately tried to forget, yet his body, and hers, were telling him something quite different. Being kissed by her was like being kissed by a stranger, though there was no part of her he didn't know! The taste of her mouth, the feel of her tongue dancing with his, the silken softness of her skin fused with the faintest lingering traces of her perfume, all so terribly familiar, yet laid over with an edgy assertiveness that rendered it, and her, utterly exotic. These responses were uniquely *Iris*, not Angelique. This was the acrobat, the free runner, the street fighter, not the Guardian Paladin lady with her laughing wit and effortless, dancing grace.

"So," he murmured, when he could finally pull his mouth from hers, "am I going to pay for *this* in the morning too?"

Her eyelids parted after a moment, and she borrowed her breath back from him for an answer, naked desire glittering in her eyes. "Maybe. But look at it this way: It's a small price to pay for getting to fuck around on your pretty baroness without actually breaking your vows to her."

Raven laughed aloud at that, then scooped her up in both arms and headed into the bedroom. "That wasn't an answer," he said, placing her on the bed with tender care.

"How the hell should *I* know," she said, sliding out of what little clothing she still wore while he divested himself of most of his. "It would be crazy for her to resent it, but *I* don't understand her. Take it up with her in the morning." Her breath caught just then at the sight of his lean, healthy male body emerging from its civilizing apparel. She thought she should have remembered something so beautiful, had she seen it before, but her memories of his stolen interludes with Angelique were diffuse, at best. It gave her all the excuse she needed to take in the sight of him, and marvel at how it made her homesick for something she could barely recall.

"For tonight, Raven," she said, a bit breathless from the emptiness that was a low ache in her belly, "you're *mine.*"

"I can deal with that." He kicked his clothes aside, then ran his hands up the length of her perfectly toned legs. In his dreams, he'd done it a hundred times just so, brushing his nose against the soft hair on her mons, his lips tingling as they caressed the baby-soft skin of her belly. Mesmerized, he traced the crease of her thigh with his tongue, but abruptly, her hands were in his hair, breaking his entranced reverie. It was Iris, all Iris who pulled his mouth up to hers, branding it with a kind of fiery hunger that burned with the need to consume him. Her legs wrapped around his waist, and he slid himself into the white-hot source of her, and all the lies, misunderstandings, hurts, and grievances that had once separated them simply evaporated.

His awareness shrank down to that single, familiar point; around it, his world centered, righted itself, and began to spin once more. He pulled her into his arms as if he could pull her into his chest, or into his heart, perhaps, to keep her safe there, beyond anyone's ability to hurt her, ever again.

She rolled beneath him, and rocked back against him, writhing in a frenzy of building passion. Each lift of her hips was answered faithfully by him, until the reach and the push were one with the breath and the body, pleasure and sorrow and need abruptly spiraling out of control. Raven gasped aloud, then began to thrust into her in desperate need; Iris clung to him as ecstasy erupted from every pore.

When he collapsed atop her at last, great, wracking sobs poured from him, unchecked. For all his running, he was right back where he started.

The Raven had come home.

Chapter 11

492 Queens Street, Merchants'
24 Vilmath, 0900 hours

Ten minutes after the flyer from police headquarters had landed at East Fork Station, a squadron of six police flyers took flight and deployed in a search pattern over their section of the city. Ten minutes after that, three blacked out transports departed the station, each headed in a different direction. Meanwhile, back at police headquarters, runners had been fanning out across Merchants', recalling officers to duty. The flyer Raven had sent to Commissioner Roland's home had returned, with orders.

Willis and three of Lucky's Lads had soon been sighted by one of the flyers. A transport was called, and a squad of six military police soon had them in custody. Four more of Lucky's Lads had been spied leaving a medical facility known to service mercenaries. They had been apprehended on Talbot Street, not far from City Hall. By the time the Clocktower had struck one bell in the morning watch, Lucky's Lads were in the city jail, charged with conducting an illegal military operation within city limits, attempted kidnapping, illegal slaving, and willful destruction of private property.

When the police runner knocked on Raven's door later that morning, he had reports on the actions Roland had taken, as well. The Top Cop had ordered a full investigation into Lucky's Lads at an organizational level. Willis commanded just one unit. There was a whole organization behind him, and Roland had sent a strongly worded request to the military police to look it over from top to bottom.

He'd also ordered police accountants to begin pouring over Louis Arnot's financial records, and the Crown Prosecution Service, in cooperation with the Urilian Ministry for Justice, had requested an official audit of every case Arnot had tried since beginning his practice. To sweeten his morning coffee, he had also put Arnot's Compton Place townhouse under constant surveillance. Both the main entrance and the carriage house entrance were being continuously patrolled by blue jackets, and they had orders to document every arrival and departure.

Roland wasn't being subtle, and he wasn't playing nice. Vincent could have kissed him!

"Thank you, lad," he told the runner after scanning the note he'd delivered. The boy had also carried in a basket that steamed with the welcome smells of warm pastries and hot coffee. He tipped the kid a shilling, then set about making Angelique the cup of tea he knew she liked first thing in the morning. He also made himself coffee, then padded back into the bedroom.

She sprawled over half the mattress, still deeply asleep. Her long hair, left loose after their tumultuous reunion, now wound messily over her face and shoulders, partially obscuring both in pale, nearly colorless strands. Weak rays of morning sunlight angled through the shuttered window and set to light the gold and silver there. There was gray there, too, he knew; much of his lover's unique hair color had been due to premature graying, ostensibly from the stresses of having lived in post-war Vin-Nôrë. From what she'd said, the night before, he realized it had been part of the truth, just like almost everything else he'd known about her. As he placed their morning cups upon the bedside table, however, what he found himself wondering who would greet him, when she awakened.

There was nothing to be gained by putting off the moment. "Morning, Burning Bright," he said, sitting down next to her on the bed. She stirred reluctantly and rolled to her back, her eyes blinking up at him in confusion. He watched recognition dawn, followed swiftly by at least partial remembrance, and then an onslaught of memories that settled over her like an avalanche.

Angelique looked around then with joyous, half-disbelieving air of a woman who found herself in a place she never expected or hoped to see again. Her gaze lit upon the old oak wardrobe with the chipped door, then the brass-banded storage chest with his monogram on the latch; the posts at the foot of the bed were scratched from hosting his belt and scabbard, and the warm, dark blue blanket under which she'd slept. It and the linens were all that was between her very naked body and a sleepy, half-dressed Sir Vincent Sultaire.

Her memories of the night before did not include returning to this place, nor anything that had happened after until his soft voice, with three little words, had summoned her out of a sound sleep. It didn't require any talent for analysis to figure out what had happened—the soreness between her legs alone told *that* tale—but without some kind of context for it, she found she had no idea what it meant, beyond the obvious.

Fortunately for them both, it wasn't the first time she'd awakened in such confusion. To Iris' credit, it *was* the first time confusion had involved a man, *any* man.

Angelique cleared her throat, and pushed her hair out of her eyes, not scrupling to hide how they caressed his face and shoulders, lingering on each of his features though she'd memorized them long ago.

"I never thought to hear those words from you again," she said at last. The D'waanese accent, as natural-sounding as any native's, colored the softly spoken words, and unlike the last time she'd seen him—at the Belton House

Ball—she saw no point in attempting to mask it. At this point, she reasoned, he either knew why she should be speaking thus, or he did not. He would question her about it, or he would not. She only knew that it was her part, now, to answer him as best she could.

Vincent swallowed what he was about to say, and instead held up her cup. "Tea," he said, somewhat unnecessarily, then watched as she somewhat gingerly sat up, then folded her legs in front of herself before accepting the cup from him with a murmured word of gratitude. Given the accent, this had to be Angelique. Iris had warned him that she had no idea how much she would remember. That seemed to be a good place to begin. "How much of last twelve hours or so can you recall?"

She thought about that as she held the cup between her fingers and blew across the steaming surface of the liquid. It was uncomfortable, still, to discuss it. "I remember everything up to that point in the taxi ride where you accused the earl of Camrose of corruption," she admitted at last, sipping her tea. "It was in reference to our situation with Louis Arnot. And that is, I believe, the latest discrete memory I have."

It was odd. The night before, Iris had pronounced his name as any other Fernwall native would have: loo-iss. Angelique pronounced it as the Norëans did: loo-wee. Perhaps underscoring the inherent oddness of that, she gazed at him steadily as she lowered her cup and asked him a question. "Did you know with whom you were speaking?"

"Iris, you mean?" he picked up his coffee cup and nestled it in his hands. The fire had burned low while they slept, and he hadn't yet tended to it. "Yeah. It was a busy night. Fortunately, I don't think there are any marks left."

"Marks?" It confused her. It was the term the Vin-Norëans used for their money, and at that moment she couldn't imagine why it should be a good thing to be out of them.

"Do you remember Lucky's Lads?"

Angelique frowned slightly and sipped her tea again. "You meant 'physical marks'. Yes, of course," she said, reflecting for a moment on what had transpired on the bridge. "I would very likely be chained to Louis' bed this very instant, had it not been for your intervention."

"Yes, well, you were in pretty bad shape after that. Flint put you back together." He thumbed in the direction of the Navy man's flat. "That would be after the Camrose discussion, though, so you might not remember it."

She nodded again, trying to rub the sleep out of an eye with the back of her wrist. "I do not remember returning here at all. And yet, you know about me, and Iris, and I'm here, not restrained in some hospital bed, so I must assume the oddness of my, ah, 'condition' has not repelled you completely."

Vincent chuckled wryly and took a drink of his coffee. "Of all the stupid things I've done in the last month, at least that's not one of them," he drawled over his cup. "I also know about Asbury, the *Boeche-Briazel* and some of your more interesting, uh, tasks there; Angel—though I haven't met her yet—and I've been told there are a few other personalities running around inside your head that I haven't yet met. I must say, when we started this, I never thought I was agreeing to marry a harem all in one woman."

After a startled moment, she flicked a wry smile at him. "How ideal for you—if you're still interested in marrying me, that is," she added, realizing only then that she didn't know. "I would not think less of you for declining, *Mar'leven*. Under the circumstances, you have reason enough."

"Yes well, I tried that," he sniffed, adding, "I ended up in the bottom of an ale barrel. It didn't help, so I guess you're stuck with me."

There didn't seem to be much regret in those words. Instead, he did seem rather pleased, so Angelique flicked a tiny smile at him and risked a jest. "Hardly a ringing endorsement, that," she said, her voice broadening into the arid drawl he remembered well. "'Well boys, I shall have to say that marrying Carlisle is better than fraternizing with what I found at the bottom of an ale barrel,'" she went on, mocking him the way she always had when what she was mocking wasn't really him, at all. "I suppose it's something."

"You're too kind." He tried to put on the airs of being offended, but the smile ruined the effect. They hadn't played together this way since that last night in her bedroom effectively ended their relationship. He found that he'd missed her dry, understated sense of humor as much as anything else about her.

"Anyway," he said, moving on before she could interrupt, "I just got a report from the office. Willis and his Lucky's Lads squad are now behind bars. Even the formerly dead ones, I understand. Roland has already started one investigation into the mercenary outfit of which Lucky's Lads is one part, two more into Louis' affairs, and is parading blue jackets in front of his townhouse doors. All in all, I'd have to say that Louis is in for a busy day."

She took that in, but frowned again. "'Formerly dead'?"

"Well, I'm fairly certain that I killed the one on the bridge outright," he admitted quietly, "but the one I hit on the River Walk probably had time to jab himself with a dose of the 'Soldier Drug', if he was carrying it. In any event, I doubt there were any permanent deaths."

"Soldiers have a drug that reverses death? That seems rather remarkable," she replied dubiously.

"Not exactly," Vincent drawled. "But it *can* keep a fatally wounded soldier alive long enough to get to medical help. At least, that was the intent."

Her eyebrows, still somewhat darkened from her appearance as "Iris" the night before, lifted delicately. "How very intriguing. Do you think Willis or one of the other survivors will offer to implicate Louis in exchange for a reduction in his sentence?"

"Maybe." Vincent shrugged, then drained his coffee and set the cup back on the nightstand. "I really don't care. I had them picked up and splattered with enough charges to keep them there for a while, mainly to keep them from reporting back to Louis."

Still snuggled under the blankets, she pulled her knees up to her chin and rested it there while she thought about that. A slow, unwholesome smile stole over her face. "I should imagine that he'll be in a froth by now," she said at last, glancing at the amount of light angling in through the shutter. "You have captured his eyes, *Mar'leven*. He'll be calling in all his informants for reports as we speak."

"And he, and they, will be dodging cops the whole time," he added with a grin. "That should complicate things. It's about time his plans suffered a few setbacks, don't you think?"

It was clear that she did. Her encounter with Louis at Morahan's had left her unsettled. "More than time. If he is kept preoccupied this morning, then perhaps you and I will have time to talk." She placed her cup on the table, then with only the slightest of hesitations, put her hand atop his. They both ignored the ugly bruise on her bicep. "Tell me you forgive me for what I've done, Vincent. I very much need to hear you say it."

It was odd to be retracing these steps again after their long talk last night, but her accent made it easier. It added context to the partially compartmentalized memories of the disparate personalities. "I do. And I hope you forgive me for being such an ass. I should have known that, whatever was going on, it couldn't be as simple as I was making it out to be. I know better. I was *taught* better, for all the good it did."

"You were hurting," she said simply, squeezing his hand a little, "and mine was the very face of the lie that had done it. I don't know if Iris knows how to apologize, nor if you had spoken to Angel, for I cannot sense her presence, this morning..."

The words trailed off, and she looked away awkwardly. "I don't know what I am, sometimes, but at least I can be enough of a Paladin to ascertain that the words have been spoken, and received."

He leaned over to kiss her. "I don't know what you are either," he murmured, leaving his lips so close she could feel his breath. "Or, maybe better stated: I don't know how this happened to you, beyond the obvious." He pulled back then, eyes lingering on her lips, still softly parted with the impress of his. "Iris did what you just did, just in her own way. You two can't seem to agree on much of anything else, but at least you're on the same page when it comes to our betrothal."

"Our betrothal?" Her eyebrows began to twitch, this time more in disbelief than in mirth. "I must confess to some puzzlement, Vincent. What did Iris tell you about our betrothal?"

"You really want to know?" he asked, eyebrow arched. "Am I going to help, or hurt things, if I get in the middle of this? You'll have to tell me, because I have no idea, and I don't want to make things worse." He took her hand and held it, possessively. "I just got you back, Angel, I don't want to lose you again to something stupid, like a fight I started in your head."

"If you were likely to lose me over that, it would have happened weeks ago, when the fights started," Angelique said wryly. "I know your appearance on Morrissant Bridge last night impressed Iris deeply, but I had no idea it meant you'd convinced her that marriage was in her best interests. If you don't mind, I'd rather not wake her up to ask. My head aches so much less without her constant, vulgar commentary."

"Maybe there will be a bit less of that now." He kissed her hand then and stood up to take their cups back to his sitting room. "And I don't know that I'd go so far as to say Iris thinks marriage is a great idea. But—how do I say this?—the rest of you does; and if it has to happen, she wants it to be an honest choice, not one based on a lie."

The only response he got, for the moment, was the rustling of bed linens, followed by the creaking of the bed frame and other "getting around in the morning" sounds. When he returned with their cups, he saw her standing in front of his vanity mirror, wearing the long-sleeved undershirt he'd worn the night before. The hemline fell to mid-thigh, leaving her legs and feet bare, and she was doing her best to tame her long hair with her old hairbrush, rediscovered among her other belongings in one corner of his old trunk.

She smiled when he handed back her cup. She couldn't help but smile, he was her own heart, standing there. "In that much, at least, I concur. You and I rushed into an engagement—a 'world-without-end bargain,' if you will—because we thought ourselves much in love, and that somehow, love would be enough." Her nose wrinkled slightly, but she reached out for his hand and twined her fingers in his. "I didn't know what love was then, clearly, but I think I know it better now. I'd rather die than see you suffer like that again. There is a fierce determination inside me to do all that I can to protect and nurture your happiness, to wake up next to your smile every morning, to make you eager to go to bed with me every night."

She twisted her head to look up at him, then reached up to cup his prickly cheek in her palm. "With all that, I would that I had not rushed into our betrothal, Vincent. I truly do wish it."

He, in turn, ran a finger along the long line of her cheek and down to her jaw, then dared to kiss her. It was a familiar kiss, and yet one only remembered, for all the kisses he and Iris had shared the night before. It was familiar for the softness in her lips, the tenderness with which she returned it, and the love that infused it, all qualities of Angelique that were alien to Iris. "Promises made in the heat of blood," he murmured afterward, "are not always the wisest of oaths made. But I will stand by my oath, even knowing what I know—maybe because I know what I know."

"Did you know you were the very first man with whom I ever *wanted* to spend time?" They were so close that their eyes were only half-open; his were smoky gray-blue in the soft light, and boring into hers with the old boldness. She remembered, in the early days of their acquaintance, wondering if he could gaze into her secrets with them, and it made her smile again. "The first I searched for in crowded rooms, the first man I ever *sought* out, of my own will, to know better?"

"No," he replied softly, a finger still tracing lines on her face. "But I can understand why. Well, maybe not *why me,* but in general, I think I get it."

His self-deprecation made her laugh again, but it was brief, and faded under his slow, painstaking regard of her every feature. "You, particularly," she breathed then, pulling his face down to hers for another delicious, languorous kiss. His lips could have made her heart jump-start back from death itself, and her mouth lingered against his for a long moment that wanted to deepen into something more. It brought to mind what she'd said about rushing, however, and she reluctantly reclaimed her tongue from him, nibbling on his chin and oddly happy about having access to the prickly, day-old beard she found there.

"I find that I'm much anticipating learning about the real you, *Mar'leven.* Not just the sides of yourself which you thought a 'noble scion of the congregation' might find *somewhat* socially acceptable. I think I should know more about this wingéd Raven and the things he does in the night—if only because he's got designs on my barony," she added with one of those flickering, here-again, there-again grins that made his eyes dance merrily.

"You have an advantage," he told her, pecking her on the nose then leading her out to the sitting room. "Most people think they know the Raven, when they don't. You think you don't, but you do."

"I do?"

"Well, better than anybody *else* I can think of."

"I hope you'll pardon me if I say that's the *second* less-than-ringing endorsement I've heard from you this morning," Angelique said, folding herself into a comfortable seat atop the sofa cushion, legs crossed. "After last night, you could hardly blame me. I doubt I'd have recognized you—at least, not so quickly."

"Doesn't make what I said *wrong,*" he said, making a show of petulance for her amusement, but the effect was marred by his smile. He hadn't stopped since he'd first heard her voice, earlier that morning.

She kissed him again for that, once again thoroughly enchanted with everything about him.

See? Ah told you so. Angel's inner presence was sleepy, and barely coherent. *This is how it was, how we are, together. It's how it's s'posed t' be.*

Angelique found, for all her attempts at caution, that she agreed. "You're telling me that I know your heart," she said, whispering the words. "I believe you, for you've completely captured mine, and all my worrries about rushing headlong into a new life with you, before I've properly put away the old one have fallen away completely."

He could almost see Iris rolling her eyes, and hear her sneering at Angelique's fickle character. He didn't agree—her proclamations had always been a little extravagant—but it made him chuckle, nonetheless. "We are still engaged," he said, taking her hand in his, "and I think it best that we remain so until the road ahead of us is clear. We have Louis to deal with, I still wear a collar, and I think it's probably what Lady Emilia would advise anyway—*especially* when she's informed of a few new facts."

"Do you suppose you'll have time to see her with me, this afternoon?" They were still so close, he felt it when she stiffened in dismay. "Lady's breath, what day is it?"

"It's the twenty-fourth," he murmured thoughtfully, and she relaxed in open relief. "I have a meeting with Roland about last night, among other things, but then yes, I will probably need to see her anyway."

"Well, then." Once assured she'd not blanked out another entire day—or more—Angelique ran over what she knew of her day's schedule in her mind, and the huge event at the other end of it. "Let me arrange that appointment, then. Would you prefer to meet me at Blakesly House when you are finished with the commissioner? Oh! You can fly! I'd nearly forgotten it!" She clapped a hand over her mouth suddenly, but her eyes were sparkling like a ten-year-old girl's. "The Raven has his wings once more! Will you ever wish to ride with me overland, in a carriage, ever again?"

"Nope," he said soberly, "never again." He held the serious, no-nonsense look for as long as he could while she waffled between understanding and an endearing pout, then grinned at her boyishly. "I dearly love flying, but it's not always the most pleasant of experiences, Burning Bright. Last night was horrid, for example! By the time I intervened, I was so cold I couldn't feel the tips of my fingers. You're lucky I didn't shoot you and not that idiot chasing you."

Her eyes had resumed their joyously speculative glitter. "You mean Iris, of course. I suppose that must be true, though forgive me for ignoring the more prosaic reality in favor of my fantasy, *Mar'leven*." It was her turn to grin at him. "Will you meet me at Blakesly House, then? Lady Emilia knows more about my situation than you might think she does, but there is still much she does not know, and it will take us both to inform her fully."

He thought about that for a moment. If Louis didn't have a spy somewhere in the house, he was a complete fool, and nobody thought Louis a fool. He was now hampered, or at least inconvenienced, by Roland's patrols, but an experienced faker like Louis also had to have well-trodden paths around standard police procedures. "Do you think it wise to inform Louis of our reunion?" he asked. "He set you up as the baroness, he hired your first household staff, he *has* to have a spy in the house."

"So Iris said, and tasked me with uncovering their identity. Be proud of me, *Mar'leven*. I delegated the task to Clarice and Verlinden—my butler. *Our* butler," she said, grinning as she corrected herself. "I'd been considering whether to dismiss her outright, or do as Lady Honoria did, during the long seige cycle in *The Charge of the Castellan,* and use her as a tool to send false information back to my enemy."

Vincent thought about that for a moment. There were certainly advantages to using a known spy to control one's enemy, but in this case, the disadvantages far outweighed them. "I think, after last night, Louis will soon grow suspicious enough to discount her information—or just kill her and be done with it. That seems to be his preferred method of dealing with liabilities, I've noticed." He made a face. Her answering nod was so matter-of-fact that it lifted the hairs on the back of his neck.

"It is a difficult tactic to use outside of a seige, in any case," Angelique said, planting a delicate kiss on his chin. "I purchased a one-way ticket on the coach to Three Sisters yesterday, and I plan to give Patsy a choice: She can be packed aboard that coach right away and sent to Three Sisters with her pay to date or she can take her chances here, on her own, without references."

Her mouth rippled again. "I'm given to understand the great merchant houses at the head of the river define 'loyalty' in ways that might give her a chance to live and support herself. In any event, it should put her out of Louis' reach."

His eyes danced merrily. "Well done," he chuckled. "I hope he paid her well, then." Then he thought of something else. "Is Louis having the house watched?"

"I wondered this, too. We think he does have tradesmen and vendors watching for Carlisle's coach at the end of the lane, but it would be much too difficult to get amateurs close to the estate on a long-term basis."

"Then I'll hire a carriage to drive up to the house," he grinned. "That should keep the prevailing narrative alive a bit longer."

"Unless Louis find a way to post bail for Willis and Lucky's Lads."

Vincent shook his head, his demeanor slowly changing from that of the urbane playboy lover to the quick-witted, streetwise Raven. "The Crown's Prosecutor should be gumming those works up for as long as they possibly can. Two can play legal games. Louis doesn't own that particular market, and Roland is putting his career on the line here. He wants to put an end to the malingering wartime crime syndicates, and last night Louis unknowingly handed him a golden opportunity to get it done. Willis will be rotting in jail for as long as Roland thinks that's where he needs to be, or he'll stick a knife in him to keep him quiet.

"We're playing a different kind of game now, Burning Bright," he finished quietly.

It troubled her, and they sat quietly for a short while, thinking their respective thoughts. Angelique spoke up to break the silence. Her thoughts weren't making her happy. "I can see why you might wish to keep Louis isolated from certain truths for as long as possible. Does this mean we must continue to deceive our peers as well by seeming to continue our quarrel?"

Another few thoughtful minutes passed. He massaged her hand, trying to decide how to answer. "I don't know how to answer you," he said finally. "I think we need to ask the counsel of our elders. I've been on both sides of the law, but never in the middle before. Not like this."

Angelique sighed quietly, disappointed but understanding the reason for it. "I'm to attend the 'Nadrean Nights Ball' at the Old Palace Hotel this evening. I'd briefly harbored a hope that we might attend together."

"And we might," he smiled. "One thing is certain, we won't be able to hide the truth from Louis forever. As you so aptly put it, we captured his eyes. Now the trick is, how best to make use of the time we've purchased." He shook his head. "That's what I don't know, what I can't see."

"It sounds as if you have done what can be done," she said, taking her hand from his and placing it on his chest, just over his heart. "Your foresight has given us an advantage, Vincent. It's the first I feel I've had against Louis since the leaves began to turn."

"It's a start," he sighed, pulling her into his arms. "I'm so glad to have you back, Angel," he murmured nuzzling his way into her hair. "This isn't going to be easy, but I'd rather be facing it with you than without you."

Milady, please...

Angelique had many memories of answering to the shortened form of her name, but now it represented an awareness distinct from her own. She'd felt as protective of that inner presence—kind, loving, compassionate, and somehow still innocent despite living through the horrors of Püran-Khir—as Iris seemed to be. Though she had come to some tentative conclusions about this disturbed inner landscape of hers, she still could not be certain what the "voices" of Angel and Iris represented. Regardless of all that, it seemed only right to let Angel have the chance to speak for herself at last. If she could.

Just relax, milady, Angel suggested. *Think about goin' t' sleep. Ah'll take it from there.*

Vincent felt it when her entire body slumped. It happened so suddenly that he'd no time to react before she was leaning away to look up into his face, smiling softly, hazel eyes dancing sea-green and gray in the light angling in from the window.

"Nothin' in my life that's been worth havin' has ever been easy," she told him, hearing the Asburine accent in her own ears for the first time since her appearance at Remington Hall. Vincent's dark eyebrow winged upward again, a sure sign that he'd caught the significance. "Ah think that's why you're the most impossible man Ah've ever met, Raven—and why Ah'm so in love with you, and never lettin' you go."

"Angel, I assume." It wasn't a question. Impulsively, he kissed her again and felt her melt into the long, slow, languid kiss so willingly that for a moment—a long moment. A *very* long moment—he was tempted to forgo the day's schedule for a return to the bedroom, and it took a ruthless act of will to tear his lips from hers at last.

"We finally meet," he said, or rather purred, for the words were soft and tickled in her ears. She flashed him a genuine, happy smile, an expression so unlike Angelique's cool amusement or Iris' barbed sarcasm that it recast her face entirely into that "Asburine poster girl" image that Flint had pointed out, the night before. Fair hair, eyes, and skin, with high cheekbones and a delicate nose; she was the very essence of the innocent, willing, biddable, serving girl in the south.

"Oh... you know me better than you think you do," she told him, openly delighted with his nearness and not scrupling in the least part to hide it. "And Ah know you, too. Ah knew that you still loved us, all along. Ah knew you couldn't leave us, that you wouldn't let Louis have us, not once you knew the truth."

"So you're the power behind the throne, so to speak?" he asked.

She shook her head slightly, reaching up just a bit to rub noses with him. "No, not really. Power's the baroness' kick, and Iris', too. Ah don't think it's made either of 'em happy. *You,* though? You've made me—us—very happy.

152

That seems more important t' me than power, or anythin' else, really."

That was an interesting tidbit that he filed away, unsure of whether it was just *that* part of Angelique's compartmentalized personality, or reflected a more widely held view. "So, who are you, then?" he asked, trying to not make it sound like a police investigation. "I mean, to put it simply, the 'baroness' rules, Iris takes care of defense matters, it seems, so what part do you play?"

The question puzzled her, for it was similar to one Lady Emilia had asked, and she hadn't a ready answer for it then, either. "Ah don't know," she finally said, knowing it was inadequate. "When Ah met Lady Emilia, she tasked me t' get you and Angelique and Iris on-side, and in the most serious terms you can imagine. Is that what you mean?"

"Did she, now?" Vincent mused. "And you've met her! Well, then yes, I guess that's what I meant. Iris and Angelique both talked about Angel," he smiled, ignoring how strange it still felt, not just be talking about this one person as if she were so many different people, but to see it play out right in front of him. "It's beyond time I got to meet you too, don't you think?"

Angel giggled softly, but what she'd been about to add was interrupted by the distant tolling of the Clocktower. "Six bells," she said, and sighed regretfully. "The mornin' has nearly slipped away. Louis' goin' t' be chewin' on his expensive carpets by now. Whatever you and the baroness were goin' t' do about that, Ah guess you'd best be about it." The mention of the name chilled her. "You won't be too long, comin' back t' Blakesly House, will you?"

Their faces were still so very close that he could read her need for that reassurance like large print. It took him off-guard. Angelique had never sought such reassurance, and Iris had seemed to need it even less. But, Lady Emilia had tasked Angel, not Iris or Angelique, to get them back together, and he wasn't sure what to make of that.

"I should get there almost the same time as you," he said quietly, not really knowing what else to say.

It seemed to be the right thing. "Good," she said, smiling softly. "We'll be watchin' for you."

Chapter 12

Compton Place, Upper Merchants
24 Vilmath, 580

Two things burst into Louis Arnot's consciousness at once. The first was the incessant banging on his bedroom door. The second was the Clocktower's distinctive bell, ringing in the hour. He counted eight and noted the dim light near the drapes at the windows. That meant it was eight hundred, the end of the morning watch.

"Come!" he commanded at last. The dark-haired woman next to him moaned in dreamy pleasure but didn't wake. The butler entered, dressed in his pajamas and an expensive satin and brocade robe. The set look on his face might have been carved out of stone. "Thackery is waiting in the morning room for you," he said in that quiet voice that people use first thing the morning. "He has a... *woman* with him. And, we have uniformed police officers watching the house, front and back."

He hadn't finished the last sentence before his boss's face was a mirror image of his own. Louis rolled the sleeping woman out of the bed and got up. She landed on the floor with a squeak, jumped to her feet, and bolted for the door. "Morning room," the butler murmured to her as she passed. Louis would expect her to be properly displayed and aroused when he entered the room. They both knew that.

Two minutes later, Louis entered his morning room. Thackery was there, dressed in the pseudo-uniform that marked him as the mercenary he was. A small, slender, austere woman dressed mostly in buckskins stood at his side, feet spread apart, arms crossed over her chest. She wore her dark hair very short and slicked back from her face at the sides, but rucked up on the top as if she'd just been blown in on a storm. Her disgusted gaze bounced from the man who'd just entered and the naked woman who'd just sprawled herself out enticingly on a pile of furs.

Thackery began barking before Louis reached the rugs. "What are you playing at, Louis?" he demanded, jabbing the cut end of a cigar in his direction for emphasis. He snapped the fingers of his other hand, and the tip of the index finger burst into flame. He lit his cigar with it while he stared

155

at Louis, waiting for an answer.

Louis arched an eyebrow, then flicked a brief glance his "lover" to ensure she was where she was supposed to be. She had apparently helped herself to another dose of slave milk, given her exaggerated attempts to entice him over to her in the furs. He didn't mind. The girl was simply trying to make sure she didn't disappoint him, which was part of what he loved about her.

The other woman snorted and took the cigar from Thackery. "*Talk, Arnot*," she commanded. Her voice was as pointed as her nose. She took a drag off of the cigar, then handed it back.

"It would be helpful if you could narrow the field down a little bit," Louis told them, knotting the belt on his robe to underscore his disheveled state. In truth, he wasn't particularly concerned. Archibald Thackery was a military-trained mage. They went by many names—soldiers and sailors never lacked for imagination—including "wonder wizard," or even "minute mage" for those the IMMC had begun turning out rapidly, with only the most basic skills mastered. The more colorful colloquialism commonly adopted by the veterans who'd formed the cadre for mercenary companies was "spell slinger." In other words, he knew how to do what he had been taught how to do, and had learned a few more things since leaving the service, but was in no danger of being one of those highly educated mages who might have turned him into a something unsavory in a fit of pique.

All this meant Louis wasn't likely to take the man, or his woman, or his threats, very seriously. "In case you hadn't noticed," he went on, yawning a little, "I *just* got out of bed."

"How *very* nice for you," the woman drawled sarcastically.

"This is Kestrel," Thackery said, handing her the cigar. "She's Lucky's air support. We've been up for the last three hours! There are *military police investigators* turning our offices upside down as we speak. Two of our men were killed last night in that operation last night—and successfully revived, luckily for you—after which they, and the entire squad I sent out, were arrested by FPD's special forces response unit! So I ask you again, Louis, *what are you playing at?*"

Unruffled, Louis removed a cigar from the case nearby, snipped the end, and lit it rather pointedly with a match, not his finger. "I assume this means your austere attempt to collect the Iris failed?"

He exhaled a great cloud of fragrant smoke, then leaned over and jabbed a finger inside the raven haired beauty, and fucked her with it for a few seconds. She squealed delightfully and doubled over around Louis' finger, a titanic orgasm roaring through her like an earthquake. Thackery watched, his face an implacable mask. Kestrel's lips lifted in a snarl, and Thackery had to put a hand in front of her chest to keep her from seizing Louis by the throat.

Louis, still watching his pet orgasm, was apparently oblivious to them both. "Well? What happened?" he asked, affecting an air of casual disregard.

Thackery's jaw worked for a few seconds, his patience with Louis' nonchalance growing thinner by the second, and from the nervous tapping of

Kestrel's fingers on her crossed arms, she was becoming impatient as well. "We just came from CSH-5." CSH-5 was a small corporation that provided specialized medical support to the city's many private military contractors. "According to the staff," Thackery went on, with a certain amount of relish, "the Raven happened."

Louis turned abruptly to stare at him.

"Yeah. That's right. They were going on about it while the men were being revived," the mage went on, pausing to puff on his cigar once, then flick the ash on Louis' rug. "Their weapons, they said, couldn't touch him. He apparently grabbed Iris and flew off with her in hand, *after* shrugging off a throw net as though it were nothing more than a spider web!"

"Also, you might have *told* us he could fly!" Kestrel snapped. "Willis should never have been out there without air support if you knew Iris had access to a flyer."

"The *Raven*?" Dumbfounded, Louis was almost stammering. "Fly?"

Thackery and Kestrel glanced at each other, smug that they had scored, and now had Louis' full attention.

"Roulston!" Louis shouted at the door. The butler dutifully appeared in seconds. "How many cops are parading around outside?"

"Between four and six," Roulston replied evenly. "Mrs. Vinge and I are still debating a couple of faces. And, this just arrived for you by air courier." He handed Louis an envelope.

Louis opened it and began to read. His face blanched, then paled even further as he read. In fancy language, his accountant informed him that all of his banking assets had been frozen that morning, and that police accountants had served search warrants on each account as well as his own records, which they were busy carrying away in boxes.

"Raven! So the boy wants to go another round." He crumpled up the paper and threw it at Roulston. "No reply. Bring coffee," he snapped, waving him out of the room.

"I'm sorry," he turned back to Thackery and Kestrel with a sneer, "you were saying?"

Thackery and Kestrel exchanged another glance. "Raven got you again, did he?" Thackery grinned mirthlessly. Kestrel smirked.

Louis glared at them both. "My business is none of *your* business," he told them both.

"Oh I think it is," the mage purred darkly. "Two of our men were killed, the entire company is now under investigation, and since your doors are being watched, Fernwall PD now knows—absolutely certain to know—that you and I are connected. You can either come clean with us, right now, or I'll turn you into a prize-winning radish."

It made Louis laugh. "You wouldn't know how," he snorted, heading for his chair. "And the day you turn me into anything is the day you'll have far more to worry about than Roland's fancy military police unit. Now sit down and quit talking nonsense."

Kestrel's lip lifted again, and this time she snarled loudly at him, her hands flexing at her sides. "I'd be careful with the threats, pretty little man, or you're going to be glancing in fear up at the skies for the rest of your pathetic little life!"

Louis glared at her. Nobody had ever called him that before, and there was something in the woman's look and tone of voice that made his skin crawl. Fortunately, Roulston entered just then bearing a silver coffee service.

"We have agreed there are six," he said, setting the tray on the side table. "Will there be extras for breakfast?"

"No," Thackery said firmly.

Kestrel's nostrils lifted again. "Not hardly. I'm picky who I take my meals with."

"We'll be leaving as soon as our business here is concluded," Thackery added, puncuating the exchange by casting Louis a dark look.

Roulston nodded, completely unperturbed, then waved in two scantily clad young women to serve their coffee. Thackery took his without seeming to notice who handed it to him, but the little patience Kestrel had left was worn thin.

"You need clothes, girl!" she drawled as she took hers, "*and* better taste in employers."

Louis ignored it and ogled the girl who served him. She pretended to be pleased at his lurid behavior, but blushed when she saw the disgusted look on Kestrel's face. At the butler's nod, both women curtsied and left.

Thackery waited until Roulston had also left before continuing. "I'd be careful with the threats, Louis. Either one of us could kill you dead right here and now in the space between breaths and the nobility would probably pin another medal on us."

Louis waved that off idly. "Oh, *Sit down,* Archie, Kestrel." He blew another cloud of blue smoke. "Military people can be so limited. Killing each other isn't going to solve our mutual problem. The Paladins might well pin another medal on you, but if you think I am unaware of your other, shall we say, more *intriguing* activities, you're wrong. I know about them and I guarantee if that... *boy,*" he spat his reference to Raven, "decides you're intriguing, then Roland, Trobiere, Remington, Winchester, Demorest, and all the rest of the peers will know about it as well. By spring, that medal pinned to your chest will have turned into a sword driven through it."

It was his turn to score. Thackery sat down, but Kestrel remained standing behind him, her arms crossed, her empty coffee cup danglingly loosely from a finger.

"You have a plan," Thackery observed. It wasn't really a question, but Louis did note with private satisfaction that he'd managed to divert their attention away from probing into his affairs. He looked over to where his raven-haired beauty writhed in dreamy, post-orgasmic ecstasy.

"I do. You need to get me the Iris. She's our golden ticket. With her, we own this town and all of this goes away!" He gestured dramatically, waving his cigar in the air. "If you really want out of this, then you have your orders. Bring me the Iris—alive."

"And this 'Raven?'" Kestrel asked. "What do you want done about him?"

"Oh, I think you're up to dealing with one young, amateur flyer," Louis said, puffing on his cigar with the kind of smug satisfaction that immediately set her teeth on edge.

"Damned straight I am," Kestrel hissed under her breath.

Thackery and Kestrel looked at each other, and something passed between them.

"Things are always about you, aren't they, Louis?" Thackery's gaze slid from Louis to the woman in the furs, drenched in sweat from her titanic orgasm. Her mind was now as gone as the rest of her life. The only thing left for her, for the rest of whatever time she had left, was sexual sensation, and like any addict, she would do anything and everything to get it. Personally, he found the drug revolting and wasn't blind to the things it said about those who used it—as well as those who worked with them.

"Well this is no longer just about you, Louis," he added, not liking how this was playing out. "We want your legal support, and you're going to give it to us for free. *And,* the price of getting this Iris you're so interested in has just gone up. One thousand pounds, in cash, up front. If not, you lose our outfit, and we *might* just decide the risk-to-reward ratio is a bit too high for our tastes and take steps to rectify that problem."

He stood up to punctuate that. Internally, Louis froze. He couldn't afford to lose Thackery's support now, of all times. Outwardly, all he said was, "Would you sit back down, Archy!"

"No," Thackery said flatly. "You claim to know of our 'other activities', as you put them. Then you'll know where to contact us when you decide, and you better bring the money when you show up."

"Thackery!" Louis jumped out of his chair. "You walk out that door and your life won't be worth an hour's purchase!"

Thackery and Kestrel stopped, then turned slowly, as one. When they looked at Louis, their eyes held no trace of fear. "You are in no position to threaten us, Louis," Kestrel said quietly. "You don't know as much as you think you do, and you're not as powerful as you like to think you are. I'd keep that in mind if I were you."

With that, the two soldiers strode from the room.

159

Chapter 13

Blakesly House
24 Vilmath 580, Noon

Young Clarice sat vigil in the lady's upstairs sitting room, near the big picture window overlooking the grounds at the front of the house. She had the baroness' fine set of prayer beads in her hands, and she worked them much as she'd watched Lady Angelique do, whispering a short scriptural verse as her fingers caressed each smooth, round pearl. Her eyes, however, were fastened upon the gate near the end of the drive, and with every pearl that slipped through her fingers, she prayed for the safe return of Carlisle's missing lady.

Verlinden and Mrs. Reynolds had been informed of the situation, so far as the girl herself knew it. The lady had disappeared at some point during the night previous. The linens on her bed had been turned down, but were not disarranged from sleeping, and no one had seen or heard her leave, the night previous. Clarice had left the lady in her chair near the fire the evening before, with the latest pouch of paperwork by her side which had just arrived from Carlisle. She'd seemed happy enough, but also tired and somewhat distracted. She had confided nothing in her maid, and that had been the last Clarice had seen of her.

The new butler had seen little reason for concern, however, and had counseled both she and Reynolds, the old housekeeper, to patience. The new carriage was still on the grounds, and there had been no sign of a struggle in her chambers. Lady Blakesly was accountable to none of them for her movements, he reminded them, and that for the moment, the wisest course was simply to wait.

The pearls had become warm in Clarice's hands and she'd lost all sense of what the words of the prayers meant when at last a public taxi cab turned onto the approach to the house. Clarice dropped the strand of pearls upon the low table nearby and ran to greet her, leaving only the sound of their clattering in her wake.

Downstairs, the footman had barely gotten the door to the taxi open before Angelique burst through it with a happy, excited smile. It was so unlike the lady's more usual, reserved expression that it set the young man back on his heels. He stammered an awkward "m-my lady!" but it, and her laughter, merely trailed in her wake.

"Good afternoon, Rion! Have the overnight case removed to my chambers," she called out, tossing the words over her shoulder, "and the larger trunk left just outside the door to the baron's suite!" With an energy more reminiscent of Iris' nightly activities than those of Carlisle's sedate, reserved baroness, she bounded up the stairs and nearly ran headlong into Verlinden as he emerged through the doors.

"Lady Blakesly! Welcome home!" he said, nearly as startled as she was.

"Thank you, Verlinden!" She took his hands, forestalling his formal bow by standing on tiptoe to kiss his cheek, instead. "I know, that is not really very proper at all. Do please forgive me. It likely shall not happen often, but I have the most *wonderful* news!"

The man was relatively new to her, and to her service, but managed a smile even as he took in her breathless, disheveled state. Before he could query further, she'd turned to find her young maid before her, scrambling to come to a stop on the waxed, marble-tile floor of the entry hall. "Oh, my lady! Thank the Lord and all his angels that you are safe, I was so worried!"

"Clarice, you are just in time." Angelique let Verlinden take her wrap, then hugged the girl to her tightly, wishing she could transmit some of her own boundless joy to this lovely and loveable person who'd given her so much, and asked so little in return. "But hold just a moment. There are duties which must first be performed.

"Verlinden, it is time. Seal the house, and summon the servants to the drawing room. *All* the servants," she said, nodding when she saw he took her meaning. "I shall burst with this news if I cannot share it soon. It is time to 'send forth the faithless... that the faithful may gather and rejoice.'"

"Oh, my lady! Have you—?"

"Not now, Clarice." Angelique placed two fingers on her maid's lips to silence her. "Follow that trunk up to my chambers," she said, gesturing toward one of the curved, up-sweeping staircases that led up to the second floor, "but you are not to open it. I shall tend to its contents personally. Send Rion down to the drawing room straight-away. I'll be up presently so you can repair my appearance for the household."

"Yes, my lady." Curtsying and smiling her relief, the younger woman withdrew, directing several loitering undermaids and a hall boy back to their duties as she did so.

"Lady Angelique, you might wish to speak with Reynolds before your meeting with the staff," Verlinden said, waiting until Clarice had complied and the entry hall was clear of servants before he spoke. "Here in Fernwall, I understand, it is how such things are done."

Her happy smile hadn't faded. "Thank you. I shall. Good, loyal head housekeepers are treasures. Think you she is? Loyal," she added, clarifying his confusion right away.

"I do, my lady," he said, nodding gravely. "Your former solicitor may have been responsible for her hire, but her loyalty is, unquestioningly, to you."

That's a relief. Iris' characteristically acerbic thoughts appeared suddenly, the sole irritant in the day's joys. *She's a sour old prune, but we don't have to care as long as she's loyal.*

"Thank you, Verlinden," Angelique said, ignoring Iris—and the headache her thoughts had started– for the moment. "Would you ask Reynolds to join me in my private sitting room at once?"

"Of course." He bowed, but Angelique had already turned for the stairs.

By the time Mistress Reynolds was let into the lady's private sitting room, Clarice had managed to turn out her lady much more presentably. The baroness was seated at her little writing desk near the big picture windows, in a simple lilac-colored day dress in one of the fashions that this newer generation of nobility like so well. In the days when Reynolds had been an under-maid, the fabric in that dress would barely have made a proper under-shift, never mind the absence of the slips and layers of petticoats that should have served to create an empty space about her as she moved, as virtuous and untouchable as the very Lady of Paladins. Instead, they used lace and beads and only the Lady knew what all else to gaud themselves up like festival poles. . .

Lady Angelique looked up in the middle of that thought, and smiled at her in the brightest, most heart-warming way. She hadn't seen Carlisle's lady smile like that since their big dinner party, and something softened within Reynolds, to see the return of it.

Not that it showed in her expression. Her keen gaze swept about the room once, in that habitual glance all housekeepers seemed to know how to deploy. The wallpaper was the palest shade of pink imaginable, with a floral pattern in brushed-velvet ivory, and the fine woolen rugs echoed those colors and added hints of mint green and lilac. Most of the furniture was constructed of rosewood and upholstered in deep rose-pink velvet or wool and embroidered with floral motifs. Reynolds thought it a fit retreat for any lady, but especially soothing for those who carried the many heavy burdens of a barony like Carlisle alone. Her keen eyes noted the silver tea tray low table and one of the lady's delicate lace shawls draped over the back of the sofa as the only two differences in the room she'd left in immaculate order, earlier.

"Thank you, Reynolds. Would you care to sit for a bit by the fire?" Angelique waved her envelope about to cool and set the imprinted wax seal, but gestured her toward the fire. "Clarice is pouring tea for us—oh, do please humor me. As I told Verlinden the other day, I am mortal-tired of drinking tea alone, and I've much to tell you."

She hesitated, knowing her mistress had funny, foreign ways. "Well. If your ladyship insists," she said, seating herself gingerly in one of the rosewood and velvet-upholstered chairs.

"As it happens, my ladyship does." The baroness joined her by the fire, taking the other chair and the cup of tea Clarice had just served her. "There are changes coming to Carlisle, and to Blakesly House, of course. I am not certain, however, that all of them will meet with your approval. I know how well you value your reputation, so I wanted to tell you here, privately, that I was able to reconcile my differences with Sir Vincent this morning. He and I are to be married, after his debt to society is paid."

Reynolds looked sour at this, but she thanked Clarice for her tea, and sipped it carefully before she replied. "Well, congratulations to you, Baroness. You'll be wanting the baron's chambers opened, I presume?"

"I shall," Angelique said, her eyebrows twitching in surprise and delight. "Does that mean you will stay on, afterward? I understand that you've been rather plainspoken in your opinions about Sir Vincent's past. I wasn't sure if you would."

The older woman flicked a disapproving glance in Clarice's direction once, but simply placed her teacup back in its saucer, then cradled it in her lap, before she spoke. "I can't say as I've approved of the young lord, to date, but..."

"Do go on. Please."

She shrugged, then drew a deep breath. "But, my lady, if you believe he'll fill his place here... if he's coming here to take some of this load from you, if he'll take on his part like a *noble man,* and not run when life gets hard, then yes. I'll stay on without a qualm. Done is done. The books are cleared when the anchor lifts, as my father used to say."

"Thank you, Reynolds." Though Angelique hadn't always felt comfortable around her hard-eyed head of housekeeping, she did feel relieved at not having to go through the arduous process of hiring another just then. "I'm so glad, truly. Vincent and I will rely on your faithful steadiness as we settle into this life, together. I did have another question for you, however?"

"Yes, my lady?"

"Have you heard from Louis Arnot, lately?"

She'd delivered the question abruptly, in the same light, conversational tone she'd been using. Reynolds' surprise at it was clearly genuine, for it startled the dour look right from her face.

"What? Oh, the lawyer? No. Not for years, now. Sent him packing early on. As if I needed his advice on how to run a house, the arrogant sod. May I ask why you wanted to know, my lady?"

I like her already. Can we keep her, Baroness?

Angelique was already chuckling. "Good. Well done. I dismissed Goodman Arnot as Carlisle's solicitor last summer, but he has since been paying one member of your staff for information on my health and activities."

The time, the pinched look was replaced with one of disbelief, followed quickly by horror. Angelique pressed on, not giving her time to protest. "Patsy's identity as the informant has already been discovered. I am moving to dismiss her, this morning."

"Why didn't you come to me about this, my lady?" Her normal look of disapproval had returned, only emphasized under the duress of true disappointment. "It was my part to assist you with that."

For the first time, that enlivening smile Angelique had worn since her return faded. "I am truly sorry, Mistress Reynolds. I doubted it was you, or that you could be involved in any way, but until I could know with certainty, I began with the two who are oathsworn to me. I did not know what else to do."

Reynolds didn't like it, but she'd worked for Guardian Paladins all her adult life, and knew how such matters were to be handled. "Very well. You're sure it's Patsy?"

Angelique looked at Clarice, who nodded. "She has no family in town to visit, Mrs. Reynolds. And, if you'll check her room, you'll find she's some new items of expensive clothing that she couldn't possibly afford on an undermaid's wages."

That sour look deepened. "Well, I'm not surprised. That one's got airs above her station, she does. And she's lazy, besides. I'll have to replace her, you know." Reynolds delivered it like a warning—the verbal scuffles between her and Verlinden over the household budget were ongoing, and the number of tales the rest of the staff related about them were growing by the week.

"You'll need to hire more than that, but not just yet," Angelique said. "Goodman Arnot's unwanted attentions are still being addressed. Until he is contained, there is a risk anyone we add to the staff at this point could be compromised. It shouldn't be much longer. After Winterfest, no later, I should think," Angelique added, her happy smile reappearing. "With Vincent's help, I feel as if I could conquer the world before breaking my fast, tomorrow!"

Reynolds didn't smile at this, but she nodded readily enough. "And we shall be filling out the rest of the household staff then, I trust?" she said, and it wasn't quite inflected as a question.

"Won't that be something, to see this grand old house fully staffed and functional, again?" Angelique stood to signal the end of the interview, concealing the sudden bout of fatigue that had just tried to swallow her. Reynolds also stood, placing her teacup and saucer carefully on the tray. "But, not a word, for now. We've much to accomplish before we find new members willing to join our extended family here at Carlisle."

"Of course, my lady." Reynolds smoothed the apron on the front of her dress, and nodded again. "Shall we be about it, then?"

"Please do precede me, if you would. Help Verlinden do a head count, then seal the drawing room. I'll be down shortly."

As the older woman left and Clarice returned the tea tray to the sideboard, Angelique stepped into her bedchamber, her own teacup in hand. Weariness washed over her like a fast-running tide, sucking the energy right out of her, but there was too much to be done this day to spare any of it for a nap. She opened the drawer in her nightstand and took up the little bottle of alchemical stimulant. If she were going to see her way through this day and into a long evening at the Old Palace Hotel—and she fully intended to enjoy every last moment of *that*—a little medicinal help to overcome the fatigue she already felt wouldn't be out of line.

"My lady?" Clarice called out from the sitting room, then poked her head through the door just in time to see her lady drop the dose into her cup. "Oh! Ah..."

"It's the doctor's prescription, dear girl. Do not fret. You will find a letter on my writing desk for Lady Emilia at Remington Hall. Please give it to Verlinden and see that it's sent off with our fastest runner." Angelique said, pocketing the little bottle.

"Of course, my lady." Once left alone, Angelique swallowed the liquid that was left in her cup, then began to compose herself for what was to come.

Verlinden half-bowed and put his hand on the latch to one of the drawing room doors as his lady approached. "Patsy is within, Lady Angelique. She appears to be unaware that she has been discovered."

"And Reynolds?"

"Arrived just minutes ago. I trust all is well?"

Nerves had driven the smile from her, but it attempted a return in answer to his question. "Indeed. She's already planning Patsy's replacements," she said quietly, with just a thread of wry humor to sweeten it.

"Very good, then. Are you ready?"

Angelique nodded, and with an answering nod, Verlinden opened the door.

The drawing room's renovations had been among the first completed in the house, and now the grand old room, with its vaulted ceilings and sculptured moldings gleamed from the crystal chandelier that hung from the ceiling to the polished feet of the furniture on the floor. Chairs and divans in cream and pale orange were arranged to facilitate conversations, and the paper on the walls had been restored with painstaking attention to detail, so that the tone-on-tone, turquoise velvet flocking was more a study in texture than in color, but somehow deepened both. The magical crystals in the chandelier had been covered, as they were for all but the darkest days, but the drapes to the large windows had been caught back to let in the natural daylight. There were several dozen of her servants standing uncomfortably in the center of the room. She could only remember the names of half of them, a regrettable lapse she intended to correct as soon as possible. Fortunately, they all looked much more nervous than she felt, except for Patsy, who seemed quite curious to learn the reason for this unusual summons.

I'd call that "smug", actually. Bitch thinks she got away with it. I'm going to love to see her face when she realizes she hasn't.

Iris' sarcasm caused Angelique to straighten her spine, and take a deep breath. She'd not gotten over her fear of speaking in front of groups of people. That these were her own staff didn't make it any easier. Verlinden escorted her to the hearth, and she smiled at him when she squeezed his arm in thanks, but her mouth was so dry she had great difficulty speaking.

Clarice stepped up to offer a glass of water. Blessing the girl privately for her thoughtfulness, Angelique took a sip from it, then smiled at her maid in thanks before turning to the rest of the staff.

Patsy stood off to the right. Verlinden had placed himself just behind her, and stood at parade rest as Angelique drew breath to speak.

"I realize this may be the first time some of you have seen me, or been in the same room with me," she began, acutely aware of how foreign her D'waanese accent must sound to most of them as she spoke, "and I must apologize for this. You'll all have heard the stories, and at their essence they are true: I was not raised to be a baroness. I am *learning* how to be one, with the good examples provided by my peers, of course, but also," she said, relaxing a little as she saw them begin to lean toward her as she spoke, "with your constant and *faithful* support. The simple, unadorned truth is that I could not do what I do without you. My hope is that I can make what I do—for Carlisle, and for all of us—something of which you all may be fiercely proud.

"Well, all but one of you, perhaps." At her change in tone, they all shifted somewhat uneasily, but Patsy most of all. "I am given to understand that someone here has been selling information about my personal life and habits to my former solicitor, Louis Arnot."

Her gaze landed on Patsy as she said the name, and Iris began to seethe. The undermaid's pock-marked face had blanched white, but she lifted her chin and stood her ground as the rest of the staff realized where the baroness' accusatory gaze was pointed, and began to sidle away from her. Everyone in the room knew the consequences of betraying their house. Realizing she stood alone, Patsy's gaze dropped to the floor and she began to smooth the front of her smock, her hands visibly shaking.

"By our rules, I must give you the opportunity to clear your name, Patsy," Angelique said at last, feeling very much as if the Lady of Paladins were somehow standing at her back, supporting her as she spoke. Hoping it wasn't just another symptom of her fractured mental reality, she forged onward, completing her part of the rite that was almost as old as the relationship between the Paladins and their serving class. "Do you have aught to speak in your defense that would explain the lies you have told to Mrs. Reynolds, or what you have done to earn the money you've used to purchase luxury items you cannot possibly afford on your honest wages?"

Patsy's fussing with the front of her smock had evolved into wringing the fabric up into her chubby hands, and tears were streaming down her face by the time Angelique had finished. "N-no, milady," she snuffled pitifully. An angry murmur made its way around the servants hall like a wave, at her answer.

Angelique held up one hand. She'd had time to think about this moment a great deal. It would have been the worst sort of hypocrisy for her to condemn a woman for lying and illicit acts when she herself had been guilty of the same. The old punishments for such an infraction had once ranged from public shaming to whipping, and even, in the worst cases, death by hanging.

We've been whipped, my lady, more'n once. An' we've seen our share o' hangin's. The memories were shared, then, or glimpses of them, but

167

Angelique pushed them away. Fortunately, she had no intentions of doing anything of the sort.

"Very well," she said, really rather grateful the wretched girl was going to go quietly. "As of this moment, you are dismissed from Carlisle's employ, without reference. However, I am the lady here, and what you have done was in part my responsibility. I was not a very good lady, or a baroness, to you. I have long put my personal troubles ahead of my duties to you—to all of you—and to Carlisle. I did not assume my place adroitly enough, nor did I work to earn your loyalty quickly enough. These were my wrongs, Patsy, and in a partial attempt to redress them, I am making you an offer.

"I have purchased a one-way ticket on the coach to Three Sisters. I am prepared to hand it to you with your wages to date and a paid taxi ride to the central coaching station," Angelique said, raising her voice a bit to be heard over the freshened murmuring of the other servants, and Patsy's muted sobs. "If you choose to take it, you will board that coach and start your new life in Three Sisters, never to return to Fernwall or communicate in any way with Louis Arnot. That is my offer. If you refuse it, you can take your wages and your belongings and skulk out the back door to make your way out there as best you can. I'd recommend seeking out a Valïan shelter as the first order of business, however. The Vilmath nights have turned bitter cold, but you will require protection from more than the elements."

Tears still streamed down the girl's pock marked face, but she was staring at the baroness before she'd finished speaking. Clearly she never thought to receive such a light sentence for her behavior. "Th-Thank you, m-m-my lady," was all she could stammer, and that could barely be heard over the din of unwanted advice Angelique was receiving from the rest of the staff, none of whom thought Patsy should be granted such leniency.

Iris didn't care for it either. Abruptly, it felt as if it were her head that were caught between that well-known hammer and anvil, and Angelique raised her hand for silence.

She got it, on the outside, at least, but swayed visibly while she waited for the pounding in her head to subside. "I appreciate your concerns," she said when the worst of it had passed. "You feel that such a light sentence will only encourage treachery, do you not?"

Some of them nodded, others looked away. "Perhaps those of you who feel this is so are correct. I do not know. I only hope that in using the Lady's compassion with Patsy, I demonstrate to the rest of you that I'm worthy of your loyalty, and your faithfulness. If I am wrong, doubtless we will all learn of it soon enough. At that time, we may have to consider if the Lord's justice is the better disciplinary choice.

"Verlinden, would you see that Patsy is accompanied at all times while she remains on the grounds? Have someone escort her upstairs and stay with her as she packs."

"I'll do it, my lady," Clarice said, fixing Patsy with a steely, unforgiving eye.

"I'll go with you." It was Hannah, who had become head maid as the household had expanded. She and Clarice had grown quite close. They flanked Patsy as she covered her face with her apron and walked swiftly from the room.

Silence descended once more as Verlinden closed the doors behind them. "Now, for a happier announcement," Angelique said. She'd nearly drained the glass Clarice had given her, and was able to reclaim some of that earlier, brilliant joy as she faced her people again. "You have all doubtless heard the gossip. Some of you may even have helped spread it," she said, flicking an eyebrow in mild amusement as some few of them shifted uncomfortably. "Allow me now to give you the news directly from the source: Sir Vincent Sultaire and I have resolved our differences. We are to be married when his sentence of indenture is completed, wherein he will be formally bestowed with the title of 'Baron of Carlisle.'"

It was still a most happy thought, though it wasn't doing much to make her feel better. The murmuring arose again as she paused, however, a jumbled mixture of surprise, concern, resentment, suspicion, and excitement. "For the interim, Sir Vincent will be taking up residence here at Blakesly House, and as long as he is on the grounds he is to be addressed as the baron in all ways. Is that clear?"

"Of course," Geran, one of the footmen said. He'd been exchanging speculative glances with a few of his friends. "Will Sir Vincent bring a valet?"

"He can't have, he's a bond-slave," another said, and was abruptly shushed by those standing nearby.

Angelique, however, simply nodded. "You are quite correct—Albor, that is your name, yes?—it is true that Sir Vincent has been stripped of most the privileges of his rank. However, here in what is to be his home, he'll be served as fits his birth rank, and that of the betrothed Baron of Carlisle." She smiled weakly. "I am certain he and Verlinden will come up with something."

She swayed again, and Verlinden took that as his cue to step forward. "My lady, you need some rest. We shall tend to the rest of this messy business with Patsy. Will you retire to your rooms?"

They were looking at her again, this time as if they expected her to shatter apart on the expensive carpets. "I believe I shall. Thank you, Verlinden. Thank you all," she added, addressing them as a group once more. "Open a few bottles of that sweet, sparkling Crecy wine this evening with dinner to toast our health, and the prosperity of Carlisle."

That evoked a general round of excited approval. Angelique winced, and Verlinden clapped his hands for attention. "Thank you. You all have duties which require your attenion. That will be all. Lady Angelique," he said, turning to her in some concern as the rest of the staff filed out, "may I accompany you to your chambers? You're not looking well at all."

She wasn't feeling well either. "Well, no, Sir Vincent will be arriving soon—any moment now, I should imagine," she said, and that thought filled her with such happiness that she smiled—dazzlingly, brilliantly—then turned abruptly.

The room spun dangerously.

"My lady?" Verlinden's startled query seemed to come from three separate directions at once. When Angelique turned her head to see where her butler was standing, the colors in the room bled into one another as her eyes passed.

"Verlinden?"

"*He's not the one you want, Baroness.*" It was a new voice, Iris' voice, coming from just behind her. Startled, Angelique whirled.

Iris, garbed in her indigo-blue suit—the color running like ink to cover the walls and drapes—sat near the big picture window, paring her nails with a knife.

"You?! What are you doing there? You don't belong—"

"Lady Angelique!" She could barely hear her butler's insistent voice over the stabbing pains that were building in her head. She straightened and turned, hoping against hope that it *was* Verlinden, and not another voice splintering her inner world apart.

"*Ah'm not sure Iris is goin' t' be able t' help you either, milady.*" Angelique whirled at the sound of that voice to see Angel curled up on the divan. She was dressed in a pair of dark trousers, and a reddish-brown tunic, her long, pale hair tumbling loosely over her shoulders. "*But you might oughta want t' sit down now...*"

"What? Angel! How did you get—?" She put the heels of her hands into her eyes, and dug her nails into her hairline, but could not seem to halt what was happening to her.

"Lady Angelique, please! To whom are you speaking?" Verlinden's voice penetrated the crackling haze of pain and confusion, but she couldn't spare breath to speak to him. Much as it had the morning after the Belton House ball, the hot blades flashing in her head felt as if they might split open her skull.

"Get them out!" she moaned, dropping to her knees, her throbbing head cradled in her hands. "Lord and Lady, this is killing me! Just get them out!"

"All of you! *Clear the r o o m...*"

Abruptly, it all overwhelmed her. Angelique Blakesly collapsed to the floor like one dead. From somewhere within the mass of colorless blond hair that fell free of its pins, however, Verlinden heard a voice he did not recognize, a voice that scratched, like dead leaves over cobblestones. It began to chant a rhyme.

"*A dragon found a dolly, then made it come to life...*"

Vincent's plans for the morning had gone awry almost as soon as he entered Police Headquarters. Roland wasn't there, and hadn't been expected to return until late afternoon. He'd gone off for an urgent meeting with Lady Emilia on the events of the night just past. He'd left Vincent a note, explaining his absence and urging him to "keep his head down," then included a warning that "Arnot will not be fooled for long."

There had also been a note waiting for him from Barbara Cole, on which she had scrawled a design that she believed to be the unit badge of the mysterious soldiers guarding the barges, which he shoved into a pocket. All in all, his trip to the office had lasted less than a quarter of an hour, so he opted to take a cab up to Blakelsy House from Three Quarters, and thought he should arrive less than a half an hour after Angelique.

Vincent hadn't been there since the previous summer, and then he'd only been there a few times in the entire time they had been lovers. In the early years of the war, it had been abandoned by the Blakesly family as they and the rest of the city's lesser nobility built more modern homes closer to the more powerful peers. The entire estate had fallen into a sad state of neglect, and Angelique had only just begun the first of the renovations when they'd met.

Perched on top of a hill some four kilometers north of Three Quarters, Blakesly House was a classic Nadrean great house, with high walls, flowing verandas, rounded towers, and grand columns. Like almost all the Nadrean great houses on Highcourt Way, the house was partially visible from the road below, which approached it from the eastern side of the hill. The peaks were given over to the most expensive estates along the route, of which Blakesly House was one. Rock walls lined the road along the western shoulder, and hedges topped that. Thus, as seen from the cab, the colorful old homes seemed to emerge from their surroundings like brightly colored flowers from a hedge.

His cab turned left off Highcourt Way onto Marina Drive, then left again a few hundred meters later, through the decorative wrought-iron gate and onto the lane to Blakesly House. When last he had been here, parts of the property were still either wild and over grown, or being reclaimed. Only the lawns and the main garden had been fully restored. Now, all the lawns and hedges were manicured, and the gardens were properly wintered-over. The stables and carriage house had been repaired and freshly painted, and the drive had been newly rocked. Vincent took it all in as his cab made the final turn of the drive, looping back up the hill until it finally revealed Blakesly House in all its refurbished glory. The contrasting dark green and white trim was chosen to accentuate the creamy yellow facade, and the newly polished marble columns that lined the great cathedral entry and veranda were very like lace trim on a fine gown. Angelique had at last turned Blakesly House into a poster image for the opulent extravagance that was the Nadrean period, and on seeing it in all its glory, Vincent thought it glorious.

He had just paid his fare when the door blew open and a footman bounded down the stairs. "You there! Driver!" the servant called, skidding to a stop right in front of Vincent.

"Excuse me?" Vincent arched an eyebrow.

"Oh. Pardon me," the footman blurted, then stammered a belated "my lord" as he saw the pin on Vincent's lapel. "Oh, my lord! I am sent to fetch the doctor immediately! You are Sir Vincent?"

"Yes."

"Lady Angelique just collapsed! She's in the drawing room, you must go to her at once!"

Vincent had reached into his pocket before the footman had finished speaking. "Here." He flicked the driver a crown. "Do as this man says, as quickly as you can. Go!" He said to the footman, jerking his head at the cab door, then bounded up the stairs and into the house.

He had only been inside Blakesly House a few times, and even then he'd only seen a few rooms. Most of the house had still been closed for renovations at the time, but the biggest reason was that servants talked, and he and Angelique wanted to minimize scandal. Fortunately, the drawing room had been open during the big party the summer past, and even if it hadn't, the uproar would have led him to it easily enough. He pelted into the grand gallery, then pushed past a knot of milling servants to find Angelique in a pile of lilac-colored cloth, her ash-blond hair spilling out of its pins to pile on the floor. One of the maids knelt at her side in an attempt to revive her, while a middle-aged man and woman, both dressed in the formal day livery of senior household staff, appeared to be discussing what was to be done.

Vincent took it all in with a show of calm, but it was counterbalanced by the heavy knot in the pit of his stomach. Like every noble he knew, he'd been raised in the midst of a large household staff. The orders that needed to be given, and given *right now!* came to him as easily as life's breath, and that was what tightened the lump in his gut. He'd seen the pitiless way in which his father dealt with such uproars at Valemont. He'd witnessed, and been powerless to stop, the abusive treatment in the house, just has he'd been unable to stop it on the land. His eldest brother, the heir to Valemont, had laughed together with his father and mocked him for treating "a mere undermaid" with simple respect. "If you want to fuck her, take her up to your room," his brother had said, laughing cruelly. The poor undermaid had exploded into tears, then ran. Vincent left the house for good less than a month later, and hadn't maintained a personal servant since.

It wasn't that he couldn't afford one. In truth, though he wore a collar, he had done well for himself in the city, and even a home nearly as fine as Blakesly House wasn't out of his financial reach. He just didn't want to live that way. He hadn't run away from Valemont only to set up another house just like it in Fernwall. He had run away because the behavior of his caste disgusted him.

"Sir Vincent Sultaire?" The man, whose accent marked him as a Vin-Nôrëan, took in the young lord's appearance and the pin on his lapel in one glance. "I am Verlinden, Carlisle's butler," he said then, sketching a hasty bow. "This is Mrs. Reynolds, head of housekeeping. As you can see, Lady Blakesly has collapsed."

Vincent's gaze flicked from Verlinden to the housekeeper and back again. "What happened?"

"She was hearing voices, and seeing angels—she demanded to know why they were here." Reynolds made the old gesture that invoked the blessing and protection of Isen, the Paladin's holy sword. "I didn't see them, but they seemed to frighten her, for some reason."

Verlinden snorted, but half-bowed an apology to Reynolds immediately.

"The lady seemed to be in great pain, Sir Vincent. She'd just dismissed one of the servants and was telling the household about her reconciliation with you when she began to . . ." The older man sighed, then gestured to where Angelique lay, head cradled in the lap of one of her maids. "She seems to be suffering from a nervous collapse, much like the state in which she was returned from the Belton House, earlier this month."

"We've sent for the doctor," Reynolds added, the lines around her eyes deepening in concern as she gazed on her mistress, who thrashed restlessly and attempted to curl up into herself, right there on the floor. "I think we should send for a priest."

"We were discussing whether to make her a sickbed right here rather than risk moving her," Verlinden added, turning back to Vincent with some relief. "My lord, I know we've not yet greeted you properly as our future baron, but it would ease matters here greatly if you would step into the role, here and now, until Lady Blakesly regains consciousness."

There it was, right in front of him. He was being asked to become *his father*—but this wasn't Valemont, and that was his life's breath, lying on the floor like a crumpled doll.

He closed his eyes and took a long, steadying breath. "Very well. The doctor's been sent for. I paid the cabby on my way in. Reynolds, is it? Get her bed turned down, and warm up the room. Where's Clarice?"

"She took custody of Patsy, the traitor. I'll see she's fetched at once," Reynolds said, dropping a brief curtsy before striding from the room.

"Verlinden?" The older man bowed, acknowledging his name. "If you'll lead the way for me, I'll carry her up." Vincent knelt beside Angelique, then gently lifted her up into his arms. She protested wordlessly, and tried to squirm away, then opened her eyes and blinked several times as she tried to focus on his face. Words followed this, half-gasped in broken sentences, but they were in a language he couldn't quite understand. Some words were in D'wan, a few others in Cascr, almost unrecognizable as they slurred and tangled with others that were unknown. She seemed to be pleading with him quite earnestly but lapsed back into semi-consciousness without seeming to notice that he hadn't understood her.

Verlinden barked orders to clear their way back to the entry hall, shooing footmen and maids back to their tasks as they circled up the stairs to the second floor. Clarice darted across the hall before them, throwing open the doors to Angelique's sitting room, then dashing through to the bedchamber ahead of them. Once the butler saw the lady safely into her bedchamber, he murmured a quiet, "If you will excuse me, I should see to the staff. Sir Vincent? May I importune you to come find me once you have the lady settled?"

"Of course," Vincent murmured as he headed over to the bed.

Clarice had thrown back the bed linens and had pulled the drapes closed by the time Vincent placed his lady gently atop the sheets. "Sir Vincent, I'm so glad you're here, but what happened? She seemed fine when I left her, and she'd just taken that tonic the doctor had prescribed—"

"*What* tonic?" he demanded as he laid Angelique out on the bed.

"I don't know!" She twitched the last two velvet panels into place, then crossed the darkened room to Angelique's side and began to pat her skirt, at the sides of her hips. "I think she put it—yes, here."

Clarice withdrew the little blue medicine bottle with the international symbol for an alchemically-enhanced solution stamped into the glass, handing it to Vincent, then unshaded the crystal lamp on the nightstand so he could examine it.

Vincent arched an eyebrow as he took the bottle and opened it. The smell was strong and pungent—and familiar to almost anyone who routinely worked the night shift. "Mule's Kick," he sighed. Iris' statements the night before now made a lot more sense. "And this has been going on how long?" he asked.

Clarice hesitated, glancing worriedly at her mistress once, then at Vincent's face. "Months," she said, blurting the word in response to the concern she saw there. "She began seeing Dr. Lagrange about her fatigue at the end of Ilian. I've only *caught* her using the tonic since the Belton House ball."

"I see," he murmured. It made perfect sense. Iris worked "the night shift" while Angelique met her social obligations during the day as best she could, considering Iris' tenacity. No mortal could go long without sleep—and as far as Vincent knew, no drug could substitute for it.

Given the alternatives, Mule's Kick—or "MOED", which stood for Military Operations Extension Drug, in the IMMC's fancy language—had been a definite advantage on a battle field. It kept soldiers alert and functional for up to three days without sleep, but even excluding the physiological effects of sleep deprivation, the side effects of MOED were problematic for civilians, especially when used far beyond even the military's rather liberal recommended dosing period.

"I'm not an expert, but given the reputation of this stuff, it very likely would have eliminated her fatigue," he went on, eying Angelique speculatively. He should have foreseen this. Why had he not? *Stupid question! How can you see* anything *from the bottom of an ale glass?*

Disgusted yet again with his own behavior, he set the medicine bottle on Angelique's vanity rather harder than he intended. "Get her changed, Clarice. I'm going to go see what Verlinden wants."

He didn't wait to hear her acknowledgment, nor, he realized, had he understood how big Blakesly House actually was until he'd gotten turned around twice trying to find his way.

On the first floor, he'd found the somewhat decimated library. A large, standing globe of Menelon in a brass frame stood between a grand old mahogany desk and the marble hearth. He'd also discovered the morning room, done up with cream-colored flocked wallpaper with forest green upholstery and pale gold rugs, but had to retrace his steps back to the grand gallery in order to get to the right part of the house. He saw then what Angelique had been doing with the paintings and sculpture she'd been purchasing regularly, for many were displayed on the walls of the long hall. It was there that he found a servant who could direct him to Verlinden, who was in the conservatory.

It was a light, airy room, decorated with green, growing ferns and furniture that seemed to be woven from some kind of reed and were padded with cushions in sage green and creamy ivory for comfort. Works of art lined the edges of the room, landscapes and sculptures and portraits on easels and hanging in places from the walls, where each could stand on its own, yet lend context and color to the next. The most breathtaking feature of the room, however, was its view: It provided an expansive view of the city of Angels, the northern branch of the Caspian river and two of its bridges, as well as most of Three Quarters.

The weak winter sun had just broken free from a thick bank of clouds, setting the room and its decor to light. The Vin-Nôrëan butler was supervising two footmen in the rearrangement of some of the decor. He looked up at Vincent's approach, however, his eyebrows lifting even as he half-bowed a greeting.

"Ah, Sir Vincent. Thank you, I had not expected you so quickly. Has Lady Blakesly recovered?"

Vincent shook his head. "I left Clarice to tend her and get her ready for the doctor's visit. I thought I'd use the time to have that discussion with you if your duties permit."

"Ah, yes, of course. Allow me, if you will, to first present Rion, and this is Geran," he went on, introducing the two men. Rion was a stocky, fair-haired young man barely out of his teens while Geran's taller dark-haired good looks were those of a more mature man, in his thirties. "Both came highly recommended from Remington Hall, and so far, we have reason to be pleased with their service to Carlisle."

The two put down the table they were moving so they could bow properly.

"Goodmen," Vincent acknowledged their obeisance, then turned back to Verlinden. "You wished to see me?"

"Indeed. Thank you, goodmen. Provide any assistance Hannah and Mrs. Reynolds may need to get Patsy clear of the house, then see to the rest of your duties. That will be all." Verlinden stood patiently while they departed, then turned back to Vincent as if he'd never interrupted himself. "I wished to postpone your formal introduction to the staff until Lady Blakesly recovers. In the meantime, I only meant to ask if the two of you have had opportunity to discuss some of the, ah, how is it said...? Oh, the 'cultural differences' in how the lady runs her house?"

Vincent arched an eyebrow at the older man. "Cultural differences?" he repeated. "She hadn't mentioned it, no."

"I see." Verlinden frowned, clearly uncertain as to how to proceed. "I do not wish to start our working relationship by offending you, my lord, however, I should like it less if you began your relationship with the staff here from a mistaken perspective. May I speak freely?"

Vincent's eyebrow climbed even higher. This did not bode well. The Vin-Nôrëan nobility had a reputation for being so arch-conservative they squeaked when they turned around. The Cascadian nobility, on the other hand, had a reputation for being... well, a lot like his father. Vain, corrupt, and often times cruel. He had the sinking feeling he was about to see two cultures politely collide. "Granted. What's on your mind, Goodman?"

"Thank you. Lady Blakesly treats with us," the taller man said, choosing his words in Cascr with deliberate care at first, then picking up in pace as he gained confidence in Vincent's perceptiveness, "in the Honorine Way, as it would be called here. If you are unfamiliar with the details, my lord, I am sure the baroness would be better suited to provide them, but in general, each of us has duties here, and she has dealt with us as if we were partners in a grand working, or project, down to the lowest maid in the scullery. The more of the burden we carry, the greater respect and privilege we are accorded, much as it was practiced in Saint Honorine's time, but even the scullery staff are never to be abused or exploited, not by any of us."

He paused then and shook his head, turning just a little to look out over city-scape just beyond the glass. "I interviewed widely for a position in Fernwall before I accepted this one, my lord. Servants do confide in their own. I, ah... have heard some tales of how servants are treated in some *noble* households. It is regrettable, and my lady has said more than once that she will not tolerate such abuses here.

"Now, it may be that your betrothal and marriage will change her thinking and practices on these matters," Verlinden said, though it was clear where his hopes lie. "In any event, it did not seem right that you should attempt to step into your role here, as I asked you to do, without a better idea of what we, and perhaps she, expected that role to be."

That last statement was rather forward, for a servant, Vincent thought. Even one given permission to speak freely, but he let it pass. The man meant well, and from what he'd just said, was probably testing him as much as informing him. "I am only vaguely familiar with the teachings of the Honorine Way," he admitted. "And most of what I've read has been—not surprisingly—presented in a negative light. The Cascadian nobility are an arrogant lot," he snorted, "but personally, I'm of the opinion that anyone with a modicum of wit should be able to see that the relationship between servant and householder as systemic, not extrinsic; and that any noble who fails to attend to the welfare of his or her people should be stripped of both land and titles—starting with my father."

The last came out almost as a snarl. In truth, he hadn't intended to divulge so much to a man he had only just met; but this was all hitting entirely too close to wounds he had left to fester since leaving home. "Does that help?"

"I am sorry, my lord. I do not know," Verlinden was somewhat taken aback, and it showed. "As you will have deduced, Cascr is not my native tongue. I did not understand much of what you said, but," and here he took a half-step back, and bowed respectfully, "I did not need to be able to define all the words to hear the pain in them. Again, my apologies, Sir. It was not my intent. I should not have interfered."

That earned the older man a smile. "It's not your fault, Verlinden. I should not have said it. But as you spent time talking to your own—as you put it—before looking for a position, I'm sure you heard *plenty* about Valemont."

"I have heard much of Valemont and its scions to trouble me." The older man drew a deep breath and cast Vincent a half-apologetic glance. "Valemont is not the worst offender, Sir Vincent, but it is not my place to say more of that. Let me add only that I am certain my lady means not to tolerate *any* of the abuses for which the ruling class, in Fernwall, is so notorious."

"In that we agree," Vincent replied dryly. He paused for a heartbeat. "Is there anything else?"

The butler bowed, and straightened his spine, assuming a more formal cadence for one of his station addressing one of Vincent's. "Did you wish a tour of the house now, my lord, or would you prefer to await Lady Blakesly's recovery?"

"That will need to wait," he decided, glad for the opportunity to move things off of the rather delicate subject of his father and Valemont. "Lady Blakesly brought some trunks with her from my flat that need to be attended to, and anything else you and Mrs. Reynolds can think of to keep the house busy for the next few hours would be helpful. Idle hands, wagging tongues— you know the rest."

"Indeed. The baron's suite is being opened and aired," Verlinden said, also plainly relieved to be back on safer conversational ground. "The baroness was explicit in her desire that you are to be treated as the baron among us here, regardless of your status just beyond the doors. Do you wish a manservant to help you dress for the ball this evening?"

His answering smile was sardonic. "No doubt, I will have to strap on the trappings of my caste soon enough," he sighed, "but not just now. It would just short you a man. I've managed to shave and dress myself for ten years. Another day or two won't matter all that much."

"Of course. If that is all you need of me, my lord, then I'll return to my duties. Convey our concerns to the lady for her health, if you would. The doctor should be here within the hour."

"Thank you, Verlinden." Vincent dismissed the butler, then made his way back to Angelique's suite. Word of his presence in the house had spread quickly, for he passed more servants in the halls, and each of them knew immediately how to address him. Most smiled, addressed him respectfully as "sir" or "my lord" with neither fear nor boldness, and he acknowledged each with a nod or a smile as he passed. They seemed *happy* to see him there, at least provisionally, and entirely confident with the safety of their persons in his presence. It was a direct and sharp contrast to his father's house, where obeisance was demanded and the fear of insufficient servility ever present.

The door to Angelique's bedchamber was ajar when he found his way back. Clarice sat in the wingback chair near the fire, watching her mistress toss restlessly beneath the blankets.

"She rouses, now and then," the girl said, rising as he entered. "And has asked after you—well, as 'Raven'—once."

Mention of his street name earned her a smile. "My grandfather's nickname was Nighthawk," he told her. "Bird names seem to run in my family. Take a break, Clarice. I'll watch over her."

Clarice said something that resembled a thank you and left. Vincent made his way over to the bed and sat. "Hey?" he ventured, brushing her pale hair back a bit. "Angel?"

She groaned a little and moved her hand to press her palm against her forehead. "Raven...? Where...?" She risked cracking an eye open to look at him, but the brilliant streamers it set off in her field of view made her regret it instantly, and she closed it.

"You're home," he replied gently. "You're safe."

With her other hand, she groped for his and clasped it to her chest when she found it. "Well, that's good news," she said, and that old Asburine accent became clearer with each word she spoke. "Safer now that you're here with me, though. What happened? My head feels like a squad of war orcs have been tryin' to claw their way out from th' inside."

"You really don't know?" he asked, somewhat surprised. He thought Angel was supposed to know almost everything about the various personalities. "Is this a secret between Iris and Angelique? You've been taking MOED, or 'Mule's Kick' as it's colloquially known, for months so that Iris could do her thing at night, and Angelique could do hers during the day."

That puzzled her. "No, Ah meant—well, of course, Ah knew about the drug, but Ah meant, how did Ah end up in bed like this? My head still hurts, but the pain does seem t' be passin'."

"Same answer," Vincent said firmly. "You took one dose too many and started fitting. Almost immediately, from the look of it. It happened just as I was coming through the front door."

"'Fittin'?' That's ridiculous," she told him, pitching her voice just above a whisper, "Ah got t' have a dray-horse t' cart my problems around, but seizures ain't been one of 'em. The drug's just a stimulant, that's all."

"It's a stimulant," he agreed, "but that's *not* all. If it was, you wouldn't have been crumpled on the floor like a broken doll, and now be in bed unable to stand even the slightest amount of light," he went on pointedly. "I had to carry you up to bed, and Clarice changed you. Just a stimulant," he snorted.

The crackling of the fire filled the silence after that for several minutes. "Ah guess it's been bein' used a bit freely, of late," she said, admitting at last what neither of her other two awarenesses would face. "There's just been so much t'do. Iris can't be drugged for what she does at night, an' the baroness can't just sleep through the days, either. The folk of Carlisle need her."

"They do indeed," he agreed, his tone softening. He squeezed her hand for emphasis. "More than many other demesnes need their rulers, in fact. But she can't be the whole government, any more than she can be the whole household staff."

178

She risked opening an eye to look at him, then opened the other when nothing more ominous happened than the aura that seemed to erupt all around him. "She's all we had, Raven. And doin' her best to make up for it. Ah lost track of all she's been readin' t' catch up, but she wasn't raised around all this." Her fingers flicked idly toward the room just beyond the bed. "And nothin' she can do will ever change that."

"She will learn in time," Raven assured her. "Just the way we all do—assuming you can keep her from killing herself before then. And I'm here now, and like it or not, I've been steeped in rulership, just like every other bloody Paladin in this country. Not that it seems to do most of them any good," he sighed.

"Has it done you any good, Raven?" she asked, risking a tiny, brief smile. "It mostly just seems t' have brought you grief. The baroness too, come to think of it."

"It's idiots like my father and Louis that bring grief," he said.

Angel blinked a few times, hurrying away the last of the strange lights that seemed to flare in her vision when she shifted it too quickly, and tried to think about what he'd said. Raven had never had a kind word to say about his father or Reginald, Valemont's heir, who seemed to be a stamped replica of his sire. She had only vague memories of the kindly, but distant old man who was purported to be her own sire, though she certainly never thought of him in a paternal way. Of all the older men in her life who'd come and gone. . .

"There's an unlikely pair t' mention in the same breath. Ah guess bein' 'steeped in rulership' doesn't guarantee a man will make a good father, no more 'n lackin' all that makes a man a bad one," she said, pausing only to kiss his hand tenderly. "Louis didn't sire me, but Ah suppose he was the closest thing Ah ever had t' a father, and as far as Ah know, he's got no morals t' speak of."

"Isn't that the truth!" he snorted. "Who *did* sire you? I don't think you've ever mentioned your family, now that I think about it."

"Iris skipped around that question last night like a bug on ice, didn't she." Angel chortled softly and tried to lever herself up into a seated position so they could speak. It made her head pound worse, but it had begun to fade again before she could think how to say so. "Ah'm not sure how much she remembers, anyway. That navy man who you took me t' see last night had the right of it. Ah was born on what the Asburines call 'Angelfest', or if you like it more formal: the Feast Day for the Lady's Angels, on the Siddoway family estates, Carolin' Dell. My mother named me Angela—probably t' remind herself of the court function she had t' miss for the birth—an' Ah got the rest of her name because there was no other.

"Angela Rose Corwin, by the way," she added, a weak, rueful grin flickering in the corners of her mouth. "Pleased t' meet you."

He grinned at her. "First we fuck, then we greet," he chortled, his eyes dancing. "It sorts well with my rakehell reputation, I suppose. So, you really are of the Rose Line? That makes you at least 'nobly-born' as I am." He made it sound as pompous as he could.

Angel shook her head—carefully, for her vision was still prone to playing tricks with the light. "Ah never thought of myself that way, Raven. Well, until Angelique came along, Ah guess. My mother is one, too. Or was. Ah assume she's still alive. She's only sixteen years older than me."

"She was only sixteen? What a question," he sighed. "Of *course* she was only sixteen. And, being a Rose herself, she was probably well aware of the rules and knew what was required of her by the men of the Siddoway family. I'm sorry," he smiled ruefully, "the Rose Line scandal is an old one, with well-worn tracks. Their behavior infuriates me almost as much as my father's and brother's does."

"Well, it's not just the men. The Siddoway women spend fortunes on contraception every year, or so Ah understand. The men just don't see any point in subsidizin' it for the servants. Pragmatically speakin'," she went on, remembering using similar words with Lady Emilia, just a few weeks past, "Ah suppose it's a way to guarantee they never run out of servants."

"It's also why, if they kept records of such things, your bloodline is probably just as noble as any of the ruling families in Cascadia. That's probably what kept you alive," he added, the thought having just occurred, "under conditions that would have broken lesser minds. How did you end up in Püran-Khir?" he asked suddenly. "Surely the family didn't *sell* you!"

Angel blinked again, and the curl in the corner of her mouth twitched once. "It's tellin' that you have t' ask though, ain't it? No, they're not quite so monstrous. My mother was more interested in the doin's at Harroweigh Court and in bein' old Lord Alnway's mistress than in whatever motherly duties she might have had. Ah don't really remember her face, you know. Ah know she had dark hair, as dark as yours, Ah think, and large brown eyes, and round, laughing cheeks.

"Well, Ah might be confusin' her with one of the nannies," Angel added with a shrug. "At some point, when Ah was between eight and ten years old, my mother had taken another lover. Ah remember him only as a towering, red-haired man with a quick temper."

It was odd to recount it, after everything that had happened between then, and speaking it to the man who seemed to still want to marry her, in spite of it all. In some ways, it was like telling the story of something that had happened to another person, entirely. "Ah don't know the details, Raven. He took me from my bed late one night and handed me over to another man with a funny accent—D'waanese, I learned later—and tole me Ah belonged t' that man now, an' that Ah'd better obey him if Ah ever wanted t' see my mother again.

"He—Jairard, that man's name was—told me later that Ah was payment for a gamblin' debt. Two hundred crowns seemed like a vast fortune, then." Angel paused and twisted Carlisle's signet ring around on her finger. "Ah think he got his money's worth before we boarded the ship in Greenock."

Vincent looked away, sadness blending almost perfectly with impotent anger. The Siddoway family and their courtiers were supposed to be the ones *preventing* this kind of abuse, but as often as not were the worst offenders.

"So, you were his little prostitute?" he asked then, keeping his voice gentle, and low. As angry as he was, this wasn't about him now, and he knew it.

"No," Angel said, exhaling forcefully. "Prostitutes get paid, Raven. Call it for what it was: Ah was his little slave."

The pained look in his eyes answered for him, for all he could do was take her hand and kiss it. His father, his oldest brother, the lords of Glouden, Trobiere, Asbury... They were all users and abusers. They were the selfish, arrogant, self-righteous narcissists he'd furiously sworn to himself he'd stop when he stormed out of Valemont. Now, ten years later, he'd just added Louis Arnot's name to that list.

The only other thing that had changed was Vincent, himself. Back then, he thought he could change the world. Now, he knew he couldn't. The world had him outnumbered.

The fire hissed and danced for several long minutes before he pulled himself out of his reverie, and Angel let him have them. She knew even better than he that there was nothing to say, nothing that *could* be said that would make any of that less awful than it was. "And then came Louis?" he finally asked, half-dreading the answer.

She nodded, but drew a deep breath, and managed to sit up a little more in the bed. "Then came the *Boeche-Briazel*, and Louis. Ah think Iris told you about that, last night." Angel looked at him then, pausing to lift the shade on her little lamp a bit so she could see him better. It was simply impossible that he could still be so handsome as worn with cares as he was at that moment. It hurt to think she'd just piled on more. "Ah'm sorry, Raven. Ah didn't want t' add to your cares, not ever again. Most of that is behind me now, Ah swear it is, and you an' Iris an' Angelique are takin' care of what's left. We do not ever have t' talk about it again, for all o' me."

He chortled at that and gave her a fond look. "Darling, if my past is anything to go by, we're probably going to be talking about this over and over for some time. The past, I've noticed, has an obnoxious way of intruding itself into the present. In trumps, in your case." He made a face.

There was a knock on the door, but Angel giggled right over it. "Lady's garters, your babies are goin' t' be adorable. Ah can't tell if you're stubborn or crazy, t' be stickin' around when most other men would have hit th' door runnin' an' not looked back. Yeah?"

The last was directed to the door, for Angel had quite forgotten that it was the baroness who was supposed to be responding. Clarice appeared, her expression both openly inquisitive and relieved that the lady and her betrothed seemed to be in such good spirits. "Pardon me, my lady, but Dr. Lagrange's coach just pulled into the drive."

Vincent turned to Clarice as she spoke. There was a silent beat when Angel should have replied but did not. When he turned back to her, she'd placed her fingers upon her brow, and was straightening up as she spoke.

"I was not aware she had been summoned," she said then, dropping her hand to look from Clarice to Vincent. He didn't need to hear the Dwaanese accent in the words to know that the persona of Angelique Blakesly had returned. It was in the tilt of her head, too, and in how she moved her hands, and the set of her hazel eyes. "On your authority, was it?"

"Yes," Vincent murmured. "Send her in, Clarice," he instructed. As the maid stepped out, he fetched the medicine bottle from his pocket and handed it to her. "I'm no doctor," he told Angelique quietly, "but I think you've over-used this. You collapsed."

Her momentary confusion cleared as she took the little bottle from him. A moment's inner conference with Angel confirmed her suspicions. "I was not the only one using it," she said, understanding it at last. "And Iris was the one who replaced it, after it was gone, some weeks ago." She clasped it in her fist tightly, closing her eyes and clenching her jaw in a bid to out-wait the anger that rushed through her, but left her nauseous in its wake.

"Yes, well, Iris and I are going to have a little chat about that—or a fight, more likely," he said grimly. "I understand I abandoned you and left you with fights on two fronts, but this is ridiculous."

"She is dangerously irresponsible," Angelique said, hissing the words because to give them voice in her current state would have been equal to shouting down the house, "and will not think beyond the moment, nor that anyone's cares can equal her own. She is secretive and arrogant and I should v—"

The pain erupted in her head again, cutting off her words and causing her to sink back into her pillows with her palms pressing into her eyes.

"Relax," Vincent completed her sentence for her. "We can deal with that *after* the doctor has finished with you."

Angelique winced again. "If she leaves anything," she said, half-whimpering the words as she sank more deeply into her pillows.

Clarice showed in the doctor, who turned out to be a tall, spare redhead with pulled-back hair and a no-nonsense look about her, from her sensible wool trousers and jacket to the medical case she carried. "Lady Blakesly, I was told you collapsed again. And you are?" she added, looking directly at Vincent in a way that made him think of specimens pinned to cork boards.

"Her intended, Vincent Sultaire," he nodded. "She overdosed on MOED, I think. If that's possible. Anyway, she collapsed right after taking a dose about—oh, half an hour ago?"

Seeing that she was not going to be permitted to hide, Angelique emerged from her blankets and nodded. "Perhaps a bit more. I did eat this morning, however!" she added, in a clear bid to win over some measure of good will from the woman.

"I believe I am the one with the training here, and the gift," the doctor said then, stepping toward them, but halting to allow Vincent to rise and pull his chair out of the way. "So why don't you both just stick with giving me the facts, and leaving the diagnosis to the professionals?"

Angelique nodded in chagrin. "My apologies, Doctor. My reasons for not sleeping last night involve Sir Vincent, but for the best of reasons this time, rather than the worst."

"I'm delighted to hear it. Do you wish for Sir Vincent to remain while I examine you, and you attempt to justify how badly you've been mistreating yourself, this time?" She was busily opening her case and retrieving a notebook, pen, her pocket watch, and some other items neither Vincent nor Angelique recognized.

"If he wishes to stay, I should prefer it," the baroness admitted. "I may need his protection."

"Shall I fetch my sword?" Vincent quipped, looking back and forth between the two.

Dr. LaGrange took his measure with a wry glance. "It seems your fetching sword has been part of the problem," she said, turning to the old Paladin metaphor and wrenching it into a sexual jest. "Although wakefulness in pursuit of pleasure is rarely ever a real problem, I'll admit."

She turned back to her patient with a considered look. "Now, you should have run out of that medication long ago, Baroness," she said then, putting one finger beneath Angelique's chin to turn her face to the light. The doctor's diagnostic talents were considerable, and with her gift she ranged deeply into Angelique's body, searching for signs of damage, and what might have caused it. "So, either you suffered a reaction, and I can clean that up fairly quickly, or, you've somehow procured more of that drug, and you and I are about to have a very long and likely very uncomfortable conversation about the dangers of obtaining medications from unvetted sources."

The doctor's eyes were somewhat unfocused as she split her attention between what her gifts were uncovering and the need to listen to her patient's words. Angelique sighed quietly, and couldn't help glancing at Vincent as she spoke.

"More was obtained for me," she said, knowing that the truth was complicated, and so she reached reflexively for that ephemeral line between truth and lies for an answer her doctor would accept.

For all the differences in the various personalities, Vincent had already begun to notice similarities between them, similarities that he assumed pointed to the larger person, the "soul" that was Angela Rose Corwin. Angelique's evasive answer was very like that he might have expected from Iris, who trusted no one, not even the other parts of herself. Angelique hadn't shared the truth with Clarice and apparently hadn't confided in Doctor Lagrange either.

"Darling, you're going to have to start trusting people, or the weight of the burdens you're carrying is going to kill you," he told her pointedly. "You may as well start, here and now, with Doctor Lagrange."

The fear-threat response was instantaneous, going through her like a wash of hot blood, and she looked at Vincent as if he'd slapped her. Her doctor, still intimately linked with her body's physiological responses, started back as if she'd been burned. Before she could sort what had happened, Angelique spoke.

"Surely that is not nec—"

"Oh, I think it is, Baroness," Dr. Lagrange said, taking Angelique's wrist firmly in hand. She pushed up the sleeve of her bedgown with her other hand, exposing the deep, livid bruise on her upper arm for them all to see. Angelique, much stronger than her doctor realized, of course, wrenched her arm away, but it didn't slow Dr. Lagrange's diatribe. "Is that why you didn't want to be sedated at night? Had someone been threatening you with such bodily harm that you couldn't even confide in your doctor?"

"You're not alone, doctor," Vincent drawled. "She hasn't been confiding in *anyone,* that I know of—even me." He sat down on the edge of the bed and took the hand she had jerked away from Lagrange.

"You were not around to be confided in, at the time," Angelique said, offering it as apologetically as she could, "and at the time, neither of us had much trust for the other."

"But this is now, Burning Bright. Look, you survived waiting for me in the carriage last night. You *trusted* me and survived. Trust Dr. Lagrange with what she needs to know to help you—to help *us.*"

The doctor's eyebrows came up at this language, and she looked at Angelique expectantly. She sat between them, deeply conflicted, unable to remember the incident of which Vincent had just spoken. Those kinds of moments hadn't been unusual, of late, and the reason why was at the root of the problem: Iris still didn't trust her, and it was more than mutual.

My lady, if Ah may suggest it, leave Iris out o' this, for the moment. Her trust issues are her problem. Angel's thoughts had strengthened a great deal since she'd been having external conversations in addition to these internal dialogs. *Raven's right. It begins here, with you, this very moment. And if you hadn't noticed? It ain't been gettin' any easier.*

Vincent was watching her closely. "You don't need to tell her everything," he pressed. "You shouldn't, in fact. It would put the doctor in danger. She just needs to know enough to do her job, part of which is probably going to be putting you back together a few times before all this is over."

They looked at him in unison, mirroring each other's dismay. His meaning dawned on Angelique only after she factored "Iris" back into the personal equation.

"He means that I have been leading quite the night life, Doctor," Angelique said at last. She glanced back at Vincent once, feeling the lacy edges fear again but knowing in her heart that he was there for her, to protect her and support her, as Guardian Paladins did for each other.

"In short, Doctor, there's a lot going on," Vincent reinserted himself in the conversation. "We're trying to coordinate with Remington, Commissioner Roland, and the rest of the Law Enforcement Committee to bring a criminal to justice. Angelique's excessive use of MOED was driven by events, as were her injuries." He flicked a glance down at the bruise on her arm, then back at the doctor significantly.

Again, both women looked at him in unison. Dr. Lagrange blinked several times. Angelique, however, exhaled the breath she hadn't been aware she was holding, and felt herself *relax* in a way she had not experienced before.

184

He wasn't going to require her to expose her fractured inner world, at least, not just then, and it was remarkable how much tension simply *allowing* him to help make these decisions had released.

That's right. It's all gonna be all right, see? Once you know who t' trust, the rest comes so easy...

"Well then," the doctor said, looking anew at them both, "it would seem you have another choice before you, Lady Angelique. You are a healthy young woman with resources. Your body will flush the drug and the resultant build up of fatigue toxins naturally. It usually takes three to five days, and I would strongly recommend a regimen that included lots of rest—"

"Doctor, there is no time for that," Angelique said, the protest in her tone as much as her words. "I am *expected* at the Old Palace Hotel this evening, and I have already missed too many events this season. My peers are relying on me, and," she added, chancing a small, happy grin at Vincent, "I'd hoped we might make public our reconciliation, too."

"Well, if you'd let me *finish,* your ladyship," Lagrange said, mocking her just a bit for exercising a rather overused noble privilege, "there is another way. With my gifts, I could detoxify you right now. It would take about thirty seconds. However," she went on, raising her voice over her patient's too-eager agreement, "it is not a pleasant experience. In fact, it's rather awful. You're going to throw up anything you've eaten in the last six hours—"

"Not enough to worry over."

"—Ha! I knew it—and then you're going to spend the next two hours or so after that sweating and shaking. Then you're going to be ravenous and quite thirsty, so I'll speak with Clarice and that imposing Verlinden fellow about what you're to be served during your recovery. It will force you to rest, but, since there doesn't seem to be anything else wrong with you that rest and good food won't fix, you *should* be ready for a fashionably late entrance to your party tonight."

She paused for a breath then, glancing between them, but addressing Angelique last. "Do you still wish to go through with it?"

Angelique looked tenderly at Vincent, who clearly regarded this one as a choice she needed to make. She squeezed his hand and smiled a little. "I've been through worse, believe it," she said at last, turning back to Dr. Lagrange with some of that dry, jesting tone in the words. "Thank you, Doctor. I accept."

Vincent squeezed her hand. "Should we send for a bowl and towels first?"

"Oh, at the least, I should say," the doctor replied, putting the rest of her kit back into her bag. Angelique had already taken her hair into her hands and was twisting it into a loose braid. "Clarice will know. Unless you've a liking for such things, my lord, you'll probably wish to wait for her in her sitting room. Truly, it's not going to be pleasant."

"No, I have no liking for such things," Vincent admitted with a smile, but he neither stood up nor released her hand. "I've been at sick beds before. I almost lost her to all of this, once," he told Lagrange. "I'm not leaving her again. Not when she needs me right here, at her side."

"As you wish, of course." The murmured response was almost unheard. Angelique was looking at Vincent as if seeing him anew, as if what she saw in him was melting her heart all over again. Even as the doctor stepped out to speak with Clarice, Angelique shifted herself into his arms and embraced him tightly. One small moment of surrender was all it had taken, but in return she could already sense the comfort, strength, and support she'd never have gained, without it. Somehow, she and Vincent were going to get through this—all of this—together. For the very first time, she was certain of it.

What Dr. Lagrange had done to Angelique's body had felt a lot worse than dying. All the thoughts within her agreed on that singular point. Dying was a little release, really—just a letting-go, the opposite of all that struggle and strife. There were too many memories of her previous brushes with that state, and they all smashed against one another in chaotic glee while she sweated, wept hot tears, cramped in every muscle, and heaved her guts, or what was left of them, into a bowl.

It was reassuring, in a macabre sort of way, to know she couldn't be dying. She clung to that, and to Vincent's rock-steady presence while her body did what it had been prompted to do. When there was nothing left, and she felt as if she'd been beaten hard and left to dry out on some barren desert, Clarice and Vincent wrapped her in bedsheets and placed her back on the bed. She hadn't been sure what happened after that, but the panic those thoughts used to invoke couldn't get much traction with her. Vincent was there, and so was Clarice. It was all going to "come 'round right," as her maid kept murmuring, until the fever and chills passed, and she slept, wrapped in Vincent's arms, until Clarice came to rouse her for her preparations for the ball.

Chapter 14

The Old Palace Hotel, Angels

As Carlisle's carriage turned into the long, paved drive that led up to the Old Palace Hotel, Vincent caught sight of the elegant arcs of glittering water that leapt up from the pool of the Princess Fountain like long-tailed sprites, winking and peeking out from between the hedges at the carriages that rolled up the drive. For the ball that evening, and for the rest of that pre-holiday week that led into Winterfest, the old hotel was cast into light from the base of its pillars to the top of its soaring turrets. Its four full stories were surrounded by skirts of balconies, their long, gently curved scrollwork backlit by magical lights, and supported by platoons of intricately carved columns. The facade was equally detailed, from the carefully crafted cornice-work to the multicolored patterns painted into the soffits, fascias, and gable ends. Like Blakesly House, the Old Palace Hotel had been built in the Nadrean Period, and was a study in its extravagances. Tonight, it gleamed like a painted jewel set atop a liquid mirror for what was widely regarded as "autumn's last, best party" of the season.

The gala's annual theme was a nostalgic, pre-war fantasy they'd termed "Nadrean Nights." It was a yearly tribute to a time long dead, if it ever existed at all. Vincent was sure it never had, at least, not the form this annual remembrance celebrated. According to his tutors, the Nadrean era began shortly after the state marriage between Princess Nadeera Ashoä M'latti Nerafahn of the Sudaani imperial family and the Winslows, Cascadia's powerful, though thoroughly disliked ruling family. Though she had never assumed the throne in her own person, Princess Nadeera achieved a high level of popularity with the people and most of the nobility. Intelligent and highly educated, Nadeera was also a vivacious and charismatic young woman with a great deal of personal energy, and an unerring eye for color and composition.

Within ten years of her arrival and marriage to Prince Altheon Winslow, Nadeera had managed to turn her personal style into a cultural movement that went on to span three decades. The ruling Paladin nobility and the Urilian aristocracy had slavishly emulated her personal style when it came to flaunting their wealth, but they had been much less ready to embrace her social reforms. The secret and ugly underbelly of the Nadrean period had been that the glittering, ornate displays had all been built on the backs of servants and workers who had been treated little better than serfs.

Vincent pulled himself out of his reflections as their carriage made the final, sweeping turn up to the dazzlingly well-lit portico of the hotel. Porters bounded down the wide steps the instant their carriage stopped. Garbed in red doublets and gold hose for the occasion, they bowed and held the door for Vincent as he stepped to the ground.

"And, here we are, Burning Bright," he said, half-bowing as he, in turn, handed Angelique out of the carriage. Her answering smile deepened, but her face turned up almost immediately to gaze at the intricately lit facade. The garish effects of the light made it look for a moment as if she were wearing her own mask, but the impression passed quickly.

"I can hardly allow myself to believe it," she said, squeezing his arm, then pulling her cloak about herself tightly as he escorted her up the steps. In truth, she was much recovered, and didn't need any further lectures to realize she had been much, much luckier than she deserved. "Do you know, I remember attending the event last year, dancing nearly every dance, bored out of my mind, secretly hoping that you'd attend. When you appeared at last," she went on, turning to him as they passed through the spectacularly large double-doors that let into the grand foyer, "that's when I felt the celebration had truly begun."

"Then for you tonight, Burning Bright, the party begins right now, at the beginning," Vincent grinned. Clarice, in a stylized costume of an old Sudaani imperial court page, appeared to take their outer garments, then passed a small stack of greeting cards to her mistress before departing.

They represented polite bids for her time this evening, but Angelique tucked them into her little purse, barely noting them. Her eyes were fixed on Vincent, and she could hardly bear to tear them away for even an instant. She leaned into him as if he'd become her center of gravity, and he brought her hand to his lips to plant a tender kiss in her palm. In that moment, she felt that her joy must outshine even the light from massive crystal chandelier that spanned nearly the entire breadth of the ceiling above them.

"Not only the party. Our life together, too." It took a moment to untangle her eyes from his, but she wasn't in any hurry. When Vincent put her on his arm to lead her through the crowded lobby, a trail of astonished murmurs wasn't all they were leaving in their wake.

In the act of shrugging on his overcoat, Louis Arnot caught sight of the happy couple entering the lobby. At first, he didn't recognize Angelique, and with a flash of shock wondered if Sultaire were stupid enough to attend such a high-profile social event with another woman. Then she turned in better profile, and he saw that it had to be her.

Finally, he had confirmation that she was still alive! She had vanished off the Morrissant Bridge the night before, and he had heard nothing since. "Blue bottles" from two different precincts had been swarming around outside his house like flies, but Roulston was able to smuggle a message out with the laundry. It had gone to one of his best, and most expensive "delivery services", asking them to fabricate any excuse to deliver a message to Blakesly House. Patsy, he reasoned, would be able to tell them if the baroness were home, but the delivery wagon was not allowed inside the gates, nor would the stable hand divulge any information to the driver.

He had intended to attend the ball anyway—it was where all the real work got done, no matter which shift one worked—but, after nearly twenty-four hours without any news at all, his very real need to ensure Angela's survival had made attending an imperative.

What he still didn't know was how he was going to get her back under his control before it was too late. The presence of Sultaire, apparently back in her good graces, wasn't going to make the task any easier. However, he and Thackery had devised a fall-back plan, and that thought helped him rein in his impatience. He drew back to stand among some potted greenery to watch her, trying hard not to scowl openly.

She was dressed in a costume that played on Princess Nadeera's legendary liking for trousered outfits, though he supposed it wasn't nearly as shocking now as it had been, almost two hundred years before. Angelique's were black gauze, trimmed with fine silver thread, full-legged, blousing at the ankles in a way that likely caressed her legs with every step she took. The bodice resembled a vest with a filmy under-blouse, but was in fact a single garment, though the opaque black satin "vest" left most of her chest and belly semi-exposed under the sheer blouse. Her pale hair was braided back, Cascadian-style, and she wore a headband with a device in silver affixed to her brow, though it was too small to make out details from where he stood. Black and silver tourmaline jewelry and silver-embroidered dancing slippers completed the set. It wasn't Sudaani garb, not really, but it wasn't "Cascadian" either. It was a blend of the two that made it stylistically "Nadrean", and she looked so good in it, so alluring, so *happy* and self-satisfied that it made him seethe.

"Shall I summon a cab for you, goodman?" A hotel footman asked, handing Louis his hat and cane.

"Ah, no. I believe I'll stay a little longer, after all." He lingered in the greenery until he heard the herald announce Carlisle's arrival, then took up a glass of thesker from a passing server and followed them.

Orchestral music embraced Angelique and Vincent as they entered, and competed with merry laughter and the rise and fall of a hundred of conversations for the ear. Angelique paused a meter or so behind the green-robed back of the event's herald annunciate to take in the sight. Guests clustered in the vaulted archways around the edges of the dance floor, garbed in the old-world glamor of the Nadrean era. She picked out round, feather-bedecked, pink-cheeked Merci'a Devon standing next to her equally round, but sallow-faced husband Lord Alren, and Anne Carter of Lansdowne nearby, fiddling nervously with the over-beaded fringe on her bodice while she laughed and doted upon an older man who might have been her husband, for all Angelique knew. The costly fabrics of their fine clothes shimmered, draped, and flowed in mottled color combinations that looked as if they had sprung from a dyer's fever-dreams. Ladies' maids and valets scurried back and forth from archway to archway, carrying drinks and snack trays to their lord or lady, dodging the number of red-and-gold liveried servers employed by the hotel itself, there to attend to the needs of the guests generally.

Occupying the center the ballroom floor, built especially for Princess Nadeera and to her specifications so that all who danced there could do so as effortlessly as she could devise. Marble had been deemed too slippery as had most woods, but the tall, sturdy ash trees from the mountainous barony of Norwood provided the solution in a bright, warm wood that could be polished to a satiny sheen, its boards laid together so tightly that the seams could barely be distinguished from the grain. Dancers covered it almost completely, concealing its beauty in order to reveal it as the rest watched. Angelique saw knights, barons, earls and countesses from dozens of demesnes with just a single glance about the floor, and realized only then that she and Vincent had just picked one of the most well-attended events of the season to come out together.

They had barely taken in the scene before the herald annunciate approached, dressed in a flowing robe of green velvet, hemmed in a band embroidered with the repeating green and silver sigil of the International Herald's Guild. A dark green sash bore the badges and awards of her rank and her calling. Under the robe she wore dark green hose and a shimmering silver-gray, satin doublet; all the formal livery worn by heralds of the Nadrean era. In the crook of her arm, she held the traditional metal-shod, oaken staff of annunciate. Neither the role nor the staff of the annunciate had markedly changed in centuries.

"Good evening, Baroness Blakesly," she said, taking the invitation card Angelique provided and scanning it with a practiced eye. Then she turned to Vincent who, lacking time to collect a proper costume, was formally dressed in a tail coat, waistcoat, and cummerbund. Her gaze drifted down to the pin on his collar. "And Valemont," she finished after a brief pause. Though her tone was neutral, and she apparently had no idea who Vincent was by sight, there was a general, albeit mild distaste for the name of the barony as she spoke it.

"Actually, that would be my father. But 'Sir Vincent' will do nicely," he said, taking the herald's hand. Before the older woman could protest, a finely stitched red, velvet rose grew in her palm, the sweet fragrance of rose oil wafting from its cloth petals. "Oh, well done! I couldn't have done it better myself!"

A quick smile broke through her professional mien. "I believe you just did," she said, tucking the lovely thing into one of her pockets with some care. Eyebrows lifted inquiringly, she gestured then toward the top of the steps. "If you're ready, gentles?"

Angelique's heart was about to burst at Vincent's antics, but she nodded permission, anyway.

The annunciate half-bowed then, and resumed her deadpan expression as she turned to face the room once more. The metal-shod end of the staff struck the marble floor with a resounding *bang!* and she delivered her lines in a voice that would have carried a distance over a heated battle.

"LADY ANGELIQUE BLAKESLY, BARONESS OF CARLISLE. AND SIR VINCENT SULTAIRE OF VALEMONT."

"Oh, well done," Angelique said, chortling as dozens upon dozens of startled faces turned toward them at the announcement.

"Wonder if she was a drill sergeant?" Vincent quipped.

"No idea, but she's certainly dropped a couple of cats among the canaries." She caught his gaze and directed it to where a throng of the colorfully dressed, openly curious were gathering, with that enigmatic smile flickering in the corners of her mouth.

Vincent's gaze followed hers, then turned suddenly to take her hand. "Darling, they're playing a waltz. Would you like dance? Our first since—"

Before he could finish it, the multi-colored waves of nobility that Angelique had spotted had almost reached the bottom of the steps. He groaned inwardly. *One evening spent reciting the official* Mâgun-Zak *talking points, coming up.*

Angelique had taken a half-step toward him as he'd spoken, but of course she'd seen them, too. "Since the Belton House, I believe, which is why some of our peers are closing in on us, this very moment. Chin up, darling man," she said, squeezing his fingers tightly, "if we want to play here—and I, for one, certainly do—then we're going to have to do some repairs to the court."

"Lady Angelique, what a stunning... dress? Is that not a dress? It is—oh, it's *trousers!*" Georgiana Dawes punctuated that with a squeal of delight and clapped her hands. She was dressed in a floor-length kirtle in deep blue, bead-embroidered velvet, with a low-neckline that displayed a stunning amount of cleavage. The blue chemise underneath was a costly thing of fine lace, and she wore it with the traditional wreath of ribbons worked into her loose brown hair. The modesty of her costume was somewhat offset by the knowing, speculative looks she was casting on Angelique's companion. "And you are on the arm of—well, we've not been introduced, have we?" she went on suggestively, crowding in close to avoid some of the dancers near the edge of the floor.

"If you're sure your old aunt won't fall over dead from the shock," Angelique said, hitting obliquely at what had yet remained unspoken among them. They laughed, though it was somewhat less nervous-sounding from the males.

"She'd just inherit before she could be disinherited," one of the other girls laughed.

"And that might spare her the tedious search for a husband!" another added.

Georgiana was also giggling, but turned her big brown eyes up to Vincent, and then to Angelique. "Well, if *you* are going to receive him, Carlisle, I think my old aunt Grafton will have to relent. Eventually. Won't she?"

It was winsomely done, and in spite of Iris' internal and somewhat unsavory musings on the girl's actual worth in a fight, Angelique managed a knowing smile. "Very well, then. Darling, this is Lady Georgiana Dawes, the heir to the baroness of Grafton. Georgiana, it is my honor to present to you my betrothed, Sir Vincent Sultaire of Valemont."

With a triumphant little smile, Georgiana offered a hand for him to take, clearly thrilled with committing an act of rebellion, however minor.

"It is an honor," Vincent murmured as he bowed over her hand. When he released it, however, she found it held a white rose, fashioned from cream-colored satin into which tiny glittering threads had been sewn, making it look as if it had been kissed by the morning dew. "A lovely white rose, for a lovely lady," he smiled.

Angelique's eyebrows flickered in amusement. Georgiana had clearly heard *all* the gossip from the summer past, and had half-expected the delicate prize she now held cradled in her hands. "I believe I'll wear this in my hair." Purring in satisfaction, she held it up to a spot on her wreath of blue ribbons. "What do you think?"

"The color is for innocence. There's some question about that," said a man from just behind her. He was perhaps a decade older than Grafton's heir, and had hooded, haughty brown eyes set in a bronzed, narrow face topped with dark brown hair. He too wore doublet and hose, his in black and gold, and topped with a heavy brocade jacket that was simply resplendent with gold filigree and pearls. It marked him as a scion of a wealthy, powerful house, and his somewhat disdainful air confirmed it.

"Paul!" Georgiana shrieked, turning to push against his chest playfully. She had to shout it over the applause that erupted around them as the waltz ended and the dancers applauded. "You're a beast and the worst gossip I know—"

"Clearly because you don't know yourself, I'd say."

"—and now Sir Vincent is going to have some very naughty ideas about me!" Georgiana had shouted past the newcomer's interruption, but then she clutched at his arm to keep the milling crowd around them from pulling him away. "Paul, have you met Lady Angelique or her betrothed yet?"

"We've met a few times," Vincent assured her. "Sir Paul," he inclined his head to the man, who nodded back and took up Angelique's hand to kiss it. "Lady Georgiana is entirely too intelligent a young lady to be an innocent— though she pretends very well," Vincent added, and cast Georgiana a wicked, knowing look. She half-shrieked in an attempt at playfulness, but a bright scarlet flush drenched her from cleavage to brow line.

"Perhaps a bit *too* innocent for you, Sir Vincent," another young woman said slyly, causing them all to erupt in good-natured laughter. She was a slender, willowy brunette with something of that classic Medini look— bronzed, hook-nosed, imposing—that seemed to accent the vaguely military costume she wore. She'd come dressed as one of Princess Nadeera's *Zhoka*, her squadron of personal household guards, with a stylized silver breastplate over a scarlet tunic and leggings. Her matching half-slung cape was lined with silvery-gray fabric, and she looked as if she might actually know what to do with the cavalry sword that hung across her back.

"Darling, this is Sir Constance Waverly-Exton of the earldom of Waterford, newly arrived from the south," Angelique said, interrupting to provide the necessary social lubricant. "Sir Constance, you escorted Sir Paul's mother and father north this season, did you not?"

"I did," the woman nodded, with a cautious half-bow in Vincent's direction. It was difficult to manage given the flux of bodies moving around them, either deserting the dance floor or seeking it out for the next set. "We came up through Valemont, Sir Vincent," she added, her chin coming up slightly. "Your father asked us to inquire of your progress in recovering the *Mâgun-Zak*."

Vincent's eyebrow came up. The first thing that crossed his mind was, *yeah, he wants to know if I've failed yet so he can say "told you so" to anyone who will hold still long enough.* But, what he actually said was "I'm sorry, Sir Constance, but for obvious reasons, information about the case is now classified, to use the military phrase. Oh, and my apologies for having to suffer Valemont, too," he added sardonically.

The older knight chuckled briefly, almost in spite of herself, but was interrupted before she could reply.

"Yes, yes, Valemont's a sewer, Vincent's better off here even if he is in a collar and we all know that." Sir Paul, Waterford's heir, brushed aside those lesser concerns with a healthy dose of the unself-conscious arrogance that tended to characterize most scions of his caste. "What *I* want to know is, what we all *really* want to know is this: Is it true you can fly?"

Everyone who'd heard turned to Vincent as one, hanging on his answer.

"It was how I finally managed to escape that sewer you mentioned," Vincent finally said, the sarcasm in it largely lost on its target.

"Only to find another, or so we hear, but yet now you're betrothed to a baroness of your own!" Georgiana could hardly bear to be far from the center of attention for long, though Angelique suspected this stemmed more from lack of intellectual stimulation than anything else. As Vincent had noted right away, Grafton's heir was too intelligent for her current station.

"Lady Angelique," Georgiana said with a winsome smile, "will you forswear Carlisle to rule Fernwall's sewers at Sir Vincent's side? Somehow, I don't think you've quite got the look," she mused, rather openly referring to the rumors going around about the women with whom Vincent had lately been spending his time. Her eyes glittered as she tapped the white rose he'd given her on her cheek, glancing among them for their reactions.

"For the love of the Lord, Georgie, your wit is as shallow as you are," Sir Paul said, heaving the words in a great, loud sigh. "Forgive her, Baroness, Sir Vincent. She's hardly ready to be out at public events, yet."

Georgiana struck back with a dazzling smile, a weapon mostly wasted on her male relations, from Paul's reaction—or lack of it. Angelique glanced between them in some bemusement, and she wasn't the only one. She sensed that Georgiana had meant her to feel uneasy and off-center by those

193

remarks, but she did not. Without Iris' constant scorn and Angel's doubts to hobble her, in fact, she found she was having a very good time among them. It occurred to her then that she was the ranking member in this impromptu little conversation, and as such, was *entitled* to put an end to it.

"Oh, your cousin and I are well-acquainted, Sir Paul," Angelique said. The orchestra was retuning itself for the next set, and more than anything just then, she wanted to dance. "I will only say, Georgiana, that it is a good thing for Vincent that I was not trained to regard such choices in absolute terms. Now, if you'll excuse us, gentles," she said, turning to her beloved with a steady, affectionate regard, "Vincent and I have a long-delayed date on that ballroom floor."

"Why my lady—I thought you'd never ask!" Beaming boyishly, he put Angelique's hand on his arm. Then, upon a moment's fiendish reflection, he paused and leveled his best rakehell look on Georgiana. "And for that 'sewer' remark, you owe me a dance." He winked at Sir Paul, who burst out laughing, followed by Constance and the rest.

Angelique couldn't wait long enough to see if Georgiana were satisfied or scandalized. She took him by the hand and threaded them through the milling dancers, and it was only her native agility and his quick-witted reactions that kept some of the more outlandish costumery from getting crumpled. She found an open spot at last by the north wall, where the three-meter tall portrait of the resplendently bedecked Princess Nadeera was displayed, then spun into his arms with a flourish of black silks.

"'Our first in much too long,' is what I believe you were saying as we entered," she said, dazzling him with a smile just as the strings struck up the introductory refrain, "and I am delighted that my first *public* act as your betrothed is to agree with you completely, my lord." The orchestra struck up the first refrain of the dance, cutting off whatever else he might have said in a thunder of noise from the music, swishing costumes, and shoes, all setting off at once.

It had, indeed been too long. Though he had a good memory, he found that time had dimmed his remembrance of the feel of her in his arms, gliding with him across a dance floor like satin flowed through his fingers. She was lithe and supple, yet her body was strong and flexible. She was the Iris, yes, but it was *more* than that. For the first time since learning of the many pieces that made up his beloved, he saw the whole *in* the pieces, rather than just the pieces themselves. This night was a showcase for Angelique in her element. The poise and grace she exhibited were all Angelique—but the precision in her movements, he now knew, came from Iris's absolute command over her body. The love in her eyes and the sunlight smile he now recognized as purely Angel, however. It was a symmetry he had not expected to find, but it made perfect sense to him, and it filled his heart to overflowing. "I do love you, you know," he said, holding her just a little closer.

It was the first time she'd heard the words from him in almost as long, and they pulled her into him as surely as his arms did. *"Mar'leven,"* she said, smiling up at him with her pet name for him on her lips, "I think you

194

truly must, for, you are here, in my arms. This is real, not a dream, however much it sometimes seems like one. And my heart is so full of you that I just want to *shout* it from the Watchman's Finial atop the Clocktower." Her smile deepened. "Could you fly me there?"

It made him chuckle for a moment as they floated across the floor. "I can think of a lot of places more fun to fly you than the top of the Clocktower," he replied suggestively. "Though the 'shouting' part is right on point, I should think."

Angelique laughed aloud at that, drawing bemused glances from the couples they passed. She didn't care. "And where would we go? Where does the Raven take his treasures to have his way with them, once he's stolen them away?"

Vincent looked scandalized. "My lady!" he gasped, eyes going wide. "Such a thing to suggest!" It drew more bemused glances from passing dancers. He held the pose for a dramatic moment, then let it drop. "It's a lot more comfortable at Blakesly House, Burning Bright, believe me," he said with a chuckle, and she burst into laughter once more.

"Oh, but not nearly as exciting," she said, managing it, at length, around her mirth. "I suppose I have had my share of excitement, and ought to crave safety and comfort rather than wild, airborne adventures with you." She glanced about them then, in particular at the men and women her age, with whom she'd been attending these balls for a few years, and recalled her dread at the prospect of having to go on attending them, for many years to come, without the keen wit and dancing grace of the dark-haired man in her arms.

They were the qualities that had initially attracted her to him. He didn't indulge in empty small talk, or try to impress her with his accomplishments, intellectual or physical. Vincent—Raven—had always spoken with her as if she were a person, with real thoughts and feelings. He *engaged* with her, right from the start.

"But, it seems like a terribly expensive and complicated way to wait around to die. I've always felt so very alive with you, Vincent."

He cast her a look so suggestive it drew more attention to them from nearby dancers. It was his "rakehell" look again, the one that had captured her attention a year and a spring ago. "Well," he breathed, "if you're going to be *that* way about it, I've always found a hay loft to be a particularly fun place for such things." Paul and Georgiana spun by them just as he said this, and the little gossip's head snapped around to stare at Vincent just as her cousin swept her away.

His suggestion invoked a cascade of fragmented memories in Angelique, however, from a long-ago time she never could quite recall. They were filled with the sting of the hot summer sun upon her skin, of the rich smell of grapes ripening in the heat, the flash of color in a dragonfly's wings, and the laughter of children in a hay-filled barn. They were Angel's memories, or pieces of them, like glimpses of a story written on tattered pages. It was a complicated feeling, but mostly a good one, and when she answered him at last, some of that Asburine summer heat sizzled in the cool, composed voice of the baroness of Carlisle.

"I confess, I *had* hoped for a ruined castle, or a deserted hill fortress, or something like that," she told him, eyebrows flickering under the tourmalines in the headband she wore, "but I swear, I would rather be with you in a hayloft than in any castle, ruined or otherwise, without you."

"Oh, we'll be busy when we get to Carlisle, then." Predatory smile flickering, Vincent dared to kiss her, right there on the dance floor, in front of anybody who thought they were somebody in the city-state. It was a brief kiss, hardly improper for a betrothed couple, but his heart was in it, and in every beat was the promise of summer after summer spent upon their own land, with their own people, in their own hayloft—or ruined castle, if it came to that.

It barely slowed their dance, and even then, they moved together into a series of long, gliding turns that swirled the ends of her black and silver sash around him. "Such kisses make it quite likely I'll be keeping you busy long before that," she said, breathing the words into his ear.

"In the embrace of such beauty, how could I *possibly* resist," he said, turning his head to brush his lips against her ear, then planting a tender kiss upon the silken-soft skin of her neck. Angelique shivered delightfully in his arms, murmuring that it might be best not to try, though the words were offered in so low a voice that he couldn't be certain. It hardly seemed to matter. They were in a crowded ballroom, dancing under twinkling magic lights in a chandelier above them to the slow, sweet strains of an old waltz. If they hadn't yet convinced all of their peers of the wisdom of their match, the radiant joy on her face as she looked up into his said all that needed to be said about her feelings on the matter.

Across the ballroom, Louis leaned against one of the huge pillars that held up the ornately painted ceiling, a gin and tonic in hand, his impeccably polished shoes gleaming, every strand of his perfectly coiffed hair creamed into place, his freshly pressed slacks and tail coat perfectly arranged, watching his property—yes *his* property—entertain another. It was disgusting. It was disloyal! Had he not saved her life? Had he not taught her everything she knew, *including* this very dance? Had he not educated her, protected her, fed her from his own meager means when they both were both grateful for every morsel of food, no matter how sickening?

And there! Look now! Look how she gazes, so wide-eyed, beguiling that young fool with kisses, fawning over him... she used to kiss me like that, not so many years ago. He could almost hear what she was saying, and how she said it. He knew all her pet names, all her favorite turns of phrase by heart. He had heard them a thousand times. She had been his, then, and glad to be so. Now, there was *him*. There was the Raven, a convicted thief who had now stolen her right from under his nose, all the while pretending they were estranged.

He was *quite* sure, now that he was seeing them together, that the quarrel had all been a ruse, and it had worked so well that the arrival of the blue jackets that morning had been a complete shock. He had Raven to thank for that, and for the money the police had stolen from his bank accounts, *and* for the argument with Thackery that he'd had to spend the rest of the day papering over. No easy task, with Fernwall's finest watching every move on both their parts. Well... It would not do. The whole plan was now in jeopardy because the foolish girl believed herself to be *in love.* No, it simply would not do!

Louis drained his glass in one swallow, then headed to the lobby to look up another. He had some emergency thinking to do.

Angelique had lost almost all track of everyone else present at the Old Palace Hotel that night, along with most of the mistakes of her past and even the vague sense of unease that seemed always to have hovered at the edges of her awareness. There in Vincent's arms, held so tenderly and dearly in his regard, it all felt so *right* that she wanted it to go on forever.

In a world with time, however, nothing could. Vincent pulled her close as the dance ended, kissing her once more as the room burst out in applause for the beauty they'd just shared among them, and they were still kissing when a rueful, apologetic woman's voice interrupted them.

"Your pardon, young gentles." It was Lady Rebecca, and she was dressed much as Angelique, in loose silken trousers, but Rebecca's was topped with a long, flowing tunic in shades of muted emerald and pink. She exited the floor on the arm of an elderly man who, like Vincent, was in traditional formal wear for the occasion. He was also quite bald, but beamed at the two of them as if they'd just invented kissing.

"Lady Angelique, Sir Vincent, may I present my brother-in-law, Lord Fallney of Three Oaks, in the barony of Malvern," Rebecca said, and they all bowed and curtsied to one another, as Paladins did.

"Delighted, delighted," Fallney said happily. His cheeks were bright pink, likely more from the good thesker he'd consumed that night than from the exertion. Angelique returned a happy nod, but Rebecca spoke up before Vincent could reply

"My dear," she said, speaking directly to Angelique then, "Lady Emilia asked me to send you and Sir Vincent to her in the great library as soon as I found you."

"*And* Sir Vincent?" Vincent murmured, turning his arched eyebrow on Rebecca. "Oh!" Realization dawned and he turned to Angelique. "You sent the Countess a note earlier, didn't you?"

"And Clarice followed it with one excusing my absence on grounds of illness," Angelique replied with a little laugh, pulling her eyes clear of his only reluctantly, then turning to Rebecca and her dance partner with a bit of that "love light" lingering in her expression. "Of course, we should see her at once. Thank you, Rebecca. Lord Fallney, how lovely to meet you. Will you excuse us?"

"What? Oh, of course!" He'd just reached over to pluck a crystal goblet from a passing server with a tray full of them. "Sister, you see to these fine young people. I'm off to find old Colonel Rivers, if he's still alive. I'll come see you at Remington before I leave town." He bent over to place an affectionate kiss on Rebecca's cheek, then with only a tiny list to starboard wandered off in search of his friends.

Rebecca watched him depart with some bemusement. He passed another crowd of young persons gathering nearby, with Georgiana Dawes once again conspicuously in the center, and most of them seemed intent on once more ambushing Vincent and Angelique into their company as the subjects of some of the hottest gossip at the party.

"If you would walk with me," Rebecca suggested then, gesturing toward a vaulted arch beneath which was an impressive set of oaken double doors, left open so that air and revelers could pass freely through the antechamber. The room just beyond was perhaps half as big as the ballroom, and also had a high, vaulted ceiling. One wall was paned glass entirely, and through it a view of magical crystal lights in trees and lit garden paths that eventually led down to the river. Two of the other walls were lined with heavy cedar shelves, laden with leather-bound books. It was one of the finest private collections of printed works in Cascadia, and was freely available for the use of the hotel's paying guests.

Upon the fourth wall was the massive hearth, its huge, air-blasted fire glowing like a miniature sun. Not far from it sat Remington's countess, flanked by some of her peers. Angelique's fingers tightened on Vincent's arm almost at once, for among others standing nearby was Valemont's liege lord, in the person of Duke Henry of Trobiere, and none other than Police Commissioner Hal Roland, himself.

"Well now," Vincent quipped into Angelique's ear as they approached. "Goodman Roland is turning in high and mighty company, tonight." As though he'd heard his name mentioned, Roland saw them approach, and looked almost relieved.

"Finally! I was beginning to think you'd find a reason not to show."

"So *that's* where all the gray hair comes from," Vincent shot back with a fond smile. "I was wondering. Your graces, and gentles all," he bowed to the assembled peers, stepping aside as he did so to allow Angelique to greet them. She nodded to them all and curtsied briefly to Duke Henry, who had half-scowled at sight of the pair of them, but straightened up immediately to take Angelique's hand, and bowed over it, in turn.

"My dear, I did hope you'd come to your better senses about this betrothal," he began, but was adroitly interrupted.

"She most certainly has, and is here tonight with her intended," Lady Emilia said, her sightless eyes turning unerringly toward the place where the two of them stood. "Well done, my dear daughter. Well done, indeed."

"Thank you, my lady," Angelique said, first casting a brief, but completely unrepentant look upon the old duke. "My lord of Trobiere, I have made many mistakes in my life, enough surely to know it when I have committed another." She turned her eyes back up to Vincent's face then, and happiness softened hers once more. "He is not one of them. That, I know."

"Any man would give up a great deal for a woman who would look at

198

him like that," a younger, slenderer man said then. He was dressed in a Nadrean sailor's costume, though no sailor could have afforded materials so fine. "Including you, Henry."

"Lady Angelique, this is Lord Admiral Jameson Calveers, IMMC northern fleet command," Duke Henry said, grudgingly performing the introduction. "Lady Blakesly is the baroness of Carlisle, and if you'd had the gods-granted good sense to show up here last summer, like I said you should, perhaps you could have convinced her to make a better marriage with you instead of this criminal."

There was an awkward beat, and Angelique drew breath to retort, but Emilia beat her to it. "Henry, you're clearly up past your bedtime, for your rudeness is beyond tolerance. Admiral Calveers, Sir Vincent Sultaire, youngest son of Valemont, is here tonight with Lady Angelique."

"I am delighted to meet anyone who can sour old Henry's mood before even a word's been said," the admiral said then, casting a wicked little smile at the older man. "He's a cousin, you know. Twice removed, on my mother's side."

"Your father's."

"Perhaps it was both. That would explain a great deal, actually," he said, laughing with the rest of them at the adroitly turned jest.

"I am pleased to make your acquaintance, Admiral," Vincent managed to say at last, extending his hand. "I wouldn't take Duke Harry's tone too seriously. My father has that affect on almost everybody, and the old boy clearly spent too much time as his playmate in his youth." The admiral chuckled, then chuckled even harder as he saw Craigmont wind up for a retort.

"Commissioner!" Vincent spun on Hal Roland, neatly cutting off the beginning of a tirade, "I don't believe you've had the pleasure." He held Angelique at arm's length, as though putting her on display. "Lady Angelique Blakesly, Baroness of Carlisle."

Some of the shine she'd carried with her since their entrance faded at the introduction, and she drew herself up with a single breath to face down one of the three men in the city-state who knew she'd stolen the *Mâgun-Zak*. "Commissioner Roland," she said quietly, extending her hand with her chin held high. They both knew he could arrest her that very moment for the crime, and from the carefully neutral look on the Top Cop's face as he took her hand, Angelique suspected he was privately considering it.

"Baroness. I can honestly say I've been looking forward to this all night." He bowed over her hand politely, then released it and stepped back. "*Chief Inspector,*" he said then, speaking the only title the younger man had a right to use in this setting. "You've been busy."

"As commanded, Commissioner," Vincent bowed to the non-nobleman who was his nominal owner, then turned to Lady Emilia. "My dear Countess," he said gently, kneeling to take one of her knotted old hands in his. "I have been saving this for you." Another rose appeared in his hand. It was red and glistened and sparkled as though it had been kissed by the morning dew, and the fragrance that wafted from it was rich and thick and sweet. It had been fashioned from the finest velvet, and he caressed the old woman's hand with it before leaving it there. "With many apologies, and much gratitude."

She smiled at this, and drew the precious thing up to her nose to sniff lightly at it. "Not as fresh, perhaps, as the ones you handed out so freely this summer past, but just as gallant. Thank you, Vincent. Your return to us cannot come too soon."

Duke Henry cleared his throat irritably. "Yes, well, that comes *after* he's served his time, and in the meantime, we've got a huge, royal-sized problem inbound on the next clipper ship from Püran-Khir. Prince Athos Mirac, the Lord's own Champion, is coming here to demand to know why the nobility and their legally deputized law-enforcement wing cannot recover what has been stolen, nor are able to arrest the thief who stole it."

"What?" Angelique's shock showed on her face, and she saw that Roland noted it before she could recover. Fortunately, Admiral Calveers took the opportunity to excuse himself from the political turn in the conversation, and immediately joined a mixed group who were moving toward the ballroom.

Vincent, meanwhile, blinked in surprise. "The politics are heating up, then." He kissed Lady Emilia's hand and stood up, putting Angelique's hand back on his arm. "But *not* a discussion for this party, I'm rather sure, Your Grace. Would you not agree, Commissioner?"

"I would not agree, Chief Inspector." Roland turned his stony gaze from Vincent to Angelique. "My apologies, Baroness. Events are moving quickly. Your... betrothed and I need to talk."

"Beyond time you've taken a sterner tack with him, Roland," Trobiere said, casting a withering look in Vincent's direction. "The LEC won't tolerate such laxity much longer, and young Sultaire's station can't go on excusing his incompetence before a prince of the Medini."

Confusion ensued as everyone involved tried to be heard at once, including a hotly incensed Angelique, but it was Lady Emilia who put an end to it. "That will be quite enough. My lord of Trobiere, we'll speak again before the committee meeting tomorrow. I'll have a word or three to put in your ear, then. For now, I hope you will excuse us. I should like to speak with Vincent and Angelique privately."

It was practically unheard-of for a countess to dismiss a royal duke in this manner, but Lady Emilia's moral and social authority remained as absolute as the Imprimae's. Trobiere huffed once and puffed up his chest indignantly.

"All right, but be there all the earlier," he told her, taking up her hand to kiss it, "because we've got much to settle before Prince Athos arrives and starts waving around that sword of his. And don't be out too much later," he added, half-whispering it so as not to be caught out in his sentimentalism. "You're not as young as you used to be, either."

"I'll be on my way up to my rooms within the hour," Emilia promised him, pulling him down to kiss his grizzled cheek. "Good night, Henry."

With a half-bow to Angelique, the duke withdrew. He nodded politely to

Lady Rebecca, who was just returning to their gathering. She dropped a half-curtsy to him out of respect, but smiled at the four who remained, and placed a hand upon her lady's shoulder.

"The Sunset Room is ready for you now, gentles."

The Sunset Room was about the size of Lady Emilia's drawing room at Remington Hall, and was decorated in the warm colors of the setting sun. The wood paneling was a light tan, and the curtains and draperies were all various shades of gold, turquoise, and rose. There were three hearths, one along each inner wall, and all were ablaze. Finely rendered paintings of the sunset—in Shanakara, and in Glorédil, from the top of Par-Isen in the holy land, and several other scenes Angelique did not recognize on sight— were displayed on the walls around them. Large, finely upholstered chairs and low tables were arranged around each hearth in ways that encouraged conversation. The only thing missing, Vincent noticed, were the people. At a party of this size, there should have been many people in this room and there were not. Such was the power of a request by the lady of Remington.

As the five entered the room, Vincent offered to put Lady Emilia on his arm while Rebecca closed the door behind them. She also locked it, he noticed, before leading them over to one of the hearths, and settling her mistress in the principle seat, near the fire. Angelique followed, and so did Roland, though she could not risk looking at him. Iris was wide awake and growling threats that made her hair want to stand on end each time the old cop came within view. Angel was attempting to shush her, and the inevitable result planted the seed of a headache just behind her brows. She gratefully snatched up a tall, fluted glass of sparkling golden wine from the tray when Rebecca offered it and took a generous swallow.

Vincent turned to her then and offered to hand her into her seat on the divan, bending over her with a mildly inquiring look. Angelique shook her head once, slightly. There was no opportunity to explain. Instead, she urged him to sit next to her and scooted a little closer to him when he did.

"I had wanted to tell you about all this privately, but Henry Craigmont couldn't define 'patience' with a tutor and three friends to help." Emilia sighed then and accepted the glass that her maid pressed into her hand with a briefly murmured, "Thank you, dear," before turning back to the subject at hand.

"It is true that Prince Athos' ship is due to make port here in about two weeks, weather permitting. There is a thin layer of the usual politics in this visit, but it is *very* thin, indeed. King Cashëmin is standing with the Santí family quite publicly in demanding the return of the *Mâgun-Zak*. I suspect that Prince Athos brings a series of escalating ultimatums from his royal brother. Do not doubt that he will take a hand in the investigation personally, if he is prompted to do so."

Roland frowned. "Prompted by whom, my lady? The king of Vin-Nôrë has no authority to order anything, here."

"Not by the king," Emilia said, sipping daintily from her glass. "By that sword."

Vincent saw Angelique's face blanch. The stories the Medini people told about "the Champion's Sword" were legion, and there were almost as many about the martial exploits of its current wielder. None of them boded well for wrong-doers. He squeezed her hand comfortingly but spoke to Lady Emilia. "Pardon me, Countess, but beyond the obvious political embarrassment— which is surely more ours to suffer than theirs—just exactly *why* is the loss of the *Mâgun-Zak* so important that the only man capable of dismantling Cascadia was dispatched to retrieve it? Beyond being pretty to look at, it's supposedly useless."

"It is, to humankind. Or, it is said to be." Emilia held out her glass, and Rebecca took it from her wordlessly, placing it on the low table nearby. "This is not widely known. In fact, I had to solicit the information directly from the documents vaults in Par-Isen. The internal structure of the *Mâgun-Zak* was created by the dwarves before there was even a place for humans to stand on this world. Where we regard the outer form they've given it as a pretty thing, they used it as a tool, of sorts. They've no need of it now, of course, so as a sign of the close relationship between them and the Vin-Nôrëans, it was loaned to the Santí family—arguably the second-most powerful family in the kingdom, after the Mirac themselves—and they are accountable for it, when the dwarves ask for it to be returned. I do not know if you've ever seen a dwarf, Vincent, but once you do, you'll know right away that you don't want them to get angry."

"I'll keep that in mind," he drawled, "the next time I find one in a bar. So," he sighed, moving on, "if it's useless to humans, and it can't be sold, then pray what does Louis Arnot want with the darned thing? Because I can draw a pretty straight line of causality between the movements of the *Zak* and the movements and activities of Arnot, but I can't put my finger on what is important enough about it to take the kinds of risks he's taking."

Emilia and Roland turned, as one, to look at Angelique. "Well?" Roland finally said, addressing her directly for the first time since their greeting. "He was your solicitor, wasn't he? You came here with him, you were part of his plans. Have you chosen your side yet, Baroness? Or should we call you 'Iris' when we're all here alone?"

Lady Emilia drew breath again to speak, but Angelique lifted her chin to speak first, and in full voice, flaunting her D'wanese-accented Cascr in the man's face. "For better or worse, Commissioner, I *am* the baroness of Carlisle. Whatever happens to me now will happen to Carlisle, so it is best that you continue to address me so."

Roland laughed, but there was no mirth in it. "Oh, that's funny, *Baroness.* Give me one good reason why I shouldn't arrest you here and now? With your testimony, and Vincent's, given under a Seer's supervision? The results ought to be enough to get Trobiere and his ilk off my back, at least."

Give me a fucking knife and I'll get this over with for you.

Shut up, Iris! You cain't fight your way out of everythin'!

You don't know that.

"Because if you do," Angelique shot back, glad for an excuse to raise her voice a little so she could hear it over the argument in her head, "you will never get the man who knows what has happened to the *Mâgun-Zak*, or what his plans are for it."

"Are you telling us that you know?"

She deflated a bit and glanced away. "I wish I did, but I do not."

Before Roland could jump on that, Emilia smoothly inserted herself back into the conversation. "Commissioner Roland, I understand and sympathize with your frustration, but the baroness of Carlisle is not the proper recipient for it. If you did arrest her tonight, I would be required to *un*-arrest her almost right away. We need her."

"You'd gut all respect for our laws if you did that," Roland retorted, and Vincent saw the tell-tale vein throbbing under the skin of the man's forehead, a sure sign he was growing agitated.

"Perhaps, but it is my task to look beyond the law, to the society those laws are meant to serve." She'd withdrawn a lovely set of amber prayer beads from her bag, and passed them through her fingers for comfort as she spoke. "I realize you set little store upon the visions that have guided me—"

"My lady, I meant no disrespect—"

Emilia waved his interruption away. "I know, dear goodman, and it matters little, in any event. What is important to know is that I have *seen* the *Mâgun-Zak* in a context that has helped me to understand the role it plays in all this, and that Angelique Blakesly's role—or roles, I should say, for she plays several—are critical to its recovery and return."

The younger woman's eyes widened, and she leaned toward her oldest friend with wonder and dismay fighting it out for supremacy in her heart. "My lady, what did you *see*?"

The older woman's mouth creased once, briefly. It would have been a smile, had there been any mirth in it. "The specifics also matter little, Angelique, though after this is over, if you wish to know, and ask me, I will tell you," Emilia said, not ungently. "What is important for you to understand now is that you and the *Mâgun-Zak* are linked together in ways I do not understand, and that are not easily explained. Some sort of 'affinity' or perhaps 'sympathy' has been created between you and that artifact, for purposes that remain equally mysterious. It seems reasonable to assume that, at some point, Goodman Arnot discovered this affinity, for lack of a better term, or perhaps he somehow caused it—whatever the case, it might explain why you were the one who had to retrieve it, and why he continues to pursue you now, in the aftermath, rather than attempt to recruit anyone else to assist him in his plans for it."

Vincent's eyebrow had gotten cozier with his hairline as the old woman talked. "That explains a lot," he muttered.

Angelique sat next to him with her mouth open. It was Iris' crude prodding from within that caused it to snap closed, but she glanced among the three of them, having difficulty crediting what she'd just heard. But with Iris' presence so close, the vagueness that had characterized her memories of the theft dropped away, and she had begun to recall with great clarity details about that night that she'd forgotten she knew: the feel of the magitech crystals in her hands, and how they had reacted as she lowered them to counteract the magical wards...

"But I sensed nothing from it," she said at last, catching Vincent's eyes with a pleading look. "From the *Mâgun-Zak,* I mean to say. The crystals, yes—though I am not mageborn, Louis checked—but nothing from the artifact, itself. Should I not have sensed it, were I... somehow...?"

Lady Emilia shook her head slightly. "I do not know what should or should not have happened, my dear. I only know what I saw. I postulate that, if I am correct, this affinity makes you uniquely qualified to retrieve the *Mâgun-Zak,* and I do not regard it as mere coincidence that you and Vincent had to reconcile before that vision was granted me."

"Wait, what?" Vincent blurted. "Me?" His father's brand of Paladinism followed the highly conservative "Moro doctrine," and he made sure that the priests appointed to the baronial churches were members of the sect. Like Lady Emilia, they too believed they had visions. Most of theirs, however, were little more than laughably predictable confirmations of their own limited ideologies. Lady Emilia, on the other hand, was widely respected as a living legend. To most Cascadians, she was both queen and high priestess in all but title. To hear his name mentioned in the context of one of *her* visions was not exactly comforting.

"Indeed," Emilia said, a fond smile deepening the lines in her cheeks, "it has been extraordinary to receive such visions about individual persons at all."

"Countess, I confess, you've lost me," Roland said, unable to hold his peace any longer. "Are we talking Paladin church doctrine here, or trying to figure out how we're going to catch a criminal?"

They looked at him as one, but as Lady Emilia had been addressed, it was her privilege to reply. "They are not unrelated, Commissioner," she said evenly, her beads clattering pleasantly in her hands as she resumed caressing them. "I must remind you that Sir Vincent is more than just a chief inspector indentured to your command. He is a noble of this land, a Guardian Paladin, and it will be his part, one day, to understand how church doctrine influences society and its laws, and how it enforces those laws. Indeed, his term of indenture has given him an understanding of the law unique among his peers. He is, in his own way, as critical to the recovery of the *Mâgun-Zak* as Angelique is."

Vincent nearly choked. "You're probably the only one in the entire city state who believes that," he drawled. Just beyond the closed doors were hundreds of people who would have vociferously challenged Lady Emilia's assertion. Were Roland able to speak freely, he was fairly sure the old cop would as well.

"One of two," Angelique corrected him at once, waiting for him to recover his composure before she continued. "But, it was you who made a believer of me."

"Right," Vincent exhaled forcefully. "The point is, most people in this town think I should be pulled from the case entirely." He looked directly at Roland. "I imagine you do, too, though you're too polite to say so, and I can't really blame you."

The older man snorted. "I don't second-guess myself that easily. With Lady Emilia's forebearance, and all the mystic visionary stuff aside, what I'm hearing here is that you, Baroness, have a dossier of evidence stashed somewhere, and that should be enough to serve some warrants on Arnot, and get him into custody. That will be enough to stop Duke Henry and his boot-licking sycophants from getting *me* 'pulled from the case entirely' while we sort out what charges to file first."

"Louis might then use the location of the *Mâgun-Zak* to bargain his way out of heavy sentence," Angelique said, her words slow as she thought her way through it. "He will also accuse me of being the one who committed the theft, and expose the truth of my birth."

Emilia chuckled grimly. "For all the good that will do him."

"Did you expect to run riot over everyone and everything you professed to hold dear and still escape unscathed, Baroness?" Roland's life had been spent in the service, first to the military, then to the law. That she could sit there before him and speak about her possible exposure as if she didn't deserve it was not something he could ever have taken lightly. "Maybe you ought to consider whether the rest of your peers deserve to know the truth about you, and what you've done."

"I doubt any of us want the whole and complete truth about ourselves and our pasts laid bare for the world's censure," Emilia said, seeming as if she were merely temporizing, as amber beads dropped through her fingers, one by one. "Angelique *is* the demonstrable heir to Carlisle, and it is time you—all of you—ceased rehashing it. None of us can afford to be slowed by the mistakes of our pasts, just now."

Silence reigned for several long minutes after that, broken only by the muted sounds of the all but forgotten ball going on beyond the doors of the Sunset Room. "Speaking of the past," Vincent finally said. "Arnot is also the syndicate's favorite problem solver and intermediary. We're not likely to have a better chance at cleaning up the old war time corruption schemes than by milking it out of their favorite solicitor."

Roland nodded and so did Emilia. She leaned toward the older man slightly. "Your chief inspector is a future baron, and it shows."

"Why do you think I want Arnot in custody so badly?" Roland chuckled. "He's been implicated in more filth than you'll find in the sewers and none of it has ever stuck."

"And he's made damned sure none of it sticks to his clients, either," Vincent snorted. "Including Baron Van Trapp."

"Get me the evidence. The crown prosecutor's office will sort it from there." Roland stood up then, and brushed down the front of his dress uniform jacket. "And get it *fast*. I don't know why he thought he could hire a mercenary outfit to conduct operations in the city without obtaining clearance from the LEC, but it tells me that he's getting worried. Don't wait for him to get desperate."

"You'll have it in the morning," Vincent assured him. "And then there's this." He dipped a hand into his waist coat pocket and pulled out the paper on which Cole had drawn the likeness of the unknown mercenary badge. "Some of the trap war tension is being caused by armed barges coming into town from upriver. The soldiers don't wear anything that identifies them. At least not publicly, but Cole caught sight of a badge and drew this." He handed the paper to Roland, who glanced it over once, then tucked it into his pocket.

"I'll have copies in every blue jacket's hands before the morning shift starts. If it's another way to vector in on Arnot, I'll send a runner by your flat with the details. If there's nothing else," he said then, half-bowing to the ladies present, "the morning's coming early, and I should be going."

Lady Emilia started to speak, but Vincent cut in first. "Not my flat, boss," he said to Roland. "Blakesly House. It's easier to secure against Arnot. My flat is now officially just a blind."

"All right for tomorrow, but don't get too far ahead of yourself, there. I'm not sure the terms of your sentence permit permanent residency out of Merchants'."

Rebecca returned to Emilia's side in time to assist her out of her chair. "The Llamázi ambassador is departing the ball, my lady, and wishes to speak with you before he leaves."

"Very well, dear. The terms of Vincent's indenture can be cleared up later, surely. If you'd keep me apprised of the progress, Commissioner, I will do my best to keep Trobiere's duke from pushing you onto the point of your own sword before we can get the matter resolved to our satisfaction. And you two," Emilia said, turning to Vincent and Angelique with a knowing smile, "go enjoy yourselves. You've earned it, even if it *does* stretch the terms of your indenture."

Vincent smiled at the old lady, and it seemed that, despite her blindness, she saw it. "Thank you, my lady." He stood up then and handed Angelique out of her seat. "I think we shall. The last few days have been horrid."

"Most of the last four months have been horrid," Angelique said, squeezing his arm slightly. She leaned toward Lady Emilia, and kissed her cheek tenderly. "I do not know what I should have done without you and your wise counsel, my lady. Thank you."

"Of course, my dear girl. Age should bring wisdom, should it not? Good night, children. Commissioner Roland, always a pleasure."

"Good night, Countess. Chief Inspector, I'd like a brief word, before you and the baroness rejoin the party," Roland said to Vincent.

"Of course," Vincent murmured. He took Angelique's hand and kissed the back of it. "I'll be with you in a moment," he promised. Her answering smile was a cautious one, but she nodded, and with a single glance at the older, larger man, trailed Emilia and Rebecca out of the room.

Vincent turned to Roland expectantly. He waited until the women had cleared the door before he spoke. "That dossier of evidence—it's not going to be easy to sell the Urilian justices on it as evidence of *ongoing* illegal activities. You know that, right?"

Vincent's brow furrowed. "As I understand it, the file is a meticulous record of how Arnot manipulated the Van Trapp evidence," he said thoughtfully. "Which means, the judges were gulled. Might that not make them a bit more amenable to such suggestions?"

Roland's craggy eyebrows twitched once. "Is it, now. Should make compelling reading then. Do you know how you're going to take him down?"

Vincent sighed and shook his head. "No, not really," he admitted. "I remember from the Van Trapp trial that he was always over-done, when he appeared in court. Not a hair out of place, not a crease in his suit. He's obsessive. The files only exist because he has to compulsively record everything, Angelique tells me. Also, that the man hates to improvise. Like his appearance, he prefers everything to be neat and tidy. So, making his world a whole lot *less* neat and tidy seemed a logical first step. But beyond that..." he shrugged.

"Hunh." The sound was more an acknowledgment of what Vincent had said than anything else, and Roland turned it over in his head for a moment before he spoke again.

"Men like that... you can't outplay 'em, Vince. Arnot is a controller, the kind of man who's had to stay three moves ahead of everyone else for all his life. He's already run all the moves and possible countermoves to this scheme of his dozens of times over. You can't beat him by trying to outplay him. He'll exhaust your resources before you can locate half of his. The best you can do is try to make him out-play himself."

It was Vincent's turn to be thoughtful. What Roland said made a great deal of sense. Louis had taken years to plan not only for the theft of the *Zak,* but what he intended to do with it as well, and if he included Lady Emilia's cryptic comment about Angelique having some connection to the artifact, he could throw his attempts to control her into the mix as well. Clearly, whatever his plans were, they went beyond merely stealing the thing. Otherwise, she'd be dead.

"So rather than pushing Arnot off-script," he said finally, still thinking, "we need to force him to write another one that plays against the first." He looked at Roland for confirmation.

The older man shrugged. "Or just try to force him to play his game harder and faster than he expected. If he runs out of his scripted moves first, he loses."

Vincent nodded, still thinking, then he chucked the older man on the shoulder. "Thanks, Boss. I'll see you in the morning."

"First thing. Sounds like I'll have some new reading to enjoy." With an answering pat on Vincent's arm, they turned to rejoin the party.

Louis watched in growing irritation as Angelique and Vincent had made their way from the ballroom to join the accursed Countess of Remington. She, of course, was already in the company of the chief of police and the irrepressible old Duke of Trobiere. Louis had hoped to lure her away from Raven when, he assumed, the besotted youth would fetch his woman something to refresh her after their dance.

He was wrong. Then, to make matters worse, Cascadia's uncrowned queen had dismissed her coterie and vanished behind guarded doors with the two of them and the commissioner, and he *knew* what the main subject of the discussion had to be. Yesterday, he thought he had managed to work things back into his favor. He was nearly back on schedule. Almost all the supplies had been delivered, construction had started, nobody had noticed, and he had every confidence Thackery's SAS troops were the equal of one slender woman, no matter how well-trained she was.

Then the Raven crawled out of his damned ale barrel and stole her right out from under Thackery's nose. Now the House of Lords was involved, Vin-Nôrë's overbred "champion" was on his way, and it appeared that Raven was worming his way back into the nobility's favor! In less than twenty-four hours, the situation had spun out of his control.

Well... it would not do! It had to stop. It had to *be* stopped!

Angelique and Lady Emilia had paused just beyond the Sunset Room's doors. Remington, as a greater earldom, maintained standing rooms at the Old Palace Hotel, and its countess intended to avail herself of them rather than make the long drive back to Remington Hall that night. Angelique requested, and was granted, permission to use one of her spare rooms to change clothing, when it was time for Vincent to become the Raven, and for Iris to take control in order for them to retrieve the dead man's trigger dossier.

"It's more discreet than trying to find an unused powder room here, tonight," Emilia smiled. "Have Clarice send your trunk up to my suite at your leisure, my dear."

Rebecca had one last tidbit to share, however, before they departed.

"Sir Eric was looking for you earlier, my lady. He did ask, if I should see you, that I pass along his request for a moment of your time."

The wine hadn't quite blotted out the ongoing, internal diatribe from Iris, which had moved on from Roland's high-handedness with Raven to the giddily partying society members who lingered late over drinks. By tradition, the orchestra would continue to play until dawn, or as long as there were dancers on the floor. There were still a fair few, but Angelique did not see Eric's tall, fair-haired form among them.

"Thank you for the kindness, Rebecca. I shall make a point of finding him ere Vincent and I leave."

With a nod, the older woman took her mistress by the elbow and, with gentle deference, led her toward the lobby. Angelique was just attempting to decide whether she had time to locate Eric when she saw Clarice accompanying him toward her, a serving tray in her hands.

Those two women collude a lot more than I'm comfortable with, Iris decided. Angelique promptly took up another glass of wine, but waited politely until Eric had greeted her before downing half of it.

"Lady Angelique," Eric bowed, taking her free hand and bowing over it in some concern. "Are you unwell? I had not thought—"

"It's just a headache, Sir Eric. It will pass."

"You should eat something, my lady. Dr. Lagrange was most insistent." Clarice's tray held a platter of the foods she knew her mistress liked most, and held them up suggestively as she spoke.

"Bring them later, my girl. I should like to speak with Sir Eric before Vincent has finished his discussion with Commissioner Roland. In the meantime, would you have the trunk that accompanied us this evening sent up to Reminton's suite?"

Clarice couldn't help glancing up at Eric's face once, but she nodded, curtsied once, and withdrew. Eric was very good at keeping his countenance pleasantly neutral, but he'd caught the reference to his rival, and it had told him what he'd most wanted to know.

"You and Sir Vincent are reconciled, then." It wasn't a question, but he did seem to expect a response. Angelique's heart suddenly ached for him. Grateful for the momentary silence within her, she touched his elbow once and then led him to one of the nearby archways, wherein seats were arranged in conversational nooks. Many of them were in complete disarray after hours of use, but Eric proved proficient at locating two seats with relative ease, and pulled his closer after seating her.

The trouble was that there suddenly didn't seem much left to be said. Angelique gazed at his handsome face with a too-familiar sense of helplessness. For all her supposed social competence, moments like these still left her feeling off-balance and unsettled, but the last thing she wanted to do was hurt Eric over it.

"May I make a confession, Sir Eric?"

He blinked once, startled at the unusual request. "Of course, my lady. What is it?"

"I envy you." Surprised again, he drew back slightly, but she nodded and pressed on before he could interrupt. "No, I do. I envy your... ease, though I am not certain of the word. Your, ah, *facility*? Your easy way with the right words, and how you instinctively know how to respond to your peers. It is... a comfort, or a certainty perhaps, that I shall never have, among the Guardian Paladins of Fernwall. I do not know if you realize how competent you are at all this," she said, gesturing toward the kaleidoscopic display of color passing by on the dance floor. "To someone like me, who is permanently a foreigner in your midst, it seems almost magical."

He shook his head, and huffed mirthless laughter. "Ah, no, you overrate me entirely, Lady Angelique. If that were true, I should have spoken to you two years ago, when I recognized my feelings toward you, and I might still have had a chance to win your heart."

His directness arrested her momentarily, and Angelique found herself caught in his earnest, penetrating gaze, unable to look away. What he read in her face caused him to remember himself, however, and he spoke again before she could.

"I am sorry, my lady. Sorry I didn't speak up then, yes, but also sorry to have said as much now. There, you see? Abate your envy. I am not as socially facile as you would have me be, and I've made a mess of this entirely."

"Don't be silly, of course you've not," Angelique insisted, leaning toward him to press her point. "You *belong* here. This is your world, you were born to it, don't you see?" She turned again to look at the dancers swirling by, and the small clusters of costumed party-goers who laughed as they conversed. "You function here because it is in your blood, and because you were brought up to it. You understand nuances that I don't. I will never have the instinctive facility that you do, even should I spend every waking moment of the rest of my life here."

"My lady, you are a baroness, and of a very old family. This is your world as much as it is mine."

She was already shaking her head before he finished. "Not so, Sir Eric. The world into which I was born and raised was not this one. It has its own nuances, its little secrets and in-jokes, its shared history and hope for the future. Similar to this, in some ways? Yes—but it is not the same."

Oh, nicely skirted, Baroness.

Leave her be, Iris. She's on t' somethin', here.

"You deserve someone who shares that fluency with you," Angelique pressed, with a quiet passion and determination in her voice that was uncharacteristic for her. "Someone who can function in this world, like you do, with you. That will never be me, I am afraid." She leaned back then, and in the periphery of her vision caught sight of Vincent, searching for her. "I hope you will one day forgive me for it, but it seems I needed another outsider to help me find my place here. I am *sorry*, from the center of my soul, that I could not find the words to tell you this, sooner."

He looked at her then, and glanced at Vincent's approach. "Tell me you're happy," he said, capturing her eyes again with his. "If you can tell me that, and make me believe it, I'll be content."

"I am." She knew she hardly needed to say it, for she could feel it pressing up and out of her like a fount. There were still many difficulties, obstacles, and dangers to be faced, but from the fractured core of her, she could never ever remember feeling so much joy. "I love him, Eric. And I am so very, very happy."

His jaw worked, but then Vincent was there, and the chance to say whatever he might have wanted to say was gone. "Sir Vincent, Lady Angelique has just told me her happy news," he said, bowing formally from the waist. "I should like to offer my congratulations to you both."

The conversation with Roland was still chasing around in his head when he approached, and it took a second for him to grasp the underlying meaning in what Sir Eric had just said. From everything Vincent knew about him, Eric was the very model of a perfect Paladin. He deserved a proper Paladin wife, and the disappointment he was working so hard to keep out of his stoic expression said louder than words that he believed Angelique was that woman. That he didn't and couldn't know the other stormy facets of her personality added a poignant sting to the sudden compassion Vincent felt for the man.

"Thank you, Sir Eric," Vincent returned his formal bow. "And may I wish you equal conjugal felicity. I have no doubt that the Lady's choice yet awaits you."

"I hope you are correct. If you would excuse me, gentles?" Eric nodded at them without really seeing them, and departed. Angelique's eyes lingered on him as he left, noting the rigidity in his spine and the stark set to his shoulders, like that of a man who'd just been ordered to march into a battle-line, and did not envy him at all for the sleepless night he was about to pass.

"I could not have made him happy," she whispered, looking up to Vincent at last for understanding, and perhaps absolution. "Not for long. I tried to explain why, but I do not think he believed me."

Vincent took her hand and kissed it again. "Because you couldn't say anything more than any other noble woman would have said under similar circumstances," he observed. "And if you had, it still would have broken his heart, just in a different way." He sighed and looked around. This was supposed to be a happy night, a night they could spend together publicly, in each other's company, simply being *normal*. It was, however, turning out to be yet another exercise in balancing truths. "Another dance?" he suggested. "We need to get back in practice."

She felt him draw the smile out of her as if he'd hooked it on a line. "Yes, please. And you did threaten to dance with Lady Georgiana, remember. Do not make the mistake of thinking she'll ever let you forget it," she said, setting Eric and his heartbreak aside for the moment.

"Oh, I'm rather looking forward to that," he admitted, grinning, "though she might not be, after about thirty seconds."

Angelique was laughing again as they reached the floor, and he weaved them through the first few layers of dancers, before turning to take her into his arms again. Despite their deadly serious meeting with Lady Emilia and Roland, and despite her having to deliver heart-breaking news to Sir Eric, her eyes were sparkling brightly, and he was sure he could see the purely liquid love of Angel in them. "How very beautiful," he murmured. "Despite everything, I don't think I've ever seen you so happy."

211

"This is because I've never been so happy," she told him, reverently touching his face with her fingers as he steered them around the other couples. "I do not think I knew what it was to be happy, until you. And you changed everything."

"Then perhaps tonight is not a total loss." He kissed her again. Another proper, Paladin kiss full of scandalous promises for later. "I was afraid that lovely little interlude with Lady Emilia and Old Grumpy might have spoiled it."

"It might, if we must discuss it further." He twirled them about, twisting her long silver-black sash about them both, and she laughed again, lightly, entirely delighted with the inquisitive looks they were drawing. "I'll have to surrender to Iris at some point so she can escort you to where the documents are kept, but until then, you are *mine,* darling man. All mine."

"And am contented to be so," he replied with a warm smile. They stepped and twirled and made a promenade around the ballroom with the other couples for several more minutes, then Vincent's brow furrowed. "Darling, why are we going to a records room? I thought you said the documents were kept by an attorney. Is that the decoy story?"

It took a moment for her to answer. She'd also thought the documents were still with the attorney, but a moment's conference with Iris had infuriated her as much as it had enlightened her. "Iris relocated the documents two months ago, when she thought they were close to discovery." Her words were nearly as clipped as Iris' might have been, and the warm sunlight in her eyes had been nearly eclipsed by surging anger. "That woman is going to get us all killed if she cannot be brought under control."

Good luck with that, Baroness. Louis couldn't do it, and I doubt you've got what it takes, either.

Vincent chuckled, then kissed her forehead. "Are you upset that she did it, or that she didn't tell you? If Louis was getting close, relocating them seems like a good thing, to me."

"It is the principle—"

Iris' angry shouts filled the vaults of her mind. Angelique bit off what she'd been about to say and waited for a long moment for it to pass. In the end, she knew that she simply didn't wish to be angry with Vincent, not on this night of all nights. Iris, on the other hand...

"I cannot safeguard Carlisle with that kind of treachery from within my own person," she said at last, glancing at him in a way that begged for his understanding, "but that is a conversation to be had at another time." Her smile tried to flicker back to life, a feat made somewhat easier by Angel's inner efforts to quiet Iris' diatribe.

"It is," he agreed, "and of course you can't. You won't, because you won't have to." He kissed her again, hoping that he was right. The truth was, he was just as in love with Iris as he was with Angelique. He dearly loved Angel too, but hadn't spent enough time with her to be able to say with any integrity that he was "in love" with her the way he was the other two personas. There was supposedly an "Angela" whom he had only heard mentioned, but had not yet met. The strangeness of it was something he determinedly refused to consider any more than he had to because he knew he didn't understand it. That Lady Emilia accepted it was enough—for now. Comprehension, and perhaps treatment, could come later.

Her hand had slipped behind his neck, and the kiss lingered a little longer, with her active help, but the sea green lights were back in her eyes when he looked at her again.

"No, I won't have to, will I?" They resumed the steps of their dance more earnestly, grinning at each other about the lifted eyebrows they were drawing. "I fully intend to *marry* you this time, Vincent. You're not getting away from me, again."

"Hmmm... Is this my cue to say, 'how about in the morning?'" he grinned. It couldn't happen, of course. At least, not without his "owner's" permission, and after this evening he was in no doubt that Roland would refuse. "I just happen to know where there's a church nearby," he finished outrageously.

"Meet you there at nine-hundred. I'll be the one in the fancy gown. You be there with the flowers."

They were eventually parted by a resolute Georgiana Dawes, who as Angelique had predicted, was not about to leave the venue that night without her promised dance with one of the most notorious knights in the city-state. Vincent escorted her to the dance floor with an unwholesome look on his face, and they hadn't even properly begun the first set of steps before the girl's face was flaming scarlet from her bodice lace to the wreath of ribbons in her hair.

Angelique refused the offer of a dance with Sir Paul, claiming with some justice that she would be better for a bit of rest. If Paul was disappointed, he hid it reasonably well, and quickly found an excuse to join his friends. His farewell barely even registered with her. Vincent's antics and Georgiana's reactions to them were vastly more amusing, and the lack of direct conversation was helping the headache left behind from Iris' hateful words was fading with each shrieking giggle she heard from the dance floor.

By happenstance, she spotted Clarice near the great glass doors to the gardens, flirting bashfully with a small group of other young persons of her station. She'd just begun to pick her way around the edges of the dance floor to reach her maid, and was passing the tall stand of potted ferns when she felt someone seize her from behind. "Angela!" Recognition of the voice came with a sudden start as Louis spun her around.

"Angela! Listen to me, you're in grave danger!"

"You!" She wrenched away from him, or tried to do so, fury erupting within her. Everyone's attention was either on the dancers, or on their conversations. No one yet seemed to notice what was happening.

"Angela. Listen to me. Listen to me now."

"Let go of me, Louis! I'm not—!"

"Angela!" he repeated The commands kept coming, rapidly, forcefully, and her will to resist him evaporated under the onslaught.

"Listen to me, now. You've been ill, Angela. We're leaving. I'm going to take good care of you. Take a step, there, now another. Keep walking, that's a girl." Her pace quickened to a normal walking pace, and he began leading her away from Vincent, Clarice, and the ballroom, to a place where he could talk to her in relative safety.

Within Angelique, all had gone still. She could hear echoes of the revelry in the room around her, and some other, dull roaring full of filtered rage from somewhere deep within her, but none of it truly registered. There was nothing to be done about any of it, and her world narrowed down to that one, simple fact. The only thing that mattered was the voice, Louis' voice, and the simplicity of that was overwhelmingly seductive.

Why are you going with him?! Have you gone mad?

My lady! Baroness! Wake up, what's wrong? You cain't leave with Louis now!

Shut up, you bitches. It was *that* voice again, languorous and sullen and wanton, all at once. *You've had your fun. Now that Louis is back, I want to have some fun, too.*

"Where are we going, Louis?" she asked, her voice somewhat like Angel's, only the Asburine accent was much more pronounced, and child-like.

Oh, this is not happening.

"Away from here, my dear," Louis replied. He knew the accent and he knew the tone of voice, so he deliberately schooled his voice to a gentle but firm parental tone. "You *do* want to play, don't you?" he asked, still leading her away from the party.

"Oh, yes," she breathed, and a little smile bloomed on her face. "I've missed you so, Louis. No one else likes to play as hard as you do."

This is absolutely not *happening!*

Iris, it is *happenin'! Ah don't know what happened to Angelique, but—*

"That's because nobody else *is* me," Louis chuckled, "and nobody is quite like you, either." The mere thought was arousing, and the arousal made him miss her all over again. "What I don't understand is why you haven't come back to play?"

Her lower lip protruded just slightly, a delightful little pout. "You sent me away," she reminded him, but whatever else she was about to add was lost when her knees buckled beneath her, briefly.

"Easy, Angela." He quickly put an arm around her to steady her.

It was a thoroughly-incensed Iris who tilted her face up to his as she regained her own legs, smiling in that vapid way that Angela always smiled at her marks. She'd had to exert a phenomenal amount of will to take control back—the mental equivalent of grabbing the stupid cunt by the hair and jerking her back where she belonged—but Louis had not seemed to notice. The ploy had worked.

"I'm easy for you," she said, delivering the words with the right amount of breathy flirtatiousness, then punctuating them with a giggle. The look Louis gave her told her she'd hit the mark. If Louis had Angela wrapped around his little finger, Angela had Louis wrapped around hers as well, and had they been more private, she was sure he would have fucked her right then and there because—well, that was Louis.

"Angelique?" It was Vincent's voice, from behind them. His dance with Georgiana had concluded, but coming up from behind them as he was, he couldn't see who had his arm around her.

Louis stiffened momentarily, then tried to quicken their pace.

"Not exactly!" Iris tore her arm out of his grasp and spun, catching him by the wrist and twisting it into a straight-arm submission hold that forced him to bend over to keep her from breaking it. A follow-up blow to the back of the neck sent him sprawling to the floor.

There were shrieks and a few shouts from the other occupants of the lobby when she sent him sprawling, but Iris ignored them. "I told you I'd kill you if you ever touched me again, you slimy prick," she hissed quietly, lunging for him as he attempted to stand.

Vincent stopped her before blood could be shed. "Oh, well done, Iris!" he said, and grabbed her by the waist. As soon as he'd identified Louis, he knew whatever was happening couldn't be good. "But, we sort of *need* yon Slimy Prick alive, though you could castrate him if you wanted, I suppose." His eyes danced merrily as he placed her back on her slippered feet, then he turned around to face Louis. He'd just regained his feet, and his countenance alternated between fear of Iris and a naked hatred of Raven.

The crowd noise around them faded to almost nothing as the rest of the lobby's occupants registered the change in atmosphere, and drew back in shock and surprise. It left little to hear but the strains of a folk dance from the ballroom, and Louis' gasps for air.

"You have our permission to leave, Louis." Vincent delivered the words with implacable calm, and Iris, fists clenched, punctuated it.

"Now," she said, tilting her head toward the front doors.

"Not without her." Louis jabbed a finger at Iris. She flipped her hand back at him, but it was a much ruder gesture.

"It would seem that 'her' doesn't want to go with you," Vincent said, completely unimpressed. "Run along, Louis. Go play with your slaves like a good boy before I change my mind and let, um, *Angelique* here carve you into tiny pieces right in front of everybody." He almost said "Iris", but then that name would have been in all the morning papers. Platoons of reporters would have followed, all banging on the gates of Blakesly House before the morning's eighth bell.

Louis fumed. He was surrounded by party-goers, most of whom were chattering about the exciting melodrama playing out before them. Raven had snatched her from his grasp once again, this time openly, publicly, and had turned him into a laughing-stock while he was at it. This would be in all the papers. His clients would find out, and they would not be happy. They were *already* unhappy that his fees had to be paid in hard currency to avoid confiscation by the police. The situation had gotten completely out of hand, but he had one ace left, and he intended to use it.

215

"This round goes to you, *boy,* but it's not the last." Mustering as much dignity as he could manage, he straightened his jacket, smoothed his hair, and strode through the front doors. The night manager's assistant pitched his overcoat out onto the steps after him.

Iris, still garbed in Angelique's Nadrean desert girl's costume, watched Louis' back until she couldn't see it any longer. Voices erupted around her again, but she could barely hear them over the riot going on between her ears. Angela's fury took the form of a screaming headache, and Cricket was helping that along as hard as she could. Angel was attempting to soothe them both, and to crown it all, Angelique had returned completely scandalized at the scene they'd just made in front of her peers, and demanding that Iris turn control back over to her *at once.*

"Get me out of here, Raven." She had no intention of surrendering to Angelique, not at this late hour, and turned to whisper the words in his ear. "Fuck this, we've got work to do."

"Don't make a scene!" Vincent hissed back into her ear. "Right now, the work is dealing with Paladin society. *Then* we go get those files. Now, let Angelique come back and do her job."

"A brain-dead dog could 'do her job'," Iris retorted, wincing visibly at the baroness' strictly internal demonstration of her command of swearing in three languages. One look at the Guardian Paladins closing in on them in the aftermath of Louis' departure, however, caused her to realize that the current state of rebellion going on inside her wasn't going to make dealing them any easier. "All right. Fine. But you *will* pay for this later. Believe it."

The change was hardly noticeable from the outside, this time. Iris was willing, more or less, and Angelique more than ready to step into her place. Still, there was an inevitable moment when her entire body slumped, and she'd have fallen to the floor if Vincent hadn't been there to catch her.

Angelique emerged to the collective gasps of dismay from the rapidly assembling crowd, led by scions of Demorest, Landsdowne, Lavalle, and even the new earl of Carcand, to whom she'd only been introduced the week before.

Vincent hastily put her back on his arm. "If you'll excuse us for a moment, gentles," he said, attempting to make his way through the crowd. "After *that* bit of unpleasantness, I think my lady and I could use a drink."

"Is there anything we should know about that man, Lady Blakesly?" It was the earl who asked. He was a short, stocky man with a chest and hands that looked like they belonged to a barrel-maker. His small, bright eyes glanced between her and Vincent, to whom he had not been introduced.

Angelique rectified that quickly, but then placed her fingers to her forehead. It was no act. Angela's infuriated shrieks echoed like ballista-fire in her head. "I am sure you and your family are quite safe from him, Lord Morgan. Goodman Arnot has some mistaken attachments to the past, but those are being addressed. He should not trouble us again. Thank you—thank you all, for your concern, but Sir Vincent is correct. After that, I very much like a drink, preferably something other than wine."

"Of course, of course. Only allow me to offer my compliments to your combat instructor. Your defense and escape were cleanly done, my lady." He turned then and spread his arms, effectively creating a lane of escape for Angelique and Vincent, and using his elevated social position much as she had, earlier, to get people to *move*. "Let us allow the lady and her lord a clear path to the bar, shall we, gentles?"

"Thank you, my lord earl," Vincent said, turning Angelique to lead her back towards the ballroom. He caught sight of Clarice and beckoned her over, then sat them down in the chairs that lined the walls beneath the balcony. "Water, or something stiffer?" he asked while he waited for the girl to make her way over.

"Yes." It wasn't much of a smile, but she gave him what she had anyway, and sank into her chair. "Both. I cannot believe he was here. I cannot believe I was just walking away with him—" *WELL, IF YOU THINK I'M TELLING YOU WHY, YOU ARE SO WRONG! WHY DO YOU GET THAT USELESS PRICK AND I CAN'T HAVE—* "but I do not remember what happened, once he grabbed me."

Please... Angel, Iris? Can't you...?

We're tryin', milady. Iris is workin' on it, right now. Keep breathin'.

"Iris does," Vincent said quietly. "As usual, she was quick and efficient. Just be glad I arrived in time or you'd be up on murder charges that even Lady Emilia couldn't get discharged. Water, dear girl," he said then to Clarice, "and a good stiff thesker."

"Cairnbrooks, please," Angelique clarified. She had no head for hard liquor, but this was a special occasion, and its sweetness would help it go down, and stay down. "And that tray of delicious looking finger foods you brought, earlier?"

"At once, gentles." Clarice scampered toward the servants' pantry. Angelique reached up to remove the headband she wore, and the veils that were attached to it. Removing the restriction made her feel better almost right away.

"He called me 'Angela', Vincent. I haven't answered to that name in years. *How* did he make me *want* to leave with him like that?"

"I have no idea," he replied, exhaling heavily. "But apparently, Iris wasn't as easily swayed as Angela, for which you owe her a thanks. He got you entirely too close to the door for my comfort."

He paused then, his mind running at a racehorse's speed, but it came up with no new answers. "This all has to fit together somehow," he grumbled, giving voice to what he felt. "Darling, as soon as you're settled, let's get out of here. Iris is chomping at the bit, and now so am I. Louis obviously needs something more immediate to focus on than kidnapping you."

Silence descended within her, and from it she guessed that Iris and Angel had successfully dealt with this "Angela" whoever or whatever she was. She drew a deep, relieved breath, and nodded firmly.

"I could not agree more. Clarice," Angelique said, looking up at her, and at the refreshments she'd brought, "is our trunk safely in Remington's rooms?"

"I had it sent up directly after you asked it," Clarice affirmed.

The baroness drew a deep breath. "Very well, then. You may take the carriage back to Blakesly House tonight, my dear. Sir Vincent and I will not be returning right away."

It was in the girl to ask questions, but she bit her lip instead, and nodded. "May I stay with my friends awhile longer, my lady, before I return home?"

Angelique smiled. "Of course you may. I shall leave the lateness of the hour to your discretion as you have proved your good judgement over and over again, of late. Enjoy yourself, my dear."

With a happy smile of her own, Clarice withdrew. Vincent and Angelique headed to the mechanical lift that would take them to the fourth floor not long after.

Chapter 15

Merchants' and Docktown
25 Vilmath 580, the early hours

It was Iris, not Angelique Blakesly, who emerged from the Old Palace Hotel that night, via the side entrance used to cart deliveries up from the river. The baroness had waited until she and Raven had reached the privacy of the room they'd been offered to use in Remington's suite before ceding control of their body for the tasks to come, but her presence hovered in Iris' mind, alert and anxious, as she plotted her route to the East-West Barge Company. It would first take her westward, along the North Caspian to Three Lions Bridge, in an easy cross-country run for the better part of four kilometers, and she'd need every meter of it to run off the seething anger she'd been nursing for over an hour. Raven's summary dismissal of her—in favor of Angelique, no less!—had stung, but it hadn't hurt nearly as badly as having to watch him *enjoying himself* as he cavorted around with those overdressed and under-exercised fools at the ball. As if he wanted to stay in that world.

As if he *belonged*.

Her rage boiled all over again at the thought. She knew he expected her to make a run for the bridge, and would be circling above to help her avoid any pursuit she encountered. Even the rank amateurs Louis had first hired to capture her had figured out that the bridges were bottlenecks for anyone traveling overland, and so tended to lie there in wait for her. Iris didn't really need Raven's help with those idiots. She'd been avoiding them for months (and said as much to him, when he brought it up), but Lucky's Lads, or those who remained at liberty, at least, had proved themselves to be a different matter entirely. In fact, she'd been tempted to start her run by cutting directly across the river by ferry in order to prove a point, but the prospect of being overpowered by professionals who'd come armed to defeat her, specifically, chilled any desire she might have had to act on that.

Her stride lengthened once she cleared the gates of the hotel, and she settled into the rhythm of the run almost within just a few steps.

Iris crossed the street, then vaulted a low rock wall to sprint across lawns and through more wintered-over gardens on her run toward the bridge, her mind ranging backward in time, trying to remember when she'd first began to run like this. There had been a childhood in Caroling Dell with kilometers of rolling, terraced hills, long rows of growing grape vines, and dozens of little brooks for jumping that flowed in the valleys between the hills. There were shallow-pitched roofs on the dormitories for the field workers, the stables, barns for agricultural storage, and row after row of wagons lined up for the harvest, and endless summer days to run and run and run until she'd dropped.

When her boot-heels struck the cobblestone streets in the business district, however, the memories changed. Those were attached to her years in Low Town, in Püran-Khir. Running there had meant learning to find her footing on piles of rubble, shattered glass, crumbling brick, and burnt timbers. There, a fall meant instant death. Slowing down or stopping meant getting caught.

What "getting caught" had meant, in those days, was something that still gave Angel and the baroness nightmares.

Iris had begun running routes across the rooftops of Angels and Merchants' almost as soon as she'd begun functioning independently in Fernwall, and had added some of Docktown and even Near Thieves' to her repertoire as her need to protect the dead man's trigger had grown. The city-state was vast; its gang territories and trap boundaries weren't marked by lines on a map. It had been a painstaking process, but she was more than a little proud of the routes she'd constructed, in the relatively short time she'd had to do it.

Three Lions Bridge, lit up at night, was a sight to behold, but Iris did not pause to admire it. Instead, she marshaled what she knew of Angels and sprinted down a side street toward the Holywell Chapel. Its rough brickwork facade facilitated climbing, and the grounds featured a long colonnaded walk. The shallow-sloped pitch of its long peak meant that she could build up enough speed to make the leap from where the colonnade ended to the bridge's northern gatehouse, without having to cover the distance at ground level. Louis' thugs—the amateurs, at least—liked keeping their boots on the cobblestones, where they had a better chance of surviving an encounter with her.

Iris climbed to the top of the gatehouse, and paused to catch her breath as she reached the first of the three lion sculptures from which the bridge took its name. Low clouds hung over the city that night, holding the warmer air down against the surface, where it melted the last patches of ice that had stubbornly clung to shaded places in the rooftops and gables of Lower Angels. She glanced up at the sky around her, but the lighted bridge paradoxically made it more difficult to penetrate the darkness just beyond it. If Raven was up there, he was well-hidden.

He was nowhere in sight because he was above the dim glow of the street lights, hidden in the velvet-black sky. No sooner had she left the hotel via the servants' gate than he'd shot a tow line to a chimney across the courtyard and leaped out the window. The Raven Wing spread out around him and he swooped out into the night sky like a giant version of his namesake. As he circled a nearby building to gain altitude, he watched her exit the hotel grounds and turn westward, towards the port district in prosperous, northern Docktown, then headed that way himself, weaving from the hot air of a chimney to follow a street, then to another chimney, as he made his way towards the bay.

That Louis had shown the temerity not only to confront Angelique, but to attempt to kidnap her at one of the largest parties of the season was a troubling development. And, given the attitude he displayed, he was getting desperate. Raven could not dismiss the very real possibility that he would try something even more drastic in the relative anonymity of the city. So, rather than following Iris, he flew on ahead to scout.

The night had become deadly calm and very dark, and heavy clouds obscured the stars and moons. It was still, and very quiet, like the deep breath before a storm. The shod hooves of the horses, clopping along the cobblestone streets seemed extra ordinarily loud, and the golden glow of the street lights gave everything an eerie, haunted cast. Few were out, at this late hour. Those that were seemed to be hurrying to get to from their social event to the safety of their homes, but he found no trace of anyone lurking on rooftops or around corners, in Iris' path.

He banked and turned back toward Three Quarters in time to spot a lithe, sleek figure casting long shadows as she sprinted between the lights at the top of bridge, at least twenty-five meters above the surface of the river. It made him do a double-take. He had foolishly forgotten his Owl Sight Goggles, so she was barely visible at that height, little more than a dark blur moving at speed between patches of light, and nothing but the night around her. Clearly, she had no fear of heights. In fact, it was possible, she feared nothing at all.

As if to prove him right, she reached the roof of the southern gatehouse and plunged, in a free, arcing dive, over the side of the tower.

Raven swore and dove after her, spending his altitude to gain speed, reaching over a hundred kilometers an hour as he streaked past the gate-house tower. *There!* He spotted her, clinging fiercely to a rope halfway through a long, swinging arc on the far side of the bridge. He banked hard and pulled up, hoping he had enough speed and momentum left to reach the hot air from the chimney stacks, unable to see where she'd landed.

Iris' momentum propelled her toward the long facade of warehouses and shipping offices at what she privately thought of as "splattering speed," given what was left of those she'd seen try it and not survive. The chill air rushing past stung her eyes into watering, and the rope was freezing her hands even through her leather gloves. She was quite literally reaching "the end of her rope," and by the time she'd released it to fling herself through the air she was whooping in pure, unadulterated joy.

The airborne arc ended as she tumbled over a second-story balcony rail, rolled out what remained of her momentum, then leaped to her feet and ran toward the trellis at the other end. The building that housed the East-West Barge Company was still two blocks back upriver, but from the thieves' highway, the side streets were narrow enough for her to jump from one rooftop to the next without having to descend to the ground. Iris hauled herself over the cornice, then clambered up the slope to the long, chimney-studded peak at the top.

There near the river, the calm, sultry air was a bit warmer than it had been up in Angels, easing any lingering concerns she might have had about black ice. After a moment to catch her breath, she focused her mind on this last leg of the route, and began to run.

The vaults between the roofs were purest joy, and the closest thing to flight she'd known until Raven swept her off the Morrissant Bridge, the night before. It didn't take her long to reach the East-West Barge Company offices. Slowing to a reluctant stop, Iris looked around carefully for signs of pursuit, or for clues that she was otherwise being watched from the ground. Finding none, she cast her gaze skyward once more for any hint of a silent black shape gliding through the night sky, and tried to ignore how her heart turned over when she saw him spiral down out of the inky black sky, flare the great wing, and land on the far side of the roof.

"*That* is cheating." Iris emerged from deeper darkness of the shadow of a chimney stack, and though the words were delivered casually, the puffs of steam from her mouth indicated how hard her body had worked to get there.

"You were considerably more grateful when I flew you off the bridge last night. Now," he said, ignoring the derision in her answering snort, "unless you have really big drill hidden in that cat suit, we'll have to get to the ground to get inside," he went on, pulling out one of his smaller line pliers. "Kiss me baby, and we'll go down together." He held out an inviting arm.

Another snort exploded in a cloud of steam. "Oh no. Kissing you is *Angelique's job*. I'll make my own way down." She turned toward the access ladder that let down into an alley, but knelt first and pulled out her flash, directing it into the dark corners to probe for unwanted company.

"You weren't complaining about *that* last night, either. But, suit yourself," he shrugged, making his way to the roof ledge. The alley was lit only by the reflective light of the lights on the main street, and using a flash would alert every flier in the air, and anybody within a kilometer or so on the ground, that they were about. Light also made the perfect target. Thankfully, as best he could determine, the alley looked to be unoccupied,

"*Last night*, you weren't prancing around a fucking ballroom in dancing slippers."

"I wasn't doing that tonight, either," he drawled, scanning the night sky for signs they were being watched from above.

Iris snapped the cap back on the slender tube to douse the light and then tucked it into the strap on her belt. "You got more than one of you in there, too?" she asked him, reaching out with a gloved finger to tap the center of his forehead. "Because otherwise, that's utter orcshit and we both know it."

"*I* was wearing shoes. *You* were the one in the slippers." He held up the plier again. "Ready?"

She cast him a disgusted look. "They sure looked like poncy little dancing slippers, to me." So saying, swung herself onto the iron ladder and descended, opting to slide down the last few meters rather than use the rungs. It put them near the side entrance to the building at about the same time.

Without a word, she moved to the door. From out of the darkness, he saw the tiniest flash of light train down onto the lock from her flash, the end held between her teeth so she could use both hands. Pulling two picks from her sleeves, she jimmied the lock's interior until the soft *snick* told them both she'd been successful.

"There's a night watch for this block of buildings. He's usually chewing on day-old pastries from the bakery just down the street at this hour," Iris murmured, gesturing him to precede her. Once inside, they were standing in a small foyer with racks for boots and coats, and a whole row of umbrella stands along one wall. The only other door in the room was opposite them.

"Which means he'll be back around, eventually, complete with sticky fingers, no doubt." Raven drawled quietly, tapping the door. He pulled his fancy lock pick out of a pocket, installed the appropriate tip, shoved it in the lock, and squeezed. The pins whirred, then came another audible *snick* as the lock opened.

"Two for our side." He grinned at her and pulled open the door. "Ladies first," he waved her in extravagantly.

"Damn. Do you have a gadget for *every*thing you do?" Iris demanded, albeit softly, shaking her head at him. "I'm surprised you don't do Angelique with a mechanical dildo."

"You'd know if I did."

"Doubtful. I don't like her taste in men." She started to brush past him, but he barred her way, then kissed her.

"I like *your* taste," he said, eyes twinkling in the low light. Something in hers glinted back at him, and she leaned in to kiss him, teasing his lips apart only to bite down on his lower lip when he obliged.

He snatched her by the hair, and the alchemically-enhanced glue that held the wig to her head pulled the skin tight against the bones of her face, giving her an eerie, feral cast in the low light. Iris caught her breath and locked eyes with him. Slowly, she unclenched her jaw, releasing his lip before she drew blood, and fighting down the rush of desire that had caught her completely unawares.

"Do you, now…" She breathed the words over his face, vacillating between kissing him again and stabbing him.

He flicked his tongue into her mouth again, then sealed it with another kiss. "Mmm… If you're not careful, we'll get distracted."

"I'm always careful." One well-placed nudge in the crook of his elbow crumpled his support, and expediently removed him as a barrier. She slid past him with a triumphant little smile to lead him through the back hallways of the shipping company's offices. No one should have been there at that hour, but to demonstrate her point, she paused to listen at each juncture in case some junior clerk had come down with a late-night case of ambition, and he took every opportunity to fondle various parts of her person at each stop.

"Look, do something *useful* with your hands and open the damned lock," Iris snapped at last, batting his hand away as they reached the end of the last hall, and were standing before the door with the words TOBIAS MATHESON-ANDRUUS, HEAD FOREMAN.

"I *am* doing something useful," he shot back. "*You* could open the lock. Then I wouldn't have to stop."

"With you jostling me at every turn? Please." She gestured impatiently, not willing to give in to his charm so easily. Grinning impudently, he took out his mechanical pick and buzzed the lock. "Satisfied?"

"Don't you wish." Iris turned the knob and pushed past him again. She pulled her flash and, filtering the light between her fingers, let it provide enough illumination to guide him around the desk and over to another door. It might once have been a closet or pantry, but those doors were usually not kept locked. "This isn't a lever-tumbler lock. Can that gadget of yours handle a pin-tumbler?"

"Can I handle your gadget?"

"Just get the damned lock open, or get out of my way, Raven. The night wears on."

Grinning at her, he opened a leather pouch and picked out a blade that looked like it had been thinly sliced. He peered at it closely under her light, attached it to the lock pick, then applied it to the lock.

The pins buzzed, and nothing happened, but he tried it again before she could push him aside. This time the pins buzzed much more slowly until...

Snick! the barrel of the lock went off -center. He turned the pick the rest of the way, and opened the door. "Glad to be of service," he smirked, shoving the device back in his pocket.

"I did it in one try, the first time." It was offered drily enough to make a man pucker, and he could just see the corner of her mouth twitch as she pulled open the door. "Don't let it close behind us," she told him, nodding at the door. "That lock resets when the door closes, and it only opens from the *outside*."

Within was a spacious closet, or small room. The walls on either side of the door were lined with shelves from floor to ceiling, and on those shelves were cylinders, books, and boxes. Opposite them, however, was the door to a wall-safe that was taller than Raven, and it was secured with a tumbler with a dial that was bigger around than his fist.

"Hold this, and keep your paws off me for a minute."

"That's no fun." She cast him a look as she handed him her flash, then spun the dial anti-clockwise once. "One for sorrow... " he began the old nursery rhyme.

Iris froze before the first tumbler fell, recognizing the words to Cricket's rhyme.

224

You cannot truly think...

Ah don't think Cricket is strong enough...

The trouble was, neither of them could be completely certain. Iris wasn't either. "Where did you hear that?" she asked, striving for a conversational tone as her fingers rolled the dial again.

"It's an old nursery rhyme," he shrugged. "I think it originated in the wine country, but I could be wrong."

"Oh, right." She leaned toward the dial again, rotating it slowly to be sure the tumblers all fell as they had the last time she'd been here. The last two fell into place. With a single, enigmatic glance as the sole prelude, Iris turned the wheel and pulled open the door.

It took up nearly the whole space of the closet, and pushed her backside right up against Raven's front as she pulled the edge of the heavy, reinforced door past.

He grabbed her from behind and snuggled her close so he could look over her shoulder. "Oh how charming," he said, fondling one of her breasts through her jacket as he looked over the cavernous vault. It didn't appear to be very organized. "The stevedore's junk bin. Perfect place to hide documents."

"I rather thought so." Iris pulled away from him, but it was an afterthought, and Angel wasn't letting her forget it. "But, take a look around. Any outfit with a safe like this has got to have some juicy secrets lying around. They keep their gold in that iron box, by the way," she added, reaching up to one of the top shelves. "Though you'll need your cheater again to get past the lock."

"My 'cheater'?" he chuckled. While she looked for her file, he fished out his own flash and began rummaging around the books and files and papers on the shelves near the door. Anybody this disorganized, he reasoned, was bound to lazy and would forgo the increased security the obscurity a large safe offered in favor of ease. Things often needed would, therefore, likely be right inside the door.

It didn't take long to find a small, pocket-sized book labeled the "bo'son's book". On seagoing cargo vessels, the bo'son was directly responsible to the captain for the ship's cargo, and so kept their own records, which were then later copied into the ship's record book. Barges, he assumed, operated on similar principles. He opened it.

"Lady's girdle!" he swore, flipping through the pages. They were all the same. A date, underneath of which were columns of letters, then numbers, then descriptions—and the descriptions were *very* interesting. It seemed straightforward enough. The letter code was the cargo class, the numbers would be manifest numbers. But in this case, the manifest numbers all started with the letter A. That matched the tidbit of information Cole had passed on to him. "Well, would you look at this," he breathed, flipping through a few more pages. "I think we might just have found a way to uncover what all those armed barges are about."

Iris turned, clutching a battered leather portfolio in her arms. "The professionals, you mean? I got chased off the river a couple of times by them. Unfriendly sorts. What did you find?"

He pointed out a manifest number, then let his finger slide down the column. "Cole found an open container when the longshoremen were offloading one of those guarded barges in River Trap. The manifest number on the box was prefixed with an A. These numbers are also prefixed with an A. Those unmarked guards—along with your charming activity—are contributing to the instability in the traps. I want to know what's coming into town that's so important an outside military group has to guard the cargo."

The hair on the back of her neck prickled uneasily, but she trained her flash on the pages and tried to make sense of what she saw. "So Cole survived," she said, the words barely above a whisper. "Full points for tenacity, I thought she'd be a deader before the blue bottles found her."

"She's alive. The blue *jackets*," he murmured, emphasizing the more polite term for Fernwall's finest, "also got a glimpse of their unit badge. Roland is going to hand that information over to the MPs to research." He closed the little book and put it in his pocket. "Let's see how much more pressure we can apply," he grinned, patting the book through his coat. "That the file we need?"

Iris shrugged. "Let's make sure." Kneeling, she unbuckled the flap and placed the folio on the floor so she could riffle through the contents. Now actively curious, Raven squatted down beside her and trained his light on her hands. The folders were clearly labeled, and he could see the court stamps on the official copies of the case, to which were attached pages of notes, all written in a very neat, precise hand.

"They're the Van Trapp case documents, all right," she whispered, browsing past them to the smaller files beneath. "There's more here. We got it by accident that night, and just left it all bundled together. Even Angelique didn't understand half of it, and she's got the best education among us."

"I can almost hear Roland's drooling from here," Raven drawled. He swung his shoulder pouch around. "I wouldn't mind reading it over myself, since I had some small part in the case."

She chuckled grimly. "I assume you'll have all the time you need to do that while Louis' rotting in a holding cell. Where to, now? You want to head up to records storage and see if we can find out what those manifest numbers are about?"

He flipped the flap open on the pouch, so she could insert the folder once she had it rebound. "Why not. It might be educational. You're no longer putting heat on River Trap, but those damned guards are."

"And, maybe old Rolly will cut the baroness some slack if she helps you hand him a nice surprise." Jerking the strap through the buckle and cinching it down tight, she stood as he did and handed it to him by the straps, which had clearly been attached so that it could be worn over the shoulders and carried on the back, or the front. "Here. You can fly this to safety afterward much more easily than I can run it."

"'Rolly' will get over it—eventually," he drawled, securing the flap on the pouch. He slid it back around beneath his cloak. "Know where the records room is? Lead on."

"Let's get this closed up. Keep your ears spread. That guard isn't the only one who prowls this area at night." She matched actions to words, then led the way out of the office, and locked the door behind them. Though she wasn't familiar with the whole building, even with her flash filtered between her gloved fingers, it was easy enough to find her way back to the stairwell they'd passed, earlier. Raven went to the street door and carefully peered out through the glass panels. The wisping of a discarded scrap of paper told him a faint breeze had come up, but the street was still quiet.

"This should do it," she said, breathing the words rather than speaking them. He left the door and joined her. "Too close to the river to risk storing paper in a basement. My bet is up, probably the top floor."

"It'll be on the same floor they cloister the blue pencil brigade, I should imagine," he whispered back. "Or one floor above or below."

She nodded, then took the first steps, pausing on each landing to listen intently before continuing. He followed, and managed to do it quietly for the first two flights. "I understand Thorin is nice this time of year," he finally said, training his flash up the stairs still above them.

He heard her snort derisively. "I'm sorry I didn't think to bring along a lift to the moons. If you need to stop for breath? Keep it to yourself."

He was going to retort, but watching her sleekly covered ass ascend the stairs in front of him was far more entertaining. Iris led him past the second story landing and up to the third. The stairwell let out into a long hall, with doors on either end. Iris paused to bypass the laughable excuse for a lock on the nearest, then led him into the large room beyond, open except for rows and rows of shelves containing ledgers and labeled filing boxes of books and papers. Tables stood guard at one end of the rows, with a few chairs around them.

"This is better," Raven murmured, looking around. "Now we need the manifest book." He started down a row of books, pulled one off the shelf and put it on the table. Then he fished the little book he'd taken from the vault out of his pocket, and opened it to the last, used page. "Let's see..." he murmured. "A934523." He flipped through the manifest book. "The bills of lading for this date should be in—"he flipped through a few more pages, "binder 451," he finally finished. "That way," he pointed further down the row.

"Oh, is this *my* job, too?" she said, though she wasn't truly inquiring. She was, however, already moving down the row, her flash trained on the volume labels.

"Any exuse to look at your ass while you walk," he replied, putting the manifest book back on the shelf.

"Enjoy it while you can." She returned with the book he wanted and placed it on the table next to him, resentment threading through the words she spoke. "Once this is over, you go back to your pretty Paladin baroness, and she won't be caught dressing like this on a bet."

"Poor wittle boozed baby," he teased, coming up behind her to put his arms around her so he could nibble on her ear. "That looks like one."

Anger flared. She shoved him away with one forearm, and pushed the book toward him with the other. "Talk to me like that again and I'll have to knife you," she told him, as matter-of-factly as if she'd promised him that the sun would come up in the morning.

He stepped right back up to her, pinning her against the table. "You're so fucking sexy when you make threats. Say it again." He leaned forward to kiss her, felt it as she reached for her knife, and *heard* it clear the leather sheath before he struck out instinctively. It flew from her hand and clattered impotently across the floor.

She'd wrenched herself away from him before it came to a stop, her left hand clenching and re-clenching on the hilt of the other knife still her belt. "I don't waste my breath on threats, you Paladin prick. Keep your fucking hands off me."

He arched an eyebrow and scanned her from eye to thigh for several long heartbeats. "I don't know what bug crawled up your ass tonight, darling, but you *really* need to get a grip before you do something you're going to regret," he finally said, and only then turned back to the binder.

The only thing that kept her from hurling the second blade was Angel's protest, shrieked so loudly that Iris was privately amazed Raven hadn't heard it. Shaking her head once to clear the ringing echoes left behind, she released the knife she held, and turned on her heel to retrieve the other. "Too late," was all she said, hurling the words instead of the knife, though it wasn't nearly as satisfying.

He opened the binder and began sifting through the bills of lading. "Not yet," he countered. As was typical, the bills of lading were only mostly in order. Shipments that had come in off of the same barge were mostly numerically sequenced, because they had been punched and put in the binder together, but that was about as ordered as things got.

"Wrong." A cursory inspection told her that the blade hadn't suffered any damage, and she replaced it in its sheath with deliberate care. "Angel won't let me cut you. That's a huge regret, right there."

What he was looking for wasn't hard to find. He scanned the through a half-dozen or so of the papers, his eyebrow arching higher as he drew from his memories of some of Master Slagter's most obscure history lessons to understand what he was seeing: This was a list of parts needed to assemble *a demon gate!*

Stunned, he was slow to process what Iris had just said, but he looked at her indignantly when he did. "Wait. You were really going to stab me because we went *dancing?*"

"Don't be insulting, Raven. I'm not a child." Iris stalked back to him, tightly controlled anger simmering in every pore. "I'll stab you for talking down to me in a heartbeat. But, for using me basically to get back into Angelique's good graces?" she went on, flinging each word at his head, "That would be why I'm *leaving* you."

"Well, that *would* be childish," he agreed amicably, "and I know you're better than that. I also know you're smarter than that."

"Smart enough to know when I've allowed lust to overrule my good sense." Iris had stopped just out of arm's reach, but wasn't sure whether it was for her own protection, or for his. "I let you mislead me once. I wanted to believe that you'd come with me, and we'd play games in Fernwall for fun and profit. I'll admit that. You don't get that kind of chance with me twice, Raven. Most people don't even get it once."

He stared at her. "Seriously? We spend an entire day patching things up so we can be together and now you're having an attack of *jealousy* over it?"

"No, I'm actually having a fit of rage. I'm just *very* good at controlling it." She reached out peremptorily and flipped the binder closed. "When I checked out last night, I thought we were going to have a life together. Instead, I find out that what you really wanted was a life with *Angelique*."

Iris, you cannot possibly be serious.

"Is that what you think?" he snorted. "Have you checked with Angelique about how that would work? Or Angel? Have you considered the personal consequences of permanently shoving the rest of yourself aside, or the rather epic consequences to everyone who depends on you, and Carlisle, for their safety and well-being? Are you really so damned selfish you'd kill Angel just to get what you want?"

Iris! Stop this right now!

Fighting back the urge to lunge for his throat, Iris ignored Angelique's directive and took an incautious half-step forward. "I'm not killing Angel over anything. I thought I could get what I wanted, and give her what *she* wanted—you, gods help her." She stabbed a finger into his chest to underscore the point. "If I'd known what you really wanted was Carlisle—"

"*Carlisle needs you!* Don't you get it?" Raven hissed. "This isn't a you or Angel, or you or Angelique, and it isn't a me and Angelique *or* me and you. Angelique needs you right here, right now, doing what you're doing, because she can't. And so do I. And Angelique needs you in Carlisle for the same reason, and so do I. Get a fucking *grip,* girl!"

"Raven!" Iris half-laughed, but it was mostly a strangled shout and they both knew it. "Are you seriously *in love* with a fucking lie? No, just shut up for a minute, because I honestly don't think you understand," she insisted. Angelique, infuriated, attempted to reassert control over their body, and the internal struggle intensified in this last-ditch attempt to rescue him from himself. "Angelique Blakesly was Louis' creation, remember? She's the lie that had to become true, and she did—once people started to believe in her. Including, most especially, you."

"Hah! What makes you think *you're* so special that you're more 'real', whatever that means in this case, than Angelique?" He closed the distance between them and the air between them crackled with tension. "Everything you said about Angelique is *also* true about you. If Angelique didn't exist until I came along, I bloody *created* you. The persona of Angelique Blakesly became real when she was invested in the lands and title of Carlisle and the

Cascadian nobility took her into their fold. Her existence was documented all over the city-state *long* before I even knew she existed, and apparently Lady Emilia has made damned sure that it can never be challenged. *You,* on the other hand, didn't come along as a separate entity until the breakup, and are documented *nowhere!* You're *mine,* sweetheart, all mine. Without me, it's *you* that doesn't exist."

Abruptly, there was nothing left within her but the silence, a horrified, expanding negation so monstrous that she could not give it voice. The baroness' presence vacillated between rapture at the defense she'd received and disgust at his "rather vulgar" display of possessiveness. Angel vacillated similarly, but it was between her need for Raven and her anxiety at Iris' likely response. There was simply nothing for Iris to seize on, no argument or weapon within her to take up in her defense against her own sneaking suspicion that he might be right.

A dragon found a dolly, and made it come to life...

NO! Raven's not like that, he's no—!

Horror turned to panic and then to rage before her next heartbeat; infuriated by what she couldn't name, Iris reached for a knife. Raven knocked her hand away from the hilt, then pulled her into his arms.

"And, I have no intention of letting you, or Angelique, or Angel, or Angela, or any part of you go, ever again." His breath, hot on her face, punctuated every word. "How many times do I have to say this? I let you go once," he went on, his lips brushing against hers, "and I didn't like it. I love you. *All* of you. Trust me." His lips brushed past hers again, leaving a feather light kiss in their wake. "Please. Work with me, darling."

Angel melted first; that was no surprise. Angelique's resistance, such as it was, melted right after that, but Iris realized that Raven had fought and won that battle long ago. It was only when she felt her own fury and indignation begin to melt away that she realized for her to do so without so much as a protest was completely untenable.

Her body had already softened in his arms by the time when she managed to draw breath to speak. "You know, Angel's always been frantic about you, and you've charmed the baroness with your pretty vows," she whispered, thrilling to how their lips caressed as she spoke, "but don't think that gives you a special pass with me, Raven. It doesn't. I *know* you."

She shifted suddenly, taking him by the lapels and forcing him back against a wall of ledgers. "You're a liar, and a con, and a thief. Faithful? Ha. You're going to screw around on Angelique every chance you get. We both know that." She was right up against him, whispering the words defiantly into the space between their faces, not ruffling in the slightest when his arms enfolded her. "You've got no more scruples than a tomcat and I wouldn't trust you any farther than I could *spit* you.

"Utterly, completely shameless." Iris breathed, brushing her nose along his jawline ever so lightly. "I happen to like that about you."

At first he was taken aback, and wondered whether he needed to think about defending himself, but by the time she'd finished he was grinning like the cat in the creamery.

"Just 'like'?" he said, breathing the words into her mouth. He felt how her lips yearned towards his, how her body seemed to lengthen inside her skin to connect her mouth with his.

"On a good day." Iris was tingling all over, inside and out, but wasn't about to surrender quite so easily. "If you'll stop pissing me off every time you open your mouth."

"You don't seem pissed off now." He dared to move his lips a few millimeters closer to hers.

She didn't move, and barely breathed, eyes and lips challenging him to close that last, scorching hot distance.

Will he dare?

Of course he will, Angel's voice sang out. *He's Raven!*

"Well... it's been a *very* good day..."

"It's about to be," he whispered, then, as Angel predicted, he closed the distance. Their lips brushed, then parted, the contact striking sparks that seemed to arc and dance about them. Iris grabbed him by the front of his jacket once more, and pulled him to her to kiss him hungrily.

His head reeled. *This* was definitely Iris, not Angelique! They were the same lips, the same lithe body. He could feel every curve under her skin-tight clothing, and yet, they were *not* the same woman. Where Angelique seemed refined and delicate, a creature to be protected like the Paladin protected the Lady, Iris was tough, willful, aggressive, a woman who needed no man's protection. Angelique lured him, seduced him, drew him in, then had embraced him with her love completely. Iris demanded and pushed, her hard body up against his, pressing him against the shelves, using her physical presence to hold him there while she kissed him thoroughly. He answered, he couldn't help it, blood and desire thundering in his veins.

Sex the night before had been on grounds Iris could understand—passionate, overwhelming, and mercifully brief. The distinct lack of sentimentality was more a relief than a concern. She didn't need romance to pretty up the fact that she wanted to fuck, and in that moment, she was *afire* with it. She strained against him, moaning insistently, tongue lashing against his in a desperate need for more of him.

He lashed back in kind, fencing with her for the thrill of the heat, which was rapidly becoming too hot to handle. Grabbing her by the hair, he spun them around, shoved her up against the books, and bit her lip to hold her still when she squirmed. The same body, yet wildly different women—the whole idea made him shake with need of her. "Tell me you don't want this," he hissed into her panting mouth.

"I hate it," Iris agreed hotly, biting his lip in return, then twisting to the side enough to draw blood. She moaned then, and kissed him again, grinding her hips against him where his rock hard erection was trapped. "But not as much... as I hate... Sir Vincent Sultaire..."

He took her by the hair again and kissed her so hard it hurt. "You fucking cunt," he retorted, tasting his blood on her lips. He bit her chin, then left a trail of bite marks to the side of her neck. "So, it's true love then."

"Save that shit for Lady Blakesly." Under his coat, her gloved fingers dug savagely into his back, frustrated at their inability to plunge directly into his flesh. It, and the sheer physicality of him, nearly drove her wild. "She'll believe it. I don't."

"Bullshit," he snorted, biting her neck again for emphasis. He shrugged off the Raven Wing, and then pulled at the fastenings of her jacket, making room when she began to help. His lips and tongue followed the reveal down over her shoulders, pushing aside the undergarments to kiss and bite her chest and breasts. It was all maddeningly familiar, and yet arousing and strange. Those breasts seemed just as hard-edged as the persona that currently owned them, and that thought was more intoxicating than a double shot of thesker. He bit down on a nipple, and shook with need at warning hiss it elicited from her.

Iris pushed into the pain, ignoring Angela and her shrieks of glee, stripping off her gloves to tangle a handful of fingers in his hair. The others found purchase in the back of his shoulder, and she moaned hotly at his groaning protest. "You're right," she gasped, so aroused that the words erupted from her like fire. "She doesn't really believe it, either."

Raven bit her other nipple for that, and held her there, by the teeth, until she stilled, and the shivers of pleasure and pain had abated. Only then did he release her, and push her jacket back to expose the iron-hard muscles of her belly, undoing her by belt and waist band to get at the pale muff just beneath her trousers. The sight of it caught him up for a moment, and he paused to stroke her sides, to squeeze the flesh with his hands, digging his nails into the skin to make her moan again.

"You can tell me how wrong you are about that, tomorrow," he said, challenging her as he pushed the fabric further down over her hips. In answer, she grabbed his hair and pulled him upright for another kiss. Taking him by the belt, she turned him back into the wall of books, pinning him there with her lips, and with hands that swiftly removed the obstacles his belts and trousers posed.

"You'll have to find me, first."

He seized her chin in his fist. "Ah, but I know where you sleep," he said, licking the words into her mouth, then devoured it like a starving man. His other hand found its way into the dampness of her cleft. Moist and inviting, and yet hungry and challenging—unlike anything he'd ever experienced with Angelique. Raven spun her around and slammed her into the bookcase.

She was still laughing unsteadily when he shoved his aching erection into her from behind and began pounding into her, and then her laughter turned into thick, hungry groans that incensed him even further.

He was out of control. She had pushed him over his limits, they both knew it—and it felt so damned good! *She* felt so good, hips rocking back against his, and snarling filthy encouragements to make him fuck her harder. It was all boiling up to a spectacular explosion when they both froze, at the same instant, all senses on alert.

A doorknob had rattled, somewhere on the floor just below them.

Iris cursed internally, floridly, but otherwise didn't move. "He won't come up here unless he hears something," she said, barely aspirating the words. Her inner muscles, however, clenched and released the throbbing, steel-hard thing inside her relentlessly. "Unless you want him to join us, don't move."

"You fucking bitch," he groaned softly, helpless unless he wanted to pull out of her completely, and he knew as well as she that he'd orgasm if he did. He took her by the hair again and twisted her head sideways to nip at the back of her neck, ignoring her hissed protestations.

Then they heard it again, this time much closer. Panting hotly, almost silently, Iris clamped down on him tightly.

"I love it when you talk like that, Raven," she whispered, squeezing and releasing and rocking ever so slightly over his rigid pole. "I love your big cock inside me, so fucking hard and hot...I want it, I want it *so bad*—"

Not bad. You were paying closer attention than you let on.

The thought ended as if it had been smothered, and it was all Iris could do not to laugh out loud.

Another, closer rattling noise from downstairs, this one sounded as if it was right below them!

Raven bit her again, *hard,* mostly to keep himself from exploding inside of her. "Keep it up, princess," he hissed into her ear after the worst of the imminent detonations had passed, "and you'll have my seed shooting out of your nose." He grabbed her breasts and pinched her tender nipples until he felt her cringe from her attempt not to squeal.

Yet another loose doorknob, and in their extremity it was impossible to tell whether it was closer or not. On the verge of a righteous climax herself, Iris somehow held her breath and body completely motionless until they both heard the next rattle. It seemed slightly farther away. Her hands clenched the shelves in front of her, and she squeezed him tightly in celebration—and whispered her final retaliation.

"Oooooh... you make it sound like a bad thing..." she said, rocking back into him ever-so-slightly.

She felt his fist clench in determination. "I'd rather not have to beat dipshit over there to death with my dick," he grunted.

Silence ruled for a beat. "That would be impressive," she said at last, choking back her laughter. Unfortunately, the muscular spasms involved weren't limited to her chest and throat, and abruptly tumbled her over the edge into climax.

That was too much for Raven. He didn't orgasm so much as detonate inside her, and clutched her to him tightly as another followed, and then a third before the need to plunge himself into her again overcame him. She keened ever so softly and pushed herself up and over him, each pulse filling her with pure, unadulterated lust, the like of which he hadn't experienced since very his first time, almost ten years before.

Iris convulsed in his arms, panting in great, heaving gasps that rocked them both. He didn't even realize he had the back of her neck in his teeth and was holding on like a male cat. He also didn't realize he'd drawn blood until the acrid metal taste hit his tongue. The epiphany made his cock throb anew inside her.

"Hey," she finally whispered, rocking back against him with more force now that the threat to dipshit's life had passed. "Wanna get your teeth out of my neck there, lover boy?"

"Maybe," he replied—which meant he did, since talking and biting were mutually exclusive activities. He kissed her there tenderly, then pulled out of her and stepped back.

"Angelique will need a high neckline for a week or so, I'm afraid," he observed. "And we've been here *way* too long!"

Chapter 16

The words filled Iris with sudden dread. It hadn't even rung midnight when they'd arrived. *And two bells have come and gone while I've sat here running my mouth and fucking around! Iris, you stupid fool, you're every bit as fatuous as that idiot Angelique!* She scrambled for her clothes and weapons as if Raven's voice had scalded her.

"I knew this was a mistake, I just knew it," she muttered, her fingers doing up the fastenings as fast as they could fly. "Malingering in one place this early, screwing around with you here, of all places. I should just surrender to Louis right now and save everyone the fucking trouble."

"I could arrange that," Raven tossed back distractedly. He had gotten himself back together and moved about the room to put things back into place. "Got your face on, yet?" He asked solicitously, and gave the room one final look over with his flash.

"Oh for the love of the Lord—shut up, Raven." Exasperated, but in truth more angry with herself than him at the moment, Iris slammed the last belt buckle closed and headed for the door in one abrupt movement. "Maybe I'll get lucky and find out Louis has used up his bad guy quota for the month."

"I wouldn't bet your new hairdo on that," he murmured, cracking open the door to check the hall. "Let's just be careful leaving, okay? I just found you, and I'm not ready to lose you."

He held the door open for her, and her eyes got tangled up in his as she passed. It was an uneven, halting beat in what was otherwise a smoothly-executed exit, and it troubled her. His words shouldn't affect her like they did, they shouldn't leave her feeling weak-kneed and fluttery, as if he'd just tenderly replaced her heart back into her chest. Those were thoughts for the likes of Angel, innocents who didn't know any better and couldn't take care of themselves.

Descending the steps ahead of Raven, her footsteps were no more than the merest whispering of air passing, but the voices swooning girlishly in her head made it feel as if she were ringing like a cast bronze bell. Raven stayed behind to reset the lock on the office door, but was only a few steps behind by the time she reached the entry foyer. She left him to reset the lock on the inner door while she cautiously opened the outer. She'd have taken an oath that the night had deepened somehow, that the earlier stillness had intensified in these earliest morning hours. Hearing nothing, seeing less, she slipped outside and by long training looked around for the way up to the roof.

At that moment, the entire world around her erupted in a strange, bright blue light. Her arms and legs went numb, followed by her feet, face and hands so swiftly that she couldn't speak. The last thing she remembered was the sound of her own gasp in her ears as her knees buckled.

Raven just manage to pull back as a bright blue-green glow engulfed Iris. It enveloped her completely and shot out in tendrils out all around as it took her to the ground. Some of them caught him too, caressing him in a way that turned his arms and legs as stiff as steel and caused his vision to blur. He leaned against the wall and fought the urge to pass out, unable to move. He could do nothing but watch as a carriage rolled up beside Iris' limp body. Something emerged from it, but in the odd blue glow that lingered behind his eyes, he couldn't be sure what it was until it became people, and one of them spoke.

"Huh. She doesn't look quite so tough now, does she." It was a woman's voice, weather-roughened and inflected like a native's.

"Bag her," another voice said, this one a man's. As Raven's vision cleared, he could just see through the curtains that he was taller, and wore a long, dark coat and a rather large hat. "Let's collect our bonus and get out of town before Arnot has us all up on charges."

Arnot! *This isn't over, boy!* he remembered Louis saying at the ball. *So this is your counter play,* he thought grimly. *You didn't waste any time, did you? Well... We'll see about* that!

Two more shapes detached themselves from the carriage. One of them knelt, and rolled Iris face down on the cobblestones. "Hey, Kestrel," he said, tying her wrists with a length of twine, "you want these blades as a trophy? They look expensive."

"No trophy-taking until the client clears it, Calder. Just get her secured, then put her on the floor in here. We need to get moving."

After they'd tied her ankles, two of them pushed her into a bag, then did as she'd said. Internally growling with the effort of making his arms and legs move, Raven managed to take a step forward, and got a better look at at the conveyance as it pulled away.

Bad move, boyo, Raven thought to himself. It was a custom coach, and wouldn't be hard to locate from the air if he could ever get his limbs back under his control! He tried another step, and this one came more easily. The two men remounted to the driver's seat, and one of them called out to the horses. Their hooves echoed against the building walls as they began to pull the coach away.

He reached for the door. It was like moving against running water, but he grabbed the latch, twisted it, and used it for support as he hobbled out into the street. No extra guards were riding in the back seat, a fact that was some relief, if not much.

It took what seemed like an eternity to fetch a line plier from his pocket, and another eternity to get it pointed to the roof top opposite, but he could still vaguely see the outlines of the carriage in the distance, where it encountered the irregularly lit street lamps. He raised his arms, fired, then squeezed the trigger. He was so clumsy he couldn't even get close to the roof for fear of hitting it, so he retrieved the line early and dove for a lower building's chimney stacks to gain altitude. By the time he'd done so, most of the paralysis had dissipated. He banked over and pointed the glide wing after the carriage.

It was a few hundred meters away, headed for the docks. He followed along at a leisurely pace, flexibility slowly returning to his limbs. The heavy clouds blotted out what little light might have come from moons or stars, so as long as he stayed above the glow of the street lights, he felt confident nobody could pick him out against that inky black curtain. And, if his nervous system was returning to normal, he was fairly certain that Iris would soon be coming back around as well. Her kidnappers might have drugged her too, if they were worried about her regaining consciousness.

They'd sounded downright dismissive of her, however. Perhaps there was hope.

The carriage turned onto a wide back street mainly used for loading and unloading wagons. It stopped in front of a nondescript warehouse in one of the busiest sections of the main port area. The immediate vicinity was unoccupied, but the port of Fernwall never closed. At the other end of the long warehouse buildings, the longshoremen were hard at work loading and unloading ships. The squeaking of blocks and tackles, the tinkling of tack and harness, and the chattering of the working men all carried eerily through the heavy night air.

They were the sounds Iris heard as she struggled back to awareness, a lunatic choir howling in her ears. Still groggy, she tried to shush the racket only to find she'd been gagged. A few black threats silenced the other voices in her head, and they settled into waiting for her to get them out of this.

She took a quick inventory. *Bound, ankles and wrists. Lying on a hard surface... and netted, or maybe bagged. And, we're not moving.* Her heart sank. *These are professionals. Damn, damn, damn.*

Silence within was the only reply. A door opened somewhere near her bound feet. Iris stayed limp while rough hands pulled her through the opening and then let her fall, stifling a grunt of startlement, and then the next one that was the natural result of impacting a stone surface.

"Hmph. Still out then," a deep, masculine voice said from somewhere above. It was answered by a woman's.

"Hope Louis doesn't mind a few bruises on his prize."

There was an a snort from nearby, then the first voice said, "You've seen how he treats them. It'll probably just turn him on. You'd better get airborne. We don't know where her backup is."

Iris hadn't needed confirmation of who'd paid the bounty for her, but she thought it was good of them to provide it all the same. She jiggled the thin cutting blade from her sleeve, caught it in her fingers and began slicing through the bindings at her wrists, hoping against hope that "backup" meant Raven, and that they hadn't killed him before they'd taken her.

High above, Raven circled once, hurriedly, to get a lay of the land, then spiraled down to the roof of the run down office building on the eastern side of the street to land. From there, he reasoned, he could remain protected while he picked off the kidnappers. Or, failing that, he could at least follow until he could find a way to steal Iris back.

Then something slammed into him from above, *hard,* driving him down into the surface of the roof. He skidded across the tiles and over the side, catching a broken brick with one hand. It left him hanging over the ledge, exposed and vulnerable to attack.

A flyer whizzed past, just at the edge of his vision. It was a woman! Whoever she was, she had already swung her lance back into strike position, and had begun to circle back around on him.

Lancer! Raven had never faced one, but their skill in the Great War was as legendary as tales of their valor. Now he knew why. He had neither seen her, nor heard her before she struck. Had the Raven Wing not been armored, he would have been very, *very* dead. He pulled himself back up over the ledge and took another look around.

"Hey! Up there. Shoot him!" With his attention focused on the lancer, he'd momentarily forgotten about the activity on the street below. Bolts fired. He tried to duck.

Iris's eyes snapped open. Through the opening of the sack, she clearly saw him take a blow to the chest and hurtle back out of sight.

He couldn't breathe and he couldn't see. Everything was hazy. He struggled to his hands and knees and nearly blacked out. Summoning every bit of will he could muster, Raven fought his way back out of a dark tunnel. Air! Why wasn't there any air here? Lord help me—the Soldier's Drug! Right! The Soldier's Drug. Nausea doubled him over, and he still couldn't see. There was blood in his mouth, and he smelled it in his nose. It made the air he had to fight for smell bad and taste worse. He rifled though his pockets for a small metal cylinder. There! He had it!

Raven flipped the cap off and stabbed the long needle into his chest. The pain made him want to scream but he forced himself to keep the damned thing on inside him for the required count of *two... long... seconds...*

The pain vanished. His chest still hurt like hell, but he could see, breathe, and move. In relief, he rolled to his back and took what shallow breaths his ruptured lungs would allow. He had just "extended his contract", as the soldiers used to say. He had been a living man who was dying, now he was a dead man whose small amount of remaining life was being doled out in tiny portions by the drug. When those portions were used up, the contract expired. He either needed to be in a surgery by then or he was a dead man.

The catch was that the contract could expire at any time. That was the cynical irony of the wartime use of the Solider's Drug. Though it had been designed and distributed to save lives in field hospitals, its more common use was to kill more orcs. The victim wasn't guaranteed a long enough life to get to a field hospital, but he might just be able to help his comrades by holding off an enemy assault for a few more minutes, or possibly hours.

That's exactly what Raven intended to do. Whatever life the drug was going to grant him, he'd use to keep Louis from getting Iris.

"Got the bastard!" Iris heard from inside her sack. Bodies had interposed themselves between her and the spot where Raven had fallen. She closed her eyes, hardly daring to breathe or to believe what her eyes were insisting they'd just seen.

"Who was it?" Asked another.

"Dunno, but he's a deader now. Saw the shaft hit him square in the chest. Probably knocked him off that roof."

Square in the chest... square in the chest... stupid thing to say, "square in the chest"... there's nothing square about it... It was nonsense, and it was enough to keep the horrified silence in her head from overwhelming them all. It couldn't have been Raven. It simply couldn't have. They were wrong.

Back to work. It's up to... work. Back to us... up to us now. Angel was the first to let loose a howl that deafened Iris internally, but it was the trigger she needed to free her from the rage and horror. She flexed her will in response, savagely, wordlessly smothering all voices until within her until a cowed silence descended.

Watch for it, she hissed to them all, fingers still furiously sawing at her bonds. *Watch for it, the chance... watch for the chance, and wait.*

"Shoot me, will you?" Raven groused, coughing as he crept back up to the roof's edge. He had one of his big line pliers in his hand. The small ones were good for capturing people, but these...?

He aimed carefully at the big-mouthed man and fired. The lead missed him by mere centimeters. A flip and a snap of the controls opened the grapnel and it flew back toward Raven. Before the man could react, the tines had cut his head off. It flew a half a meter, and flopped onto the ground. The other two men froze, speechless.

These line pliers could kill.

The lancer sprang to life immediately and jumped into the air, her wings clawing the air for altitude. Raven shot again before she could clear three meters off the ground. The lead caught her full in the chest and slammed into the building behind with a loud *thack!* The woman crumpled to the ground in a pile of disheveled feathers. *That's for the crash!* he coughed, seething in satisfaction.

Iris's wrists had come free the moment her ears registered the tell-tale thud of a decapitated head hitting packed dirt. *Told you they were wrong,* she quipped into the internal silence, then paused to listen as the commotion erupted around her.

A coughing fit prevented Raven from shooting a third time. He spat blood and bile, and glanced down at his chest. He was bleeding so badly his shirt and jacket were soaked. He had never been a soldier, but he knew what "terminal" looked like. By the time he could look over the roof ledge again the remaining men were ranging. They had seen the results, but not the cause of the two kills.

"There!" Shouted one of the men, the driver, he thought. "Here come the others." Another wagon had just made a turn onto their street. The driver started waving wildly at them.

This was getting complicated. Raven took aim and fired the grapnel again, this time hitting the bowman in the chest with the lead. That man probably wasn't dead, but he was down and not moving. For the moment, that was good enough. Now Raven knew he had to get to Iris.

She'd just managed to slice through the first cord at her ankles and was able to twist free of the second. She used the little blade then to part the canvas sack with a sharp buzzing sound and she caught a glimpse of the man towering above her. He was wearing large-brimmed hat, a long coat, and a crossed weapons-belt over his chest.

It was all she had time to note. Iris used his distraction against him and rolled for the shelter of the carriage. From the corner of her eye she saw him fling his arm out at her and point. *Something* unnatural left his fingers and hit the ground where she'd just been, exploding into a tangled, bright blue mass that swirled and dissipated harmlessly into the ground.

Cursing, Iris rolled to her belly and scampered under the rear axle, readying herself to run for the nearest cover. Just then, the head of a familiar-looking grapnel buried itself into the dirt less than a half-meter from her head, showering her with pebbles and mud. Without pause for either breath or thought she rolled to her feet and yanked the grapnel out of the ground with both hands, all in one motion.

Above her, Raven braced himself against the edge and squeezed the trigger. Iris sailing up towards him, her gleeful laughter ringing out as she rode the line to her freedom.

In the street below, the man behind the carriage emerged with his cross-bow loaded. This time Raven had the second line plier in his other hand and fired it at him. The tines raked the big brute's arm as he retrieved the line, but that was all. He'd effectively missed.

"Here," he turned to help Iris onto the roof. His voice sounded like he was talking through pond water with a throat full of gravel. She was still laughing as she clambered up beside him, mirth that withered in her throat once she saw him, and smelled him.

Iris knew what death smelled like. No one survived the streets of Püran-Khir without that smell becoming part of them, and there was a long, thick shaft protruding... her own chest felt hollow and for that horrified moment, so did her head, as wide and silent and dark as the depths of the sea.

"Raven?" She whispered it, gaze fastened on the enormous bolt in his chest because she couldn't bear to see that death was in his eyes. "Oh, what have you done...?"

The incoming wagon had reached the carriage, and the big brute he'd just winged. "Later," he wheezed, stowing his gear. He nodded at the street, spat out another mouthful of blood and bile, took her hand in his, and began to stagger toward the opposite end of the building.

She, too, had seen what he'd seen, and knew they weren't yet safe. She went with him, forcing herself to think where the nearest source of medical help could be. "Hey, take it easy!" she urged him, picking her way along the roof behind him. "We don't have to hurry this hard, Raven! This is our turf... we can take them up here, slow down!"

"Girl," he half-coughed and half-gagged, "my next breath may be my last. That's not a good place to be in a fight, with you outnumbered." They had to stop while he suffered another coughing fit. Iris held him through it because she didn't know what else to do, and thinking too hard about that would have unhinged her entirely.

"Don't talk like that. We've got to find help—"

"Let's use the time I have to get away." He almost inserted a "you" in there, but thought better of it. Angelique might have taken orders from him. Iris would not. "If I'm alive when we're safe, we'll get me some help."

Her answer stuck in her throat and for the moment she was oddly grateful for the return of the horrified silence. In it, she could at least think. "Then let's head that way," she managed at last, assisting him to his feet. "The closest I know is the Holywell Chapel, upriver, closer to Three Lions Bridge. And that's only if Matria Margret is there. You?"

"Soldier's Drug," he wheezed, hurrying them along again. "Any old army medic might do—if he still has his field bag. Here." He handed her one of the smaller line pliers. "I can't carry us both. That rooftop." He pointed with the plier, shot it off and hooked the grapnel. "Like that. Squeeze the trigger and it will pull you. The harder you squeeze the faster you go. See you there," he grinned—or tried. The gore pouring from his mouth ruined the effect. He clutched the towing device with both arms and let it pull him ahead of her.

A bit longer, Vince, and she'll be safe, he told himself, hanging on to the line with every shred of strength he could muster. *She's right. We know this ground, they don't.*

Iris bit back several curses, and especially at that last. No pro ever tried new equipment during a job, let alone an escape! *Unless they're out of options,* she corrected herself, squeezing down on the trigger as he'd instructed. Sounds of pursuit erupted from the ground level behind them. *And it seems that we are out of options.* She squeezed too hard, and it yanked her off the building unceremoniously, but her eyes were more on his progress than her own. Her landing on the roof nearby was clumsy, but successful.

"Okay, next one," she said, almost before she'd retracted the grapnel. If he wanted to get to help, well then, she'd hurry him along, half-convinced that damned drug was going to give out on him in mid-flight. "Come on, Raven. Don't quit on me now."

"There's..." He started coughing again. It might have been his imagination, but it seemed he was having to work harder to do almost everything. "Fireman's drop on the other side. We... can get to the street from there. Alley. Hopefully it's safe."

"No problem at all. Let me carry you?" She suggested, taking the larger mechanism from him, then firing off the line as she'd watched him do earlier. "I'm stronger than I look. Come on."

He didn't argue. He could feel it now, like someone had pulled a stopper from a drain. He wasn't going to make it. Things weren't going dark yet, but he knew they would, and soon. He just hoped he'd lasted long enough. In a few moments, he'd know. He just had to hang on that long. Just a few more minutes...

"Shit!" Iris swore, grabbing Raven before he toppled over the ledge. One arm around him tightly, she tried for an even pull on the trigger, but panic fueled her strength. The resultant pull on the line nearly tore her arm out of its socket. She grunted hard through the pain, holding on to both lover and line until they had something solid under their boots again.

It got them across, even if it wasn't pretty. Even as she retracted the grapnel, however, her gorge was climbing into her throat. He wasn't going to make it.

"Raven!" She held him so he wouldn't fall, cradling what was left of his torso as he collapsed to the roof. "*Raven*! Hey come on, you can't die now, Angelique will never forgive me. Raven!"

He tried to look around but nothing happened. On reflection, he doubted it would have done any good as he really couldn't see much. It was like looking through a fog. "You're safe," he whispered. "My Burning Bright... for now... Hope it..." He coughed again, never having understood before then just how much strength it took. "Makes up a bit... for the trouble..."

"Stop that!" Iris wanted to weep, but even more than that, she wanted to scream. She did neither, instead stripping off her gloves to hold his face in her hands, as if by touch and will alone she could stop the light from fading from his eyes. "You're can't go anywhere. You said I was yours, remember? You can't leave without me! Without *us!* Raven? *Raven!*"

At first he said nothing. Finally he gathered the last of his strength and looked at her, there in the dark, his blood smeared across her face. She was so beautiful, so strong, so vibrant. "I love you, you know," he finally said, his voice naught but a whisper. "Kiss me... kiss..." Her face had faded into the darkening mists, or perhaps he had. At least the pain was gone. *Come on, Vince. One last push. For her.* "Kiiiisssss..."

Iris kissed him, taking the last word and the last breath from his body, then kissed him again as if she could give it back. Again and again she kissed him, as all the voices within her screamed for him to stay, and then as they began shrieking in grief and denial when he couldn't. She had only one body to channel the storm of all that weeping, and it incapacitated her. Stunned, staring at him as if he'd taken the light from the world with him, Iris let Angel and Angelique carve out entire river valleys with their tears, unable to summon even a single idea, or thought, or direction to go that would somehow change what had just happened. Transfixed by the lifeless body of a man she'd sworn she hated only hours before, for the first time in her life she could not summon any way to think of what must be done next.

His sudden absence rang in the hollow shell she'd abruptly become. He'd been right all along, and she'd realized it much too late: Her life meant nothing without him.

* * *

𝔄𝔐 *From the Desk of Dr. Albert Martin*

25 Vilmath
Goodman Christóphe Verlinden, Blakesly House
For Immediate Delivery

As you love our Lady, upon receipt of this letter you must do the following things as swiftly as you can. I will answer all questions later today, assuming I am alive and free to return to Blakesly House.

Wake Clarice and tell her to assemble my toilet and clothing for today into a packing case. She was to have used that case to take some of my gowns to my seamstress this morning, but instead she must now escort that case to me here at Dr. Albert Martin's home in Angels.

Close down the house. No visitors permitted in, and none of the staff are to leave except for you and Clarice.

Stay vigilant. Pray for us.

-Angelique Blakesly

* * *

𝕬𝕸 *From the Desk of Dr. Albert Martin*

25 Vilmath
Lady Emilia Fauré-Nielsen, Countess of Remington
Old Palace Hotel, Angels

My dearest Lady,

I know of no polite or genteel way to say this that might also frame the depth and breadth of my need for your help. I must ask you to set aside some time for me at eleven hundred hours at Remington Hall. I will also be sending a strongly worded request to Commissioner Hal Roland to join us. What has happened this past night concerns the matters we discussed at the ball, and the fate of his charge, Sir Vincent Sultaire.

Even were I not in desperate need of your help and counsel, I would be that much in need of your wisdom and strength.

I cannot say more without saying all. Pray for me.

Pray for Vincent.

-Angelique

* * *

Lady Angelique Blakesly, Baroness of Carlisle

25 Vilmath 580
Police Headquarters, 1100 Caspian Square, Fernwall
Commissioner Roland,

No doubt you are surprised to receive this note from me, rather than from Vincent. Believe me when I say I wish it were he writing it too. As he cannot, the duty falls to me, not only as his betrothed, but also as the woman who was present with him last night, when events in the case he has been investigating came to a violent and deadly turn.

You will understand that I cannot commit the entirety of what happened to writing at this time, nor will events allow me the leisure of visiting you at precinct headquarters to speak with you. I request of you, most urgently and sincerely, that you will instead make time to come to Remington Hall at noon to attend upon Lady Emilia and myself, where you will hear the whole tale, as fully as it may be told.

I realize and regret that this leaves you with little time to make the journey up to Angel Heights. Please hurry.

-Lady Angelique Blakesly, Baroness of Carlisle

–End Book 2 of The Raven & The Iris–

Dear Reader,

If you read this far without hurling your book/device against the wall, thanks for that. If you're in tears, that's okay, too. Alesia still can't make it through the end of this one without blubbering like a baby.

As the authors, we wanted to take this opportunity to tell you that we are so very grateful for your time and attention as a reader, and that we always try to honor your readership in our storytelling. It's important to us to let you know that we do remember that this trilogy is a love story, and that we remain faithful to that, in spite of the very sad endings of the first two books in the series.

But, as Master Shakespeare said in one of his own fantasies: *The course of true love never did run smooth.* As writers, we intend to stay faithful to that timeless truth in telling Vincent's and Angelique's story. We hope you'll find that it bodes particularly well for the tone of the ending of the trilogy.

What wouldn't you do for a love that could conquer death? Angelique is about to discover it for herself in the third and concluding book of the trilogy, *Seven for a Secret.*

We'd like to ask, now that you're finished with *Dead Man's Trigger,* won't you please leave us at least one review?

Your honest review supports us as indie authors and publishers more than you can possibly realize unless you are one, too. It doesn't have to be long, and it doesn't matter if you "liked" the book or not—just tell your fellow readers what you think. Even a "negative" review, given thoughtfully and constructively, is going to be helpful to us in the long term, so please take this request to heart and leave at least one review on one of the pages linked above.

Lastly, if you liked what you've read here, we do have an email newsletter that's only sent out to subscribers when there are updates to the world of Menelon and the stories written there. We do not sell or rent our email addresses to any other party (though we might sometimes send you notice of things we think you might find relevant), and hope to have the chance to prove to you that your email address is safe with us. Please consider signing up via this link!

Thanks, and ever thanks for your readership. We do hope you're enjoying the story, and will tell your friends about what we're doing with the series, too.

—Alesia & Michael

www.ingramcontent.com/pod-product-compliance
Lightning Source LLC
Chambersburg PA
CBHW060422180626
46817CB00007B/2631